AFTER ADAM FELL, GOD MADE EVE TO PROTECT THE WORLD

Every god, from each of the world's pantheons, mythologies, and religions—they're all real...

Adam has pursued Eve since the dawn of creation, intent on using her power to create a new world and make himself its God. Throughout history, Eve has thwarted him, determined to protect the world and all of creation. Unknown to her, the Norse god Thor has been sent by the Council of Gods to keep her from Adam's influence, and more, to protect the interests of the gods themselves. But this time, Adam is after something more than just Eve's power—he desires her too, body and soul, even if it means the destruction of the world. Eve cannot allow it, but as one generation melds into the next, she begins to wonder if Adam might be a man she could love.

ㅇㅇ

PRAISE FOR *FORGED BY FATE*

"A beautiful, sweeping story that puts on display the power of every interpretation of love, and the truth of what can be accomplished when people choose peace over strife. I couldn't put it out of my mind for days."
—Trisha Leigh, author of *The Last Year* series

"A fascinating and artful blend of myth and legend that makes for a rich story of transcendent courage and hope. Not to be missed!"
— Saranna DeWylde, author of the *10 Days* series

FORGED BY FATE

Fate of the Gods Trilogy
Book One

AMALIA DILLIN

World Weaver Press

FORGED BY FATE
Copyright © 2013 Amalia Dillin

All rights reserved.

This is a work of fiction; characters and events are either fictitious or used fictitiously.

Published by World Weaver Press
Kalamazoo, Michigan
www.WorldWeaverPress.com

Edited by Eileen Wiedbrauk
Cover designed by World Weaver Press

First Edition: March 2013

ISBN: 0615738559
ISBN-13: 978-0615738550

For my family and friends, who read, and reread, and read again; and for Adam, who always believed this day would come, and encouraged me, every day, to put on my authorpants and go to work.

ACKNOWLEDGMENTS

This book would not have been written if it had not been for my husband, of course, who told me over and over again that staying home and writing was a completely legitimate contribution to our household. Thank you, forever, for giving me the freedom to chase after my dreams and supporting me while I learned how to fly with them.

But it also would not have been written without my Alpha Reader, Dan, who read each chapter as I wrote it and was always eager for the next one and ready to talk to me about whatever plot-problem was festering in the back of my mind, always with the proper level of enthusiasm. I left him hanging more than once for an unforgivable amount of time, but he never lost faith.

After Dan, the book went to my even more patient betas, who read and reread and read again tirelessly, fell in love with my characters, and showed me how to make my book even stronger by helping me take it apart. In particular, Diana Paz (whose book, *Timespell* is available April 2013), Zachary Tringali (who also writes amazing fantasy), Mia Hayson, Cait Peterson, Sarah Walker, and Tom Hale. Thanks must go, too, to all my non-writer friends, who stuck by me, even when I got lost writing, and celebrated all the small victories with the unwavering belief that one day it would all add up into an actual book in their hands (I am looking at you, Drew the Third).

And I have to thank my mother, who must have read the first five chapters of this book a dozen times before I finally presented her with an actual novel, and the rest of the family, most especially my aunts and uncles, who read for me, book after book, and get more upset than I do when I get rejections. You have given me every validation and support during this journey, without which, I would never have come this far. Thank you.

Not to be forgotten either, are Bjarni Bjarnason and his father who took the time to correct my Icelandic and Old Norse. Any errors within that language are born of my own stubbornness and my inability to focus long enough to learn it properly. Slowly but surely! Thank you for your patience!

Finally, a huge thanks to Eileen and Elizabeth at World Weaver Press for giving Adam, Eve, and Thor a place on their shelves and the chance to be on yours.

… FORGED BY FATE

CHAPTER ONE
Present-Day France

Eve stood under the water, letting the heat relax muscles tense with worry. Showers were one of her favorite things in the modern world. All indoor plumbing, really. She loved not having to fetch water in buckets, heat it over flame, and dump it into basins to wash. It took forever, and the water became so filthy so quickly. Showers were much more efficient.

She massaged the shampoo into her scalp, closing her eyes and imagining one more layer of the filth from her past washing down the drain. Some of her last lives hadn't been nearly so set on the value of cleanliness. South America hadn't agreed with her, certainly. And the asylum of her last life had hardly been ideal. She rubbed at her wrists, but the scars were gone, and she shook her head, forcing her thoughts away from that memory. She didn't want to think of that any more than she wanted to dwell on her argument with Garrit.

The way he had looked at her last night, as if she were a stranger. Only it had been mixed with betrayal too.

Eve sighed and turned off the water. She hadn't expected him to take it so hard. After all, these were all truths his family knew, *her* family, too. These were her people in a way no others were. If anyone should have been able to understand—but he had been gray-faced when he left the night before. And he hadn't yet come back.

She twisted the excess water from her hair and stepped out of the tub.

Garrit leaned silently against the sink, his arms crossed over his chest, dressed in a crisp gray suit for work. His lips were pressed into a thin line but he unbent enough to pass her a towel. She wrapped it around her body, suffering the feeling of exposure with little joy. Self-consciousness was not a gift she had ever learned to appreciate nor was the feeling of nakedness. Adam's fault, both.

"I didn't realize you were back," she said quietly, using a second towel to blot the water from her hair.

"I slept in one of the spare rooms." He studied her for a moment, his eyes narrowing as if he were looking for some outward sign of the truth that he had missed during the year they'd lived together. "Why didn't you tell me, Abby?"

She should have. A month ago when he proposed. She should have told him then that she was Eve, before she had accepted. "It doesn't change anything. I loved you before I knew you were a DeLeon, and then I loved you even more because of it. And now, knowing I'm Eve, you're looking at me as though I'm some kind of monster."

Exactly what she hadn't wanted. In her experience with the few husbands she had trusted with her secret, there had always been a period of adjustment. Denial. Misunderstanding. Betrayal. It was to be expected. But he was Ryam's descendent. His family knew the truth. Kept boxes of her things in a vault in the basement. That was supposed to make all of this easier. He wasn't supposed to be looking at her this way. He was supposed to love her, still, in spite of it all.

"You're my ancestor." His jaw tightened and he looked away, seeming to stare at the tile. "It's incestuous."

She shook her head. "That's ridiculous. You don't know what you're talking about."

His head came up, dark eyes made darker still with emotion. "Maybe you should enlighten me then, Abby, because this is all just a little bit overwhelming."

She forced herself to swallow the angry retort that came to mind, and spoke evenly. "It was over five hundred years ago that I married into this family, Garrit. So many generations removed, that I can't even count them. And even if it weren't, even if I were your sister, I'm genetically perfect. Our children would be healthy, more resistant to disease, with strong minds."

He stared at her again, and she saw in his face that he was wondering how many brothers she had married in her past lives. Enough that she knew what would happen if she did. Maybe that was too many. She tried to ignore it and twisted the towel around her hair, flipping it up over her head. She shivered now that the steam had dissipated. Freezing didn't improve her mood.

"I don't understand any of this."

She recognized that tone. The honest confusion and fear. Her whole body softened and she reached for him, hoping something of the love she felt for him could cross between them, reassure him. But he shook his head, raising a hand to ward her off. He paced halfway to the door and stopped.

"Most people wouldn't even bother to try to understand." She kept her voice gentle, though she didn't think he noticed. He seemed too wrapped up in his head, trying to unravel the knot of their shared history. Her existence, after all, gave new meaning to his. "But you know the story, Garrit. Your family has the truth. Nobody could have known that I would turn up now and meet you."

"It wasn't supposed to be truth. It was supposed to be *légende*. Family lore, *rien de plus*."

They'd had enough arguments for her to know it was never a good sign when he slipped into French. He'd always done her the courtesy of speaking English in the past, no matter how irritated he'd been. He preferred to save his French for flirtation and similar intimacies. Not that he wasn't above using it to exclude others, either, knowing she spoke it as fluently as he did, but alone with him in the bathroom, that clearly wasn't the case this time.

Maybe she had been away longer than she'd realized. Too long away from her family. From home. Or maybe this modern world just made everyone forget the truths of the past. Was that the price of hot running water? She rubbed at her wet face and wondered if it was worth it, even while she tried to find the words to make him see reason.

"All legend is based on truth. I thought that you of all people understood that. You're part of an incredibly illustrious family, going back all the way to Creation, to the Garden—"

"It's *myth*, Abby. Creation is a myth!"

"Part of your myth is standing in front of you in a towel!" She was wet, and miserable, and he hadn't even had the courtesy to shut the bathroom door before shouting at her. "Tell me that the thousands of lives I've lived are all lies."

He shook his head. "I don't know what you are."

She bit her lip. "This is why I didn't tell you."

"It's all been a lie, then? From the moment you knew my name."

"I hardly run about the earth advertising my reincarnations!" Her voice had risen, but she couldn't bring it back under control. Of all people, he should have known better than to think such a thing. "My feelings, me, our relationship, none of that has been a lie."

"I'm just supposed to accept this? *Sans hésitation,* without reserve?" he asked.

"Your parents didn't seem to be upset by it."

"*Mon Dieu!*" She flinched. Cursing in French was even worse than grasping for words. "That's just great, Abby. You tell my parents but you don't think to tell your fiancé."

"I didn't tell them. They put the facts together themselves, just like you." Only faster. And with less drama. They, at least, had understood and been happy.

His jaw clenched. "Your portrait. In the hall."

"Yes. My portrait." He would come to terms with it, or he wouldn't, but she was shivering and he was blocking the door. "If you don't mind, I'd like to get dressed."

He shook his head, and stepped out of her way. She knew he was still staring after her, even when she had shut the door to the bedroom they shared.

The towel had loosened, and she rewrapped it over her breasts, leaning against the door. She half-hoped he would follow, but even if he had wanted to, he was already late. He'd leave, go to work, see to his business and give them both space to breathe. Time to settle.

She sighed. That damned portrait. She'd known it was only a matter of time before he noticed, but somehow she hadn't seen him responding this way. She probably should have, but she hadn't wanted to believe it would be a problem. She was still the same woman, after all. Abby or Helen, Anessa or Mary. She was still Eve. Names were nothing more than a different way to count her lives.

All things considered, it could have gone a lot worse. She was always pleased when the result of her confessions was not the threat of an insane asylum and medication, or an attempt to burn her at the stake for witchcraft. But this was her home. The land she had settled in with her people after leaving the Garden behind. The one place on this earth where she was permitted to be Eve, always. To be rejected here, however slight, made her heart ache.

§

That evening, Eve sat alone in the family library. It was her favorite retreat. The best place to lose herself for hours, determined as she was not to crowd Garrit. He'd find her when he was ready to see her. When he could look at her without seeing her as a ghost.

The shelves were overflowing with books, except for the one glass case from which she'd chosen the volume in her hands. That set of shelves was devoted to family history and impeccably maintained. Copied and recopied editions of books and manuscripts and even what had once been scrolls, every one given the space to air.

Eve turned the page. It was a reproduction of an old manuscript, written by her second DeLeon husband, Lord Ryam, centuries ago. Still, the volume was musty and old in its own right, and the leather binding flaked in her hands. Mostly, it tallied sheaves of grain and calves born, but there was the occasional personal reference. The births of her own children and grandchildren, and the incredible wealth of crops during the first year of their marriage. There had been so much rain, that year. She remembered it distinctly. But somehow the land had absorbed it all and turned it into a rich harvest.

Their estate had been very wealthy, then. Garrit and his father still cultivated the vineyard, of course, and the wine they sold had afforded his parents a good living, but Garrit's real wealth came from investments and banking. Things she knew very little about, despite the significant advantages of reincarnation and telepathy. Or maybe it was because of them that she never found the accumulation of large amounts of wealth to be important. It wasn't as though she could bring it with her.

The book was dry, but it kept her mind off other things. Filling her thoughts with easy noise without resurrecting memories. She'd been dreaming about the mental ward again. When it had felt as though she had been lost in her own mind. She certainly had a new sympathy for those diagnosed with dementia.

A knock on the door interrupted the thought. Garrit hesitated for a moment in the doorway before he crossed the room and sat down in the matching wingback chair opposite her own. She closed the book in her lap and set it aside. He looked less tense now that he was home from work, though he hadn't changed out of his suit yet, which wasn't exactly the best sign.

He pulled his tie free from his collar and draped it over the arm of his chair. "I'm not here to apologize."

She leaned back in her seat. "I wasn't expecting it."

He seemed to stare at the fireplace. Eve couldn't get used to the fact that it was gas instead of wood, and rarely lit it. What was the fun in flipping a switch on the wall? Even worse, it came with a remote control, which Garrit took from the end table beside his chair, toying with it.

"One minute, the woman I was making love to was just a woman, and then I happen into the hall and see you staring at me from a canvas." He pressed a button and the fire whooshed to life, the flicker of light and shadow playing across his cheek, turning his frown into a scowl. "I don't even know how I missed it all this time."

"I'm still just a woman, Garrit."

"*The* woman." He tossed the controller away and ran his fingers through his hair. "Eve. The mother of all of us. Literally and figuratively."

"I'm just the only one who lived," she said gently. "Not the only one who mothered."

"But you're still our mother, our *grand-mère*, as Anessa, wife of the Marquis DeLeon." He laughed and shifted in his seat. His face was almost gray. "I'm sleeping with my grandmother."

"Five hundred years is at least seventeen generations removed. You would lose count before you finished listing the greats before my name. I've been born a squalling infant, grown old and died five times since."

He studied her for a long minute, and she followed the emotions behind it, but not the thoughts. Discomfort. Embarrassment. Admiration. She had learned long ago how to filter the words from the feelings, and only hear what she wanted to listen to. She'd never yet heard Garrit's thoughts, projected accidentally. But she felt his love, his grudging acceptance.

"I just need some time to get used to the idea."

The ache in her chest eased. "I understand."

He cleared his throat. "My parents called."

"How are they?"

He shrugged. "*Plutôt bien*. They're on their way here for dinner. And they're bringing someone, they said. What would you like to serve?"

Eve tried not to smile. How many more thousands of years would it be before men stopped asking her to make dinner? Or before she tired of playing that role? "Why don't we order something in from town? Turkish, perhaps."

He rose, moving to the door, then paused. "Lord Ryam's journal is in the cabinet. If you want to take a look at something other than bunches of grapes and genealogy of the livestock. He had plenty to say about you."

"Thank you."

Garrit shut the door behind him.

Drumming her fingers on the arm of the chair, Eve stared at the cabinet. She'd shared this house with Garrit for over a year, in that time making liberal use of the library for her entertainment. How had she missed a journal written by her husband? For that matter, how had she not known about it when she lived as Ryam's wife?

She crossed the room to the cabinet, carefully opening the glass door and walking her fingers along the spine of each book. The journal was bound in plain leather, the only marking on the spine an imprint of the dates he had lived. Now that she knew to look for it, it was clear what it was.

She removed it, letting it fall open in her hands. Clearly, it had been reproduced; it wasn't written in Ryam's hand, though his name appeared on the inside of the front cover. She wondered what had become of the original, if it was kept somewhere sealed in a cabinet in the basement with the other relics of her past, locked away from the general populace. Trinkets and tokens she had wanted to keep and shipped or mailed over lifetimes to this house to be stored.

She went back to her chair and sat down, holding the journal in her hands. As if it held some piece of the man who had died so long ago. The man who had loved and protected her, regardless of the shame she had brought with her.

It had only been her last life when she had lost herself in those lives, her pasts twisting together, crowding out sanity with memories of days long gone, men long dead. Only this life when she had felt herself whole again, grounded in the present, her fractured mind healed. She missed Ryam, missed the comfort of her memories. Missed the life they had lived together, indoor plumbing notwithstanding. She missed it, but she wanted to stay whole for a little longer; she wanted to keep her sanity.

She couldn't bring herself to read it.

CHAPTER TWO
Creation

Be Filled With My Spirit, And Breathe.

She gasped. Blood rushed through her body, pricking and tingling and roaring through her ears. Air filled her lungs, too much, too thick, too full, each breath more suffocating than the last. The comfort of darkness shattered into blinding light and the world pressed down upon her in all its living glory. The void, the blessed void, was gone.

"Eve?"

The light became blurred, round shapes and pink colors, and a pair of hard gray eyes. She touched her face, then stopped and stared at her fingers. Her hand. Her arm. Body and blood and flesh. She was flesh.

Another hand, darker and thicker than her own, pushed her arm away. "Can you hear me?"

She looked back at the eyes. The face. The wide, moving lips, just that much darker than the rest. There was another noise, whimpering and sorrowful. She was making it.

"Don't be afraid, Eve."

Arms slipped beneath her, cradling her and lifting her up. The world spun and Eve closed her eyes to stop it. Darkness. She knew darkness, the absence of everything, but even with her eyes shut, light still reached her, faded and flickering and red. She could still feel the movement, but at least it was only a gentle sway.

"There's a storm coming." The other spoke, holding her close, warm skin pressed to her own. She tried to concentrate on the voice, but there was so much noise. The roar of her blood, the thumping in her chest, steady and dull, and more voices, indistinct and buzzing. "We'll be safe in the caves, even without God to protect us."

Eve was set down on cold earth and she opened her eyes. Cave, she thought, shaping the word in her mind around the stone and the dirt that swallowed her. She curled up on the ground, feeling the grit beneath her cheek, pressing her fingers against the cool, damp rock.

And then there were more of them. Legs and feet and hushed tones of conversation. A flash of light turned everything white and a boom shook the earth. She yelped, her tongue thick in her mouth. Her heart raced and the pink and brown bodies moving past her blurred as moisture filled her eyes.

Something touched her head, soothing as it moved through her hair. "You're safe, Eve. It's just the storm. Breathe now." The same firm hand pulled her arms away from her face for a second time. "And sit up."

She was forced into a different position, her back supported against the rock. The man sat beside her. He stroked her hair again, then touched her face, her cheek.

"Who?" The word was rough and felt strange on her lips. She swallowed and tried again. "Who are you?"

"I'm Adam. First among men."

The way he studied her made her tremble. She looked away,

flinching from another flash and the crash that followed. The others huddled together, arms around one another. Adam's arm encircled her, pulling her against his side. He was warm, almost uncomfortably so. A howling began and then a rushing even louder than what she had first heard.

"What's happening?"

"It's just thunder." His hands stroked her body, her breasts, her belly. Not like before, with his hand in her hair. Her chest and cheeks flushed and she tried to shift away but he held her close. "The cave will protect us and the rain will pass."

She pulled her legs to her chest so that his hands couldn't reach her there, and wrapped her arms around her knees. The rain beat upon the earth with a constant rumble, thick and heavy. A gust of the storm blew into the cave, spraying everything with fine, cold droplets. Tiny bumps rose up on her skin, beneath the soft brown hairs on her arms and legs, and she smoothed them, until Adam stopped her.

He was still watching her, his lips curved slightly. His eyes were the color of the storm. The same shade of gray but hard as the stone, filled with cold heat.

"It's confusing at first, I know," he said, and he stroked her hair again. "Everything is so disconnected. Overwhelming. It takes time for understanding to come. But the important thing is you're alive. I wasn't sure you would be."

Some of the things he didn't say out loud echoed in her thoughts.

Elohim is dead. The words wriggled into her thoughts, Adam's voice, though his lips didn't move. It was almost like the voice in the void, telling her she must breathe, waking her from darkness and bringing her into light. Into the storm. But unlike the voice, there was no warmth, no love, swelling in her chest. *The Garden is mine.*

She shook her head, covering her ears with her hands. He pulled them away, his fingers hard on her wrists.

"You must listen to me, Eve." There was a weight to his words, and a heat that made her stomach twist as it crept from his hand into her body, slithering its way inside her, as his voice had a moment before. "You and I, we're more than these others. We're meant to rule them, to lead them. I can see it in you, that same spark. His spirit is in you, like me."

"I don't understand."

He made a noise that she hadn't heard before. The sound was harsh, but she thought, for some reason, that it wasn't supposed to be. That it could be friendly and joyful too.

"You don't have to understand me, Eve. You have only to obey." *And sister or not, I will have you as my wife.* His hand in her hair pulled, her scalp prickling, but he released her again before she felt the need to cry out. *There is no God to stop me. His laws will die with Him.*

He looked out into the rain, his gaze unfocused. *The fruit. That must be the priority. I'll find the fruit first.* He balled his hand into a fist as she watched, wishing she could move away.

His head jerked up and he stared back into the cave, where the others were half-hidden in the dark, as far from him as the space allowed. Adam stood and moved to the group, grabbing another man by the arm and pulling him away from the others.

"Go, find me the body. Take a second man to help if you need it, but don't come back without Him."

The man glanced at her before he nodded. She didn't hear what he said when he spoke, but a third man stood, glancing outside, his shoulders hunched. They left the shelter of the cave, flinching beneath the rain.

Adam sat down again beside her and she felt his satisfaction crowding against her thoughts.

"We'll be very happy together, Eve. You and I." He smiled. "The world will be at our feet. Every man, woman, and beast will be at my command."

There was an edge to his voice that made her shiver and she wrapped her arms more tightly around her body. He was watching her, and when he touched her, she saw herself for a moment through his eyes. His gaze followed the swell of her breasts and the curve of her hip, flushing her skin.

My lovely Eve. God could not have really meant to give you to any of the others. You are mine. He pulled her closer to his body. *You are mine.*

The thoughts echoed in her head and she closed her eyes, leaning away from him against the cold stone of the cave. She wished he would let go. These words made her uncomfortable, these words he didn't say. The feelings behind them crept up her spine and fogged her mind. She wished she were still in the darkness without the air and the noise and the light. Without this man who sat beside her and called her his own, his own, his own.

It all felt wrong, but she didn't know why.

CHAPTER THREE
1280 BC

⚜

Thor stood beneath the shade of his mother's tree and wiped the sweat from his brow. It had taken them months, but Odin's great hall was finished. Valaskjalf was large enough to accommodate the rest of the Aesir when they arrived, though few beside Odin's wife, Frigg, would remain longer than it took them to build their own halls. Thor's small *skáli* had been built first for shelter while they hewed the larger stones needed from the earth and labored to erect the vast walls.

Odin had lifted the land and cloaked the mountain in mist, sealing it within its own pocket of time. From Asgard, they could watch the earth, but the earth would not be able to watch back, and no foreign god would be able to reach them without Odin's permission. It was a precaution they had taken before, though this was the first time they had ever chosen to share a world with other gods. A Covenant of Peace had never been achieved in the five cycles Thor had known, but he was glad of it, and gladder, too, that Odin had seen the wisdom in agreeing.

Thor was weary of the wars and the stench of death, mortal and immortal alike. New worlds were growing harder to find when the last was drained of life. Soon there would be nowhere else to go, and no people to worship them. It would make for an empty existence; even the strongest of the gods would die trying to create life from the dust, a feat the True God of this world had accomplished, and then some.

"You'll go to the others, Thor," Odin said, joining him with two mugs of mead.

They sat down on the stone bench beneath the tree. Always the first thing established in any new Asgard, Thor made sure all the proper respects had been paid. The world-tree had been his mother's last gift before she had left them.

"Bring them gifts of gold and let it be known we have settled here and sworn our vows for peace."

Thor took a drink of the mead and stared into the amber liquid. "Baldur would be a better ambassador. They would have only to look on him to know his words were sincere."

"But Baldur is not here, and I dare not wait to learn what I can." Odin shook his head. "Let it be you. And let these other gods realize the might of the Aesir, in case they entertain ideas of breaking the Covenant."

"Of course," Thor agreed.

Baldur was good and genuine, but he lacked the necessary presence for subtle intimidation. That underestimation had served his brother well. No one expected Baldur to be a *vígamaðr*, and they certainly didn't expect him to cleave a body in half, but the Aesir were all warriors and Odin had trained his sons on the battlefields of five worlds.

"You'll leave in the morning," Odin said, his gaze on the tree.

The red leaves fluttered. The first crop of apples had already grown and dropped, ripe and sweet to the grasses beneath. They had eaten some, until the rest had hardened and they could trade the gold for goats, sheep, pigs, cows, and chickens. Thor had been forced to go all the way to Egypt before the gold had been worth anything in barter. The smaller villages in the north could not use anything which did not feed or clothe them directly.

"You'll give Sif my regrets, that I could not meet her myself."

Odin smiled. "Sif will be too busy settling into her home to miss you, I think. But if there is anything she requires, I will provide it."

As much as he missed his wife, he was curious about this world and the gods within it. He looked forward to meeting the others. Sif would understand; he had journeyed often in the old worlds. "Give her my love."

"If she doesn't know she has it by now, then my words will be of little consequence, but I will tell her." Odin clapped him on the back and rose. "Take as much of the gold as you can carry. We will wait for your return."

Thor nodded and finished his mead, counting the apples left on the ground. He would go back to Egypt and turn some of it into goods. Food and clothes, and perhaps a good horse to make the traveling easier. Egypt was full of gods. He had caught a glimpse of the old one, Ra, when he had been there last, and it was only right that he pay his respects to the vow-holder of the Covenant first.

⸙

"You and your people are most welcome to the Northlands, Thor," Ra said. They walked the dusty streets of the capital city. Ra had given Thor a tour of the Pharaoh's palace earlier, and the temples to the gods, all filled with gold and bright murals showing the history of Egypt. "Tell your father his claim will be known, and he can rest assured none will challenge him there. But you know the people are few in that area?"

"There were none left in the world we came from," Thor said. "Odin is a fair god, good to those who would follow him. Word will spread, and the villages that already exist in those lands will be nurtured."

Ra nodded, his brown face lined from the sun. "You would be surprised how many gods have not learned the value of patience."

Thor smiled, his eye caught by a woman carrying a water jug. She was very beautiful, her eyes a striking shade of green he had never seen before. He paused to watch her, and felt Ra stop with him. There was something odd about her aura. Something not quite right about the shift of light and shadow...

"She is very unusual, isn't she?" Ra asked, a smile in his voice.

The woman stopped at the well, setting down the jug, and for the first time, Thor saw the small swell of her stomach. But a pregnancy did not account for the golden glow, or the presence he felt from her. She was sunlight and spring rains. "She's not mortal."

"No," Ra agreed. "Not at all. But she lives like one. And seems not to realize our presence in the world."

He grunted, watching her lower a bucket into the well and struggle to raise it back up. "Do you know her?"

Ra shrugged. "Only from the time she has spent among my people. She's rarely born here."

"Born?" Thor frowned. Once born of their parents, gods lived eternities. Longer still, if they possessed the right magic. Like golden apples and ambrosias, or better, the belief of a people. Prayers were powerful.

"She's the True God's daughter, from what I can tell. He made her to age and die like a mortal, to be reborn again somewhere else, every century or so. In this life, she is known as Yocheved." Ra began to walk again, and Thor had no choice but to move with him, though he wished he could have stayed another moment. "In the tradition of the Hebrews, she would be called Eve. There's another, a man who would be called Adam. But he is not so benign a presence."

"I've never seen anyone like her." Thor glanced back, but she was no longer in sight. He could still feel her there, and leaving her behind made him feel colder, somehow. He straightened, and forced himself not to drag his feet.

"It's a shame about the baby," Ra said absently, his eyes unfocused and distant.

"What about it?"

Ra shook his head, the lines of his face smoothing. He flicked his fingers in dismissal. "The Archangel Michael began a rumor among the slaves which has reached the Pharaoh's ears. He claims the True God has heard the cry of His people, and a male child will be born to the slaves who will deliver the Hebrews from the yoke of Egypt."

Thor stiffened, thinking of the babe barely large enough to be noticed in Eve's stomach. So not only was she a goddess living as a mortal, but she was a slave as well. An odd life to choose, but at least it seemed for a purpose. "And who better to bear the child than the True God's own daughter."

Ra frowned. "Michael does not say who will carry the child, and Pharaoh will not risk losing his slaves. He's ordered all the children born within the year to be killed, along with every boy under the age of three."

"How many?" Thor asked, feeling the pain of it already in his heart.

"Hundreds, if not a full thousand."

His jaw tightened. So many, all innocent. But it was not his place to argue. "That is a great shame."

They walked on in silence and Ra led them back to his temple, between towering obelisks, brilliant as the sun. One of the priests saw them and genuflected, bending so low his forehead touched the stone as he mumbled a prayer.

"Will you join me for refreshments?" Ra asked, waving the priest to his feet.

Thor shook his head. "I have some business in the markets, and much else to do for my father yet. My thanks for your hospitality. I hope one day I will be able to return the favor." He bowed.

Ra smiled and returned the gesture, causing the priest to stare, wide-eyed at the sight of his god humbled. "It is my pleasure, Thor of the Aesir. I wish you a successful journey."

He stood outside the small hut, shifting to catch a glimpse of the interior. It was all shadow and brick, a half-filled loom the only furnishing he could see beyond the bed, itself not much more than a mattress of straw. But from the soft, fretful cries, it seemed Eve had finally given birth to her baby.

Thor had watched over her for months, hiding himself from the Egyptian gods and gleaning what information he could from Eve's daughter, Miriam. It had been an easy thing to cultivate a friendship with the young girl as her mother became heavy with child and Miriam had been sent to the well in Eve's place. He had stopped her from being whipped at least half a dozen times, disgusted that anyone would raise a hand against a girl of seven simply for struggling to raise water from a well.

"A little brother!" Miriam whispered into the dark where he had cloaked himself outside the window.

"A great blessing," he murmured back. Neither the midwife nor Eve noticed. Their heads were bent together over the baby, and Eve wept as the child nursed. The sound of her suffering had been like needles in his heart until it was broken by the babe's wail, healthy and strong.

"It will be impossible to hide him, Yocheved. If you wish him to live, he must be sent away. Smuggled from the city," the midwife said.

"We'll be stopped if we try. The Pharaoh's soldiers will find him."

Thor didn't dare try to manipulate Eve—such a thing would violate every law of conduct between the gods—but it took only the merest thought to influence the midwife. *The river,* he told her.

"Let Miriam take him to the river," the midwife said. "The soldiers will not stop a little girl, and if you lay him in a basket, it will float long enough to take him out of the city. If it is God's will that the baby live, he will be saved."

God's will or not, this child would live. Thor had already seen too many die in this world. Too many lives wasted for nothing but the pleasure of their king. He would not allow the child of a goddess to suffer the same fate. Eve hesitated, seeming to stare straight at him through the window of the hut. He held his breath and emptied his mind of all thought but the baby's safety. If she felt him, let her feel his reassurance, nothing more.

She dropped her eyes to the baby at her breast, and then kissed the small round head. "My boy," she said. "Know my love."

Eve hummed softly while she wrapped the boy in his blanket, laying him in a basket of reeds. The tune stirred memories of milk and warmth in Thor's mind, and he shook his head to clear it. He had no time for distraction. If it was to be done, it must be done quickly. He urged them on silently until Miriam slipped out the door, the basket an awkward burden in her arms.

"I'll carry him," Thor said, stepping out from the shadows. Miriam was strong for a girl her age but the basket was a third as big as she was. He took her hand, cradling the basket in his other arm. "Quickly now. The fastest way to the river."

She tugged him to the right down an alley, and he let her lead. If he used his power to travel through lightning to the water, it would give his presence away, and he could not risk being found by Ra or any of the others. They slipped through the dark streets and Thor did what he could to ensure that they were empty. When they did cross the path of one of Pharaoh's guard by the water, he caused the man to think he had heard his wife's voice, and they passed behind his back down the bank and out of sight.

"Did God send you to save my brother?" Miriam asked.

He looked down at her small face, lit by the moon, and squeezed her hand once before letting go. "Yes," he lied. "But you mustn't speak of it to anyone. Not even your mother."

"Mother says that it's the angels who do God's work, now," Miriam said, her forehead creased. "Are you an angel?"

He shook his head. "Just a friend. Will you keep this secret, Miriam? So your brother will live?" She frowned, but nodded, and he smiled. "Good girl. I'll take him to safety by the water. Go back to your mother, now. She'll have need of you."

Miriam pressed her lips together, turned, and ran.

Thor followed her flight with a light touch in the back of her mind to be sure she did not meet any trouble, and then waded into the water with the basket. He knew exactly where he would take the baby, where he would be safe even from the pharaoh. After all, why would the king question his own daughter if she presented him with a child gifted to her by the gods?

CHAPTER FOUR
Present

"Abby?"

Garrit's mother stood in the doorway when Eve looked up. She hadn't meant to lose so much time, sifting through her memories.

"Juliette." She rose from her seat to greet her with a kiss. "I'm so sorry. I didn't realize you were here already."

Juliette smiled. She was stunningly beautiful, with bright blue eyes and dark hair. Charming, too, which she would have to be to marry into the family. The DeLeon men had always had an overabundance of charisma, but they generally preferred women who weren't bowled over by them when they took wives. Eve had never been sure if that had been a result of nature or nurture.

"Garrit told us you had a difficult day. I hope you don't mind the interruption, but Ethan was most insistent that you would wish to see him right away."

"Ethan?" Eve frowned trying to remember anyone by that name. The door swung open the rest of the way, and she saw the man standing behind Juliette. Her pulse jumped as he locked eyes with her, an arrogance pulling at the corners of his lips. "Oh!"

"*Merci, Madame* DeLeon," he said, smiling with so much power that Eve took an involuntary step back.

Juliette nodded, returning the smile and stepping out of the way. "I'll leave you to your business. We'll see you at dinner, Ethan?"

"I would be thrilled to join you." He watched her leave before slipping into the room and shutting the door behind him. His attention turned to Eve, then, and he studied her with stone gray eyes she knew too well.

"Eve."

She straightened under his inspection and raised her chin. "Adam."

She would not give him the satisfaction of fear or discomfort. Not in her own home, among her own family. Even though looking at him brought back the memories of Michael's threat. She closed her hands into fists to keep them from shaking.

He wasn't supposed to remember. Michael had promised her that much, and she had witnessed it for herself in past lives. Never before now had Adam ever recognized her, ever known to come looking for her, ever remembered who he was. Not since Creation. The punishment for his sins.

"What are you doing here?"

"Your family was kind enough to share with me the details of this part of your past." He was glancing over the books in the library. "Or at least some of them."

She stepped behind a table, keeping it between them. "Because you forced them to."

He inclined his head. Not quite a nod, but an admission. "It was no small effort. In particular, your future father-in-law. His mind is quite strong. *Madame* DeLeon was no trouble though, and very informative. It appears René keeps no secrets from his wife."

The idea that he had wriggled his way into their minds, manipulating and controlling her own family made her taste bile.

"You have no business here, Adam. And frankly, I'm not sure how you remembered to find me at all."

"Time heals all wounds, Sister."

"I'm your sister now, am I? I thought you had intended to have me as your wife."

"Clearly you're otherwise engaged at the moment." He smiled that smug and powerful smile again. "Not that I would object if you changed your mind. He's not good enough for you."

"That line is getting old."

He picked up the journal from the table beside him and opened it. "Your late husband's?"

She nodded stiffly, resisting the urge to rip the book from his hands before his very presence in the same room could taint it.

"'Anessa has agreed to become my wife. Her father was glad to be rid of her, and I am relieved that I can save her. We will depart directly for my estate. The sooner she is out of the public eye, the better. I can keep her safe in the country.'" Adam stopped reading aloud and laughed. "So noble of him to rescue you. What were you then? A nobleman's daughter?"

"I was."

"And what was your crime that your father was so happy to see you gone?"

She shrugged, not wanting to give him even that much information. Her hands closed around the edges of the small end table. At this point, she wasn't above throwing furniture.

He stepped forward, all of the smugness leaving his expression, replaced with an earnestness she had never thought to see in his face. It was more terrifying than the arrogance, and for a moment she remembered another life, when if it hadn't been for the war and the angels, and knowing what would come, she might have welcomed him. But not today.

"I can give you more than this, Eve."

"More was your dream, not mine." She sat down in a chair, hoping he would do the same. That he would be forced to keep some distance between them.

He did, but barely, perching on the edge of the seat across from her. "Yet here you are, about to become the wife of a very rich man. If you want money, I can make you a queen, Eve, an empress."

They'd had this conversation once before. In a golden city, while his memory had still been lost. Did he realize it? It made her head spin to hear the words again. She would never forget any of it. "That has never been my ambition."

Adam closed the book and set it back down on the table. He leaned forward, placing his hand on her knee. "We were made for each other, Eve."

She tried to ignore the way his touch clouded her mind. Heat spread up her thigh, tempting, inviting. More of his games. It had to be.

She brushed his hand from her leg and rose, needing more space between them. The last of the sun cast a red glow through the window. She watched it set, hugging herself and waiting for her mind to clear and her thoughts to organize into the truth she had known for too long.

Michael would not like this. She could still see the angel's cold face as he whispered the punishment he would rain upon her and all her line if she forgot the lessons of the Garden and let Adam into her body.

If Adam had come to her in her last life? She shook her head. She couldn't even think of it. He hadn't, and she hadn't. Besides, she had been too distracted by her past husbands to have noticed him anyway, lost and drugged into memory and dreams. If it were a choice between Thorgrim and Adam, it would always be Thorgrim. Regardless of her sanity.

She kept her tone even and cool and hoped he didn't notice her trembling. "Michael would as soon see us both dead than allow it. He'd rather burn the world himself than give it into your keeping."

"Michael has been absent for millennia. This is what you were made for, Eve. For me. To love me."

"I was made to correct your mistakes. So that our people would survive and live to their potential, instead of being ground beneath your heel. I was made to love everyone but you."

His silence was the sound of a thousand men marching out from Troy, and she felt his eyes on her, staring, searching for some weakness to exploit. No. She wouldn't remember that now. She wouldn't give him a way in. Whomever he had been then, as Paris, he wasn't the same man now.

"At least help me find the Garden. I'll go there and bother no one. Exile myself to prove that all I want is you."

She turned back to him, frowning. Even if she had believed him, and she didn't, it made no sense. He honestly thought the Garden could be found? Perhaps time hadn't healed everything, after all.

"It was burned to the ground, Adam. Gone, all of it, wasted."

His eyes hardened to slate, and the room was suddenly too warm. She felt his mind touch hers, insinuating itself into her consciousness like a worm burrowing into freshly turned soil. She clenched her jaw and shut her mind of everything but the memory he searched for. The Garden, scorched to ash, flared brightly into her mind. He was unbelieving at first, then angry, trying to force himself deeper, pressing against her thoughts and the image of smoke and cinder. She imagined her thoughts, her memories into stone, forcing him back.

"Not like that, Adam." She couldn't keep the resentment from her voice, or the anger from her face. Her nails dug into her palm, but she didn't dare touch him even to slap him. "You won't violate me. Not then and not now."

He crossed the room, and had her by the arm before she even

thought to move. His anger, his frustration, washed over her in pounding waves of red light and burning heat. Her breath caught, her mind throbbing.

"You will give me what I want, Eve." His grip was hard, and he twisted her elbow. "It has always only been a matter of time."

Then he let her go and left the room. She rubbed her arm and wilted against the windowsill. Her head ached from his attempted invasion, but he hadn't managed to break through her defenses. Whatever power he had, he hadn't quite mastered it. Of course, he'd probably never needed to learn any kind of subtlety.

She followed the black cloud of his anger as he stormed out of the house and drove off, until he recognized that she was following his mind, and he was gone.

§

Eve joined the others for dinner. The dining room table was covered with take-out boxes of various sizes, serving forks and spoons sticking out of them. René, Garrit's father, had heaped his plate high already. She sat down in her usual seat beside Garrit, and he smiled.

Juliette glanced behind her. "*Où est Ethan?*"

She didn't meet Juliette's eyes. "Ethan had another engagement."

Garrit passed her a carton and she served herself. He'd ordered beef adana kebabs and there were already two of them on her plate. Probably to keep René from eating them all. Garrit knew she loved them.

"*C'est bizarre.* I was under the distinct impression he wished to spend several weeks here," Juliette said. "He seemed adamant about it."

Eve tried to smile with some kind of reassurance as she served herself from a container of tabouleh. She could have used another hour to herself before dinner, crying with relief that he was gone and no one would die today, but she didn't have it. And they needed to know. It would be their lives and their blood spilled, in the end.

"Ethan was not exactly the man he led you to believe he was. It's no fault of your own. My brother has always been brilliant at games of deceit."

There was absolute silence. Eve could feel them absorbing her words, and then winced at the white-flare of their shock. After fighting against Adam's invasion of her thoughts, filtering out their emotional responses took more effort than she had the patience for. She pinched the bridge of her nose against the throbbing behind her eyes. It had been a very long time since she'd had to exercise those particular muscles.

"We had no idea, Abby, or we would never have brought him." René said.

Eve let out a breath, steadying herself. She didn't want them to see her fear or her worry, and absolutely not her pain. "I know."

Garrit was watching her, but she kept her gaze on her plate. The timing of all of this was atrocious.

"Am I the only person at the table with no idea of what's going on?"

She flinched at his accusation, bitter and needling, more than his tone. If she didn't meet his eyes now—she lifted her gaze, her expression carefully neutral.

"The man your parents brought to meet me, Ethan, is Adam."

Garrit's jaw tightened and his mouth thinned into a line of frustration. Better than anger, she supposed. He pushed his plate away and stood up, his gaze going from Eve to his father. Garrit shook his head just once. "Excuse me."

She watched him leave the room, and sighed. "I'm sorry. He only discovered last night I'm Eve, and he's upset I didn't tell him myself, earlier."

"He needs only time, Abby. He loves you," Juliette said.

"*Quel imbécile,*" René mumbled. "You are the same woman, still, and he should not blame you for not seeing what was before his nose."

Eve tried not to smile. René was the same sort of man that Ryam had been, from his dark eyes to his imperturbable attitude. It helped to remember that. Ryam had always kept her safe.

"I did point that out to him. I'm afraid it didn't make it any easier for him to swallow."

René laughed, his eyes warming. "You are good for him, Abby. A man needs a woman who will speak plainly, though at times he may not care for what she says. DeLeon men, doubly so."

"René will speak with him," Juliette said. "He is not so stubborn he will not listen."

René nodded, unfazed that his wife had volunteered him to an unenviable task. He served himself another helping of hummus.

"Thank you," Eve said.

Juliette smiled. "*Bon.* Now, tell us what you have planned for the wedding. Garrit says you would have it here, at the manor? I think the courtyard would suit you, with the chapel doors thrown wide. Is that what you had in mind?"

"Yes." Eve glanced at René. He rolled his eyes and went back to his dinner. But it was a relief to change the subject. To think about her marriage. She'd be safer then. They all would be. "Garrit was worried about the weather, but I think if we rent a pavilion tent, it would be just fine."

"*Oui, parfait!* You will want the shade from the sun, in any event. Have you thought of what you will serve? I know a pastry chef *trés bon*. He would be pleased to create your cake."

Eve grinned. "Would you be willing to arrange an introduction? I'd love it if we could do some of this together."

"*Ma chérie,* I've only been waiting for you to ask."

§

Garrit was reading Ryam's journal when Eve found him in the library. She hesitated at the door. Giving him space was all well and good, but she hadn't exactly counted on Adam's arrival.

He looked up at her and smiled. "It's all right, Abby. I was waiting for you." He set the book down.

"I wasn't sure you were ready to talk to me yet."

He shrugged and then waved her to a seat across from him. It was the seat Adam had occupied not hours earlier. She sat down and tried to pretend her brother had never come, but her hands were shaking, and she pressed them against her knees to stop it.

"*Papa* found me after dinner," he said. "He was worried you and I were having problems. He called me a damned fool." Garrit grinned.

"Your father has never been one to mince words."

"No. And he makes it very difficult to argue." His gaze drifted back to the book. "The truth has always been staring me in the face. I just chose not to see it."

She looked at her hands, forcing herself to open them from the fists they had become. "I should've told you."

"I should've *known* you." His tone was grim. "What kind of DeLeon am I, if I can't even recognize you for who you are?"

"The kind who wasn't looking." She shrugged. "You had no reason to see me coming. I didn't come to you for sanctuary. I didn't use any of the traditional phrases that should have alerted you. I didn't even mean to find you. It was pure happenstance that we ended up in the same university at the same time." She grimaced. "And the last time a man learned what I was, he had me locked up."

"Lord Ryam knew you on sight."

She sat back in her chair and rubbed her forehead. There were more pressing issues than her late husband's insight, but it bothered her anyway. "I'm beginning to suspect Ryam had more secrets than I did. Which is saying quite a bit."

He studied her for a moment, his lips pressed together to keep from smiling. "I thought you could read minds."

"Ordinarily, yes. Among this family, it takes a bit more work. And Ryam had a stronger mind than many."

"But Adam had no problem with my parents."

"Adam has no respect for the privacy of anyone else's mind, though he left me with the impression it was mostly your mother he mined for information. Your father he only had to charm."

"It would take much more than charm to make my father break his vow. Aren't you familiar with it?"

She shook her head, but had no trouble imagining it. "I can't say I'm completely surprised."

Similar vows had been made periodically, but she didn't recall telling Ryam anything that might provoke him to that kind of measure. Of course it didn't have to be Ryam; the last time she had met with this family, she hadn't been in her right mind. She might have said anything.

He opened the journal to a marked page, and handed it to her. "Our family heritage. I was made to take it also, though I never really understood it until now."

Eve read the page he indicated. She read it again, to be sure she understood, and swallowed against the tightness in her throat.

Watch for Adam, it said. *Now that he has his memory, he will come, and he cannot be allowed near to her, for the sake of all the world. Guard her!* And there was more. More of the same.

She would have remembered if she had told Ryam any of this. She was certain of that. It wasn't the kind of conversation that was easily forgotten, nor was it anything that wouldn't have come up if it had been known generally within the family. For a dizzying moment, she wondered if Thorgrim had haunted her more than once. It was a long moment before she trusted herself to respond to what she was looking at, and not to the ghost of insanity breathing in her ear.

"How is this possible?"

"*Quoi?*"

She looked up, clearing her throat and forcing herself not to think of men who should have been dead having conversations with the living. "Until today, when he arrived here, I had no clue that Adam's memory had been restored. He isn't supposed to remember anything, Garrit! From one life, to the next. He isn't supposed to know me, never mind be able to find me this way! But here in this passage, written over five hundred years ago, is a statement by the man I was married to, of his foreknowledge of the very event that took place today. How is it possible?"

"Did you not tell him yourself of the danger?"

She shook her head, staring at the page again. "There are many things in this world I have no trouble taking on faith, Garrit. But this—" she reread the passage again and, putting aside the peculiarities of her last life, tried to consider things reasonably, logically. "It says he received word. Who could he have received word from? I couldn't have missed an angel knocking on our door. And I can't imagine Michael deigning to do so, or bothering to speak with a mere mortal, regardless."

She didn't quite repress the shiver that ran down her spine at the idea. She would not have been unaware if the angels had come a third time. Michael had made it very clear that if she ever saw him again, it would mean her death. Ghosts would have been preferable.

"I think he would've mentioned an angel coming down from on high." Garrit smiled wryly. "Maybe it was just something he guessed at. Deduced from something you said."

She regarded him for a long moment. It was clear he didn't find the *how* important, only the application of the knowledge. "Perhaps."

It wasn't important right now. What Ryam knew or didn't know five hundred years ago, what Luc, Garrit's great-grandfather, had thought when she had arrived on his doorstep out of her mind, none of it mattered. She forced herself not to think of the distraction. And absolutely she couldn't afford to lose herself in that past life and those memories. Adam himself was the problem now and she couldn't afford to court insanity.

"As it happened, you seemed perfectly capable of dispatching him on your own," Garrit was saying. "I wonder why we swore a vow at all, if it is so easy as that."

"He left because I was engaged to you. But he'll be back, Garrit. If not in this life, then the next. He will keep coming for me, any time he thinks he has half a chance." Until Michael grew tired of it, and killed them both outright, along with who knew how many countless others. Would she be reborn if he killed her with the sword? Her stomach twisted. If Adam knew, he had never told her. "He is nothing if not persistent. Pig-headedly so."

Garrit leaned forward, taking the book from her and setting it aside, covering her hands in both of his. "You will be safe with me, Abby. I promise you. I will keep you safe."

"Because of your vow." She heard the sorrow in her own voice, and looked away.

He brought her face back to his. "Because you will be my wife, and I love you. The vow has very little to do with that."

Some of the tightness in her chest lifted, and she breathed more easily. As long as he loved her, she was safe. She had to believe it. "Then you've forgiven me?"

He pressed a kiss to her knuckles. "If you'll forgive me for being such a damned fool about it."

"There's nothing to forgive." She leaned forward and let him pull her into his lap, her forehead resting against his. No, the past didn't matter. Not as long as she had Garrit now. Not as long as they were getting married. Adam wouldn't touch her if she was happily married. He would have no chance of drawing her away. It would be useless, once the vows were exchanged in sacrament, with love. And if Adam was gone, the angel would not come.

For the moment, they were safe. And safer still once she was married.

CHAPTER FIVE
Creation

☙

The men returned, dragging something awkwardly between them. Adam stood and she sighed with relief to be free of the press of his body against hers. But her relief fled, replaced with a cold knot in her stomach, as they came closer. They carried a man, dripping from the rain, grizzled and empty. Adam pressed his fingers to the neck below the jaw, frowning at the closed eyes of the body.

She took the opportunity, with Adam distracted, to move farther back against the wall into a corner. The rock was cold and damp, but it was welcome against the flush of her skin. He had not let her move more than a finger's width from him, holding her fast against his side when she tried to shift away.

"Take it away." Adam turned from the wrinkled, gray man and dropped back to the floor beside her. "There's little enough space for shelter without keeping the dead. Let the angels have what's left, if they want it."

The two men who had carried the body between them glanced at one another, but they stepped back into the rain, returning a moment later without their burden. Water dripped down their bodies from their hair. One of the men glanced at her as he passed, his eyes dark like the earth, and soft. Softer still when she met them, holding his gaze. His lips thinned, lines wrinkling his forehead. Would his hands be as warm as Adam's, if he touched her? Somehow, she did not think they would be as hard, pushing and twisting and drawing her too near.

He settled back into the dirt and shadow on the other side of the cave where she could no longer see his face, and she did not think she would learn the answer soon.

Adam covered her knee with his hand, still staring out the mouth of the cave into the rain. "You'll see, Eve." Though he said her name, she wasn't sure he expected her to listen. "We'll be gods among them."

"Gods?" She shifted her position and brought her knees back to her chest again. His hand dropped away, but she rubbed at the place it had been. The warmth of his palm had seeped into her skin. It made her feel too hot. Too hot and too close to him.

His lips curved. "I forget that you weren't welcomed to this life the way we were. Elohim was already gone when your eyes opened. Only a husk remaining. Just as well." The last was mumbled and the smile left his face. He studied her again with his hard eyes. "You are the last woman made, Eve. The last and the most important. Elohim made you. He made all of us, all of this. Trees and grasses, flowers and moss, birds and fish and dogs and all the other animals to please me and give me joy. But you above all were made to be my companion. My equal. Made for me more than any of the others."

She shivered, but it had nothing to do with the cold of the stone on her skin, or the chill in the air from the rain and the wind, or the thunder that rolled through the stone into her bones. "Will you not make others?"

"No." His eyes flashed and he scowled at the rain. "I don't have the power to wake life from the dust." His voice was tight and clipped, each word ground from between his teeth. His jaw tensed and something twitched beneath the surface. Then it stopped and he seemed to exhale all the rest of the strain in a long breath. "But it's only a matter of time. When I find what I'm looking for, it will be within my power to do anything."

He touched her cheek then, and she heard what he didn't say. *With the fruit, not even the angels will stop me. I will know their secrets, too. Elohim meant it to be this way. This was his gift to me. Every plant, every animal. Including the tree. Or else why would He have made it at all?*

She turned her face away, leaning her head back against the cool stone and closing her eyes again. The storm had been going on for so long. The rain thundered in her ears, and her head ached. The darkness helped. But then he took her hand in his and she could see herself through his eyes, the curves of her breasts, the rich brown of her hair when the lightning flashed. It was starting to get darker now. Less light was coming through the storm into the cave.

She tried to pull away, but his grip hardened, twisting her fingers until they popped, and she cried out, looking up at his face. It was expressionless, and he tightened his hand further for just a moment, staring into her eyes. There was nothing soft about his gaze.

He let go and rose. "Sleep, Eve. Think about what I've told you. What I'm offering."

He leaned against the wall of the cave, near the mouth, his back to her. When he stayed there, she crawled away into the dark. Where he would not see her to touch her. Where he would not see her to pull her close. Where she could close her eyes without seeing through his.

A hand on her shoulder, warm and rough, startled her awake. Sleep felt so much like the peace before she had come into being that she choked back a sound of pain upon waking from it. Her eyes burned and what little she could see blurred. She rubbed her face, and her hand came away damp.

"Forgive me." The hand fell away. "I didn't mean to frighten you." It was a man's voice, but lower than Adam's.

Fear. Was that what it was when her heart beat so heavily against her chest? What she had felt when Adam pulled her close and wouldn't let her go? She sat up and searched for his face in the dark. The whites of his eyes were just barely visible.

She reached to touch him, this man who wasn't Adam, to feel where he was. "Who are you?"

"Reu." He caught her hand and brought it to his face. His hair was damp, and his touch was light, soft. She wished she could see his eyes. "Are you well?"

He was right beside her. Closer than she had realized. But now she knew where to look, she could almost see him there, kneeling. "Should I not be?"

"He hurt you," he said, quiet still. There were others speaking, their voices low, barely audible above the noise of the rain. "I heard you cry out."

She pulled her hand back and it slipped from his. He didn't tighten his hold like Adam had. Just let go. "Where is he?"

Even his eyes disappeared in the shadows when he moved. "He went to his chambers. You're safe for now. Until morning. He wasn't pleased you crawled away."

"He told me to sleep."

He sighed and she saw his eyes again, flashing in the dark. "You have to be careful, Eve. You shouldn't upset him."

She pulled her knees up to her chest, searching for his face. "What happened to that other man? The one with the gray hair."

"Elohim." His voice hollowed, making her chest tighten strangely. "He gave the last of His strength to you. To bring you to life from the dust and make you immortal, like Adam."

"I don't understand." They kept telling her these things, but it felt like it was only pieces of the whole. She wasn't sure what any of it meant. What it meant to her. For her life. What it meant even to live. "Adam said I was made as his companion."

"Adam is blinded by pride. Spoiled by God's indulgence. You were made to live. Not to be his slave, used and abused for his pleasure. None of us were." He spoke the way Adam had, when he had told her he lacked the power he desired. Anger, she thought.

But even naming it made her uneasy. Anger wasn't something she should know so soon. And fear. Why would the voice have brought her here, torn her from the peace she had known? She could not shake the feeling of wrongness, so thick in the air.

"The other things that were made," she asked, because Adam had said it was not only her he owned, "what about them?"

"Adam believes we are all his to grind back into the dust. But Elohim never meant for things to be this way. That's why He made you. We're meant to be free, Eve. To love and to laugh. To be unafraid."

She closed her eyes. It wasn't that much darker than the cave, but it was more comfortable. Choosing not to see, rather than being unable to do so. Her eyes ached from trying to find the shape of this man in the shadow.

"I don't understand." Nothing made sense. Not the things Adam said, or the things this Reu told her, or the things Adam didn't say. None of it seemed to fit together. Adam said the confusion would pass, but it hadn't. It was getting even more twisted and her head felt slow and thick. "I don't understand any of this. Am I supposed to? Was I made wrong, that I don't understand?"

"No." She felt his hand on hers, warm and dry, but gentle. Adam had touched her gently, too, at first. But it hadn't lasted even this long. "Forgive me, Eve. It's easy to forget how difficult it is in the beginning. How hard it is to understand everything that's happening before you even have the words to describe the sky. And it's been a long time for me. Several moons. I should have waited to speak with you, but I didn't know when I would have another chance. Adam will keep you close. He's made that clear."

She only really understood the last part, and something inside her twisted. "He says that I'm his."

"You're not." And she heard the anger in his voice again, and a new hardness. "You don't belong to anyone, Eve. Least of all him. Don't let him tell you otherwise. Don't let anyone tell you otherwise."

She shook her head. "How can you be so certain?"

"I was second made. Sometimes, Elohim even asked me to walk with Him." From his voice, she thought this was important, but she didn't know why. "At the end, He spoke with me more often. Before you were made. He said that you would be cast in His image, as Adam had been, but He meant to give you His Grace as well."

Grace. The word tugged at something inside her, something from before, when she had floated through the void, but she could not grasp it. "Perhaps in time, this will all make more sense to me."

He sighed softly, his hand tightening around hers. Then he let go. She missed the warmth when it was gone, and even the pressure of his fingers. When he touched her, it didn't hurt. She just felt…calmed.

"I hope it will." She heard him stand, a darker shadow in the black. "Rest. It will be easier in the morning. I promise."

She curled back up against the earth, and closed her eyes. But in the dark, she saw the warm brown gaze of the man who had carried Elohim's body out into the rain. A man very unlike Adam.

CHAPTER SIX
1026 BC

§

Thor took his time returning from the east, knowing he could not avoid stopping in Egypt. Word of the Hebrew exodus had reached him even on his travels, and he had not been much surprised to hear they had been led out by a man who had once been a prince named Moses. The baby he had saved.

But Ra grinned when they met at last, clasping hands with him. "It is good to see you again, my friend. Very good. How was your trip?"

"I was received warmly." Thor returned the older god's smile. Either Ra did not suspect his part, or did not care, and Thor was surprised how happy it made him to know they could continue in friendship. "Word of my coming had reached Bhagavan-Shiva ahead of me. He said you had promised me safe conduct and I was to consider myself his most honored guest as your friend."

Ra nodded. "Some wine to rinse the dust from your throat?"

"I would be most grateful." Thor went to the window, which looked out on the river, and ran a hand over his face. Egypt did not seem to have suffered much for the loss of its slaves. The temples still shone with gold, silver, and jewels.

A servant appeared at his elbow, offering a cup of wine with a bow, and Thor accepted it. This throne room was part of Pharaoh's own, a back room known only to those who served Ra and to Pharaoh himself. Every whisper of request was attended to almost immediately, the servants anxious to please their god.

"And how did you find the company of the Olympians? I imagine Zeus was quite interested in you, as similar as your strengths are."

Thor shrugged. Zeus had been determined to see Thor drunk beneath his table, and the other Olympians seemed eager only for whatever gossip he could share. "The goddesses seemed pleased by my gifts. I had not realized how fond they were of golden apples."

Ra chuckled, joining him at the window. "I did hear that someone had inscribed a message on one. For the fairest, it said."

"Indeed." Thor had never met a vainer group of goddesses than those living on Olympus. Aphrodite and Hera in particular. He glanced at the other god's face, but Ra did not meet his eyes. "What happened?"

"It must have been after you left them. You did hear about the Trojan War, I trust?"

"Only that it devastated the Greeks to win."

Ra smiled, but it was thin. "That was the least of it. We came very close to losing the world, Thor, simply to relieve Aphrodite's boredom. There are times I wonder if allowing the Olympians to settle was worth it, but then Athena comes to see me and I'm reminded why I was convinced."

"She is a brilliant goddess, to be sure. The best of the lot." But Thor's thoughts were still distracted by Ra's comments about the war. "What do you mean, about losing the world?"

"Aphrodite gave Eve into Adam's hands. Eve was Helen of

Sparta, of course, though how she was born a child of Zeus will give the Olympians nightmares for centuries. And Aphrodite helped Adam steal her."

"Is that so terrible?"

Ra looked up at him, his face gray. "Their child would inherit this world in its entirety, and have the power of the True God to change it, or destroy it utterly. Everything we had built would be lost. At best, we would be cast out of this plane, at worst wiped from existence."

Thor set down his wine, his stomach gone sour. "Why would the True God allow such a thing?"

"He is old and has not the strength even to govern his own creation, or else none of us would be permitted here. I think his children are the only hope he has left, but the risk is too great. Even Michael and the angels fear it." Ra's gaze remained distant, his expression grooved with some remembered pain he did not share. "Perhaps it would not be so terrible a thing, but for Adam. We should all be grateful he does not know who or what he is, or nothing would stop him. He is a much more agreeable creature, living in ignorance."

Thor shook his head. He had met Adam briefly, on his way east. The flicker of his aura, like the glow of electrum, impossible to miss after Thor had watched Eve for so long. Adam was a selfish man, and ambitious to be sure. Thor had lingered long enough to see him turn a village against its chief with nothing but charm and charisma. Adam had negotiated his marriage to the man's daughter, placing himself in the best position possible before beginning his campaign, and then it had only been a word here and there in the right ears, each argument carefully chosen to undermine the chieftain. He had worked as smoothly as Loki to reach his goal, and Thor could well imagine the man could be dangerous in the wrong circumstances.

Eve on the other hand, he could not imagine as a force for

anything but good from the little he had seen of her. She did not seem to search for power as her brother did, or want anything but peace in her own life. But if she could end the world it was his duty to learn all he could about her.

"This True God. Is he a threat to us?"

Ra still stared at the river, his face lined and brittle. "The angels are the ones you should consult about God's plans, if they'll bother to speak with you," he admitted. "But if what you really wish to know is the truth about the girl, I may be able to point you in a more fruitful direction. There seems to be one line she returns to, often enough that it's been noted. The House of Lions. After escaping Troy, she fled there. She doesn't like war."

"Odin will wish to know of her, I am sure." Thor scratched at his jaw. It was more than he had hoped for, but he had no wish to appear too eager. "Can you direct me to these people?"

"You'll find them on the other side of the Alps, not terribly far from the coast, somewhere in the foothills. I'm told they live quite alone there, apart from any others." He smiled, but there was no humor in it. "I cannot promise they will receive you warmly or that they will give you the information you wish to know about the girl. The rumor is that the bloodline is descended directly from her first husband, at the dawn of Creation. They appear to be quite protective of her."

Thor ignored the warning. If these Lions did not accept gold, they would certainly accept the information he could offer them, and being a god with power over rain and storm made him a valuable ally if nothing else. "I thank you, Amun-Ra, for your hospitality."

Ra inclined his head in the slightest of acknowledgments. "I will be curious to hear what you discover."

Thor bowed and showed himself out.

He traveled by foot, for the most part. It was easier to explain himself that way, with the dust and sweat of the journey on his clothes. He could have called the lightning to take him as far as the Etruscan lands, but Odin's order was to learn and Thor had done this duty often enough to know the best way to learn about a world was to live in it.

He sailed with traders from Egypt across the sea, giving them good winds and clear skies to Ra's greater glory, and then made his way north over land. He was grateful to be leaving the desert behind. The arid lands had not appealed to him—all yellows and browns. And the gold with which Egypt chose to drape itself served only to remind him of Sif. Her golden hair, warm and soft as silk, wrapped around his hand. The scent of her skin, gleaming in the firelight after their lovemaking. And her eyes, glowing with gold fire as she looked at him, bathing him in her light.

Thor smiled as he trudged over another rocky hill. Sif would be waiting for him, even now. As soon as he finished this final journey to learn what he could about the Lions and Eve, he could return to her. It had been more than two centuries, now. Far too long for any god to remain celibate. Sif would be very pleased to see him, and he had no intention of stirring from her bed for the next year, if he could get away with it. Odin owed him that much for his service.

"Meh!"

The noise startled him from his thoughts, followed by soft scuffling. A nanny goat stood on the slope, beside a crevasse in the rock. The scuffling noise came again from behind the nanny, followed by a pathetic bleat.

"Meh-ehh!"

The nanny was fat, its coarse brown fur shining, with a tattered piece of twine tied around its neck. The animal was heavy with milk. Heavy enough that it should have found its way home to be milked. When he stepped forward the goat didn't start, but stared at him with narrow eyes.

"Lost your baby, have you?" He crouched down, letting the goat catch his scent and reaching out to scratch between its horns. The scuffling sound came from the pit again, and he leaned over to look. The nanny stiffened, but he stroked her soft ears and kept scratching, murmuring reassurance.

"Meh!"

As he had thought, her baby was caught in the crevasse. The kid's front leg was stuck straight out, though at its mother's call it tried to shift and rise. The leg gave, and the kid fell back to the dirt with the goat equivalent of a whimper.

Thor grunted and lay down against the stone on his stomach, reaching down to grab the kid. It was a long fall, and he could only just reach the animal himself from the rock above. He caught it by the hind leg, and it bleated anxiously, exciting the nanny which promptly bit his ear.

He growled, and the mama left off with a shudder. The kid stopped squirming at once, and he pulled it up, setting it down in the scrub. "There. You ungrateful *geit*."

The nanny scrambled toward its young as soon as Thor rose. The kid tried to climb to its feet to suckle, but it didn't put any weight on its front leg, holding it off the ground oddly. Thor rubbed at his ear, but it had been more nuisance than anything else, and he didn't think the nanny would try anything similar a second time.

There was little sign of the rest of the herd. The area had been picked over, most of the green stripped from the branches of what plants had grown, but if there had been other goats here, they'd moved on. Judging by the nanny's bag, it couldn't have been more than a day. The animal might have been left behind this morning when the rest of the herd left, unwilling to leave its young.

The kid wouldn't be able to walk very far in this landscape with a broken leg. If he left it, they were both more likely to be eaten by a lion or wolf than to find their way home. But he was close to where Ra had told him he was likely to find Eve's people. He sighed. When the kid had finished suckling, he picked it up and nodded to the nanny. "Go on. I'll follow."

The nanny's eyes narrowed to slits again, but it shook itself and started off down the hill, pausing every few steps to be sure that he followed. They hadn't gone very far when he heard a voice calling, and the nanny goat picked up her speed and called back, recognizing its keeper.

Thor pushed through a line of brush and the nanny led him around a small stand of trees into a meadow. A young girl stood, shading her eyes from the sun with her hand, watching for them. Or at least watching for the goat.

When she saw him she reached for a staff, abandoned on the ground, and whistled sharply. A large white dog lumbered to its feet amidst the goats and barked. Thor gave it a look and it whined, its hackles raised along its back. The nanny bleated and trotted to its mistress.

The girl dropped a hand to the goat's head, almost absently, her eyes not leaving Thor's face. "What do you want?"

He smiled and nodded to the nanny, the kid still in his arms. It took him a moment to find the language and lift it from her mind.

"I found your goat on the hill." The words did not fall as easily from his tongue as he might have wished, though it was only a slight variation from that which was spoken in the southern peninsula. He cleared his throat. "This one has a broken leg, I'm afraid, but I thought you might like it back."

The girl hesitated, her fingers tightening around the staff. The dog was at her side now, its ears perked forward and its head low.

"Meh!" the nanny said. The kid bleated back, and the girl's gaze shifted, softening at the sight of the animal he held. She set the staff aside and reached for the kid.

"Thank you," she said, her fingers moving over the bones of the front leg. She frowned. "What happened to him?"

"He fell into a fissure. By the look of the leg, it can't be too terrible a break. If you set it, he should be just fine in a few weeks."

"Can you find me something to splint it?" She sat down carefully on the ground, the kid in her lap, and began to tear a strip of cloth from the bottom of her skirt. He didn't think she could be more than twelve years old, though she worked with the seriousness of someone older.

There were plenty of branches to pick from, though the younger and greener the more it would bend. He settled on one as thick around as the kid's leg, and snapped it into two lengths. It was another moment's work to strip the twigs. He pulled lightning through his hand and burned the bark free, leaving the wood slightly charred but smooth.

"Oh!"

She was watching the smoke rise through his fingers, her eyes wide. He smiled again and crouched down in front of her, handing her the wood. "If I'd left the bark, it would have worn rough against his leg. This will be better."

She took the wood without looking at it. "But how did you do that?"

He opened his hands, showing her his palms, then brushed the soot from them. "I just can."

"Didn't it hurt?"

He shook his head. "Not at all."

Her forehead creased and she dropped her gaze to the kid in her lap, taking the branches and the cloth and splinting them against the leg. He could hear her mind, buzzing over what she'd seen, trying to understand. But she was young enough, he hoped, that she would believe.

"What else can you do?" she asked, after she had finished tying the splint, and set the kid back to its feet by the mother.

Thor helped her up from the ground, and glanced at the sky. It was sunny and bright, clear and cloudless. "See that tree, there?"

He pointed toward a medium sized oak, its boughs heavy with green leaves, and she nodded. Torching the hill would not make him a very welcome guest, and while he could have chosen one already dead, it would be more likely to catch fire.

"Don't blink," he said. "And don't be frightened."

Thor closed his eyes, and called to the static in the air, drawing it together and focusing it into the sky around the tree. He could feel the moisture following, like a sweat breaking out on a hot day, and didn't stop the cloud from forming, though he could have. He opened his eyes and traced the path from the cloud to the tree in his mind.

There was a flash of white where the lightning followed, crawling over the tree and into the earth, singeing leaves and branches on its way. The thunderclap was immediate, startling the goats and causing the dog to start barking. But Thor paid no attention to the animals, his gaze on the girl.

Her face was white as bone and she did not turn to look at him. "You did that?"

Smoke rose from the tree, and he rang the moisture from the cloud that had formed, focusing the rain into a deluge over the area that had been struck and leaving the animals and the two of them in sunlight.

"Yes."

"And the rain, too?" she asked.

He smiled. "The rain, too."

She turned to look at him, almost shyly, as if she wasn't sure if she should. "Are you an angel?"

Thor grunted. It bothered him to be mistaken for one a second time, but he didn't let it show on his face. These people could hardly be expected to know him for what he was, and the Aesir were too new to the world to be known at all this far south, but for the word he had spread himself.

"Do angels summon lightning and rain?" he asked.

She bit her lip and brushed her hair out of her eyes. "Not exactly. Grandmother Eve told us that the Archangel Michael can call lightning and fire through his sword though." She frowned and glanced at his side. "Do you have a sword?"

"No." Grandmother Eve. Then he had found them, the House of Lions. It did not seem possible that two Eves could exist with particular knowledge of the angels. "But in the city where I live, I have goats."

The girl smiled, and it lit her face and eyes. Yes. These were Eve's people. And this girl was of Eve's blood. He could see the resemblance in that smile, the closeness of the line to the goddess they called grandmother. "What are you then, if not an angel?"

He met the girl's eyes and let his own glow white. "My name is Thor," he said. "God of thunder."

§

Her name was Evelia. For weeks he met with her, helping her to tend the goats, and bringing rain and sun to the village to ensure a bountiful harvest. Freyr might have done better, making the grapes grow larger and plumper, and the wheat taller and sweeter, but Freyr was by now in Asgard, building his home with the other gods who followed Odin, and Thor did what he could do. It wasn't inconsiderable.

When the time came to harvest the wheat and the other grains, he asked Evelia to take him to the village. Visitors were always more welcome in times of plenty, hospitality less begrudged, and he would be able to help in the fields while he gave them good sun.

"Mama and Papa will be happy to meet with you, when I tell them what you have done." Evelia said, prodding one of the goats with her staff to keep it moving. The young kid he had rescued had long since grown out of his splint, and charged about the hillside over the slippery stone as if he had never fallen. "Papa won't believe that you're a god, of course. You'll have to show them. Like you did with me."

"I'll give them any proof they require. As I have already." Thor nodded to the wheat field outside the village, more valuable than gold for farmers. "Eve's people, of any, should know the truth. And I can protect her, if the need arises."

Evelia frowned. "From the man with the stone eyes. Adam. That's why we're supposed to be wary of strangers. No man with gray eyes is permitted on our lands. It's one of the laws."

"Is that how you know him?"

"That's how Grandmother Eve told us we should. She said we would feel him, too, like fire on our skin, but if he got that close to us, it was probably too late."

"Too late for what?" he asked, keeping his eyes on the goats.

He nudged a nanny that had stopped to graze on a bush. How she could eat anything more with her bag so heavy with milk, he wasn't sure. They were nearly to the village now, though, and he could hear the sounds of the people within it. Laughing and shouting, barking dogs and bleating animals. The goats heard it too, and for the most part, they sped up, anxious to be milked and stabled.

"Too late to stop him from hurting us," she said, as if there was no other answer.

Thor grunted. Evelia's knowledge was vague in regard to Eve and her brother, but valuable all the same. He imagined her parents must know more. He hoped they did, or else this trip to the village would be wasted effort. The golden wheat reminded him too much of Sif, and he wanted to return to Asgard.

"When Eve came here last, what was her name?" he asked.

Evelia looked up at him and smiled. "Mama says she was called Helen, and her hair was the color of sunshine. She was glorious, Grandpapa says. Like an angel from God. But even Mama and Papa were not born yet when she lived here."

He returned her smile. Helen. Then she would have come out of desperation and fear. Yes. These people would know. He would stay as long as necessary to earn their trust, as a god and as a man. And then he would return to Odin, and be very grateful for the loving embrace of his wife.

CHAPTER SEVEN
Present

☙

Eve frowned and rubbed her face. It had been weeks since Adam's intrusion, but she could not shake the feeling that he still hovered around her, somewhere just outside her immediate perception. It left her unsettled and worried she'd wake up in the night to see Michael and his sword standing over her bed, ready to put an end to the threat she was to the world. An old nightmare she could not stand revisiting. Worse even than the nightmares from her last life, of the mental ward, and the blood.

She set aside the invitations she'd been addressing and leaned back in her chair, letting her eyes lose focus while she concentrated on the distinct presence of her brother. There was a steady buzz of thought surrounding her. The town, which had sprung up near the DeLeon estate when she had been married to Ryam, had not grown too terribly large. But it was distracting and difficult to sift through, peppered with so much of her bloodline. A perfect place for him to hide.

Garrit touched her arm lightly. "Maybe we should take a break for tonight. We've finished more than half of them. My hand is beginning to cramp, and you look like you're years away."

She opened her eyes, drawing back to herself and pinching the bridge of her nose to forestall a headache. "I'm all right."

"You're worrying again. I can see it in your face. I promise you, you're safe as long as you stay here. Forget him."

Eve wished she had as much faith in the security of the manor, and Garrit's ability to protect her, if it came to that. She was sure there was something they were keeping from her, but had not yet had any luck discovering what it was. Juliette had only smiled, when she had asked, telling her to leave that sort of thing to the men, so that they would not feel useless. But if something protected the manor, it had not stopped Adam from finding her within it already. She couldn't trust that it wouldn't fail a second time.

If she could just keep Adam away, there would be no threat to anyone once she was married. Adam couldn't violate her marriage, as long as she loved the man, by God's law. And from what she had seen of him in the past, Adam's ego would not suffer a wife who could not worship him, regardless.

"I can feel him, but I don't know where. Like he's haunting me when I'm not paying close enough attention."

Garrit's expression darkened. "You think he's still in France?"

She nodded. He was concealing himself well, but the echo of frustration hadn't left her mind in weeks. How had he regained his memory? It couldn't have been the angels. Michael would never have risked it.

"What can I do?"

"I don't know. Probably nothing."

He sighed, scrubbing his face. "I'll call my father in the morning. I'm sure he knows a man who can help."

"I'd appreciate that. I hate the feeling of being watched." By Adam, anyway. The ghosts of her past husbands had been more reassuring than anything else, aside from being a reminder of her own insanity, but that was hardly something she could admit to Garrit now.

"Just worry about the wedding. Let me worry about your brother. We'll have his picture posted in town to discourage his return, and a reward for any information offered. He can't hide himself so well as to escape the notice of so many, every day."

She shook her head. "It would only be possible if he weren't hiding from me too. I suspect that takes the majority of his concentration."

"Good." Garrit dropped his hands to his knees and stood, smiling. "And in the meantime, we're both going to put aside these invitations for the evening. I'm going to make some coffee." He kissed her cheek and left the room.

She stretched and went to the window, staring into the dark. Was this some new way to punish her? For leaving the ward, in her last life? For meddling in the minds of men without conscious thought? She pressed her hand to the cool glass and tried to remember, but the drugs had left that life more of a haze than she wanted to admit, and the things she did remember made no sense. Men long dead, alive and well, appearing to her, comforting her. Thorgrim's warmth beside her in the bed. Delusion or not, her heart had been convinced, and it still ached to think of him.

Surely Michael wouldn't risk the world just to frighten her, though, and not just the world, but his dominion over it. For all his power, Michael was still part of God's creation, subject to its destruction with all the rest. Any child she gave Adam would threaten the angel, too.

Lightning flashed, striking the trees at the edge of the property, and thunder boomed so near the glass vibrated beneath her palm. She blinked and rubbed her eyes. For a moment, she had been certain she saw the figure of a man outlined by the flash. She must have imagined it, though. And even if she hadn't, the figure she had seen was much too tall and broad shouldered to be Adam. No wings, either, outlined by the white light. Her mind playing tricks on her. That wasn't a good sign.

One of the trees smoldered and she had a distinct feeling of déjà vu. Rain beat against the window pane. Enough, she thought, to put out any fire that may have started, but she'd mention it to Garrit. She turned back from the window and put away the finished invitations, organizing those left to be done. Her eyes ached, and her head too, and she didn't want to think about what it meant if she was seeing things that weren't there.

Garrit was in the kitchen, standing in the dark. He stared out the window while the kettle steamed on the stovetop.

"I think I'm going to skip the coffee." He stiffened at her voice, spinning on his heel to look at her, and she frowned. "Should we check on that last lightning strike? I saw smoke."

In the dim light, she couldn't be certain, but it seemed almost as though he paled. "I'll take care of it."

She kissed him. "I'm going to go to bed."

"Good," he said, glancing back out the window. "*Bonne nuit.*"

§

The next morning, Garrit was sitting at the kitchen table. One look at his face told her he hadn't slept, even if she hadn't noticed his absence from her bed. His eyes were glazed, and barely tracked on her when she entered the room.

"Are you okay?" she asked.

He blinked blearily for a moment. "*Oui*, fine. I'm fine."

His shirt looked heavy and damp on his shoulders, and his hair was ruffled into a mess. He dropped his gaze to the teacup before him. There was a second one, across the table, and the chair opposite had been pulled out. His father must have arrived early and left before she had come down but it was barely eight in the morning.

The kettle began to whistle.

"Did you talk to your father? Was Adam found?"

"No. Not *Papa*." He hesitated before going on, looking out the window. "I received word that Adam was still in the town, as you suspected. But he should be gone by now."

She crossed to the stove and took the kettle off the heat. The idea of Garrit confronting Adam made her uneasy. The look in his eyes when he glanced at her only intensified the feeling.

"You didn't see him yourself, did you?"

"*Non.*" He stood and cleared the two cups from the table, placing them in the dishwasher.

She opened the cabinet, retrieving her own mug; blue, with soft yellow baby chicks clucking at the sun. She filled it with hot water, and dropped in a teabag. Chamomile. It seemed like the kind of day that needed a little bit of extra relaxation. Garrit was still fussing over the dishwasher, rearranging the dirty items more precisely. She watched him, and worried, leaning against the counter. Something was bothering him, and if it wasn't Adam—

"Did the tree catch fire?" Eve asked.

"What?" He shifted a cereal bowl to a different position, then turned a mug and moved the bowl back again.

"You said you'd check on the tree that was struck last night. You didn't forget, did you?" She looked out the window, but nothing seemed to be scorched. In the morning light, she couldn't even tell which tree it had been.

"Ah." He cleared his throat and kept his eyes on the dishes. "The rain put out what was smoldering."

She frowned into her mug, raising it to her lips and blowing across the surface of the tea. She had never had cause to mistrust

Garrit. She had always respected the privacy of his mind. But if Adam had touched him, subverted him, none of them were safe.

There was only one way to know. She closed her eyes, letting her mind open and touch his softly. Just enough to know that it hadn't been Adam he had found by the tree, but another man, tall and heavily built, standing in the rain as though he belonged there. Just enough to reassure herself Adam hadn't tainted him, or poisoned his mind. She withdrew immediately, opened her eyes, and sipped her tea. It was still too hot, and burned her tongue, but she was too distracted to care. Her stomach had turned to ice at the silhouette she had caught from his memory.

"I guess if Adam's gone, there's no reason to call your father."

Garrit's lips were pressed into a thin line. "*Non*. Everything should be taken care of. You're safe here, Abby. Safer here than anywhere else."

She nodded once, and looked out the window again to where she had seen the lightning strike the night before. It couldn't be Thorgrim. Not again. He was dead, and she was sane.

She had to be sane.

CHAPTER EIGHT
Creation

§

Light woke Eve the next morning, shining bright and warm on her face, in spite of the shelter of the cave. Adam sat nearby, staring out at the Garden. Another woman entered, bowed, and placed a large leaf down within his reach. Eve sat up, aware of a knotting in her stomach. Whatever was on the leaf, she wanted it.

Adam glanced back at her movement and passed her the leaf. She stared at rounded brown shapes, then looked up at him. Now that she had it, she was uncertain what to do.

"The nuts make a good meal. I'm sure you're hungry." He picked one up and brought it to his mouth.

It was just the two of them inside, now. She wondered where the man she had spoken with last night had gone. Reu. She put one of the nuts in her mouth and chewed. They tasted pleasant, earthy, and her stomach growled. The knotted feeling eased as she ate. "Thank you."

"The storm knocked much of the fruit from the trees, and I've set our people to gathering it." His gaze raked over her body and she dropped her eyes to the leaf, hating the way her skin flushed beneath his scrutiny.

She studied the nuts, the different shapes and sizes, each with its own individual flavor. She tried several, and then began sorting them. Anything to keep from thinking of him, of the way he watched her, of the heat that blossomed through her body.

"You slept well?" he asked.

"It reminded me of the void." The wrinkled lumps of brown tasted the best, and she had almost finished them before she realized Adam was watching her fingers more than her body. She hesitated. "Do you want some?"

"I ate before you woke." He was studying *her* again, lingering. "Tonight you'll sleep with me in my chamber. You don't belong with the rest of them, sleeping in the dirt."

"They don't seem that different," she said, careful not to meet his eyes.

He laughed. "You're still so new. The difference isn't something you would see, I suppose. They're far more fragile though. If not cared for, they'll die. You and I won't. We'll keep living. Coming back again and again, life after life. Elohim made us immortal in ways they can only dream of."

She ate a few more of the nuts and considered his words. "You said you saw the difference in me, yesterday."

"Yes." But he didn't elaborate, and another woman entered the cave, bowed, and presented them with a second leaf. Adam took it and waved the woman away again, offering the leaf to Eve. "Here, try one of the berries. They're very sweet."

They were red and plump, dotted with seeds and capped with green leaves. She took one and tasted it. The flavor was almost overwhelming, and the moisture soothed her throat and mouth. She sighed with pleasure.

He smiled. "I thought you'd like them. They're my favorite."

It startled her. The smile. It changed his face and for a moment she thought she saw the person he had been when he was first made. When everything was new for him too. She smiled back.

He shifted closer to her, and their shoulders touched. *When she smiles, it's like seeing the sun break through the clouds after a storm. Elohim outdid Himself.*

She flinched and leaned away, lowering her gaze to the nuts and berries again.

"Why do you do that?" His voice was hard now, and his eyes were stone.

She swallowed. "What?"

"You cringe from me as if you're afraid." She could feel his anger, black and burning, even when they weren't touching. "Why?" He grabbed her arm and jerked her toward him. "What did they tell you?"

The nuts fell from her hands when he grabbed her. She tried to pull away, but he only held her more fiercely. "I don't know. I'm not doing anything!"

His fingers dug painfully into her arm. "Who spoke to you?"

She shook her head and clawed at his fingers. Her heart raced, thudding in her ears. "I don't know!" Something in the way he stared at her made her keep Reu's name to herself. "It was dark, and I couldn't see anything. Please! You're hurting me, Adam."

He searched her face. *Of course, they wouldn't give their name. They know not to defy me.* His hand slid down her arm, gentle again. "You're right to fear me. I am Lord now."

She shivered at his touch, and that seemed to please him. He raised his hand to her face, cupping her cheek and drawing his thumb along her cheekbone. She forced herself not to look away. Not to move. But everything inside her twisted. She wanted to crawl away into the darkness, but there were no shadows now to hide her. His face was so close she could feel his breath on her lips.

"Lord Adam!" She jumped, though the voice was familiar. *Reu.*

Adam closed his eyes for a moment, then turned his head slowly. "What is it?"

It was easier to breathe with Adam looking at the man, though he still held her face in his hands. She shut her eyes.

"The fruit has been laid out for your inspection, as you wished," Reu said.

The fruit. Yes. The fruit first. Adam's hand dropped away from her face. "Excellent. Set the women to making a bed of fronds for Eve in my chambers. The others may do as they wish now. I have no more need of them."

"Yes, Lord."

She felt Adam's breath against her ear. "Later."

It made her shiver again, and she kept her eyes closed until she felt him move away. He brushed past Reu, leaving the cave.

"Are you well?" Reu was studying her with warm brown eyes. The same eyes she had dreamed of.

She was trembling. She pulled her knees to her chest again, trying to stop it, and hid her face in her arms. Later, Adam had said. Later, what? He kept touching her. He kept touching her and she didn't understand what she was feeling.

She heard Reu step toward her. "You don't have to let him touch you, Eve."

"He was angry with me for pulling away." She rubbed her arm, lifting her head to look at him. Her skin was red where Adam had grabbed her. "He hurt me."

Reu dropped to the ground beside her. "I'm sorry."

"The way he touches me—" she hesitated, brushing dirt from her hip. "It makes me feel cold, even though his hands are like the sun."

"He hurt you because of me."

She shook her head. "No. Because of me."

"He has no right." Reu's voice was hard. "He has no right to force you. God's laws are clear."

"I wish someone would tell me," she said softly. "What I'm supposed to do. How I'm supposed to act. I keep waiting for some understanding, but everything gets more confused."

"Eve." It was a sigh, more than anything. He covered her hand with his, just for a moment. Then the warmth was gone and he rose back to his feet. "It wasn't meant to be this way for you. You shouldn't have to fear, to weep. I'll do everything I can to help."

"How was it meant to be, Reu? Please."

He shook his head, stepping back, toward the front of the cave. "I hope someday to be able to show you." But then he turned and walked away.

§

She spent the rest of the morning alone for the most part, though Adam made her leave the cave when the sun reached its zenith. She sat in the shade of a large tree in the thick, green grass spotted with small purple flowers, and watched the others, not knowing what else to do with herself.

Some of the women brought her food and water, and sat with her while they ate their own. They laughed often among themselves as they talked about the men.

"Seth promised to marry me. He means to speak with Adam this evening." The woman's hair was the color of the sun, and Eve thought her name was Sarah.

Another woman, Hannah, glanced to where the men stood together. Her hair was almost black, and her eyes were a darker green than the grass they sat in, almost brown at times. "I wish that one of them would marry me. If only to keep Adam from touching me. Every time he sends us off to bathe, I'm tempted to coat my skin with mud before I come back, just to disgust him."

"You mean you wish Adam would marry," a third woman said. Eve thought she was called Lilith.

All three of them glanced at Eve. She felt their eyes, even if she pretended not to notice. Sarah's voice lowered. "Seth doesn't think he'll stop even if he does marry."

"We're his," Lilith said. "To do with as he pleases."

"Reu doesn't believe that," Hannah said, catching Eve's eye. The dark haired girl smiled at her tentatively. "He says that we're meant to be free."

"Reu should be more careful what he says." Lilith says. "If Adam hears him, he'll be punished. Talk like this will only get us into trouble." She stood and walked away.

Sarah sighed and watched her go. "I don't understand her, sometimes."

"Reu told me that Adam took her right after she was made." Hannah spoke softly. "He isn't sure what happened, but God was upset."

"You know Reu well?" Eve asked.

Hannah smiled, her eyes warm. "He helped many of us, when we were made."

"He confuses me."

Sarah laughed. "Everything is confusing in the beginning."

Eve frowned, her gaze going back to the men, and Reu. They were taking turns throwing long sticks. Every so often cheers went up. They clapped each other on the back and laughed together, the way the women did. All but Adam. Sometimes his lips curved, but his gaze was always hard, and none of them touched him. Because he was Lord. That was what they called him when they bowed and served and scraped.

"How long does the beginning last?" Eve asked.

Hannah's slim fingers curled gently around Eve's wrist. Her hands were delicate in a way Adam's would never be, but her skin shared the same tones, closer to brown than pink, as if her body had been kissed by the sun. "You're already doing better than any of us did."

It was a kindness, Eve thought, this touch. As if Hannah meant to show her she did not have to be like Adam. She could be one of them, included in their laughter, in their games.

"Thank you," Eve said.

Hannah smiled, and studied her for a moment. Eve thought perhaps she would say something more, but then Adam walked toward them, and Hannah pulled her hand away. She stood up, mumbling something about having work to do, and Sarah went with her.

"Did you enjoy your meal, Eve?" Adam extended a hand to her.

She took his hand reluctantly. "They were very kind to me."

He pulled her to her feet. *Kind.* "They should be. They're here to serve you." *And they should be grateful to do so. Grateful that I keep them to serve. I could have cast them out. Perhaps I still will.*

She let go of his hand as quickly as she could without offending him, hating the sound of his other voice in her head, the feeling of his thoughts twisting their way inside her mind.

"Sarah said Seth was going to speak with you about marriage."

He flashed a smile and put his hand on the small of her back, guiding her toward the caves. "Yes, I've been waiting for it." *He can have her. They can all have each other, now that I have you.* "I expect they won't be the only ones."

She walked with him, though she wished he'd drop his hand away. "Why?"

"They were only waiting for me to choose." Reu watched her, his eyes dark, as they passed by the men. "Now that I have, it is only natural they might do the same."

Adam led her through the main cave into a tunnel, which opened into a large chamber. Sweet smelling grasses were spread over the stone floor, and two large beds of fronds lay side by side. There was a crevasse in the ceiling that allowed light to filter into the room, but there was no other way out than the way they had come.

"An improvement from the dirt, isn't it?"

"Should the dirt have bothered me?" She wrapped her arms around herself. There was no safety here. And Adam's hand burned hot against her back, slipping around her waist and pulling her against him.

"It won't now." He turned her to face him and lifted her chin, staring into her eyes. Images of the two of them filled her head, their bodies interlocked, moving together in the bed of fronds. "We won't be interrupted here."

Her heart beat faster, and her breath caught. She closed her eyes against the images, but it didn't help. They intensified without the backdrop of what her vision told her. Damp skin and too much warmth, his body atop hers, pressing her down. Something uncoiled inside her, and the heat of Adam's hands spread lower, lower, lower.

"I—I'm not bothered by the others." Right now, she would have given anything for someone to find them in the cave. To have some need of Adam and call him away.

His hand moved to her cheek. "Open your eyes, Eve." *I'll not have you thinking of anything but me.*

The images became more powerful. She could feel his hands on her. Smell their sweat and something else mixed with it. Eve struggled to breathe, to separate herself from his thoughts. She looked at him, driven by the desperation to free herself more than his command. His eyes were hard and gray, lit with something she didn't know, and then his mouth covered hers, crushing and demanding.

She tried to gasp, to pull free, but he only forced his tongue into her mouth as her lips parted and pulled her more tightly against his body. He pressed against her, hard and lean and searing, his thoughts burning behind her eyes, impossible to escape. She sobbed and turned her face away, but his mouth only moved along her jaw instead, his fingers digging painfully into her waist.

She felt his distaste a moment before he shoved her from him, wiping his mouth with the back of his hand. It was enough to keep her from stumbling to the floor, but only just.

His eyes raked over her body and his lip curled. "I should've had one of the women bathe you first."

She wiped at her own mouth and face, leaning against the cool stone wall. Her heart still pounded against her chest and her whole body trembled from the loss of his heat.

"Go. Find one of them. Tell them I require them to help you.

You taste like sand and dirt, and I want none of it." He spit into the grasses on the floor and turned away from her.

She didn't wait for him to ask her again.

CHAPTER NINE
985 BC

※

Thor stood on a wooded hill, looking down on one of the simple fishing villages of his people, of Odin's people. Would they ever rise to the same potential as the other civilizations he'd seen? The Egyptians. The Assyrians. He grimaced, thinking of all the wars of those nations. He almost wished they wouldn't. That they might be spared that heartache and live their lives in peace.

Booming laughter was punctuated by the shrill shouts of women. The fields glowed golden with wheat inland, and beyond them, goats and cows grazed peacefully. In the village itself, dogs and children barked and played together outside their huts. He smiled slightly. At least they were happy. Certainly the men seemed to be. He could not be sure of the women, but after spending time with the House of Lions, it was hard to look on any other people without imagining how different things could be for them.

It had been a fruitful visit, to be sure, but he had been forced to stay much longer than he intended among Eve's people, in order to convince them of his honesty. It was years before they had come to an agreement, and in exchange for the information they had given him, he had promised them good weather, and protection for Eve for as long into the future as the gods remained present in the world. It hadn't been an opportunity they could refuse, though they took their time about it.

"Thor!" A hand clapped him heavily on the shoulder, and he turned to see Odin. The god's scarred face was split by a grin. "Baldur was beginning to worry you would not find your way back to us." Odin chuckled, his eyes, as gray as his beard, crinkling at the corners. "And it goes without saying that your wife has made us all miserable in your absence. Another year and I might have sent her in search of you, just to spare the rest of Asgard."

Thor frowned. Perhaps it wasn't for all women to be left to rule their own lives. "I will see her first, of course. I had not anticipated being gone so long, but I believe you will be pleased with everything I have learned."

"I am always pleased with you, Thor. Come." Odin's grip on Thor's shoulder firmed and the air around them thickened, the view of the village melting into the stone of Asgard, high above the earth. They'd done so much since he'd left. Carefully tended gardens had been built around Yggdrasil and a new crop of golden apples winked between dusky red leaves. His mother's tree welcomed him home with its bounty.

He took a moment to breathe in the scent of its fruit, like honey and wine, his gaze traveling over the halls that surrounded these central grounds. A building that could only have been Baldur's work stood beside Odin's great hall, modest in size, but made of white marble and roofed with shining silver. A smaller *skáli* standing opposite was gilt with gold, dwarfed by a greenhouse behind it which was filled to overflowing with plants from across the earth, all in full flower and heavy with fruits and nuts. Two boars rooted in the dirt of the gardens out front, one with golden bristles, and a pair of tuft-eared cats lounged in the sun by the doorway.

"I see Freyr and Freyja have made themselves comfortable," Thor said, nodding to the hall. "The others have settled well?"

"As well as they always have. Freyr and Baldur are disappointed that living in the heavens keeps them from the sea, but such is the cost of sharing a world. Better that we keep our safety and our skins," Odin said. "Go find your wife and assure her that you missed her. The rest will wait until supper."

Odin slapped Thor's back and strode off toward his hall without waiting for a response. A raven cawed and swooped at the sight of its master, landing on the stone windowsill nearest the entrance. His father stopped to give orders to one of his Valkyries, and then Odin collected the bird and disappeared through the great silver doors. Thor could already hear the stir in the kitchen as news of his return spread and servants began preparations for the celebration. Odin would not permit anything less than a feast in honor of his first son's homecoming.

"Sif," Thor said to himself, wondering what trouble she had caused while he was away. Surely she could not have been too difficult. He had made sure the home he'd built for her was furnished with everything she could possibly desire, and Odin had promised to provide her with anything else she might need.

He turned toward his own home, and followed the stone path around Yggdrasil and Valaskjalf. Sif had planted a garden of her own in front of the cottage, and he smiled to see his goats, Tanngrisnir and Tanngnjóstr, grazing. Thor stopped to let them remember him, and Tanngnjóstr butted his hand with its head, bleating, until he scratched the goat around the curled horns and behind the ear. At least the goats had been some company for Sif in his absence.

He settled the animals and opened the door to the cottage. "Sif!"

The front room was homey, a fire burning low in the hearth, and filled with the things he recognized from their old world. Tapestries she had woven, of his mother's tree and the old Asgards, hung on the wall. She had found fabrics in bright colors to cover the armchairs he had made, stuffing the cushions with wool.

Thor pushed open the door to the bedroom, a smile on his lips. It was as though she divined his needs, to be waiting for him there. Perhaps one of the Valkyries had sent word while he stood with Odin beneath the tree.

And then he froze, his mind catching up to the sight that greeted him. He felt his eyes burn white, washing all color from the room.

Thor's hand closed around a war-hammer he did not hold, aching to bring it smashing down on the black-haired head that hovered over his wife's breasts as she arched her back with a moan. Thunder cracked so loudly the stone foundation shook beneath his feet, and the goats outside began to bleat.

Loki glanced back over his shoulder, a sly grin on his face as Sif cried out with pleasure. The Trickster did not even pause, his eyes glazing as he moaned his own release.

Responding to his fury, dark clouds formed, blotting the sun, which had previously streamed through the windows of the cottage. Loki's sharp chuckle snapped him free of his paralysis and Thor crossed the room in one long stride. He grabbed the Trickster off Sif's body by the back of the neck, throwing him through the window. Stone, glass, and wood shattered, leaving a gaping, splintered hole.

Loki still laughed as he picked himself up off the stone-cobbled ground on the other side of the wall. The Trickster smirked and brushed himself off, unashamed by his nakedness, though under the storm clouds his skin had a sallow hue, and the shadows beneath his eyes were so dark he might have worn a polecat's mask. Thunder rumbled and Thor stalked toward him, unwilling to so much as glance at his wife, sputtering objections and imprecations from the bed.

"What do you expect, Thor, when you leave Sif for centuries to live among humans?"

Thor didn't trust himself to speak. The sky overhead darkened even further as black clouds swirled over Loki's head. A single lightning bolt, charged with his hate, was all it would take. Once, Loki might have been his friend, even an uncle in his youth, but those days had ended long ago. It had taken only a single cycle of Ragnarok for Thor to understand the Trickster's true nature. Jealous and cruel, Loki had been a thorn in his side for millennia, but never had he believed him capable of so base a betrayal.

"Thor!" Sif's voice distracted him, drawing his attention from the Trickster. "Control yourself!"

He growled and turned back to Loki, even more intent to destroy him, but Sif had given him the moment he needed to slip away. Without a focus for his anger, the thunder boomed and the lightning dissipated between the clouds.

Thor spun to grab his wife by the arm, broken glass crunching beneath his boots. He hauled her bodily from the room, ignoring her squawk of protest. Loki might not be in sight, but he would be lurking, listening, ready to twist the words he heard into lies. When Thor released Sif in the front room of the cottage, she all but fell into one of the armchairs.

"You *dare* to chastise me?" Part of him recognized he was shouting more loudly than the thunder that still rolled overhead, but he could not quiet his voice. "You *dare* to allow that filthy *rakki* between your legs?"

Sif righted herself and stood, proud in all her naked glory. Her golden hair cascaded down her shoulders to her navel, covering her left breast. She closed her hands into fists and raised her chin in defiance.

"You couldn't even be bothered to wait until I had arrived before satisfying your curiosity about these feeble creatures, and you object to the fact that I found my own interests in your absence?"

"I was ordered, you fool! By Odin's command!" He grabbed her again by her arms and shook her. He was barely able to moderate his tone, but when he continued, it was with a volume which did not cause the walls to shudder. "To return home to this betrayal! This faithlessness!"

"As if you weren't planting your seed among the mortals while you were away," she sneered.

He found himself growling again, and his hands tightened involuntarily on her body until she hissed. Thor forced himself to relax, open his hands, release her. He took a deep breath and stepped back.

"Unlike you, Sif, I do not cast aside my vows so easily for the first pleasure which presents itself. Could you not have chosen someone less offensive, at least? He is not even Aesir!"

Her eyes flashed gold in her anger. "Loki's reputation as a lover is hardly undeserved, as he proved to me repeatedly."

His hands balled into fists and he clenched his teeth so hard that the bones creaked under the stress. "Get. Dressed."

She glared at him. "And if I refuse to take orders from a man who abandoned me for more than three centuries?"

"I'm your husband!" The window rattled, but he didn't care. He didn't care if all of Asgard was listening to their argument. He would not suffer this. Would not accept it.

"Are you?"

The coldness in her voice was like a knife in his stomach, and he felt his knuckles crack as he stepped toward her, as if her words were a challenge and he must fight. It was all he could do to transport himself out of the house to keep from striking her in the rage that consumed him at the blow of her words, but he managed. Just. Lightning flashed brilliant white, crawling over his skin and dissolving the walls around him, the stone floor beneath his feet, and Sif. Out of his reach at last.

Valaskjalf materialized around him, with servants in the midst of the preparations for his homecoming.

Odin looked up, the gray eyebrow of his false eye rising. He had lost the eye long ago, but he did not often show the scar. Twice in his life, Thor had seen the gaping black hole where the eye should have been, both times deliberate reminders of Odin's right to rule. But Thor had yet to master his father's trick of utter calm, and his own eyes bled white, burning hot.

"Ah," Odin said. "Yes. Perhaps I should have warned you to knock."

He stood and crossed the room, causing the large raven on his shoulder to launch itself into the rafters of the building with a loud croak. Odin guided Thor to a seat and called for drink.

"I will kill them both with my bare hands."

Odin shook his head. "You will not."

A serving girl appeared at Thor's elbow with a mug of mead. He wrenched the mug from her hand and brought it to his mouth so quickly the drink did not have time to slosh. He held the empty mug out to her, glaring, for more. She filled it again at once.

"And why not?" Thor did not immediately pour this second dose down his throat, but stared into the amber liquid. "It is my right. She is my wife. Loki has given me grave insult."

Odin shooed the girl away and when Thor looked up, his father's expression was unmoved. "You will not, for it is not my wish to have two of my number struck down before I am sure of our safety in this world. Loki will be forbidden to touch your wife again, and cast to the earth to walk among men for a century, unable to touch their women as well. Sif's punishment I leave in your hands, but it will not be death. This is my command, Thor."

He downed the second cup of mead and glowered at his father.

"You ask much of me."

"You will obey, nonetheless."

Thor threw the mug across the room. It crashed into the far wall and clanged against the floor, sending the other servants bolting for the kitchen. "Then I must go."

"You've only just arrived, Thor. The banquet is already being prepared."

"I do not trust myself not to kill him. If you wish me to obey, I must leave. My fingers itch to encircle his throat even now and I will not sit with him at table and share food and drink!"

Odin sighed. "And Sif's punishment?"

Sif. Faithless Sif. He found his hands in fists again. After all this time, she would turn from him? Deny their marriage? "Cut off her hair. And let no god touch her until I have returned."

"As you wish." Odin studied him for a long moment, his expression still reluctant. "Return as swiftly as you can. I am anxious to learn what you have discovered."

Thor stood, relieved that he would not have to stay a moment longer. "Thank you, Odin-Father."

Odin gripped his shoulder once more in farewell, and then released him. "Go. Find what peace you may."

Thor closed his eyes, searching the earth for the bright light of her familiar presence, not knowing what it would bring him, but needing at least that much purpose, at least that much distraction. And then the lightning wrapped around him and he was gone.

§

Her back to him, she knelt along the bank of a stream, scrubbing cloth against stones to remove the filth. She hummed softly to herself. Thor watched her for a long moment, the way her hair caught the sunlight as it danced between the branches of the trees, the way her body moved with grace even while working at such a menial task. She sat back and he realized she was washing her own clothing, naked from the waist up but for what modesty her hair allowed. He inhaled deeply, catching the scent of juniper and sunshine, and the tension left his shoulders.

Thor had no idea where he was in the world, did not care in the slightest. He pulled the language of the area directly from Eve's own mind, and he bent to the ground to darken his hair and his skin with dirt as well as he was able. Perhaps he should have begged Odin to alter his appearance before he left, but it was too late now, and he hadn't really known what he was doing until he arrived here. He would make do. As long as he remained calm, his eyes would stay an un-alarming shade of blue.

He stepped out from the cover of the trees and called a soft greeting.

Eve spun, her humming abruptly cut off, and looked at him with wide eyes. She pulled the garment from the water and covered herself with it.

"I didn't mean to startle you," he said, still keeping his voice gentle.

She searched his face, and Thor stayed where he was, trying not to scare her further. He wasn't sure what he was doing. But it felt right. More so than anything else he could have done.

After a moment, she relaxed enough to smile. "If you would turn around, please, so I can dress."

Thor nodded and turned his back to her, concentrating on his reflection in the water. The surface rippled, and he frowned as he saw his hair darken from the dirty red-gold, to a natural light brown. There was movement reflected in the trees and he searched for the source. A raven croaked. Odin, then. The rest of his body altered as his hair had, his skin darkening to a bronze tan over paler skin.

Why? he asked, silently.

Find what peace you may, and return. Until then, do what you must. None will be able to find you until you reach once again for Asgard.

Odin was gone as quickly as he had come and Thor studied himself in the water. The changes were enough. No god of the North would recognize him at once. But there was something more to the change than just his appearance. The sky did not respond to his touch. There would be no flash of lightning to give him away if he lost his temper. No dark clouds forming in a clear blue sky to alert anyone of his location. He lacked the powers which marked him as a god.

"You can turn around, now," she said.

He turned immediately, and there she was. Eve. Lovely, loyal Eve. "I've never seen someone as beautiful as you."

She smiled again, her cheeks dimpling, and a flush creeping up her neck into her face. "You're a stranger to us."

"Yes." He had to stop himself from reaching out to her. Touching her just to reassure himself that she was real, and he was present. "I've traveled from the north."

"Will you stay very long?"

"If I am welcome, I believe I will." It wasn't until he said it that he realized it was true. He would stay with her, for her. He wanted so much to know her, as he could not have until this moment. He smiled. "I am skilled in the art of crafting. Have your people any need for boats?"

Her eyes lit and she took his hand. "Come. My father will want to speak with you. You are like a gift from the gods."

How she managed to speak so casually of other gods, he wasn't sure. The House of Lions had shown him she believed none of it, but it sounded natural from her lips.

She led him through the trees, and with a shock, he saw the same small fishing village laid out before him, the hill upon which he and Odin had stood just that morning in the distance. Women sat together in the sun, mending nets with quick fingers. Men laughed raucously, drinking mead and wine, before going out to work in the fields, while others left with spear and bow to hunt. No wonder Odin had changed him, hiding his godhead. In the heart of the Northlands, it was the only way to keep Sif from knowing where he had gone, and Loki from searching him out.

She glanced back at him when his steps slowed and smiled encouragement. "We will be grateful for any help you can offer us. Please. My father will make a place for you here."

Thor returned her smile and matched his pace to hers. He would have time to consider the ramifications of his actions later. For now, he was with Eve and she seemed to be pleased to have him there. Her hand was warm within his and his heart eased. Perhaps, at least, they could know one another, and some good could come from all of this.

CHAPTER TEN
Present

§

Eve hugged her mother and father, kissing their cheeks. Her parents were the last of the line of well-wishers who had filtered through the house and out into the courtyard for the wedding rehearsal. A broad white canopy shaded the guests from the sun, and what looked suspiciously like storm clouds in the distance. The small chapel at the other end of the yard stood with its doors wide open, and Garrit's father, René, was laughing with the priest. He was a friend of the family, she'd been told, not at all acquainted with the peculiar beliefs of the House of Lions. As a rule, the DeLeons were not religious, but the Catholic Church had held influence over France for a very long time and allying themselves with it had been the prudent choice. Eve couldn't blame them, even now, and avoided speaking to the man altogether when it was possible. When it wasn't, she limited herself to comments on the weather.

But guarding against offering some accidental heresy in conversation was almost a pleasant distraction from fearing for her sanity. Almost. Thankfully, she hadn't seen anymore ghosts framed by lightning, and she wasn't aware that Garrit had either.

"How was your trip, Mum?" Eve asked.

"Pleasantly uneventful," her father replied, waving off the question. Her mother had already turned to Garrit, hugging and kissing him.

"Garrit, the wedding will be so lovely. We're so thrilled to have you join our family. Abby has been so lucky to have found you," her mother said. Anne Watson had little love for France, nor did she care much for the French themselves or anyone who claimed to be Catholic. Eve tried not to wonder if her mother would have loved her new son-in-law quite so much if he hadn't been so wealthy.

Her father grinned and shook Garrit's hand. "Glad to have you, son. Glad to have you." His nose was already beginning to turn pink with the pre-dinner drinks.

"Mum, Dad, why don't you go sit down? I want to just double check and be sure we have everyone."

"Of course, of course." Her father pumped Garrit's hand once more and then hustled his wife away. "Let's not embarrass the boy, now," he mumbled to her mother as they went.

Garrit flexed his hand dramatically. "*Bon Dieu*, but your father has a grip. I'd forgotten."

"I wish René hadn't shown him to the port quite so soon." She watched her parents greet others on their way to their seats, rows of chairs neatly arranged for the wedding rehearsal. Her father tripped over one of the chair legs, knocking three others out of line before righting the first and taking a seat. As if she weren't already on edge, now she had to babysit her father.

"Just a few more hours, Abby. Then he can get as drunk as he likes, and no one will know the difference but us."

"Until tomorrow at the wedding when he's hung over and blustering."

Garrit grimaced. "I'll have *Maman* watch him."

"I'd appreciate it."

Garrit's family clustered together in smaller groups on the groom's side of the aisle. Her family, sparse enough already, seemed even smaller in comparison. Not that it mattered, really. For Eve, family had always been a strange imposition, bonds to be balanced against lifetimes of knowledge she couldn't share. Unless she had the good fortune to come home.

The DeLeons laughed together, every now and again shooting glances her way. René's sister, Brienne, the matriarch of the family, had identified her the first time they had met. René's two brothers had been a bit slower to catch on, but just as pleased when they had learned the truth. The House of Lions could not be happier to welcome her back into the fold.

It was Brienne who suffered from her father's attentions, now. Juliette had probably asked her to keep an eye on the Watsons. Garrit's aunt bore it well, though Eve could feel her bemusement. John Watson was an odd sort of man, especially after he started drinking. Better than her mother's disdain, Eve supposed.

Garrit slid an arm around her waist, turning her slightly away from the door, just as one of the caterers opened it. Where had they found someone so immense? And with that shade of red-gold hair?

"I think that's everyone, Abby. *Père* Robert is ready to begin whenever we are."

"Of course." She swallowed hard, her throat tight, but when she glanced back over her shoulder the man was gone. She wasn't sure she liked the idea that it had been her imagination any better. But now wasn't the time. They had a wedding to rehearse, and Eve directed her attention to finding her maid of honor in the mob.

Her sister stood in the midst of a crowd of DeLeon cousins, a bright spot of red among the navies and blacks of their suits.

"Mia! We're ready."

Her sister winked at the men and excused herself. Garrit kissed

Eve's cheek and started herding everyone into their seats, collecting his best man, Luc as he went.

"Sorry about Dad, Abby." Mia said, still flirting over her shoulder. "I really did try to keep him from the port. Have you seen Garrit's cousins? They're absolutely stunning!"

"A little bit of focus, Mia, if you don't mind." Eve snapped her fingers in front of her sister's face until she had eye contact. "You'd think you were still in grammar school."

"Easy for you to say—you're marrying one of them." Mia grinned at the group, which was still entirely too focused on her for Eve's liking. One of them was mentally undressing her.

Eve tsked softly and gave him a pointed look until he noticed and grinned, dropping his gaze. Garrit's cousin, Jean, his uncle Ryan's only son. No doubt he had just remembered that one of Eve's many gifts was mindreading.

She smiled slightly. "I'm sure you'll have plenty of opportunity to get to know them later. At the moment, perhaps we can get through this rehearsal."

"Oh, fine. Yes. Although the longer you drag it out the more sober Dad will be before the dinner starts and he can drink himself drunk again."

"*Merveilleux,*" Father Robert said, raising his voice to be heard above the hum of conversation. "If we could have the bride and the groom up front, as well as their attendants. Everyone, please, take your seats." The DeLeons quieted quickly at the call to order by the minister; the Watsons a bit slower.

Eve let Mia pull her by the hand to the front of the assembly, trying to ignore her father's over-loud and absurd comment to her mother about Catholic mass.

Garrit took her hands in his and lowered his voice so only she could hear. "Just let it all play itself out, Abby, and we'll be done here in no time."

She leaned forward to kiss his cheek and whispered softly. "Your cousins are thinking very unchaste thoughts about my sister."

Garrit chuckled and the priest cleared his throat before nodding to her parents. "Now, Mr. Watson, you'll have walked Abby down the aisle and released her into Garrit's capable hands. And the service will begin with a reading from the Old Testament."

There was a chuckle from somewhere on the DeLeon side of the aisle. Garrit turned a snicker into a cough, and Eve tried to hide a smile.

The wedding would certainly be interesting, with the house full of Lions.

§

A few too many glasses of wine later—a pre-emptive attempt to keep her father from getting his hands on them—Eve blinked blearily at the large man who didn't appear to be mingling. The same man she'd glimpsed before the rehearsal, and she still hadn't made up her mind if she was imagining things.

He wasn't family, of that she was certain. None of her progeny had that odd shade of red-gold hair. Or that kind of height and breadth of shoulder. And yet, Garrit and René had been speaking with him earnestly at the beginning of the dinner, their lightly built height dwarfed by the man. He looked too familiar though, and even drunk it was making her uneasy. God, but she hoped it was just the drink making him look familiar at all. She really didn't want to lose her mind again, not with Adam haunting her footsteps.

"You don't think Jean is too old for me, do you? Really, it's only four years. Garrit's almost two years older than you, isn't he?" Mia was saying. "Dad can't really object. I'm old enough to make these decisions on my own by now. And he's so delicious. Those dark eyes—I could swoon."

Eve shook her head once. The room spun slightly, but it distracted her from the man who looked much too much like a long dead husband. She would *not* allow herself to think of Thorgrim on the night before her wedding.

"Mia, he's practically undressing you with his eyes. If that's the kind of relationship you want, I don't see a problem. But don't fall in love with him. It's not what he's interested in."

"You really think so?" Mia almost squeaked in her delight, and Eve winced. "Wonderful! If Mum asks, tell her I just went out for a walk or something. I'll be back before too long." And then she was gone, walking straight to Jean and standing on her tiptoes to whisper something in his ear. He at least had the grace to be surprised before he offered one of the most charming DeLeon smiles Eve had ever seen in her long association with the family.

Eve shook her head again and looked back to the large man, now in deep discussion with Garrit's aunt, Brienne. If her family was talking to him, he couldn't be a figment of her imagination, could he? Or a construct of her subconscious mind? If he was, wouldn't he have been talking to her instead? Thorgrim had never been shy about talking to her, when she had imagined him. Maybe if she went to sleep he wouldn't be there in the morning, and she could stop thinking about it. Or perhaps when she was sober she'd realize there was no real resemblance at all. It wasn't like she wasn't capable of that sort of trick.

Garrit chuckled softly in her ear, startling her. He kissed her cheek. "*Ma chérie*, I believe your sister has bitten off more than she can chew."

"She's resilient. And she could do much worse than Jean. At least he'll be respectful for the duration." She leaned back in her seat and smiled at him. "I had too much wine."

"Your father did as well, in spite of our best efforts." Garrit nodded to where he was passed out on a table. "How many glasses did you take out of his hand and down yourself?"

"Too many. I'm going to have a miserable headache in the morning."

He smiled. "Plenty of water and an aspirin before you go to bed tonight will have you fixed up. Raw eggs and Tabasco, if necessary."

"At least it's nearly over."

"Mmm." He helped her to her feet, guiding her toward the exit. "Let me get you into bed before you imitate your father."

"If I weren't exhausted, I'd be offended by that remark." But then she stopped, her gaze still on Brienne and the man. Those blue eyes were straight out of her memory. And his face. She knew his face. It definitely wasn't just the wine. "Who is he, anyway?"

"Who?"

She pointed.

The large man looked up at her. His eyes flashed white and she stumbled in shock.

Garrit caught her, picking her up off her feet and continuing on. "Just an old friend of *Papa*'s. You might say that he's acting as our security for the event tomorrow."

"Security, huh? He looks the part." She must've imagined his eyes. She was certainly drunk enough to be seeing things, and there was no reason at all that she would have brought him here. Not now. She wasn't insane anymore, and even Thorgrim's ghost had refused to come to her in France after she had escaped the mental ward and left America in her last life.

Ghost. She closed her eyes and tightened her arms around Garrit's neck. Delusion, more like, if she was honest with herself. Hearing voices, seeing people who didn't exist, those were symptoms of schizophrenia at best. If Garrit saw him, and René knew him, she had to believe it wasn't just her mind this time. Except that other people had seen him last time, too. One minute she'd been unconscious in her cot, and the next she'd been in

France. She couldn't have done that alone.

"The best offense is good intimidation at the outset," Garrit agreed. "Shall I carry you all the way up to the bedroom? Call it a rehearsal for tomorrow."

"Don't strain yourself."

He chuckled again. She liked the sound. It was the most relaxed he'd been in months. Weddings did that to people, though. There was something to be said for eloping. Perhaps in her next life she would insist upon it.

She rested her head against his shoulder and he pulled her closer against his chest. "*Merci,*" she murmured.

"*Pourquoi?*"

"Letting me be me. For giving me this life, as Eve."

He almost overbalanced them as he climbed until he braced against the wall. "I didn't give you the life, Abby. It was yours for the taking. Always. You don't have to marry me or any of us to have it. We're your family."

She smiled. "You know I can't resist the DeLeon charm."

He laughed and took the last steps from the stairs across the hall to the door. "Do you suppose you could get the knob? I can't quite manage that without dropping you."

She obliged him and he crossed to the large four poster bed, tossing her onto it. "Oof!"

"Don't worry, tomorrow I'll be nice," he said, grinning as he began to loosen his tie.

"Sometimes niceness is overrated in these circumstances." She climbed to her knees and pulled him close enough to help. Her fingers fumbled with it, but the knot came free and she started on the buttons of his shirt. If she could just put it all out of her mind, let Garrit distract her and forget until morning. Forget that she might be insane again. Forget what it had been like, with Thorgrim. What she would never have again, even with her family.

Garrit pulled the fabric from his collar and kissed her. "I'll keep that in mind."

"Do you suppose you could lock the door, and then help me out of this dress?"

"I would love to." And then he leered at her. It was a far cry from the too-charming smile of his cousin, but she liked it all the more for its artlessness.

He kissed her again and they both forgot about the door.

§

"Water for my beautiful bride." Garrit opened his palm, sitting stark naked on the edge of the bed, and revealed two chalky white tablets of aspirin. "We're breaking the rules, you know, it's after midnight now."

Eve propped herself up on an elbow and took the pills first, then the water. "Don't be silly. It's only bad luck if you see me in my dress."

His gaze traveled over her body, as bare as his was amidst the tousled sheets, and he smiled. "No danger then."

"*Non.*" She swallowed the pills and drank the rest of the water. She was feeling much more sober now that she had sweated off most of the alcohol, and her mind kept returning to the man at the rehearsal dinner with the blue eyes that had flashed white. There was no help for it. "Tell me something?"

"*Oui?*" Garrit was trailing his fingers along the line of her ribcage, and instead of looking up, bent his head so that his lips could follow.

She shivered and wound her fingers through his short hair. "It's important," she said, though for the life of her, when his teeth grazed her breast, she wasn't sure she remembered why.

He stopped, and she made a soft sound of disappointment.

Garrit chuckled. "You said it was important."

"I didn't mean it." She tried to pull him back, but he lifted his head and lay down on the bed instead, leaning on one elbow to face her, his eyes sparkling with amusement.

"*Non.* You have my attention now. *Dis-moi?*"

She felt her cheeks flush. "It's about the man downstairs. The friend of your father's?"

He frowned, the humor fading. "Our security man. What do they call them in England? Bouncers?"

"That's American. In England we call them door supervisors."

"Ah." He smiled, but it seemed forced. "Door supervisor, then. What else would you like to know?"

She bit her lip, but she had to know. Needed the reassurance that she wasn't losing her mind again. "What's his name?"

"Owen," he said. "*Monsieur* Owen."

She let out a breath she hadn't realized she'd been holding. "Oh."

"Why do you ask?"

She shook her head. "I thought I recognized him from somewhere, but it must have been someone else."

When Thorgrim had come back to her, in the ward, when she had imagined him, he had called himself Donner. Not Owen. Though, that name reminded her of something else. Maybe the resemblance had less to do with seeing ghosts, and more to do with genetics. She had given Thorgrim a son, once, a very long time ago, and if the DeLeons could keep the resemblance to their forefathers, Thorgrim's line could have done so as well.

"Mm." Garrit grunted, rolling off the other side of the bed. "Another glass of water for you, I think, and then we should both get some sleep. Tomorrow will be busy."

She felt herself relax, staring at the ceiling while she waited for Garrit to return with her glass. She didn't have to be insane. The man could just be some family of Thorgrim's, three thousand years removed. Why hadn't she thought of that before? The realization was a balm, and she felt her mind drift away from any other possibility, secure in this one.

When Garrit came back to the bed, she kissed him, curling up against his side. He was warm, and she trailed her fingers through the hair on his chest. "Thank you."

He kissed her forehead. "Next time, remind me to ignore you when you say it's important."

She smiled, resting her head against his shoulder. "Only if we're in bed."

CHAPTER ELEVEN
Creation

§

Reu caught her by the arm before she made it into the trees. "Eve? Are you all right? Did he hurt you?"

"Let me go." She pulled away from him. "Please. Let me go."

His hand dropped. "Of course. Forgive me."

She darted into the trees, glancing back to be sure Adam wasn't watching.

But Reu followed. "What did he do?"

"I don't know."

The moment raced through her mind, and she doubled over as her stomach heaved. Her meal burned the back of her throat and she swallowed convulsively. Reu caught her before she fell, supporting her against his body. She tried to steady herself, her thoughts, her stomach.

"He covered my mouth with his." She pressed her hand against her belly, willing it to calm. She felt as though she could still feel the heat of Adam's hands on her body. "And then he threw me from him."

Reu's grip tightened. "Did you want him to touch you, Eve? Did he give you a choice?"

She shook her head. The warmth was gone from his eyes, and now they just looked black with anger.

"Are you hurt? Did he do anything more than kiss you?"

"No." She wiped her mouth, and closed her eyes. The image of their bodies moving together swam before her, along with the flare of…of something she didn't understand, warming her belly, and spreading lower. "No. But he meant to."

"You stopped him?"

She shook her head again. "I tried to, but he was too strong. I couldn't push him away. He sent me to bathe."

Reu rubbed his face with both hands. "I have to stop this. I have to stop him."

"He'll hurt you." Then the words came back to her. Adam's thoughts about how they should be grateful. "Cast you out. I don't understand what that is. Out of where?"

"The Garden. Into the barren lands outside to starve." Reu's face was dark again, and he looked back the way they had come. The caves weren't visible through the trees, but she was sure that was what he was trying to see. "When did he say that?"

"After the meal. I told him the women were kind to me. He thought they should be grateful he let them live at all. That he might cast them out anyway."

"He said all this to you?"

She leaned against a tree, her stomach still twisted. "When he touches me, I hear more than he speaks aloud."

Reu murmured a word she had never heard and took her by the arm again, though gently, pulling her deeper into the trees. Leaves pawed at her, bushes grasping at her arms and legs. It wasn't until they had traveled some distance that he stopped, sweeping back the drooping branches of a willow tree.

"We should be safe here." He guided her inside. The sun filtered through the branches, turning everything green. "Please. Explain to me what you mean."

She blinked. Reu had seemed so wise. But Adam had told her she was different. Was this how? "You don't understand?"

He almost smiled. "I'm not all-knowing. None of us are. Can you explain?"

She sank down to the ground, her legs unsteady. All she wanted was to curl up somewhere safe. To hide in the shadow, in the dark, in the void. There was no comfort in this world. She rubbed her cheek, thinking of Adam's rejection. Dirt and sand had saved her. That was something. She dug her fingers into the dirt and leaves. It was cool and soft and damp, clinging to her skin.

"When he touches me, it's like there's another person in my head. I hear so much more, feel so much more. It's uncomfortable. Overwhelming."

Reu's voice was very soft. "Does he know?"

She looked up. "What?"

He was studying her, his eyes gentle again, but still dark. All the anger had left his face. "Have you told this to Adam? Does he know?"

"No." She dug her fingers deeper into the soil. "I haven't said anything. I thought he knew. That it was the same for everyone else."

He crouched in front of her. "That's why you don't like to be touched, isn't it? Why you keep pulling away from him." He held his hand out to her, palm up and waited.

She shook her head. "It isn't the same."

"But you feel something?" He closed his hand.

"Feelings, sometimes. Emotions." She lifted her gaze to his face. "Is there something wrong with me, Reu?"

He laughed. It was short and sharp and nothing at all like Adam.

"You're supposed to be the most perfect of us all, Eve. If you can do this, feel these things, it isn't because there's something wrong with you."

"But you don't hear or feel anything."

"No." He frowned, looking away, his face darkening again. "If Adam could hear us, surely he would have acted. Done something to punish us."

"Why? What would he do?"

Reu shook his head. "He'll be looking for you. We should get you back, or he'll be angry."

She closed her hand around the dirt, the images from Adam's mind racing through her thoughts again. She tried to breathe, but it was too hard. "I don't want to go back. I can't do this, Reu. I can't."

He took her hand, and she let him pry her fingers open and brush away the earth. "I'll think of something to stop him. Stay close to the others in the meantime."

"He'll hurt you."

"It wouldn't be the first time. Or the last. But better that he turn his power on me than you."

She searched his face. "Why would you do this for me?"

He raised his hand and she thought he would touch her, but he only brushed her hair away from her eyes and dropped his hand again. "God said I should protect you. That I had to keep you from him. And I will."

※

Reu sent her back to the cave alone, promising he would follow. Adam would be angry enough that she had disappeared and not followed his command. She had seen the stream on her way back but couldn't bring herself to wash. The dirt was the only protection she had.

Eve hesitated at the tree line, watching the other men and women as they ate together, sharing gourds of water. Hannah was sitting with a man Eve didn't know, using a sharp rock to split a melon. It was quieter than it should have been. No one was laughing or smiling the way they had earlier in the day. Hannah scraped the seeds from the melon without looking at her companion.

As she watched, Adam grabbed a woman by the arm. She could see the anger in his face as he spoke, but his words were lost to her. Eve stepped out from the trees and moved closer so she could hear.

"You were supposed to be serving her. Seeing to her needs. Where is she?"

"You took her into the cave, Lord. And I went to fetch water. I thought she was with you." It was Sarah, with the golden hair.

He slapped her, the sound carrying even to Eve. Sarah dropped to her knees in the grass with a sob, but he hauled her back to her feet. "You're not even worth the air you breathe. What do I keep you for if you can't do what you're told?"

He pulled his arm back as if to strike her again. Eve's stomach twisted and she lurched forward. "Adam, stop! Please."

He spun, dropping Sarah and crossing to her so quickly she didn't even have time to step back. He grabbed her by the arm, his fingers bruising her skin. "Where have you been?"

"I got lost in the woods." It was what Reu had told her to say. "I'm sorry."

He jerked her away from the others. *Lost in the woods. And even dirtier now than she was earlier. I should've taken her then.*

"You had no business in the woods. You were to bathe and return to me."

She tried to pull her arm free. His anger clouded her mind, making it difficult to think. "I'm sorry. I just wanted to see the Garden. I just wanted to see what was there."

Insolence. His fingers dug even deeper into her flesh. "You will do what you're told in the future, Eve. Do you understand me?"

"I didn't do anything wrong." She saw his hand rise but didn't flinch, his anger so strong that it washed her own fear away.

Until he struck her.

Her head snapped to the side beneath the blow. His hold on her arm kept her from falling as Sarah had, but she didn't consider it a mercy. Her skin burned and her eyes watered. She covered her cheek with her hand and gulped back a sob of her own.

"Don't ever contradict me in front of the others again." *She has to learn. They all have to learn. I am their god now, and they will obey!*

He flung her away from him and she stumbled back, almost falling, but for Reu who caught her. She cried out once in relief and clung to him, more shocked than hurt. He folded her into his arms and mumbled a soft apology into her hair. She hid her face against his chest, his skin cool on her cheek where Adam had hit her.

"You're safe, Eve," he murmured in her ear. "It's all right."

Somehow she believed him, though she felt Adam's eyes on her back and she shuddered. Reu held her closer, stroking her hair.

"He's walking away."

For some reason, the words were hard. She looked over her shoulder and caught sight of a woman disappearing into the cave with Adam. Lilith. Reu's jaw tightened, muscles twitching below the surface.

"I'm sorry. I didn't intend for things to happen this way. For you to be hurt." He tilted her chin up so he could see her cheek, his fingers gentle. "If I'd only been a moment earlier, I could have stopped him. You're going to be purple and green by morning."

She pressed her face against his skin and let him hold her. She wasn't sure there was anything she could say to reassure him. Or what it meant that another woman took her place with Adam tonight. She closed her eyes against the images springing immediately to her mind, making her shudder again.

Reu lifted her into his arms, carrying her against his chest the way Adam once had. When she had been so new and so innocent.

She didn't feel innocent anymore. Things were starting to make sense, but it wasn't an understanding she wanted. Her stomach twisted into knots of fear and she longed for the confusion she had left behind. When she had not known cruelty or pain or fear. And she was beginning to understand, too, what Reu had said her first night.

This wasn't how they were meant to live.

§

The sun sank behind the trees and the sky turned red, then black. Reu drew pictures for her in the stars shining down, telling her the stories God had shared when He had lived among them. He traced the outline of a great man with a spear, and an eye that had been lost in the search for the wisdom to save his son and his people.

"The most worthy of sacrifices," Reu said, then fell silent.

She felt his discomfort and turned her head to look at him in the moonlight. He was frowning, and though he stared at the sky, she didn't think he saw the stars.

"How so?" she asked.

"God said seeking wisdom for the benefit of those you must provide for is never a sin, but so often we will find ourselves searching for glory alone, and it's then that we must stop ourselves."

Eve shivered and Reu wrapped his arms around her in the grasses, tucking her head beneath his chin. Somehow, as the silence stretched, she was certain they were both thinking of Adam.

CHAPTER TWELVE
984 BC

§

"Fresh water, Thorgrim?" She slung the skin from her shoulder and held it out to him.

Thor grinned, taking it from her and drinking deeply. "Not as good as mead, but thank you."

"Better for you than mead, when you've been sweating in the sun all day." Eve took back the water skin and sat down on the nearby rocks. "Your boats are better and faster than any others, but you spend so much time working to build them, I wonder that you've even taken the time to sleep."

"I've taken time for more than sleep, Tora." He smiled. Odin help him, but she was even named for him in this life. He wondered who above him was struck with such a sense of humor. Or perhaps it was something else. The True God trying to lure him into her arms. He was perilously close to succumbing.

She returned his smile, a blush creeping up her neck and into her cheeks. "Yes, you've taken time for mead, as well," she teased.

He put down his hammer. It was crude, and more often than

not, his fist made shorter work of the job, but appearances had to be kept even if Odin had not taken his strength. Eve came to watch him almost daily, bringing water with her, or a small meal of bread and cheese they might share together. He had come to look forward to her teasing, and her laughter when he returned it.

"What else should I find time for?" he asked, letting his gaze drift from her face. The tunic she wore did not quite reach the top of her string skirt, the wide neck leaving much of her shoulders bare, for all the sleeves met her elbow. Often, when she sat, he struggled to keep from staring, hoping for glimpses of her ivory thighs, dusted with soft, fair hairs. He was beginning to think she struck such poses just to tempt him.

Her face flushed a brighter scarlet, but she said nothing, only looking out over the water as if it fascinated her.

Thor walked around the half-finished boat and she shifted to make room for him upon the rock she'd claimed. His tunic did not reach his knees, with the same wide neck of her own and belted at his waist. If he was guilty of looking at her, he had caught her watching him in the same manner more than once. And he had surely tempted her, time and again, when he had stripped off the heavy wool to bathe in the sea after a long day spent sweating beneath the sun. Once he'd even thrown the garment into her lap before launching himself through the water, her laughter in his ears.

But he'd had enough of teasing now, and he thought, perhaps, so had she. "I do not love building boats as much as I do the excuse it gives you to bring me water. And the excuse it then gives me to speak with you." Thor took her hand in his and kissed it. "I wish to remain as useful as possible to your father."

Her eyes were wide when she looked up at him. "Is that why you work so hard? To prove yourself to my father, that he'll give me to you?"

He thanked Odin silently for removing his power to control the storms, because if he hadn't, his eyes would've flashed with lightning then, and given him away. As if she could be the property of any man. As if she weren't glowing with immortality before his eyes.

"I seek to prove myself to you, Tora. That you'll allow me to care for you, whether your father wishes it or not."

Surprise flitted across her features and she studied his face. "You are a strange man, Thorgrim. So unlike the others here."

He smiled, releasing her hand to caress her cheek softly. "Would you prefer I declare you my property and steal you away?"

She laughed. "Father might expect it."

"Is that how your father met your mother?"

"Their marriage was arranged. To make peace with another village. But he will expect me to marry a strong man, to lead our people." She frowned, her forehead creasing, and looked away again. "He still wishes for a son. Perhaps the gods will grant him one yet."

"The gods," he repeated. He didn't know what to make of her when she spoke this way. If she meant what she said, or simply offered what was expected. "Do you pray to Freyja for a baby brother?"

Something about her body stiffened and she stood, collecting the water skin. "I should go. I've kept you from your work for too long."

He chuckled at her discomfort and caught her by the wrist before she had gone far enough to evade him. He had to hear the truth this time. If he was going to stay, she had to know she could trust him. He wanted her to trust him.

"Is Freyja not your preferred goddess of fertility? I know there are others. In the south they pray to Isis, or Aphrodite. Hera?" He couldn't bring himself to name Sif, though it was much more obvious. He couldn't let the thought of her poison this moment, this happiness. "I suppose you could pray to Frigg, instead."

"It's not that." She twisted her hand to try to free it. "I'm sorry. I really must get back to my weaving."

"Please, Tora." He didn't let her go, pulling her back to him instead, relieved that she allowed it. "Why does this upset you so?"

She stared at his hand on her wrist, her shoulders hunched. He tugged her closer, until she stood between his legs, so he might see into her eyes, even if she would not meet his gaze.

"These gods you speak of," her words were a whisper. "That I speak of. They're not real. They're just myth and legend and men explaining things in the world which they can't understand."

Thor laughed, struggled to stop, and then laughed again even more loudly, startling a rabbit from its hiding place and sending it careening out of the brush toward the forest. Eve pried at his fingers to free her arm, no doubt misunderstanding the reason for his amusement.

"Oh, Tora," he finally gasped. "Dear, sweet, lovely Tora." He released her wrist and stood, wrapping his arms around her and tucking her head beneath his chin. She fit there so perfectly, melting against his body. With relief, he thought. "You confess this to me so urgently, as if you fear some retribution for speaking it. Who do you fear if not the gods?"

"My people." Her voice was still soft, thick with misery and muffled against his tunic.

"Ah." He held her for a moment longer, pressing his lips to the top of her head and breathing in the scent of her hair before releasing her. She still smelled of sunshine to him, and spring rains. "They would never trust you to lead them if they knew you didn't believe."

She looked up at him, her eyes narrowed and her lips pressed into a thin line. "So you see, Thorgrim, perhaps I am not very much like the others, either."

He chuckled. "I'm sure you can't be the only one who believes that way. Nor will you be the last."

"And if I were born anyone else, it wouldn't matter."

"And is being born someone else so simple a thing?" He couldn't stop himself from goading her on, though she stepped back and looked away. How long had he been waiting for this opportunity? This moment? "What else are you hiding?"

"It hardly matters." She stared at the water. "You won't believe it anyway."

"Won't I?"

The wind had picked up from the sea, and her hair caught in it, whipping across her face. She brushed a piece away from her mouth. "Do you know much about the southern gods? You mentioned Aphrodite and Isis."

"A bit." He didn't take his eyes from her face. "When I traveled, I learned what I could of other people, other faiths."

"In your travels, did you ever hear of the god without a name? Sometimes they call him Elohim or Yahweh."

He shifted uncomfortably, not wanting to lie, but not sure how much of the truth he should tell. "Is that your god? This Elohim?"

"I have no god." She looked back at him, frowning, and her hair flew wild, the sunlight lending it shades of red. "But sometimes, I wish I did. I wish I could have that comfort. Feel the presence of something greater and know myself safe within its power." She wrapped her arms around her body, hugging herself. He didn't think it was from the chill of the wind. "I envy them that, no matter what god they worship. Delusion or not."

He stroked her hair from her cheek. She closed her eyes and pressed her face against his palm. It was something that he could give her, he thought. Now. Later. Even if she didn't know it for what it was. Didn't know him for what he was. Even if, for the moment, he was barely more than a man, he could be that presence in her life. If she would let him.

Thor closed the distance between them and raised her face to his. Her eyes were still closed, but her hand covered his, holding it against her cheek. When he brushed his lips over hers, she sighed, and he felt her body soften against him.

He kissed her again, wrapping her in his arms, and she kissed him back, eager, hungry. It made him ache for her even more, knowing that this, whatever this was between them, was the exception, not the rule.

She made a soft sound, her mouth warm and inviting, begging for more. He deepened the kiss, tasting her. Honey and fresh, clear water, on her lips.

He pulled away, though he could not let her go, not completely. Not kissing her was bad enough, like a physical pain in his chest. He wanted her, wanted to keep her at his side forever, wanted to make love to her on the pebbled beach, but if he was going to do this, if he was going to stay, he would do it right.

"Oh." Her hands clung to his shoulders and she hid her face against his chest.

He chuckled softly. "Oh?"

"Oh," she said again, then took a deep breath and exhaled slowly, relaxing her hold on him and looking up at his face from beneath her eyelashes.

He groaned at the look in her eyes, his hands tightening involuntarily around her waist. The soft, bare skin between her tunic and her skirt, like silk to his fingers. Letting her go when she looked at him like that was impossible. "I'm going to besmirch your honor if you don't allow me to wed you."

She smiled, and he thanked Odin that amusement overtook the hunger in her eyes. "What's to allow? All you need to do is throw me into one of your boats and away."

"I will not take you forcibly." The words were feeble. Already he was tempted by the thought. What would she do if he called for his power and stole her away to Asgard? Odin would find her a fascinating creature. They could be married beneath his mother's tree and feast in the great stone halls. He stopped his train of thought there, shying away from the problems it would cause. The things which stood in his way. He could not think of Sif, now.

"Then you'll have to go to my father, and risk his refusal," she was saying. "I'm not sure he'll allow it, Thorgrim. And if he refuses you, there will be no other way. I'll be forbidden to see you, to even speak with you."

"You deserve better than to be stolen away in the night."

She raised her chin. "If I wish to go, I have not been stolen. Is it not my right to give my heart to you?"

It was cowardly, taking her this way instead of facing her father, but she pulled him toward the fishing boats waiting above the tide line, dragging him by the hand. Someone shouted for her behind them, from the village, and he glanced back. Her father, he thought, wondering what kept her.

"Please," she said, turning to face him when he hesitated.

He growled and swung her up into his arms, carrying her to the boat he often used to fish in the evenings. No one would think it odd if it were gone. He dropped her onto the bench and shoved the boat off the beach, scraping against the rocks. He waded into the water to his knees before jumping in with her.

"How far?" he asked.

She smiled and worked the crude oars, taking slow easy strokes out to sea. "A few villages away will do. If we hug the coastline, I can tell you when to stop."

He eyed her for a moment. She was strong for a woman, and he'd made sure she was no novice with an oar, but he was stronger. Faster. It was best to get out of sight before whoever had been calling for her came down to the beach to look.

"Let me row."

She slid out of the way and he took over. Their speed nearly tripled. The wind shifted, and another call carried to them on the water. He turned the boat, sending them further up the shore. If they could get around the wooded headland, they would be safe from discovery.

Eve sat across from him, her back to the beach. In the sun, her skin glowed, and her aura was bright with joy and love. Golden with immortality. And yet she lived so simply as a woman within the world, not as a goddess, as she could.

"We don't have to return," he said. Even if he could not bring her to Asgard, it did not mean she should be trapped by the customs of men. "You can leave all of this behind. Live freely, independent of any village, any people."

"And if I were to go, what would happen to my father's people?"

The beach was out of sight now, and he slowed the pace of his oars. "Your father would choose a new heir. Someone else to lead, where your husband might have. Adopt a son, perhaps, though the gods might still grant him one."

"The gods," she repeated softly. "And what gods do you worship, Thorgrim?"

Her face was turned away from his, and he wished he had not spoken of them, but it was too late now. "None of them."

She looked up sharply, her eyes wide with surprise. "But you speak of them as if you believe."

He took a stroke with the oars, and then stopped, meeting her eyes. "So do you."

"But—" She bit her lip, her forehead furrowing as she stared at him. "I don't understand."

He smiled. "I have traveled a long way, for years on end, and heard many stories of many gods. But faith requires doubt, Tora, and I have none." He shrugged and began to row again. He did not wish to be on the water after night fell. Even if the chill of the wind did not bother him, the cold would bother her.

"You're speaking honestly." But by her tone, she did not seem to believe her own words. She was staring at him so hard now, he thought he felt her eyes piercing through his body. "How can you have no doubt? No question?"

No. She wasn't staring at his body, but trying to search his mind. His eyes narrowed as he realized what it was he felt. The familiar pressure upon his thoughts, and the vague ache at the base of his skull. How had he not realized it before? Of course she would have some power. Some ability to help adapt herself to her people, or else she would never belong to them, her past experiences overriding her present.

He kept his mind calm and his tone mild, burying the thoughts as quickly as they had come and hoping he was fast enough to keep them from her. "What answer are you looking for, Tora?"

She flushed, dropping her eyes guiltily, and the ache disappeared. "I just don't understand how you can be so certain. Or what it is you're certain of."

"Don't you?" Had she been able to read his mind? It certainly didn't seem as though she had. He pulled the oars in and reached for her, turning her face back to his and looking into her eyes. Without his power, he couldn't be certain. Couldn't find the truth in her mind for himself.

She looked troubled and confused, a wrinkle appearing between her eyes, and the thought that it was because she had seen his godhead worried him. But surely she kept her own secrets. If she knew his, too, he did not think she would speak of it. If she even believed it. She might very well consider it delusion, as she did the rest.

"You said if you told me what you hid, I wouldn't believe you. Do you still think so?"

Her eyes darkened, and she turned her face away again. "You

wouldn't. You'd think there was something wrong with me. Or that I was a witch."

He heard the bitterness in her voice, and it reassured him. If she had seen his own immortality, she wouldn't worry. She would have no reason to worry. "I would never think you were a witch, Tora."

"You say that now, but you don't know the truth." She shook her head, and when she looked up at him, her eyes were filled with tears. "I had no right to ask you to take me away. To ask you to bind yourself to me this way. There are so many things I wish I could tell you—that I want to tell you before it's too late for you to stop this, but I don't want to lose you. Lose this feeling of being loved. Not again."

"Shh." He pulled her to him, gathering her into his arms and holding her on his lap. She was crying now, her face hidden against his neck, her tears hot on his skin. "You won't lose me. And I will always love you." He stroked her hair, kissing the side of her head. "No matter what, Tora. Do you understand?"

"But you'll die," she sobbed, her words garbled by his shoulder. "You'll die, and I'll be alone again."

He wanted to tell her that he wouldn't. That she would never be without him, but it wasn't a promise he could make. Someday, he would have to return to Asgard, but he would not do it before her death. That wasn't something he could explain now. It would only disturb her further.

He held her closer, pressing his face against her hair. "Tell me. So that whatever it is, I can protect you, and whatever it is, you'll know I love you for it."

She took a breath, gulping the air, and he felt her begin to calm. If she could read anything from his mind, she would see the truth of his words now. That he meant to love her, no matter what. The hand that had been a fist in his tunic relaxed, and she smoothed the rough wool.

He caught her hand and held it to his chest, over his heart, waiting. It wasn't just that he wanted to know her, though he did, but that he wanted her to know he knew her and loved her all the same. Loved her more, for her immortality, for the things that made her more than human.

"You really don't have any doubts, do you?" she asked softly, wiping the tears from her eyes.

He kissed her forehead, glad it was a question he could answer honestly. "Not about this."

She sniffed, and then took another breath, as if to steady herself. "Elohim was my father, when this world was made. And my name…" she hesitated, and raised her eyes to his. He could see the fear in them, the worry, but he stroked her hair from her face and held her, and she went on. "My name is Eve."

CHAPTER THIRTEEN
Present

§

"Where is she?" Eve paced the small room she had chosen to dress in. The sitting room was filled with antiques, including a bright red fainting couch, but more importantly, it was just off from the courtyard, which was now filled with guests, all waiting patiently.

Juliette caught her as she crossed the room for the fifth time. "Abby, *s'il te plaît*. Sit, *ma chérie*. Garrit has sent René to find her. I am certain she has only lost track of the time."

Eve let herself be coaxed to a seat. She rubbed her forehead. "This is just so Mia. Couldn't she have been late to the rehearsal instead of the wedding? Jean ought to have more sense."

Her mother patted her arm. "Don't be so hard on your sister."

Eve rolled her eyes.

Someone knocked on the door and then Mia burst in, breathless. "I'm so sorry, Abby. I didn't have a watch." Her dress was wrinkled and her hair fell from what used to be an organized pile on the top of her head. She went straight to the mirror and started pulling out bobby pins and sticking them back in. Half a dozen of them appeared in her mouth almost immediately. "Did you know this mansion has a hall of portraits? Like a proper English manor!"

Eve froze, her gaze sliding from her sister to Juliette, whose eyes had narrowed.

Mia kept talking around the bobby pins in her mouth. "It's amazing. All of the DeLeon men have the same dark eyes. They're all so handsome. Have you ever seen that portrait at the very end of the hall? Their matriarch or something." Mia looked at Eve, studying her face. "She looks remarkably like you. I wonder if that's why Garrit fell in love with you. Some weird Oedipus complex." She turned back to the mirror and only then seemed to notice Juliette. "Oh! No offense of course, Mrs. DeLeon."

"Less talk, more putting yourself back together, Mia," Eve muttered, exchanging a look with her future mother-in-law. "Please."

Juliette smiled. "I'll just tell *Père* Robert we are nearly ready." She slipped out of the room.

"I hope I didn't offend her. I was just saying."

"Mia, please. Can you focus? We're already a half hour late. There are two hundred people out there waiting on you."

Mia grimaced, and even that expression was somehow seductively attractive. Eve sighed. After all these generations, still, each new set of siblings managed to drive her mad. Mia pulled the last pin from between her lips and secured the final strand of hair back into place, then reapplied her lipstick. "Ready!"

"You look beautiful, Mia," their mother said, hugging her. "And Abby, of course, you look wonderful. Garrit will be beside himself."

Eve stood and smoothed her dress before picking up the bouquet. It would be a relief to have this over with, and go back to being with her family. Her first family. It was so difficult to be Abby, when she was just getting used to being Eve again. "Mother, why don't you go out first? Luc will be waiting to seat you."

"Of course dear." Her mother kissed her cheek, squeezing her free hand. "I'm so proud of you, Abby." She opened the door and the sounds from the courtyard drifted in.

Eve could've sworn she heard René's voice speaking urgently nearby. But then the door swung shut again, and it was quiet in the room.

"I really am sorry, Abby." Her sister offered an apologetic smile.

Eve sighed. "You always are."

"You look absolutely stunning. If that makes a difference."

Eve shook her head. "I live with DeLeon men, Mia. I'm immune to flattery."

Mia hugged her. "Jean will be so distracted by you, he won't even look at me, I'm sure."

"Now I know it's flattery." Eve smiled and pulled the door open. "At least wait until after the reception before you run off with him, would you?"

Mia flashed a grin and took up her own bouquet. "I think I can manage that."

Eve waited another minute or so until the murmur of conversation died down outside, and then left the room. Her father stood at the back of the tent, for once his face not showing pink.

He blew his nose loudly into a handkerchief, stuffed it back into a pocket, and then took her hand. "Lovely," he sniffed. "I'm so proud of you."

She never had understood the pride of a parent in the marriage of a child. But she squeezed her father's hand, and they turned toward the aisle. Garrit stood at the far end, and he was looking at her as though he'd never seen her before. Heat flushed her cheeks, and the wedding march began to play.

They started down the aisle, but Garrit's gaze shifted slightly and his mouth firmed. She looked back over her shoulder to see what had distracted him.

Adam had just slipped into the courtyard.

Monsieur Owen, Garrit's supposed doorman, moved quickly toward him and Adam's eyes widened in surprise. Owen caught him by the arm and hauled him back roughly. They disappeared almost as quickly as they had come.

Garrit had stepped away from the aisle to speak to Brienne, who rose and slipped into the manor through the kitchen door. Eve's heart raced, and the room began to spin. Garrit moved purposefully down the aisle toward her.

And everything went dark.

§

"What did you do to her?"

"I did what had to be done, Garrit, as you requested. Had I known what her response would be, I never would've—" the voice broke off. It was oddly familiar, but she couldn't quite put a face to it. "I must go before he wakes. I'll keep him in my custody as long as I can."

"Abby?" Garrit took her hand, squeezing it gently. "Are you all right?"

She groaned and opened her eyes just as the door shut behind the other speaker, blocking him from her sight. The fainting couch was narrow and she clutched at the edge to steady herself before she rolled off the edge. The last time she had passed out like this—the most immediate memories were from the ward, when she had been so desperate for relief, she had bled herself dry. How often she had prayed to Michael for death, then? But of course he hadn't come. She blinked, and then finally focused on Garrit; his forehead was creased, and his face looked gray.

"What happened?" she asked.

"Your brother decided to grace us with his presence. Our security man removed him a bit more violently than we had anticipated. You passed out. Or got knocked out. We're not certain why."

"Adam." She remembered the shock in her brother's face when he saw the man who grabbed him. As if it was someone he knew, though it made no sense to her. "Why?"

Garrit shook his head. "He was rather too unconscious to get any answers at the time. He's been removed from the manor by now. You are *sain et sauf*, just a bit less married than we had hoped."

"All those guests. I passed out in front of all those guests." She tried to sit up, and Garrit helped her. "Can we still get married today? I'd hate to have to go through all of this again."

He laughed and kissed her forehead. "You haven't been out that long. *Père* Robert was kind enough to wait. *Maman* suggested she had strung your corset too tight, perhaps. She's very upset about it. Your mother is reassuring her that it was your own fault for not saying anything."

"Jean!" One threat made her think of the other, though she had nearly forgotten. "He showed Mia the portraits!"

"Shh." He laughed again. "*Maman* told me. He will not behave so foolishly again."

"I miss all the fun." Her head was throbbing, but when she felt it, she couldn't find any lumps. "What I would've given to see Adam get thrashed properly."

He frowned, studying her. "I'm not sure you would've seen much of anything, Abby. We think perhaps that was what made you pass out. Is there some connection there we didn't know about? Unless your corset really is too tight."

"It doesn't even have laces." She closed her eyes for a moment, trying to remember any time something similar had happened. Her head was pounding. She couldn't make any sense of anything over the roaring in her ears. "I think I need some aspirin."

Garrit put a glass of water in her hand but the rattling of pills in their bottle made her wince.

She grimaced. "Let's just get married, shall we? And worry about the rest when we don't have a house full of people to entertain. Or explain the delay to." She sipped the water and swallowed the pills. "What on earth could Adam have been thinking to show up like that?"

"I thought you just said you wanted to get married first, and worry later." Garrit helped her to her feet, half-smiling.

She wrinkled her nose. If he was gone, she didn't have to worry. At least that's what she told herself. It was an effort not to look out the window to be sure there weren't any angels descending from the sky.

He brushed a curl of her hair back into place, and looked her over. "No one would ever know you'd fainted if they hadn't seen it. *Tu es ravissante.*" One hand on the small of her back, he pulled the door open. "When you're ready."

Mia peeked in. "Thank God, Abby! Are you all right? Is the wedding still on? Mum, get Dad."

"I'm fine, Mia." She took another deep breath and sighed. "Now that I've got my clothing right."

Garrit chuckled. "Tricky business. *Maman* will be relieved." He kissed her cheek. "I'll meet you at the altar."

Eve nodded, and he walked away.

Mia attached herself to her side. "You should've seen Dad's face when you dropped like that. And Garrit. It seemed like he got to you before you even hit the ground. I've never seen a person move that fast. Abby, he was so worried." Mia led them to the courtyard while she spoke, barely even pausing to breathe. "And what was with that guy who got hustled out right beforehand? Did you see that? Garrit looked furious. Jean would only tell me he wasn't invited. I know the DeLeons are rich, but are they really so rich they have paparazzi sneaking in and out?"

"I don't know about paparazzi, no, but I'm sure the press would have liked to cover the wedding." At least Mia could be counted on to come up with her own explanations. "Do you mind walking down the aisle for a second time?"

Mia grinned. "You're joking!" She detached from Eve's side and skipped over to their father. He stood at the back of the assembly again, watching Eve with a look of concern. "Ready, Dad? I think she'll actually make it this time."

He offered Eve his arm with a smile. "I hope so. I'm not sure poor Garrit could stand it if we had a second disruption. We wouldn't want him to take it personally."

"No, we certainly wouldn't." Eve smiled, and then the music began, and Mia moved gracefully down the aisle. Garrit looked at Eve like she was the only thing in the world that mattered, as if nothing had happened to interrupt this moment.

Her father walked her toward him. At the front of the chapel, they stopped together and he kissed her cheek, dashed the moisture from his eyes, and left her to take his seat.

Garrit took her hands in his, and they turned to face the priest together.

§

"But for *Père* Robert speaking of how Eve completed Adam, and that unfortunate business before, I will call it a success." René raised his glass to them and smiled. Drinks had been distributed almost immediately after the ceremony had concluded, the servers weaving through the guests while the chairs were cleared from the dance floor and arranged around tables in preparation for supper. "*Félicitations*, and best wishes."

"*Merci.*" Garrit raised his own glass and took a sip of champagne. The first toast of what was sure to be many. René had released the best of his private stock for them, but the majority of the wine was made from DeLeon grapes. Wine-making was one of the few pursuits that hadn't changed since Ryam's day. "If you and *Maman* would do your best to keep *Monsieur* Watson out of the worst of the drink?"

"*Oui, oui.* Your *maman* watches him as the hawk studies the field mouse. Have no fear, Abby. We will see to it."

"I have no doubt. You DeLeons seem to think of everything."

"Not everything," René admitted with a sad smile. "Forgive us for earlier, *ma chérie*. If we had known what it would do to you, we would have taken more care in how we handled your brother."

Half of the Watson contingent was at the bar which had just been set up in front of the chapel, now closed and barred, the other half were finding their tables. The DeLeons were circulating, greeting each other with enthusiasm and making comments about the minister's lack of tact. No one who would understand a rapid exchange in French stood near enough to hear.

"About that," she began. French was one language she never forgot, and she spoke it as fluently as any DeLeon. Not that she hadn't let Garrit think otherwise, at first. "How exactly did you handle my brother?"

"Knocked him out, of course. We didn't dare do anything else, or risk more manipulation. One swift blow to the head." René grinned as though he wished he had been the one to deliver it.

"It's going to make it difficult in the future, won't it?" Eve asked. "If knocking him out knocks me out, too?"

"My dear girl, brute force is hardly the only defense we have. Don't worry yourself. As long as you're here, you'll be protected." René leaned forward to kiss her cheek, then switched back to English. "I suppose I should *mêler aux invités, oui*? Save me a dance, Abby."

Garrit wrapped an arm around her waist as his father slipped away to mingle. "He's right, you know. It's not worth worrying about."

"Easy for you to say," she grumbled. "You get to do the worrying."

"Not anymore." He grinned in a predatory fashion she had no trouble interpreting. Garrit liked nothing more than to put his cousins to work. "I'm placing that concern firmly in the hands of the rest of the family while they're present. As should you. It's not every generation you get a DeLeon wedding, and have you seen the cake yet? It's absolutely stunning. *Maman* was right about the pastry chef. Amazing work."

She slanted him a narrow look, trying to decide if he meant it. "You're just trying to distract me."

"A husband's prerogative." His grin softened then and he leaned down to kiss her. "Isn't that a novelty?"

She smiled. "I'm sure you'll get used to it. Just remember, being married isn't all flowers and kittens."

"Who said anything about kittens?"

"Puppies then."

He laughed. "That's more like it. I thought for a moment you had forgotten that your Watson family is British."

"My family is Lions, Garrit. I'm a great fan of felines."

"Were there any European lions left, I'd gladly offer you one as a wedding gift. As it happens, I'm afraid this is the best I can do." He waved to a man standing just inside the courtyard who stepped forward carrying a puppy. A Belgian Shepherd, she thought, one of the long haired versions, the color of aged bronze and all awkward limbs and wagging tail.

Eve laughed and scratched the pup behind the ears. It was desperate to lick her face. With all that dark fur, she didn't dare hold it in her wedding gown, but that would be remedied soon enough.

"He's darling, Garrit. Absolutely perfect!"

"He'll be waiting for you in the kennel in the morning. I'd rather not have a cold wet nose in the bed tonight."

She smirked and scratched the dog under its chin. "I think I can go along with that. Unless you do something awful to offend me before the night is out."

He chuckled and kissed her cheek, pulling her away from the dog and its handler and toward the dance floor. "I'll try not to."

CHAPTER FOURTEEN
Creation

❦

"Reu," the voice was soft, urgent and female. Eve rolled closer to the warm body next to her, without opening her eyes. "Reu, you must wake up. If Adam can't find her this morning, or worse, finds her here with you…"

She felt him move beneath her, carefully withdrawing his arm from beneath her head. She heard herself mumble an objection, but he removed himself anyway with a soft apology.

"Is he awake yet?"

"No," the woman said. "Sarah and I slept in shifts so we would be sure to wake you before dawn. He's going to be furious, Reu."

There was a sigh, and then Reu touched her on the shoulder, shaking her gently. "Eve. Wake up."

She opened her eyes. Hannah stood over Reu's shoulder, her expression anxious. "Forgive us, my lady, but if he doesn't find you, it will be a bad day for everyone."

Eve rubbed her face and let Reu help her sit up. "Don't call me that, Hannah. Please."

"Adam insists." But she smiled. "Thank you, for what you did for Sarah, yesterday. He would've beaten her if you hadn't stopped him."

"Go back, Hannah. We'll be along in a moment. Once he's awake, you'll need to check on Lilith. I don't expect she'll be well. Bring her some of the bark from the willow tree."

Hannah nodded and left.

Eve frowned. "What do you think he'll have done to her?"

Reu shook his head, his face tense again. "Adam uses her poorly when he takes her. He's convinced her that she has to let him, and none of us have been able to tell her otherwise. Because she allows him, it doesn't violate God's law, but it doesn't make it right." He stood up, taking her hand. "We need to get you back."

She let him pull her to her feet and kept her hand in his as they walked. "I don't understand what you mean."

He sighed and looked at her, his eyes dark. "You'll see, soon enough. Though I wish I could keep it from you. Make sure you go with the other women to bathe today. It will be safer for you that way."

"Safer than what?"

"Than if he takes you himself." His hand tightened around hers. "Remember what I told you, yesterday. Try not to let him separate you from the others. I'll keep close, but he'll be looking for my interference. He might try to send me away."

The cave was still deep in shadow. Hannah sat near the mouth, grinding the bark between two stones. She smiled at Eve as they passed inside, but said nothing. The others were still sleeping. Reu sat down in the dirt and she dropped to the earth beside him. After sleeping in the grass, the stone chilled her. She shivered and slipped beneath his arm.

He sighed again and tucked her head beneath his chin. "He'll be angry if he finds us this way."

"He'll be angry no matter what." She curled up against his body and closed her eyes. It was still dark enough to sleep, and she was tired and cold. "I'll protect you. I'll tell him I made you keep me warm."

Reu laughed softly in her ear and wrapped his other arm around her to draw her closer. "You can try."

Then he fell silent, and she listened to his heartbeat, and the way his breathing slowed. The warmth of his body lulled her back into sleep, but his voice followed her into unconsciousness.

"It's worth any beating he might give me."

§

Something hit her hard in the side, painfully, and she twisted away from it with a gasp even before she opened her eyes.

Adam was standing over her, his expression hard and his eyes like stone. "Get up."

Reu helped her to her feet, putting himself between her and Adam when it looked like he might strike at her again. "Lord Adam. Did we disturb you?"

Adam ignored him, staring at her.

"I was cold. The stone chilled me."

His eyes narrowed. "We'll search the Garden today. I trust that will settle your curiosity from yesterday. You'll have no reason to get lost in the trees again."

There was no question in her mind about why he was doing this. It wasn't for her curiosity. It was for him. For the fruit. Whatever that meant.

Adam's gaze flicked back to Reu again. "Organize the others and send them into the Garden in pairs. I want a sample of every fruit from every tree brought back. Anything unfamiliar. You're to taste nothing until I've seen it. Is that understood?"

Reu nodded, though his forehead furrowed. Adam stared at him until he left, but Reu glanced back at her from the mouth of the cave before he disappeared and she saw the promise in his eyes. He wouldn't be far.

Eve dropped her gaze to the dirt, hoping Adam hadn't noticed. He tilted her chin up, forcing her head to the side to look at her cheek.

She didn't stop him. Even as his thoughts flooded her mind. *Next time I'll be sure to strike her below the neck. The bruising mars her beauty.*

"I wish you hadn't made me hurt you, Eve. I've only ever wanted to honor you. To keep you by my side."

"You didn't have to hurt me, Adam," she said softly. "You don't have to hurt any of us."

He grunted, his fingers tightening on her chin. "If you had only waited to speak to me privately, instead of challenging my authority in front of the others, all of this could have been avoided. Look what I offer you, now. A chance to do all the exploration you like. Because you desired it. I would always give you what you desire, if you would only ask." He shook his head, his eyes hardening again. "And then I find you here, sleeping in the arms of that dog. He's beneath you."

She pulled her face away. Reu had promised to keep her from Adam, if it was what she desired. Promised to protect her as well as he was able. But at what cost to himself? Would Adam cast Reu from the Garden when she refused to join him in his chambers, when she refused to let him have her body beneath his? Would he make her watch while he beat Reu for his kindness to her?

"I was only cold. The stone was so cold on my skin after the heat of the sun all day. It wasn't his fault. I commanded it of him."

"It's cruel, Eve, to make a man love you when you already belong to another."

She looked up then, studying him. They were alone in the cave. "I thought I was your equal."

He sighed and stroked her arm. *She still doesn't understand.* "And that's why we belong to one another. Because we are equals. Because I am the only one who can love you the way you deserve. And you're the only woman who can satisfy me. We're meant to be together, Eve. We're meant to rule them."

"Is that what Elohim told you? That we were meant to be together?"

His eyes flashed with anger. She saw it clearly in his mind. It was the voice from the void, the same voice that had called her to life and put air in her lungs.

'She will be your sister.' The voice belonged to the old, gray man. The body Adam had abandoned to the storm. But in Adam's mind, Elohim's forehead was creased with troubled lines, his expression grave. *'Your twin in every way. Made to complement you perfectly. And she will live on as long as you will. Reborn in every life as you are. But you cannot take her as your wife. Not now. She cannot love you, yet, and you are forbidden to force her. Teach her everything you've learned from me, but let her live her own life.'*

She felt Adam's frustration, his anger, and then his determination, and his knowledge that God could no longer stop him. It was involuntarily thought and he shoved the memory away just as quickly as it had come. But it was too late. She had seen it. The truth of it. She was not his.

She pulled away from him and stumbled back into the stone wall of the cave, wrenching herself free of the memory and the thoughts and feelings that had followed. Adam's possession. She would not be his.

Adam frowned, "Eve?"

She braced herself against the wall. "I'm not supposed to be your wife."

"You don't even begin to understand what you're talking about." He was angry again and he grabbed her by the chin, forcing her to look into his eyes. "You are what I say you are, Eve. All of you are bound by my words, now. You'll do as you're told."

You'll love me. She felt that same heat again, as it burned her cheeks and her body where his hands touched her, leaching into her through his fingers and his palm. Her heart began to race and she couldn't breathe. Couldn't even look away. He pulled her closer and she felt him hard and hot against her. It burned inside her, body and mind. His will, his command, searing itself in her thoughts, forcing its way through, trying to take root. *You'll love me, and you'll want me as much as I want you. There's no one here to stop me. God can't save you. Just like He didn't save Lilith.*

She shoved at his shoulders with a gasp, clawing at them, digging her nails into his skin.

He jerked away. Blood beaded from a crescent moon on his arm and for a moment, he stared at it, his expression so strange, so different from anything she'd seen before. As if he could not understand, could not comprehend. Then he looked up, his eyes flashing with anger, his jaw set with rage.

He grabbed her again, twisting her by the wrist until she cried out. "You'll learn your place soon enough, Eve. It's only a matter of time."

Adam threw her from him, and turned away.

She landed on her knees, skinning her palms in the dirt. Tears pricked her eyes at the sting, but she climbed to her feet and ran from him. Ran from the heat and the desire he had flooded her with, but had never been her own, would never be her own. When Reu called her name, she didn't stop. She didn't care if he followed her. She didn't care if she ever saw any of them again. She didn't want to do this anymore.

She didn't even want to live.

CHAPTER FIFTEEN
903 BC

Thor held the hand of his wife as the last breath left her, pressing it to his face. Even knowing she would be reborn, watching her die was the most difficult thing he had ever done. Without his power, he could not follow the journey of her spirit as it left her to find its new home. He could not close his eyes and search for the bright light of her immortality among men. He was even too old and too decrepit in this body to carry her to her burial.

Soon, he promised himself, gently removing the ivory bracelet from her wrist. It was the only thing he would allow himself to keep, a token of their marriage, of their love.

He closed her eyes for her and let in the women to prepare the body. Tora, his Eve, had not wished to be buried as a Chieftain's wife had the right, in a hollowed oak beneath a mound of earth. She had begged him to send her empty body out to the water on one of the fishing boats he had built with his own hands, and let it burn. He had agreed. Her body didn't hold her spirit; there was no point in treating it as though it might.

He walked to the boat prepared for the funeral. It was nearing dusk, now, and when it fell, the night would cloak his features to the others. He waited on the rocks where they had spoken of their marriage for the first time. Long ago, he had passed the leadership of this village to the son Eve had born him, a fine man, with very little of his father in him. His hair was Eve's, his eyes were Eve's, even his build was slighter and less powerful than his father's. Some trick of Odin's, he was sure, to keep him from betraying himself with a godchild and exposing this village to Sif's wrath and Loki's treachery.

It mattered little. Owen had been a strong man and a good leader, and Eve's blood was as potent as any god's—certainly more suited to life among men. Owen had never thrown lightning bolts in his rage, or spoken into the minds of others. He had never traveled through lightning to far-off lands or exhibited uncommon strength. All for the best. Owen's people had never had cause to distrust him. Nor did they distrust his son, when he had taken the leadership of the village at Owen's urging, or his grandson, who stood as priest and chieftain now.

Owen lived a long life, like his mother, but each generation after aged less gracefully with the dilution of Eve's blood. Even so, they were a healthier people, stronger in all the ways that mattered. Her granddaughters bore children more easily than any of the other women, and her grandchildren's children and grandchildren rarely suffered from the illnesses which plagued the rest of the village during winter and spring. Even if they did not live a century at a time, they still lived longer; to sixty or eighty winters, instead of forty.

One more task, and then Thor could leave them all in good conscience. The women carried the body of his wife to the boat, and laid her down gently. He stroked her silvered hair as it fanned out behind her head. They had wrapped her in old woolen blankets, the better to burn, and put sweet smelling oils on her skin. There was nothing of his Eve left here. Nothing more to tie him to this place, to this humanity he had taken and worn as a mask.

Others had gathered behind him, called by Owen. They were silent now; the only noise the shuffling of their feet on the pebbles that littered the beach, and the hushed movement of the wind from the sea through the trees.

Thor pushed the boat out into the water, wading with it almost to his waist before giving it a final shove. Then he turned his thoughts to home. To Asgard. To Odin, his father. He waited for the changes to begin.

Thunder rolled from far off, and all at once, he felt the power he had lived so long without flood through him, lightning in his veins. His eternal and immortal youth returned with his strength, and he bade the wind blow the boat out deeper into the water. He watched it until it was almost lost to him in the dark, and then he looked to the heavens. Great storm clouds blotted out the moon and the stars, making the sea black. He called the skies down upon it.

Lightning cracked through the darkness, bathing them all in white light and igniting the little fishing boat in the distance. Those behind him on the beach murmured in surprise, some even speaking brief prayers for his ears. *Thor, god of thunder, god of the skies, bless us and protect us.*

These people had no need of his blessing, and they had been given the grace of his protection for some eighty years while he lived at Eve's side. More, they had Eve's blood. Was that not enough of a gift?

He turned from the boat, now a mass of licking flames, and looked toward the shore and the people there. Owen stood before them all, staring now at his father with dawning comprehension. He was a wise man, a respected elder. Perhaps there was too much of his mother in him, for his perception often bordered on mindreading. Eve had never whispered a word of heresy to her son, not wishing to make him an outcast to his people, and he had grown up loving his grandfather's gods. Odin the Allfather and his wife Frigg, Thor the lord of thunder, Loki the mischief bringer, Heimdall the guardian, Freyr of the fields and fertility, Freyja, and Sif, the patronesses of fertility and women, beauty and prosperity. Never once had Owen had reason to believe his father was more than a man, until this moment.

Thor wanted him to know, to cement his faith in a way that Eve had never been able. Truth was the last gift he could give the boy who had been his son. The gods were present. The gods were watching. The gods walked among men. The gods loved.

Owen bowed his head.

Lightning struck again dancing across the sea and dazzling the eyes of any who looked in Thor's direction. He let it take him.

By the time their sight had cleared again, he was gone.

§

Thor sat in the great hall of Asgard, his head bowed and eyes closed. It had been a full day since he had returned. Odin had not spoken to him except to welcome him home, not even going so far as to suggest he see to his wife. The old raven croaked at him from the back of the Allfather's throne and Thor sighed, opening his eyes and staring into the mug of mead in his hand. So much for peace.

He drained the mug and rose. Even if Odin had not said it, Thor knew his duty. Sif waited, and the longer he put off approaching her, the more suspicion would arise. Loki still had not returned from his expulsion into the world of men. His sentence would last another 18 years. It reassured him, nonetheless, that he need not fear finding the dog in his home, making love to his wife.

His wife. His heart twisted in agony. He had left his wife in heaven to take one on earth, and she had been more goddess than Sif would ever be. True, Sif's beauty had no match among mortal women. What he had seen of Aphrodite could not put his wife to shame either, though the Olympian was beautiful in her own right. Once Thor had looked upon Sif as the loveliest creature he would ever behold. But the eons had changed her, distorting her beauty into pride and vanity. What depth she had once possessed was gone, and that was made more apparent by the time he had spent with Eve.

What a fool he had been to think a single lifetime with Eve would be enough. He could not prevail on Odin to change him again, and the only others with the power were Loki and Sif. Even if they would—an impossibility—they could only change his form, not take away his immortality. He would be lucky if he could spend ten years in her company before her people began to notice he did not age. And his temper alone would wreak havoc on the illusion of humanity. Storms rolling in from clear blue skies did not go unnoticed, even by the most oblivious of humans and gods.

The cottage was dark when he got there, his goats not even stirring. Of course. He had not paid any notice to the darkness. Sif would be asleep. He shut the door behind him as quietly as he could and entered the bedroom.

Sif was curled on her side in the wide bed, one hand beneath her flawless cheek, the other curled loosely beneath her chin. Her hair, long grown back, was neatly plaited in a braid, which coiled over her shoulder and disappeared beneath the blankets covering her. In sleep, she was as beautiful as the day he had first laid eyes upon her. There was no cruelty in the half smile which curved her lips, no vanity in the arch of her brow. He touched her skin lightly, trailing his fingers over her cheekbone and down her jaw. She stirred, rolling onto her back and falling into a deeper slumber.

Perhaps it would be possible to be satisfied by his true wife once more. Perhaps if he simply turned his thoughts from Eve, he could love Sif again as he ought. He would try. He owed her that. He owed them all that much, to be content with his purpose in this world. His people needed him. Odin needed him. It was long past time he focused on the lands which belonged to the North.

He did not disturb her by joining her in the bed, but left her to sleep and went back to the main room of the cottage. He sat facing the window and waited for the sun to rise. In the morning, he would make amends with Sif. For now, for the last time, he closed his eyes and searched for Eve's presence on earth. He brushed her mind, a squalling infant, and soothed her cries, comforting her thoughts until she fell into a slumber.

Thor sighed, rubbing his forehead with his knuckles, and withdrew. He buried his love for Eve away where Sif could never find it.

The only thoughts he would permit himself now would be those involving his report to Odin. There was much to tell the Aesir of the world in which they lived.

CHAPTER SIXTEEN
Present

The manor overflowed with DeLeons for weeks after the wedding. Eve could only be grateful the Watsons had felt no need to stay. Eve's parents left almost immediately. Mia however, begged permission to stay for another month, and under pressure from her mother, Eve reluctantly granted it. Garrit shrugged and gave her a room at the opposite end of the manor house, near his parents' room, and Juliette promised to keep an eye on her. The portrait of Lady Anessa, Eve's previous DeLeon incarnation, was removed from the hall for the duration, replaced with a framed photo from the wedding. There was no point in tempting Mia's curiosity.

"Won't you go on a honeymoon, Abby? Didn't Garrit plan some exotic vacation for you?"

Eve stared into her coffee cup. Facing her sister first thing in the morning was a trial. With the addition of Mia's unfailing ability to raise all the most awkward subjects, Eve was starting to hope Jean would marry her just so that she would go somewhere else for a while. Poor Jean. He wouldn't know what hit him.

"Unfortunately, Garrit's business forced us to cancel it. Maybe in a few months." Or never. Until they were sure Adam had given up on trying to infiltrate her life, an exotic vacation seemed incredibly unwise.

Eve picked a fresh croissant off a platter and began pulling it apart. Mia had already devoured one, and judging by the dirty plate beside her sister, Jean had already come and gone. The crust was a bit rubbery. She could've made better breakfast breads, if the man Garrit had hired to cook while the manor held guests would let her near the ingredients or the oven. She wasn't sure if that had been Garrit's idea, or the cook's.

"What a rotten job, then. Even if he is worth a fortune."

"The kind of work that makes that kind of money usually is rotten. Money isn't everything, Mia. The sooner you learn that, the better off you'll be."

Mia rolled her eyes. "Because you're learning it so well now, what with being disgustingly rich."

"I didn't marry Garrit for his money."

"That's what everyone says when they marry rich men."

She sighed. "Mia, really. Do you really think Garrit would ever marry a woman who was only after his fortune? He's not stupid. None of the DeLeons are."

Mia snorted, but then Garrit joined them, stopping whatever else she had meant to say.

He kissed Eve on the forehead as he sat down. Plate, silverware, juice and water glasses were set before him by one of the staff. Eve had only allowed him to hire them on the condition that they did not serve *her*. Garrit took a danish, and the newspaper appeared by his elbow. He smiled at Eve, but she looked away. If she met his eyes she would only frown, and it really wasn't his fault her mood was so foul. Keeping a staff when the manor was acting as a glorified hotel made sense, but it didn't make her want to smile back and exchange pleasantries.

He cleared his throat. "*Bonjour,* Mia. Are you enjoying your stay?"

"Oh, it's wonderful. Jean is taking me sightseeing today, in town."

"Is he?" Eve asked. Garrit glanced at her sidelong. She ignored him. "Did Jean happen to run that by his Aunt Brienne?"

"Abby, you're so ridiculous. Why on earth would he need to ask his aunt for permission?"

"*Oui,* Abby." Garrit smiled. "Why does he need Brienne's permission?"

She glared at him. "Brienne did mention that she needed some supplies from town. I'm sure that if Jean is going, she'd appreciate if he picked them up for her."

"Ah, *naturellement.*" He hid a grin from Mia by sipping his coffee, but Eve saw it and scowled. He cleared his throat again and opened the paper to the business section, seeming to have realized his error.

"Abby said your job is keeping you from your honeymoon, Garrit."

He shot Eve a look, and she pretended not to notice. It was his turn to fend off her sister's questions. "*Oui.* Regrettably."

"But I don't understand. How could you let them keep you? It's your *honeymoon.*"

"I'm at the mercy of my clients. And while you would think a wedding and honeymoon are life events deserving some time off, not all of them are so reasonable. The rich rarely are."

"Your family is perfectly reasonable."

Eve winced. "Mia! Would you please mind your tongue?"

"*Non,* Abby, *c'est pas grave.*" Garrit covered her hand on the table, squeezing it once. She wasn't sure if it was a reassurance or an admonition. "We are rather well off, as far as these things go."

"It doesn't mean it's polite to comment," Eve said.

"But I'm his sister now! Aren't I allowed to know the family secrets?"

Garrit stiffened, and Eve busied herself grabbing Mia's plate and stacking it with her own. "Help me with the dishes, Mia. Then you can go run around the countryside with Jean."

Mia sighed. "Please. You have people to do the dishes for you. Especially now, with everyone and their brother in residence."

The plates clattered to the table top and Eve prayed for patience. "Don't be rude, Mia."

Mia's mouth dropped open as if to argue but Garrit cut her off. "It's all right." He picked the plates back up and passed them off to one of the servants. "We are not easily offended by truth. And Mia is a guest."

"Which is it, Garrit?" Eve asked. Didn't he realize how closely Mia skated around the truth? And if she did find out, through some carelessness of Jean's or even their own, it would only make it all a bigger mess. "A guest or a sister?"

His jaw tightened. "A sister who is staying with us as a guest. If she wants to help, she's more than welcome, but as she's never been here, it is only natural her first priority should be to enjoy the activities we have to offer."

Mia rolled her eyes. "God, Abby. You've been so on edge. I thought marriage was supposed to mellow a woman."

Garrit pinched the bridge of his nose. "Mia, why don't you find Jean? I'm sure he'll be happy to get an early start. The traffic can be terrible, midday."

"Oh, fine. Not like I want to sit here in the middle of your first fight anyway." She stood up and flashed a smile. "Enjoy making up."

Eve watched her leave the room, half tempted to cancel Mia's plans for her. The fact that Garrit found her just as aggravating was almost gratifying—or would have been if she hadn't forced him into accepting Mia's presence in their home during what should have been their honeymoon. She sat down again and hid her face in her hands.

"Abby." Garrit pulled her hands gently away. "She's right, you know. You have been terribly tense. Is it the family? I can send them away. Put them up elsewhere."

"No, it's not the family. The family is wonderful. Everyone who doesn't know who I am has already decamped, and the rest really do try to make themselves scarce."

"You can't let her get to you. She really doesn't know what she's saying."

Eve shook her head. "That's exactly the kind of justification my mother would have used."

"And we all know she's spoiled. But no one expects you to step in as her parent. You're her sister. You don't need to police her. Let her enjoy herself until she's bored with Jean, and she'll return home."

She took his hands in hers and stared at them for a long moment, trying to decide how best to phrase what she wanted to say. "Do you know why I married Lord Ryam, Garrit? Centuries ago?"

He shrugged and squeezed her hands in his. "You couldn't resist the DeLeon charm."

She smiled. "Partly true, of course. But not the whole truth."

"His journal says you were in some kind of trouble. Bringing you to the country was meant to keep you safe."

She nodded, searching his face now. Ryam evidently hadn't shared the details of this particular drama. Small favors.

"I had a sister. She was my best friend in the world. We told each other everything."

He frowned. "As is the way of sisters the world over."

"I told her everything, Garrit. Because I loved her so much. Because we were so close. I thought she would understand. That she would see how much I loved her. I had told others in the past. A husband here or there. People I could trust. And I wanted so much to be able to trust my sister. My Aimee. I couldn't believe she would betray me."

His expression was full of sorrow, and he reached out to brush her hair behind her ear. "She's the reason Ryam had to whisk you away?"

Eve swallowed around the tightness in her throat at the memory. It had been a very near thing. A day later, and Ryam would have been too late. As it was, they had been forced to leave in the middle of the night, slinking out of the city like rats. "She used me, used everything I'd told her to turn me into her scapegoat. Not because she thought I was evil, but because she thought it would make our father love her. Because she thought he would forgive her, if he hated me."

"Mia isn't Aimee."

She shook her head. "I won't risk it. I don't want to lose another sister."

He caressed her cheek. "*Je suis désolé,* Abby. I can only imagine how difficult it must have been."

"It brought me home. It brought me Ryam." She forced a smile so he wouldn't think she was still agonizing over that part of her past. It didn't fool anyone.

"If having Mia here under these circumstances is causing you distress, I'll send her away with *Oncle* Ryan and Jean. She can hardly complain about it if the reason she's staying goes with her. *Tante* Clair would love to have her. We could offer it to her as an opportunity to see Paris."

"I feel badly saddling your poor aunt and uncle with Mia."

"Abby, she's a very biddable girl as long as you don't expect her to be on time to anything. Clair has complained for years that *Oncle* Ryan never gave her a daughter."

"And Jean?"

"Jean will be happy for an excuse to return to what he refers to as the 'real' city."

Eve looked out the window. Mia and Jean were just climbing into a car for the drive into town. They were laughing at something together. "Perhaps if Juliette suggests it, Mia will be more willing."

"I've never met a woman who could turn down an all-expense-paid trip to Paris." He squeezed her hand and then stood up, taking an orange from the fruit bowl with him. "I'll make the arrangements."

It would be nice to have a few less people in the house, and a bit more privacy. She sighed and stood, collecting what was left of the breakfast dishes from the table and taking them to the kitchen. It would be nice not to have a staff lurking about, giving her dirty looks when she wanted to cook something for herself, too.

Maybe, if she was lucky, Mia and Jean would start an exodus.

CHAPTER SEVENTEEN
Creation

☙

"Eve!"

She heard him calling but didn't respond. Knees pulled to her chest and eyes shut tight, she rocked back and forth on her spine. The tree behind her groaned and rasped, and the leaves fluttered in the breeze.

"Eve?" He was getting closer, she thought, listening to him crash through the brush. And then the sound stopped. She pictured him as he stepped into the meadow. He would see her in a moment, curled up at the base of the tree. But maybe not. She stopped rocking and held still. She didn't even breathe.

Leaves crunched beneath his feet as he moved closer. "Eve."

She didn't speak. But she felt his presence and then the heat from his body as he knelt beside her. He brushed her hair back from her face, and she opened her eyes when she realized he wasn't going to go away. His expression was dark with worry.

"I'm not supposed to be his wife."

Reu studied her face. "You heard something?"

"God called me his sister. He's not allowed to have me. He's not allowed to force me. God told him that." God. God, who had brought her forth into this world. For what? Breathe, the voice had said. And she had, but she wished she could take it back.

"Did he force you?"

She buried her hands in her hair, clutching her head. Adam had known what he was doing. It had been different than the other times she had heard his thoughts. It was a demand. A command. Imposed over her own will. And the heat burning through her body had been his, too. She understood now why Lilith believed as she did. He had forced himself on her, not just physically, but mentally too. Only Lilith had no power of her own. No strength of mind to stop him. No way to protect herself from the way his words twisted her thoughts to his bidding. She wouldn't understand what was happening.

Eve wasn't even sure she understood.

"He tried." But it wasn't something she was ready to explain. It wasn't something she had the words to describe. "I won't be his wife."

Reu nodded and stood, glancing up at the tree sheltering her. He frowned and reached up, plucking a piece of fruit from a branch and staring at it. His forehead furrowed and he dropped the fruit as if it had stung him, stumbling back from beneath the boughs. He stared at the tree, his jaw tense and his face white.

"What's wrong?"

He shook his head, searching the clearing now. Then he stopped, his gaze fixed on something over her head. The tree rasped again. "Eve, come toward me. Slowly."

There was a hissing behind her. Like laughter. She turned to look and then scrambled out from under the creature hanging above her head. A legless kind of lizard, only so much larger than anything she'd seen in the Garden, longer than her own body and patterned with green and brown diamonds. It slithered through the branches, its body rasping against the bark as it followed her movement to the edge of the canopy, the hissing laughter in her ear the whole way.

A tongue flicked quickly in and out of its mouth and it stared into her eyes. "Sheltered as you've been you've already learned to fear." It hissed another laugh, louder this time. "And God thought you'd be safe in the Garden."

She couldn't look away from the creature. Even breathing became a labor as it stared at her, suspended from the lowest branch of the tree. "What are you?"

"Reu knows." The creature's gaze shifted over her shoulder and the weight lifted enough for her to breathe again.

"You're Lucifer," Reu said.

It hissed another laugh. "And I didn't even need to give you any hints."

"What do you want?" She didn't like the way it laughed. The way its tongue slipped in and out, tasting the air. She had no idea who or what Lucifer was, but the way Reu spoke the name made the hairs on her arms stand up.

"What does anyone want?" But the creature narrowed its pupils as it looked at her, and she felt as if it tore through every thought she'd ever had. Her skull ached. "Poor Eve, still struggling to understand this world you've woken to. I want to live. Undisturbed. Free. Without fear. Just as your Reu preaches we all should."

"What do you want from us?" Reu's voice was rough. Eve thought it was dismay to have his words turned by this creature, though she didn't know why, or what about it offended him.

"Defy Adam. Bear sons and daughters of wisdom to protect us all. *Eat of the fruit* and live."

She stepped back, jerking her gaze from the creature and staring at the tree. The boughs were heavy with brilliant red leaves, hiding its bounty. At first glance, she had mistaken them for apples; the same fruit Hannah had offered her at midday the day before. But now she could see they were brighter, more luscious. And shining a polished gold so brilliant they reflected the red leaves around them.

"The fruit?"

The creature hissed again. "She knows more than she's admitted, Reu. Picked it from the mind of God's favorite son. Will you still love her when she can read your thoughts as well?"

"The fruit is forbidden," Reu said, glowering.

"Do you really think he's searching the Garden just for Eve's pleasure?"

"No." She only realized she'd spoken out loud when the creature hissed with its awful laughter. She cleared her throat. "He's looking for the fruit. It's been in his thoughts since I've known him."

Reu shook his head. "The angels will never allow it."

"The angels will wait until God's law has been broken before they act." Lucifer said. "They won't help you. And then it will be too late. Adam will destroy us all, determined as he is to have her."

The creature's golden eyes were black slits as it stared at Reu, who had fallen silent. She could feel his tension, so thick it was like a weight in her heart. If the creature could inspire such dread, why did it need them to act?

"You will not stop him?"

"It is not in my power to stop God's chosen ones from doing what they desire. I may only suggest, only beg, only plead." The creature said it bitterly, and its long body drooped between the branches. "Adam will not be constrained by God's law, and you cannot cower behind it for much longer. Make your choices carefully." Its gaze shifted back to Reu, and the tongue flicked out and in again. "Or it will be your death. Not that it will matter for long. Creation will be undone soon after, and God's sacrifice will have been made in vain. Will you not make the sacrifice of this small sin to save the whole world, when He gave His immortal life for you?"

The creature pulled its body back into the crimson leaves, disappearing completely into the tree as though it had never been there.

"Wait!" Eve called. But there was no response, and Reu hushed her, his head turning away from the tree. He pushed her behind him and stepped back, his shoulders squared against what came.

Lilith crashed through the brush on the other side of the meadow with Lamech behind her. Reu swore, some of the stiffness leaving his body. He let Eve go, and when she moved to his side she could see the deep furrow of his brow.

"The tree." Lamech's eyes were wide, and he glanced at Reu before his gaze returned to Lilith. His face paled.

She was staring at the tree with eyes rounder than the moon, and then her gaze fell to the ground and the golden fruit there. She stepped forward, reaching down to pick up the shining apple Reu had dropped.

Lamech made a strangled noise. "Lilith, no. You mustn't. It's forbidden."

"Nothing is forbidden to Lord Adam." Her fingers caressed the golden skin. "He will be pleased with me for finding this."

"It won't matter, Lilith." Reu spoke gently. "Even if you bring this to him, it won't make him stop hurting you."

Lilith shook her head, staring at the fruit. "You don't understand."

"I do." Eve stepped forward.

There was a ring of purple around Lilith's neck, black and blue marks in the shape of hands on her arms and splotches all over her body. This was what Reu had meant. What he hadn't wanted her to see. What Lilith had suffered in her place. But she hadn't seen this in Adam's mind when he had kissed her. It had been different, and yet…

"The touch of his mind, the heat that sinks into your bones, bending you to his will. I understand, and what he's done to you is wrong."

"He is Lord! We are his to do with as he pleases."

"He'll destroy us all, Lilith," Reu said. "He'll hurt us all. Is that what you want?"

"You should be careful what you say, Reu. He's already angry with you. He thinks you're trying to take *her* from him."

"Eve is free to make her own choices, just as you are."

But she wasn't. Eve could feel the way Lilith's emotions had been twisted. Adam's power was like a cloud over her mind, his presence thick in her thoughts. It wouldn't matter what Reu said to her. It didn't matter what God's law once might have been. Lilith would answer only to Adam, would follow only Adam. Eve pitied this woman. For the woman she might have been if Adam had not taken her. Was this what they would all be, once Adam had the fruit? When he had the power he thought would come by eating it?

"It's too late, Reu." She could feel the ripple of Adam's pleasure from across the Garden, crawling up her spine. "He knows she's found it."

"You're certain?"

She nodded and turned away. If presenting Adam with the fruit would spare Lilith another beating, another night of pain, so be it. There was no stopping the rest. Even if they took it from her and sent her back without anything to show, he would still find it now. Lilith would lead him back here. She would tell him they had stopped her, and he would punish them. Reu and Lamech would be made to suffer, or cast out.

Yes, she was certain.

Reu was watching her, searching her face. "What will you do?"

Eve stepped toward the tree, and the low branch from which the serpent had hung. One of the fruits, hidden in the red leaves, winked with a flash of sunlight. A faint tingle traveled down her arm as her hand closed around it and the fruit came free. The branch swayed, relieved of its burden, weeping the broad scarlet leaves in a shower around her.

The fruit was heavy in her hand. Much heavier than an apple would have been. She wondered briefly about the angels. Who they were, and what they would do to her when they realized she had broken God's law. Sin, the creature had called it. But was it, really? Or was it wisdom, for the greater good, like the story Reu had told her about the one-eyed man in the sky?

She raised the fruit to her lips.

CHAPTER EIGHTEEN
650 BC

In the North, the ocean currents shifted and beneath the surface, magma channels altered course. A frozen fist closed around their people, and even Sif forgot her anger for a time, as the gods worked to save the lives of those who looked to them. It had come upon them without warning, as though the Aesir were bedeviled by a higher power. Thor did not like to dwell on the possibility that this might be a punishment sent by the True God, Eve's Elohim, nor did he so much as breathe the suggestion to Odin. If it was the True God, the fault was his for meddling with Elohim's daughter, and Thor did not dare speak of Eve to Sif. There was no room for strife in Asgard, not while their people starved. There was no room for anything but what might be done to save them.

Freyr ensured what crops remained gave a bountiful harvest, but the vines could not survive the cold for long. The summers had been easier, but no matter how well Freyr tended the crops, or how much rain and sun Thor gave the fields, there wasn't enough to see the people through the lengthening months of barren cold with so little hunting to supplement their meals. Fighting against snowdrifts taller than a man made game hard to find, and as the winters lengthened, more plants began to fail.

Sif spent her days in the storehouses, blessing meager harvests of wheat to protect them from spoil, and Freyja spent long days and nights, shepherding the dead to their final rest. Men so weak they died hunting in the snow, desperate to find game for their wives and children, starving at home. Frigg consulted the runes and her visions of fate, but she saw no end in sight.

On Odin's order, Thor left for Egypt to beg for grain. But the North lands did not suffer alone.

"War," Ra told him, his ancient face looking older still. "Eve's brother is King of the Universe in Assyria, and he is determined to crush us beneath his heel. Bakare did well for a time, but Thebes is sacked now. I fear the dynasty will not recover."

"Surely the Assyrians cannot mean to displace you?"

Ra stood with him by the window, looking out over the city. Egypt reflected its god, Thor thought. Worn and tired, but still living. Still strong in the ways that mattered.

"It is not the will of Ashur, no," Ra agreed. "But Assurbanipal—Adam—he has no respect for man or god, and Ashur is unwilling to act against him for fear he will leave. In truth, I do not blame him. As long as Adam makes the proper offerings, Ashur's power grows. It is a heady thing, to be worshipped by the son of Elohim."

Thor grunted. Eve may not have known him for a god, but the love she had given him had been as powerful as any sacrifice. Truly, even more so. When they had made love, her power had spilled over the whole village, leaving peace in its wake. He could only imagine what Adam's worship might bring.

"Did you find her family?" Ra asked. "You could not have come so far to speak of Adam's foolishness."

"I fear I did not come to speak of Eve, either," Thor admitted.

"My father sent me in the hope that you might have grain to spare, but I could not ask it of you now, even in trade."

"Nonsense," Ra said, the lines of his face growing deeper. "You would not come if the need were not desperate. It is for your people?"

Thor nodded stiffly. "The climate has shifted and our people starve. Half the crops have failed, already. We have done what we can, of course, and begun moving our people south, but it has been a hard adjustment, and the southern and coastal villages cannot feed so many on their own stores."

"Of course," Ra said, staring out the window again. "When Elohim stirs, the world awakes. But He has slept for so long, I did not think even to warn you."

"Then it is His way?"

Ra shook his head. "It happens rarely. As I said, He was greatly weakened by Creation. Before the Covenant, it was much more common. He feared for the world, you see. As long as we are at peace with one another, it is nothing to Him if we remain. But He could not rest, knowing we might tear the earth apart. Was there some sign of unrest among the Aesir?"

"No," Thor said, thinking guiltily of Eve. "None among us would violate the Covenant. Odin would not stand for it."

"But there is something else?" Ra asked, no longer studying his city, his Egypt. Thor felt his gaze, sharp and searching, and he dared not lie. Not to Ra, who had treated him always as an honored friend. And at least if he spoke with Ra about his fears, it would not return to Sif.

"I married her," he said. "I had not meant to do it—only to know her better. But she is without equal. And when she began to love me! She is made for it, Ra. Made to love so perfectly that I wonder at the True God's power. She has no idea of her perfection. Not truly. No understanding of her true godhead. And after Sif's betrayal…" His jaw tightened until his teeth ached. "It is my fault, what has happened in the North."

"Enough," Ra said gently. "She has suffered through more marriages of pain and abuse that I cannot imagine Elohim would stir himself against your love. But it is dangerous, Thor. She does not belong to us. A goddess she may be, but this road you walk will only bring heartbreak to both of you. You would be better served seeking comfort in Athena's embrace."

"Athena?" Thor snorted. "What has she to do with any of it?"

Ra flicked his fingers, dismissing the suggestion. "I mean only to say there is no future to be had with her. Will you find her in every life? Court her every century, as if it were the first? Be husband, father, brother, and child to her as she grows from babe to child to woman to decrepit hag once more?"

Yes. The thought startled him all the more for the way his heart twisted with longing. To spend eternity with Eve—it tempted him in a way he had never imagined possible. He had Sif, after all. He was married, and until they had come to this world, he had been content. They both had been. His affair with Eve should have ended with Tora's death. He had promised himself it would be so.

"Perhaps for a century or two, you would have peace with her," Ra went on, as if knowing his thoughts. "But she is not made to love you, Thor. She is made to love mortal men, who will age and grow as she does, die as she does. Would you interfere, thwart the will of her Father? Teach her the love of a god so that she would be spoiled by it, ruined for any mortal who might come after?"

"My ability to love is far from perfect," Thor said, unable to stop himself from arguing like a sullen boy. "My inconstancy has already been proven. I am twice damned by my wife. Would loving Eve so imperfectly be a crime?"

Ra shook his head, his old eyes filled with compassion. "She is of the world, Thor. You are merely in it. Do not forget that, whatever you decide."

Thor wanted to snarl, to growl, to thunder his frustration. But these were not his lands, and he had not come to Egypt to fight with Ra over Eve. He had not meant to think of her at all. She would not have wanted him distracted by this while his people suffered. And if she had known he was married...

"I have gold to trade," he said at last, his tone dull even to his own ears, "if Egypt can afford to part with any of its bounty."

Ra nodded. "Even in times of war, we can spare a little for our friends in the North, but you might have better luck with the Olympians. Speak with Athena and she will see Zeus agrees."

"And how might I reach her?"

Ra smiled faintly. "Take yourself to Athens and she will find you."

Athens. Thor grimaced internally. Eve had spoken far too much of Athens. Going there would only remind him of what he should not want. But he had lost too much time already, and he had promised his father he would seek out Poseidon, besides. Odin hoped the Olympian god of earth and sea would know some secret that might help them. But if it was Elohim who had changed the course of the currents, and the flow of magma beneath the surface, Thor did not have much hope.

"My gratitude, Ra," he remembered to say, offering a short bow. "I wish you good fortune in your conflict with Assyria."

Ra waved the sentiment away. "We will rise up again. Another century or two, and who can say. Perhaps it will be Adam leading Egypt's armies in conquering Assyria instead."

The thought brought him little comfort.

"Thor of the North!" Athena smiled, taking both his hands. Unlike Aphrodite, she did not try to greet him any more warmly. "I had not expected to see you again so soon. Ra sent word ahead of your needs, and if I must give you grain from Athens' own stores, you will have it for your people, but I expect my father will see reason. He will like having you in his debt."

"I have gold—"

"Please," she stopped him, her expression suddenly grave. "The last apples you gave us resulted in more grief than I wish to remember. No. If there is any trade, let it be in some other currency."

The Athenians had directed him to a shrine, nestled in the heart of an olive grove. A low stone altar stood beneath the oldest tree, with a spring fed pond reflecting moonlight beside it. Athena seemed to shine with the same light, between the silver breastplate and the white of her simple gown. Snakes curled around her upper arms like so much gold. She brushed olive leaves off the altar and sat upon it like a bench, making room for him beside her.

He pressed his lips together. Virgin goddess or not, she seemed to know her beauty and how best to display it with simple elegance. Her skin glowed, moon-pale and perfect, in contrast to the rich brown of her hair, so dark it looked black without sunlight, but she wore no ornamentation, nor did she paint her face as Aphrodite might. Thor dared not give offense, and sat beside her, as far from her as the stone allowed.

Her smile mocked him. "You cannot be nervous of me? If you could resist my sister's wiles and all of Bhagavan's court, there is nothing I can offer that would tempt you, were I so disposed."

He inclined his head politely. "You do not give yourself the credit you deserve, Athena."

She laughed. "Are all the Aesir so generous? Perhaps I should insist on accompanying you back to Asgard in exchange for grain—

but no, you do not have time for such foolishness, and I would not tire you with it."

"You have my gratitude," he said. "For anything you might offer us."

"In Athens we have not much. Perhaps it would see three of your villages through the winter." Her eyes narrowed just slightly, shrewdly, and he wondered what it was she looked for. One of the snakes slithered from her arm to her wrist, and she stroked its head. "Are you willing to trade more than gold, Thor of the North? Zeus has no sense of urgency for pursuits other than his own, but if you can persuade him, your people will not go hungry this year or the next."

He arched a brow. "What must I do?"

"There is a feast this night upon Olympus. If you can keep from offending my family, I believe my father would be most likely to grant his aid come morning. Do you suppose you can manage?"

No doubt Sif would take exception to an evening spent carousing with Olympian goddesses, but he had come for grain, and he would not leave without it. And truly, it would be better if she believed him unfaithful in their company than Eve's.

"Do I have the promise of your support?" he asked.

Athena rose, offering him her hand. "I fear you will not succeed without it."

§

With Athena's help, Thor returned to Asgard with grain for two winters, at least. But even that was not enough. The interior lands became inhospitable, and the Aesir shifted the populations to the coasts and further south. As a result of such migrations, the small fishing village where Thor had lived with Eve swelled with refugees. Where children were too weak to travel, Thor hitched his goats to a cart and drove them, leaving them in the care of Owen's bloodline until their parents might follow. But the people there told stories of Thorgrim, and those stories were heard by gods, and more than once, Thor saw Sif's eyes narrow, flashing gold before she banked her fury.

The weather settled, and so did their people, finding new ways to live off the colder lands. And with the crisis past, the Aesir fell back into easier days and older habits. Feasts and celebrations and long nights of drinking in Odin's hall. Thor remained by his wife, among his people, and waited for Sif's anger to rise.

For Sif, goddess of beauty and desire, wheat and prosperity, did not forget any slight. And once she learned he had turned his heart to another, loved anyone but her, all peace in Asgard would be shattered.

It was only a matter of time.

CHAPTER NINETEEN
Present

Eve curled up in the library with Ryam's journal and a cup of hot tea. After the departure of Ryan and Clair with Jean and Mia two weeks before, the rest of the DeLeon's had started to disperse in dribs and drabs. The only family left was Brienne's, now, and they were arranging their own departure with Garrit for the next day. Eve didn't mind having the family in residence, but the cooks and the maids and the other staff required to make the manor run on such a large scale challenged her patience. Servants and maids smacked too much of Adam's first oppression, and Adam was already on her mind more than she liked.

She frowned and flipped open the journal, scanning the pages for anything that might be about her. One page was taken up completely by the sketch of a man's face, preserved in a sleeve of plastic. It was roughly done, as if the artist was in a hurry to put it to paper before the image faded in his mind. Even aged and cracked, she could see clearly who the sketch was supposed to be. Something about the jaw line and the shape of the eyes. Eyes which would have been the color of stone, had Ryam been provided with the mediums to color them.

Adam's face stared at her from the journal. No explanation. No notes. Just the face, and underneath it in the tight script which she recognized as belonging to her late husband, a warning. *Prenez garde! Il se souvient d'elle.*

Beware! He remembers her.

She closed the book and stared out the window. She had never described Adam to Ryam, never given him the image of her brother, always changing. But there were others who could have. Ghosts who walked when they should be dead, figments of her imagination, projected into the heads of others without purposeful thought. That was how it had begun, in her last life. Her mind had conjured those she had loved in the past into living, breathing men. There one minute, whispering in her ear, and gone the next. And nothing but insanity could have caused her to manipulate the doctors, forcing them to see the phantoms too. She had deserved to be locked up for that. She had deserved every punishment those twisted men designed for her.

No, she hadn't described Adam to Ryam, but what if she had projected the man who did? Meddled in Ryam's mind, without even realizing it? She rubbed her eyes and tried to think. Surely she would have remembered if she had been talking to Thorgrim's ghost. But she hadn't needed to be present for Thorgrim's ghost to talk to others in her last life, and had no memory of anything he'd told anyone other than herself. But why would her mind have betrayed her and worse, betrayed him?

Every time she opened the journal she ended up with more questions than answers. Ryam had been much too far removed from her own offspring to have inherited some fluke of telepathy. Aside from his appearance as if from nowhere to make a marriage offer to her father, something she had attributed at the time to the work of rumors spread about the charges she faced, he hadn't done anything that could have been termed rash. He fought for his king when it was required of him, and minded his own lands the rest of the time. The only way he could have created that sketch was if someone had deliberately implanted the image of Adam in his mind. If it had not been the angels, she was the only one who could.

A knock on the door jerked Eve from her reverie and she looked away from the window, setting the journal aside. Her tea was cold, but she drank it anyway.

Garrit let himself in and shut the door firmly behind him. "I'm not sure you're ever going to forgive me for sending Mia to Paris."

"Forgive you?" She watched him drag his fingers through his hair, his agitation palpable enough to make her stomach lurch. "What on earth is there to forgive? Sending her to Paris was an inspired idea."

He made a sound very near to a snort, as near as a Frenchman came to one, in any event. "Inspired, but not very well thought out."

"Garrit, what on earth are you talking about? With Ryan, Clair, and Jean, I find it hard to believe that she was able to get herself into any serious trouble."

His face darkened. "So did we. But somehow, Mia managed."

She searched his face then, noticing the worry lines around his eyes and mouth for the first time. "Tell me."

"Adam found her."

The mug in her hands smashed on the tile floor. All she could see was Lilith, the first woman made in the Garden, shattered in body and mind. Unable even to think for herself, when he had finished with her.

"I don't know how." Garrit said. "He was supposed to be in our custody. Safely away. No one ever could have foreseen this. What interest could he possibly have had in her?"

"Garrit, what did he do? Is she all right? Has he hurt her?" It all came out in a rush. She had a horrible picture of Mia, bruised and abused crying somewhere.

He took her by the arms and pushed her back into the chair she had been sitting in. She didn't even remember having stood. "He doesn't appear to have harmed her. Yet."

"My God, Garrit. Any detail at all? Or do you not have any information?"

"She met him at one of Jean's clubs and he hasn't left her side since. No one even realized who he was until it was too late! I should never have let her go off with them. Between Ryan and Jean, we may as well have spelled the whole thing out."

She hid her face in her hands and tried to focus on not hyperventilating. As long as he didn't hurt her. What was he after? "He probably did it on purpose. Prevented them from recognizing him. I can't imagine he isn't fully capable. Especially after what he did to your parents to get himself here."

"I am so sorry, Abby. We should have been looking, tracking him somehow. We should have known he was free."

She stood up, holding her hand out to stop him. "I never should've let my guard down. I knew he wasn't through with me. It was only a matter of time. If I'd been keeping tabs on him, this never could've happened."

"Jean says she's convinced herself she's in love. It's been a week, Abby. What the hell are we supposed to do about this without exposing everything? Mia's smart. She's caught on to far too much already."

In love? Adam didn't know the meaning of the word, never mind forcing someone else to feel it. Lust, perhaps. But not love, and not in any way that he was capable of maintaining. Not even Lilith, brainwashed as she was, had loved him. But what could she say? Telling Mia she didn't love Adam would only make her more stubborn.

"I can't, Garrit." The words caught in her throat. "We can't do anything."

He stared at her.

"I can't police her life and I'm not her parent." Her mind raced while she considered what she could actually do. Much too little that did not turn her into her brother. If she used her power to force Mia from him, then what? She had spent a lifetime struggling against moving down that path, even in her subconscious mind. She would not take free will from her sister, of all people. She wouldn't let Adam do it either. But if Mia really loved him, Eve had no choice now.

"Adam would've married someone else's sister, or daughter or cousin and we wouldn't have been the wiser. If it's Mia he wants, and Mia who wants him…" She went to the window. The sun had disappeared behind black clouds and thunder rumbled, like an ache in her bones. The land outside looked gray, and even through the window she could hear the dogs barking, and the horses in their stable objecting to the coming storm.

She pressed her forehead against the glass and closed her eyes. She could protect Mia, at least. If she kept her sister close enough, Adam wouldn't dare to violate her. That was the best way. The safest way.

"I can't risk everything for one person, and people have to make their own mistakes. Stepping in now will only make her more determined. If we invite them here, I'll be able to tell if he's manipulating her. I can make sure he isn't hurting her. But I can't stop her from loving him, if it's what she wants."

"What if this isn't about her?"

She sighed. "Then congratulations to him, he's won the first round. But maybe we'll get lucky and Mia will get bored with him before this goes much further. Her attention span is notoriously short."

"You can't believe he'd let this avenue into your life slip through his fingers if there was anything he could do to prevent it."

She turned back to her husband, studying his face. "Making someone love you against their will isn't easy. He won't be able to keep it up." She would make sure he couldn't, as long as she lived and breathed. "Mia will either love him of her own free will, in which case it is not my place to stop her, or she will abandon him in time, and perhaps exercise a little bit more caution in her future romantic entanglements."

Garrit's gaze shifted to the journal. "I have to believe that you know what you're talking about, but this situation makes us all uneasy. The family is coming back. Brienne's already cancelled her flight. *Maman* and *Papa* are on their way."

"I guess that means we'll want to keep the staff on for the duration." Rain was starting to fall in heavy drops against the window. Lightning flashed, blinding in its intensity, and she scowled into the distance as the thunder clapped so loudly it shook the house. "What is it about that tree? It's been struck again."

Garrit stood beside her, one hand at the small of her back. "*Malchance,* I suppose. I'd better make sure nothing's caught fire." His eyes were trained on the tree line and worry wrinkled his forehead. He glanced down at her and his expression cleared immediately. "Why don't you go make arrangements with the cook? We'll have at least two more for dinner, if not more."

"Sure." Smoke rose from the tree, and lightning flashed again. The thunder which followed made the windows rattle. "Wait for the rain to ease up first."

"Better now than later. I'll take care of it. Go on."

She glanced up at him again. His face had fallen back into the same troubled lines. He didn't even look at her as she turned to go, his gaze locked on the tree once more.

Maybe it was genetic. Ryam had always been driven to distraction by thunderstorms too. The familiarity was almost reassuring, all things considered.

CHAPTER TWENTY
Creation

§

It tasted like warm sunlight and strawberries, liquid and sweet and smooth. The fruit filled her mouth with the same tingling that had crawled down her arms. Juice dribbled over her chin and she wiped it away with the back of her hand as she swallowed. The tingling moved with the fruit into her stomach, radiating out from there to her limbs, to her fingertips. Like the prickling of nettles against her skin. Her body felt as though it had been lit from within by the sun.

Lilith turned and ran, the fruit she had taken held tightly in her hands. Eve paid her no mind. It was only a matter of time now, anyway. Wasn't that what Adam had told her? That it was only a matter of time?

Reu's face was white, but he took the fruit from her hand, not waiting for her to offer it. Lamech still stood with them, his eyes wide with fear as Reu took his bite.

"Go, Lamech," Eve said. "Before Adam wonders what keeps you."

He hesitated for another moment and then sprinted after Lilith.

Eve's vision blurred and shifted, and she was looking at herself. The ground seemed unsteady, and somehow she knew she was in Reu's mind, looking through his eyes. But she had never seen so clearly before, not even when Adam had touched her. She clutched at her head, stretched and bruised. It was too much. She tried to step back, to put space between them, but her body felt sluggish and unbalanced.

Reu supported her when she began to fall, easing her to the ground. "Are you all right?"

She closed her eyes, but she could still see. Her face half hidden by her hair, and her hands. It was odd to see herself this way. Odder still when the sight stayed even after Reu pulled his arm away. She stared at the red leaves beneath her hands and knees to clear the vision. Her head pounded, and the roaring from her first moments returned to her ears.

She could feel the same from Reu, though he didn't make a sound as he sat beside her. And she could feel the creature in the tree above them, watching closely, waiting to see what they would do next, and what would be done to them.

Every bird, every animal in the Garden touched her mind. With a thought she could see through their eyes, as she had seen through Adam's, but there were so many that the world around her fractured and she fought to keep her own sight. And comprehension. All at once and slowly over time, everything was brighter and sharper. All the things she had seen, witnessed, felt and heard in the last two days became significant. She understood, at last, what God had intended for her, and what Lucifer had tried to explain. Live, he had said. Whatever this power was, her children, her people, would need it to survive. Perhaps it was not what God wanted for them, this knowledge of life and death and evil, but he had seen the need to provide the path. To give her and all her people the strength to stand against Adam.

"Eve?"

Her whole body flushed at his nakedness, all muscle and tanned skin, and thatches of rough, curly hair. She blushed and dropped her gaze again. "Yes," she said. "Are you well?"

"Well enough, I think. To go back."

"You shouldn't have eaten the fruit." She climbed unsteadily to her feet, crossing her arms over her chest to cover her breasts. She kept her back to him, too, so that he couldn't see her womanhood. "He won't forgive it, Reu."

"I did what had to be done, just as you have. But if we don't return, there is no telling what he might do to the others. And I can't—I cannot stand by, Eve. Even for your sake."

"I don't know what's worse than the things he's done already. To Lilith." She crossed the clearing to the trees. There was a banana tree on their way back, with broad enough leaves to cover her body. She didn't want to face Adam so naked and exposed.

Reu followed, holding back branches that might scrape her. "I wish you hadn't had to see her that way."

"What you see is only the least of the pain he's caused her," she said softly. "The worst of it is in her mind. He's taken her will with the power God gave him. As he tried to take mine." She found the tree and stripped several leaves, wrapping them around her chest and hips. It made her feel much more comfortable to be covered, and she was finally able to turn and face Reu again.

It was impossible not to notice the way he looked at her. The adoration in his eyes. How had she not seen it before? When Adam had spoken of making him love her, she had dismissed it. When the creature, the serpent, had asked if he would still love her, she had been more concerned with the other things it had said. But it was true. She flushed again, her cheeks burning, and looked away again, adjusting the banana leaf at her hips.

He put a finger beneath her chin and tilted her face back up to his. "I will not let him harm you ever again, Eve. And when I am gone, my sons will protect you from him. And their sons, after them. Forever."

"You love me."

He smiled, caressing her cheek. "More than my life. From the moment you were made."

She covered his hand with her own, pressing it against her cheek and closing her eyes. It seemed only fitting that she see herself through his eyes in this moment. "Why didn't you tell me?"

His gaze lingered on her mouth while her eyes were closed, drinking in the sight of her face. "I wanted you to be able to choose."

But there was something else behind his words. Some knowledge he hadn't shared. She saw her forehead wrinkle in concentration while it eluded her.

She opened her eyes. "You're hiding something."

"It isn't important." His jaw tightened and he took her hand, walking with her once again toward the caves. Toward Adam. "Just know that no matter what you choose, I will always care for you and protect you."

But the truth rose to the surface of his mind, where she saw it clearly. He had walked with God.

He had bargained with God.

"Oh, Reu."

He hesitated, his whole body stiffening at her tone. "The serpent asked if I would love you still when you could read my mind as easily as your own. You can see now it is so. I will, always. No matter what."

"God made you love me?" She tightened her hand around his when he tried to let go of her.

He sighed. "So that you would be protected."

She looked up at his face as they walked. His eyes were dark again, and she could feel his discomfort. "But you, more than anyone, believe so strongly in free will. In choice."

"This was my choice, Eve. God did not force it on me without my permission. Free will was his greatest gift to us. And I wouldn't trade my love for you for anything. Even if you never return it."

Her heart ached for him. The sin of eating the fruit was not the only sacrifice he had been called upon to make, yet he had done so willingly. Without complaint, without hesitation.

"You deserve all good things, Reu. I am honored by your love, though I'm unsure if I am worthy of it."

He glanced down at her, his eyes soft and dark. "You are worthy of so much more than I can give you, Eve."

They paused at the clearing before the caves. Adam was speaking with Lilith and Lamech, his face growing darker with every word. He held the fruit in his hand, but it was unblemished, whole.

Eve felt relief from a dread she had not even known she was carrying. Adam's anger hung thick in the air even from this distance, made all the more bitter on the back of her tongue with the fear of the others and the confusion of those who did not yet understand the significance of what had been found. Reu held the branches aside for her, and they stepped out from the cover of the trees.

Adam's eyes locked on her the moment she was in the open, traveling from her face, over her body, pausing on the crude coverings she had made for herself, and back again. She blushed at the sight of Adam's nakedness, and didn't dare let her eyes stray from his face. Then Adam's gaze settled on Reu's hand holding hers, and Eve flinched from the jealous rage that washed over her, black and stinging in her mind.

Adam shoved Lilith and Lamech out of his way and crossed to them, the fruit still in his hand, though Eve thought in that moment, he no longer remembered it.

"You lust for power, and yet you deny me. You eat of my fruit, but refuse to sleep at my side." He raised his hand to strike her, and she braced herself for the impact.

Reu's hand wrapped around Adam's wrist before it could come. "You will not lay a hand upon her again, Adam."

Adam stared at him, his open hand turning into a fist. "You forget yourself, Reu." He twisted free from Reu's grasp. "I am lord here, and Eve will be my wife."

"I will not." She raised her voice so the others who had begun to gather would hear more clearly. Her refusal would be known to all of them. "I will not be your wife, Adam."

"You dare?" He tore his gaze from Reu to glare at her. His anger was a force against her mind, but the fruit had given her greater strength, and his will did not touch her. His eyes narrowed and his voice was cold and hard. "You are not just refusing me, you are giving up the world I offer you. Your only chance for happiness. None of the others will give you what you need. Do you forget I am your only equal?"

"You're right," she said softly, and he began, almost to smirk. But she went on. "Reu is not my equal. He is my better. And yours as well."

He lunged at her, dropping the fruit to wrap both his hands around her throat. There were no words now, just incoherencies as they fell to the ground. Images of her body bruised, her face bloodied until she huddled, whimpering in the dark—the punishments he would inflict on her for such an insult, seared upon the backs of her eyelids.

She clawed at his hands, trying to pry his fingers away as she choked. It was worse than anything she had ever experienced before, and tears flowed down her cheeks into her ears. She dug her nails into his skin, drawing blood.

Reu drove his fist into Adam's face, and she could breathe again.

Adam's lip split open, but he smiled a terrible smile.

Eve saw what he meant a moment before he acted, but her wordless shout wasn't fast enough to stop Adam from kneeing Reu hard in the groin. Reu dropped like a rock to the ground, on his knees, bent over and wheezing with pain.

Adam kicked him in the ribs, sending him shoulder first into the dirt.

Eve's vision swam. She crawled to Reu and cradled his head in her lap. He groaned.

"You chose wrongly, Eve." Adam grabbed her by her arm and dragged her away from him through the dirt, pulling her roughly to her feet. "But I am merciful. Change your mind now, and I will pretend none of this happened. Marry me, and perhaps I'll even let Reu stay in the Garden as your pet."

She shook her head. "No."

He threw her back to the ground and spit in her face.

She wiped it from her cheek, staring at her hand. Beads of blood rose from the scratches and scrapes on her palm, skinned again when she fell.

"Then I have no use for you. Seth, Lamech. Take her and her dog and cast them out of the Garden. Bar the gates behind them. If I'm lucky, the angels will kill them for their sin." He picked the fruit back up from the ground and turned his back on her.

She felt hands grab her, but she pulled free and climbed to her feet without help. "Maybe you should wait to see what happens before you eat the fruit yourself, Adam. If they kill us, they'll surely come for you, too."

"Anyone else who defies me will suffer the same fate as these two." His voice was even and cold, and he pretended that he didn't hear her, even as she felt him consider her warning. "Eve will watch Reu starve and die outside these gates, as any of the rest of you would in his place. Assuming the angels don't interfere before then.

For they have sinned, not by eating the fruit, but by denying their God. Elohim is dead and gone, his rules with Him. I am your God now, and you will all obey me, or you will die. That is your choice."

And then Lamech grabbed her again, and Seth lifted Reu to his feet. The two men dragged them to the gate and threw them out of the Garden without another word.

CHAPTER TWENTY-ONE
460 BC

There was nothing odd about a god leaving Asgard to walk the earth, Thor told himself. He repeated it when he did not find Sif feasting with the others in Odin's hall, and again when he saw no sign of her in the cottage they shared. He repeated it a third time when a word with Heimdall confirmed that she had taken the rainbow bridge to earth, and Loki had been whispering stories of Thorgrim in her ear.

"But not only that," Heimdall said. Thor had found him on the bridge, of course. It was not for fear of the other gods that he guarded it, though Bifrost was the only way they might come in or out of Asgard without the express permission of Odin. Heimdall guarded against the gods that had not yet come—those who searched for new worlds to claim as their own, after tearing the last apart with war. And he guarded also against the dead, for Bifrost was the only path left to that realm, and it had been filled with enemies of the Aesir. Somewhere in Niflheim, Surt still longed for vengeance and destruction, though he had lost his flaming sword.

"Loki spreads rumors of a goddess, a daughter of the True God who walks the earth," Heimdall told him. Every rumor whispered in Asgard travelled to Heimdall's ear, and from there, to Odin's. "The Trickster claims she is the reason you remained so long away."

Thor grunted, pretending disinterest, but his blood ran cold. "And Sif?"

Heimdall shrugged, his golden teeth flashing in a joyless smile. "Sif goes in search of such a goddess, to see the face of the woman who be-spelled you."

"Sif travels on a fool's errand."

Heimdall said nothing, but even his silence spoke volumes. Thor was only grateful Heimdall would not speak of anything Odin did not wish shared freely. What Heimdall had seen or heard of Thor's affair with Eve would never pass through his lips to any other.

"If she travels beyond our lands, she is bound to cause trouble when she meets this supposed goddess," Thor said.

"I have no doubt that is her intent," Heimdall replied. "Loki has accused you of affairs with no less than three other goddesses, though oddly, he did not name Freyja. It seems you prefer despoiling virgins."

He ground his teeth. "If Sif truly believes I am capable of such, I am surprised she returned to my bed at all."

"None in Asgard would court her while she remains your wife, Thor. If she wishes revenge, she will have to find a partner elsewhere, now that Loki is forbidden from having his way. But I have heard there is a Trickster god among the Celts. Did you not meet with them in your travels?"

Lugh. Yes, he had met with him and his brethren, but he had not cared overmuch for any of their ilk. They were worse than Bragi when it came to plain speech, and fought fiercely among themselves. Lugh had not been the worst of the lot—a thunder god as well as a mischief maker and god of war. But the combination of powers made him unpredictable in the extreme. If Thor was considered short tempered, Lugh's temper was kindling, already sparked, looking for an excuse to blaze. There was always the chance the right wind would blow to bank his anger into laughter, but it wasn't something to be relied on.

"Is that where she went?"

Heimdall cocked his head to the side, his eyes narrowing as he listened. Behind him, his hall stood on the steep cliff that marked the edge of Asgard's open fields and rising mountains. His hearing was too acute to give him any peace closer to Odin's hall, and for as long as Thor remembered, the guardian had always lived alone.

"If so, she has been and gone. I hear her voice in our lands, now. In Thorgrim's village. She asks for stories in exchange for blessings upon their grain and stores."

Of course she did. And if he followed her now, demanded to know what she had learned, it would only make her all that more determined. Thor gazed out over the bridge, heat and light shimmering and distorting the curving earth below. As long as she did not find Eve, that was all that mattered. And Eve was well away from the North Lands. Beyond even the Olympian lands, he thought, from the pulse of her light, burning in the back of his mind.

All these years later, he could not shake her from his thoughts, and when she grieved, he felt the pull of her pain, the ache of it echoing in his heart. Late in the night, after Sif slept, he found himself reaching for her, soothing her dreams, offering her what solace he could give, drawing the memories of their life together to the surface to give her peace when she struggled. All these years later, he loved her as much as he ever had, no matter how hard he fought against it.

"The Olympians do not take kindly to trespassers. When she leaves our lands, I would know of it."

Heimdall bowed his head. "As you wish, Odin-son."

But it wasn't as he wished at all. Five hundred years, and all he wanted was Eve.

Five hundred years, and he was no longer certain he loved his wife, nor that she held any love for him. The Trickster still lay between them in the bed, Eve within his arms, and what he had once shared with Sif was gone.

Perhaps the goddess he had married was gone, too.

§

"So sullen, Thor," Loki said, seating himself across the table in Odin's hall. "Surely you cannot still be angry about that mischief with your wife."

Thor curled his lip, hiding the expression behind his mug.

"I see," Loki said, when Thor had not responded with anything more than a long drink and a glower. "A shame, really. I thought I might travel East, and as often as Sif has been away, it seemed to me you might wish for an excuse to do the same. I have heard wondrous things about the Olympian goddesses." His green eyes glittered, feral in the firelight. "Perhaps I should ask Magni and Modi to accompany me, instead. I'm certain they would enjoy themselves immensely."

Thor growled. "My sons have better taste than to choose you as their companion."

Loki laughed. "There was a time you did not find me so contemptible, Thor. Or do you forget that once you called me uncle?"

"An error in judgment, corrected by Jarnsaxa's grace." To his younger eyes, Loki had seemed so much wiser. Brilliant and daring and, even better, always willing to embark on some adventure or another, taking time for Thor while Odin had been too busy with his own affairs.

But that had been before Thor had recognized the malice behind the Trickster's "mischief." Before he had met Jarnsaxa, who had borne his sons while he had still believed Sif would never have him. Jarnsaxa had died in the wars on Jotunheim, the world where Thor had been raised, where they had fled with his mother's aid after Surt had destroyed their own lands. But Jarnsaxa had not died before she had told him all she knew of the Trickster and his role in what had come to pass, fearing for her sons. Even so, Thor had not believed Loki would go so far as to meddle with Sif, and he was not certain which stung him more: that Sif had been taken in by his silver-tongue, or that Loki had betrayed him so completely. Sif, at least, might have been fooled. Loki had known precisely what he was doing.

"Just as well," Loki said, smiling slowly. "Sif would never forgive you if she learned you'd gone off in search of Elohim's daughter, though it is not only I who finds it strange you did not mention such a goddess in all your reports. Surely you had heard of her."

Thor said nothing, his jaw tense with the need to keep his silence.

"I can only imagine you had some reason for keeping her a secret," Loki said, reaching casually across the table to take a piece of bread from Thor's meal. "A lovechild, perhaps? It would not be your first."

"Magni and Modi were born long before I married Sif," he growled, catching Loki's arm by the wrist before he touched his plate. Thor threw his hand away, his eyes burning with lightning. The color had already leached from Loki's face and the warm yellow of the wooden table had turned gray. "Nor have I fathered any godchild since, but for Thrud."

"And then there is that pesky business with Ullr," Loki mused, grinning now. "Did finding Sif in my arms not make you wonder in the slightest? Sif is as much a warrior as any of us, to be forced—"

"Freyja bore witness," he said, grinding his teeth on the words. And Sif had loved him then, as he had her. She would never have betrayed him. Not so soon after their marriage, and not while they warred against the Vanir. She was not Aphrodite to take lovers among their enemies.

"And Freyja is so reliable when it comes to these things." Loki rolled his eyes. "Poor Jarnsaxa. She tried and she tried, and all her efforts came to nothing. You're still as thick as you ever were."

Thor's knuckles creaked around the mug's handle, and he felt the metal give beneath the heat of lightning in his hand. That Loki would dare so much as breathe Jarnsaxa's name made his blood boil and the room shift into shades of gray. He, who had told the Jotuns of the children she had borne, who had led them to her cottage against the cliffs. She had nearly died, because of Loki, Magni and Modi with her.

"I've changed my mind." Loki rose from the bench, filching the bread in one swift motion as he did so, and laughed. "I'd rather not compete against you for our fair goddess's affections. I think I'll take this journey alone, after all."

It took all Thor's strength not to follow, not to so much as rise. He watched the Trickster weave through the tables and the men and the Valkyries, serving mead, and forced himself to be still, to calm, to allow the sun to shine through the storm clouds. Only after Loki had gone, and Thor was certain he had his temper leashed, did he stir from his seat. He even smiled and clapped his brothers on the shoulders as he passed them by, for in any gathering there were those who served as Loki's spies, witting or not, and Thor did not mean to give the Trickster any sign of his plans.

He went to Ra, first, traveling by lightning instead of foot. Egypt was at war again, attempting to overthrow the Persians who had laid claim to the fertile lands of the Nile. But Ra only laughed when Thor expressed his regrets to find it so.

"I told you, did I not? First Adam conquers us, and now he fights to free us! It is a blow to the Persians, this uprising." The old god smiled, indicating that Thor might sit. "Adam will fail of course, even with the Athenians at his back, thank Athena. But it is for the best. I would not have Adam made Pharaoh, no matter how much he has done for us as Inaros."

"And what of his sister?" Thor asked, taking his seat. "Would you trust her with Egypt?"

Ra waved a hand, and a boy came at once with wine and fruit. "To Eve, I would entrust the world. And have, all these many years. The nearest she has ever come to betraying it was that Trojan nightmare, and even then, she had no lust for power, only escape. Though I am certain you know her reasons more intimately than I, by now."

Thor grunted. "I do not care to think overmuch on what she told me of those days. Theseus was a fool to lose her, knowing what he did."

"You cannot blame Theseus for falling into Aphrodite's trap. And he did return for her, broken though he was, and saw her safely delivered from Paris' hands. A true hero."

"As you say," Thor murmured, taking grapes from the tray. He did not want wine now, but he could not refuse all Ra's hospitality without giving offense. "But I have not come to argue Theseus' virtues, and I dare not stay long, besides."

"No?" Ra took a cup of wine, his eyes dancing over the rim as he drank.

Thor ignored it. To be jealous of a man so long dead served nothing, he knew, yet he still could not think of Theseus without irritation. His name had been too much on Eve's lips while they had been married. "Loki and Sif both search for Eve."

The humor drained from Ra's expression, his eyes narrowing. "Did not your Odin-Father command that secret kept?"

"He did," Thor said. "But Loki has ever been skilled in collecting knowledge he has no right to, and Sif—Sif is convinced I am faithless in every possible way." He grimaced. "I only wish she were wrong."

Ra's gaze grew distant, his lips pressed into a thin line. "Eve is in Ahura Mazda's lands—a true Persian, living east of the Olympians. Might Loki be distracted from his cause? Surely Sif will not travel so far from home, if only to know you have not slipped away for some purpose of your own."

"Aphrodite might delay him, if she were willing."

"And Hathor before that," Ra agreed. "I will speak with her at once."

Thor nodded and rose. "Then I must go on to Olympus. Perhaps Athena will have pity on me, and I will not be made to beg at her sister's feet."

Ra's eyes crinkled. "Athena will not turn you away, Thor, nor leave you to the mercy of Aphrodite. On that you may rely."

§

She met him in the olive grove, taking his hands and smiling warmly, her gray eyes bright. "If you risk your wife's displeasure, it must be for good reason," Athena said. "Though, I have heard she has taken to wandering herself. I am sorry for what came to pass—your love for her was so clear to all of us, I fear I do not understand how she could have doubted it."

He squeezed her hands and released them. He was not certain his own guilt did not pain him more, now. Just because he had not meant to love Eve did not make him innocent of the same betrayal. "What is done is done," he said.

But Athena was studying him, her pale forehead creased. "I had not thought to credit that story with any kind of truth."

A trickle of fear slid down his spine, but he forced himself to smile. "Has Ossa travelled so far North to hear our boasts?"

"Not a boast, exactly. But you would be surprised what the Celts hear, and certainly Rome does not miss any opportunity to curry our favor by passing along the choicest news. And my cousin often chooses not to sort the truth from the lies, no matter how bold. Is it true, then? You married a mortal woman?"

He froze. If the story had spread to Olympus, how widely was it known in his own lands? Heimdall, of course, and Odin. But had the others any proof beyond Loki's accusations? At least if Sif believed it—if she thought Tora had been mortal, Eve would be that much safer.

Athena gripped his arm, her nails biting his skin, and something more—a nudge against his thoughts. He growled, tearing his arm from her grasp. "If you thirst so desperately for wisdom, you search the wrong mind to find it."

She flushed, dropping her eyes. "Forgive me, please. It is only that I am unused to confusion, and in truth, I have never been so baffled by a god as I am by you."

He forced himself to calm. A goddess of wisdom would not admit to confusion lightly, and all the more difficult for a goddess of both wisdom and war. Athena should never have admitted weakness, and yet…

"I will tell you what you wish to know, Athena, if you will grant me your counsel on the matter."

"You need not speak as though I would not share my wisdom gladly, Thor. We are friends, you and I."

"Yes," he said, meeting her clear gray eyes. "And as a friend, I must ask your help, though I fear you will think poorly of me, once you know the truth."

"Whatever you have done, it cannot be worse than the behavior of my own family." Athena sat upon the altar, a flick of her slim fingers indicating he might do the same.

Instead, he sat upon the ground, dusted with olive leaves and dry grasses. The touch of the soil on his hands brought him some comfort. It had been too long since he had walked the earth, but he had not realized until now how much he had missed it. He gathered a handful of the rocky soil and let it fall again through his fingers.

"I did not marry a mortal," he told her, slowly. "I married a goddess. Elohim's daughter."

Athena did not gasp, but he felt some shift in her emotions which he could not name. As if his admission had stung her. "All those years you walked the earth, invited into the bed of every goddess between Brittania and the Far East, and none could tempt you from your wife."

"I was angry, after I found Sif in bed with Loki."

She made a sound of derision in the back of her throat. "And in anger, you turned to the one female who did not know you at all? Elohim's daughter of all women, Thor! Better if it had been a mortal, a human who might die and be forgotten, than her!"

She rose, her sandaled feet pacing toward the spring, white ankles gleaming with each stir of her hem. Athena had a way of holding the light, drawing it in and glowing like moonlight. Even more so now, in her anger. It reminded him of his brother Baldur, the shining god of Asgard, but Baldur was more silver and starlight than milk and cream. Athena was all fair skin and soft curves.

"And I suppose that it is true, also, that you gave her a godchild," Athena said, her back to him.

"No," he said, tearing his gaze away from her body. Perhaps the next time he came, he would bring Baldur. "The son I gave Eve was just a man, for my part. What she gave him of her own divinity, I do not know. Odin had stripped me of my godhead."

Her hands were fists at her sides, the snakes curling tight around her arms, hissing in response to her agitation. "Did you love her?"

"If she had been truly mortal, I am not certain I would have returned to Asgard," he said softly, digging his fingers into the dirt. "But what purpose would it serve to sacrifice my life while she lived on?"

Athena shook her head. "Sif could not forgive this, if she knew. Her dalliance with Loki was nothing more than a cry for your attention, but to love another—I could not have believed it, had you not told me yourself. Not after seeing how you cherished her, your steadfastness in refusing all others."

"Can you forgive me?"

She spun, her gray eyes dark with something—pain. He rose at once, conscious of the weight of her grief. He had thought it only his own guilt until he saw her face.

"Athena, I did not realize."

"How could you?" She laughed, but it was bitter. "I am a virgin goddess, after all. And you are married. Twice-over, now. No, Thor. Blaming you would be unreasonable."

He reached for her, then stopped himself, letting his arm fall back to his side. How much crueler would it be, if after confessing so much, he offered her comfort and false hope? He closed his hand into a fist.

"Reason does not often hold sway over the heart." He could not ask her, now. He dared not ask her for help in guarding Eve.

"So I am learning, to my dismay." But she smiled. "You need not worry. I have known from the start I had no claim to you, no right to expect you might treat me as anything more than a friend."

"If I had known—if I had been free—of all the goddesses who invited me to their beds, Athena, you would have been the hardest to refuse."

She touched his cheek, stroked his face. "You are kind to say so, Thor. Truly. But I will not hold you to your word this time." Her hand fell away, and he made no move to stop her when she turned back to the water. "Let us forget this unpleasantness. You came for some purpose, and I would not distract you from it further. How might Olympus serve you?"

He hesitated. Even for a goddess of reason and wisdom, it could not be so simple to put aside the affairs of the heart, and he had no wish to pain her further. But Loki would come, he was certain. And he could not turn his back upon Eve. Not after they had shared so much, and he had promised himself, when she spoke of faith and gods…

He had promised himself, she would not be alone.

"I come to beg a favor of Aphrodite, if she would indulge me."

Athena lifted her eyebrows, a mocking smile curving her lips. "Aphrodite drives a hard bargain for her favor."

He was not fooled. "I mean only to ask her if she will offer her distractions to our Trickster, when he passes through. To keep him from continuing further for a time, that is all."

Her eyes narrowed, but if she suspected his reasons, she kept it to herself. "One day, you must come to a feast simply for the pleasure of it. Zeus is likely to take exception before long if you continue on this way."

"I am, of course, at your father's service."

Athena snorted, linking her arm through his. "You make a very fine ambassador for your people, Thor. But do not think, even for a moment, those pretty phrases of yours will fool me. We are friends, you and I."

He smiled. "We are that."

CHAPTER TWENTY-TWO
Present

◈

Mia climbed out of the car, pulling Adam with her. The man had the gall to smirk as their eyes met and Eve resisted the urge to throttle him.

Garrit stood stiff beside her before the main entrance, at the top of the broad stone stairs. She didn't have to look at his face to know he was glaring. For centuries, the DeLeons had been guarding their lands against Adam, and Garrit was less than thrilled to offer him hospitality. But this wasn't the first time Eve had met with Adam this way, negotiating with him for the safety of those he had drawn under his influence. She just hoped it would be the last.

Firmly now, she repressed all memory of Troy and her life as Helen. When, for the briefest lifetime, Adam had nearly held her sympathy. If he hadn't remembered himself now, if he had not remembered her, she would not have been nearly so worried about Mia. Paris had been capable of kindness, even affection, misguided though it was. But Adam wasn't Paris anymore.

Something glinted off Mia's hand and Eve felt her throat tighten.

They couldn't have. She wouldn't. Not even Mia could be so foolish as to run off and marry the first fool she found! But to have that man be Adam was so horrifying Eve found herself trying to will the ring from her sister's finger.

It was unfortunate that God had not seen fit to grant her that kind of power.

Garrit's hand tightened around hers as Adam put his arm around Mia's shoulders and murmured something in her ear. Mia laughed and the two climbed the stairs, coming to a stop less than a meter away.

"Mum and Dad are going to be furious, Mia."

Her sister pouted prettily. "I don't see why you can't be happy for me, Abby."

Eve raised an eyebrow. "I'm supposed to be happy that you ran off and eloped behind everyone's back? To someone you don't even know?"

"I know him perfectly well." Mia looked up at Adam and smiled. "Ethan, this is my sister, Abby, and her husband Garrit DeLeon."

Adam smirked. Again. "A pleasure to meet you both." He extended a hand to Garrit, who ignored it completely. Adam dropped his arm back to his side, and Eve felt his amusement. "Mia's told me so much about you and your family, Abby. I feel as though I've known you for years."

Garrit ground his teeth next to her, and she felt his hand spasm in her own. She imagined the other was balled into a fist by now.

She tried to keep herself calm. The entire charade was a bit much, even for her. But she didn't want to think what Garrit would do if she left the two of them alone to drag Mia off. Or what Adam might try to do to him.

"Aren't you a little bit old for my sister?"

"Mia told me that you and your husband are two years apart, as well. Let me reassure you that I have every intention of making your sister as blissfully happy as possible."

She glared at him, but he only smiled and pulled Mia closer against his side. Eve turned away, closing her eyes against the memories that surged through her, when she had stood at his side as Helen in Pharaoh's court, where they had stopped before continuing to Troy, hoping to confound her husband. For all of that, avoiding Paris's importunities had been a relief after Menelaus. That's all it had been, she told herself. Paris had just been kind in comparison.

"We're so looking forward to getting to know you better." Her voice sounded flat and dead even to her own ears, but it was the best she could do. "Won't you stay for dinner?"

Mia latched onto her arm and led her into the house, leaving Adam and Garrit a few steps behind. "Really, Abby. Won't you just give him a chance? Please. For me?"

Eve looked into her sister's eyes, using the physical contact to search her mind as she did so. There was no aura there, no cloud of Adam's influence over her thoughts and feelings for him. Either he had been very subtle, or Mia was just so ridiculous that she had fallen in love with the most indecent man who had ever lived.

"I'll try, Mia." She glanced back at the men. Garrit was staring at Adam with black fury, and the foyer felt much too narrow to hold the two of them. "This is all just a little bit insane. And you know Mum is going to blame me for letting it happen. It wasn't fair of you to do this to any of us. Me, or Garrit, or his family! And poor Jean!"

Mia waved a hand dismissively. "Jean and I were never serious. He knew that. You were the one who told me not to fall in love with him. So I didn't." She smiled over her shoulder at her new husband. "I fell in love with Ethan instead. Isn't he gorgeous? And look at his eyes! Have you ever seen anything like them?"

"No." She didn't look. She didn't need to. Those eyes had

haunted her for millennia. There was no other man on earth with eyes exactly that shade of gray. "They're unique, to be sure."

Eve searched her sister's face again, hoping for any sign that she had been coerced. If only Adam had forced her, then she could act! Break his hold on her and send him away again where he couldn't bother her and she wouldn't have to see him, or wonder what he was doing to her sister and her family.

"Mia, please promise me you'll be careful. Don't let him talk you into anything you don't want. You can't know him as well as you think you do after only a few weeks. Are you sure this is what you want?"

Mia was still looking at Adam, her eyes alight. "I've never been more sure of anything. And did I tell you, he's filthy rich! Maybe not as wealthy as your DeLeon family, but certainly well off. We'll never have to work a day in our lives if we don't want to. Mum and Dad are going to love him once they've met him and gotten to know him. And you will too. Just wait!" She squeezed Eve's arm and then skipped back to Adam, taking his hand and pulling him away from Garrit and off down one of the hallways.

Eve didn't miss the wink that Adam threw in her direction before he disappeared around a corner. "Mia! Dinner is in an hour. Please don't disappear!"

There was a noise that sounded like something between an assurance and a laugh, and then Garrit was at her side. "Well?"

She looked up at his face; it was still dark with anger. "Nothing." She sighed and shook her head. "She's honestly in love with him. Completely of her own free will."

He raised both eyebrows, some of the anger replaced by surprise. "And your brother?"

She glanced back down the hall where he had disappeared and frowned. "I don't know. But I'm going to find out."

It was storming again and Eve waited to see if that same tree would be struck. In the last month, she'd counted it hit four times. It had been unusually rainy this year, too. She considered herself lucky to have had a clear day for her wedding. But this evening, there wasn't any lightning yet, just thunder, rumbling and booming intermittently. The windows in the library offered the best view of the storm, and the rising land, and the smell of the books always comforted her.

Eve rested her forehead against the glass of the window and closed her eyes. She had sent Garrit to bed hours ago, along with the rest of the family. He had resisted at first, but she could see how tired he was. None of them would sleep easily with Adam present, even if it was necessary. The only safe place for Mia now was under Eve's roof, at least until she was certain that Adam wouldn't harm her. It was the only protection she could offer her sister.

Adam had been pleasant, even charming at dinner, amused by the hostility of the DeLeons around him, and perfectly attentive to Mia. Eve had hated it.

The door opened, and she spun away from the window. Adam was framed in the light from the hall, and Eve realized belatedly that she stood in the dark.

"I trust I'm not disturbing you," he said.

She snorted, and turned on a lamp. "I'm not sure you could disturb me any further if you tried."

He raised an eyebrow and shut the door behind him, but he didn't cross the room, just strolled casually toward her favorite chair, picking things up off the end tables and putting them down. "You think I'm not trying?"

"I have no doubt you have some ulterior motive for all of this. Whether it's purely to aggravate me, or something else, I haven't quite figured out." She stepped back against the window, leaning against the sill. The urge to bleach everything he touched was ridiculous, but she hated having him in this room. Her room, more than any other.

He looked away, trailing his fingers over the leather of the journal that still hadn't been put back. His suit was in disarray. The jacket open, his tie loose around his neck, part of his shirt pulled free from his pants. She could just imagine Mia being responsible for it, making out with him in some hallway like a teenager, and it caused her more irritation than she wanted to admit.

What was it to her if Mia loved him? Women must have loved him throughout history. She'd never bothered to give it a second thought until now, and he had lived, married, fathered children, just as she had. But she hated every whisper, every caress, every gesture he made to Mia. Knowing the man he was, the things he was capable of, it would make anyone sick.

Anything would be better for Mia than him.

So why was she thinking about Paris of Troy? And the feeling of those same hands at her waist?

"I can feel that, you know," he said, still looking at the book. "All that hate and mistrust in your heart. I thought you were supposed to be loving, Eve? I'm supposed to be the monster."

She was torn between taking the book from him, and staying as far away from him as possible in the room. She would not tempt the Archangel, if he was watching. "What do you want?"

He smiled. "Poor Eve. You were always a little slow to understand."

Yes, she had liked Adam much better when he hadn't known who he was. "I'm sure I would've caught on faster if you ever said what you meant, and hadn't been so twisted in your logic."

"I'd like to read this." She stiffened and he smirked. "Oh, I won't steal it, Eve. Just look at it while we're visiting."

"No." She snatched the book from his hand and retreated to the windowsill. "I don't understand why you even care. Why are you here? Again. Why Mia?"

"Mia is a very lovely woman. Spirited, but willing to be led." She wanted to slap him. He grinned. "You're so easy to provoke, Eve. You know why I'm here. Why Mia."

She shivered. "Me."

"Of course." He shrugged. "It's long past time that we got to know one another again, after so many years apart."

She saw a flash of the angel's eyes, as he detailed how he would kill her. First, any child in her womb. The sword plunged straight through her stomach. She pressed her hand against her middle and focused on keeping her voice steady. "Not enough years, Adam."

"Ethan, please. Since I assume you don't want me to enlighten my lovely wife about our relationship." He flashed her that smile again. Full of imposed charm and power.

She would have taken a step back, except she was already against the window. "Ethan. Fine. But I think if you had wanted to explain yourself, you would have already. If she knew you were just trying to find a way to get to me, she'd never have you. Maybe I should tell her myself."

"You could. But it wouldn't keep me away, and it would hurt her tremendously."

He was right, and he knew it, and there was nothing she could say otherwise. Telling Mia would be disastrous for everyone. Her sister wouldn't believe her. Mia would accuse Eve of jealousy, in the best of cases. And if Mia did believe her, it could very well be worse. At least they weren't burning people at the stake anymore, but her memories of the mental ward were much too recent, and all it would take to remove her from Garrit's protection would be the suggestion that she wasn't of sound mind when she married him. Even if Mia couldn't supply proof, Adam could make any official, any doctor, believe whatever he wanted them to.

"I'm supposed to believe you're just here to get to know me? That's all? And you're not going to hurt my family, or me. Not going to cause any of us to be hurt."

"A little bit of trust, Eve." Lightning flashed and thunder rumbled like a low growl. Adam's gaze flickered to the window, his smile fading. Something in his face changed, his arrogance slipping into sincerity. "I'll be good."

She glanced behind her, but there was nothing there except the rain. She reached for his mind, threaded through his thoughts and felt his honesty on the surface. But there was more there, that she couldn't see, couldn't reach, couldn't feel. Had Michael threatened him, too?

"If you hurt her—"

"I won't."

"—or my family—"

"They'll be safe."

She frowned at him. "What are you keeping from me?"

He locked eyes with her then, gently forcing her from his mind, separating himself from her thoughts and stepping back. "God gave us the world, Eve. I just want to see it through your eyes."

CHAPTER TWENTY-THREE
Creation

§

The lands were barren. Rough grass grew pale and scratched her feet as she walked. There were no fruit trees here. No bushes overflowing with berries. No fallen nuts to be cracked for their meat. Reu led her through the golden grass, though he still favored his side where Adam had kicked him. There was a large willow tree along the bank of a stream, some last stray piece of the Garden's bounty, and they sat beneath it to hide from the burning sun. It wasn't anything like the tree they had spoken beneath in the Garden. This one looked as though it had suffered to grow, and the leaves were spotted and blemished, its branches not reaching the ground.

Eve found rocks by the water and scraped off a section of bark to grind as she had once seen Hannah do. Reu leaned against the trunk and looked out at the grassland with haunted eyes.

She offered him some of the powder and his gaze shifted back to her, lingering on her neck. "You should have some, too."

"I'm well enough, Reu."

He pinched a portion of the bark and let it dissolve on his tongue, turning his eyes back to the land around them. "I'm sorry I couldn't save you from this."

She moved next to him, wrapping her arms around her knees and letting her shoulder brush his. "Sometimes, I think we have to save ourselves." She sighed at the dry land and rested her head on her arms. "We'll find a way to live. At least we have the help of the fruit. And there are animals here. They must live off something."

"Each other." His tone was grim. Reu lifted his arm, and she settled against him under it. "They kill to live. God only kept the animals that would not harm us inside the Garden, but I saw many of them as they were made. Fierce things, with claws that rip through skin as though it were dry leaves, and jaws that crush bone as easily as we would the fruit of the banana tree."

She picked the images from his mind as he spoke. With his arm around her, it was easy to see exactly what he thought. Unlike Adam, he tended to speak the things that came to his mind. "Will they try to eat us?"

"I don't know." It seemed to upset him that he didn't, and he pulled her more closely against his side. *I should've taken better care of her. Protected her from him.*

"Reu. This isn't your fault."

He grimaced. "I wonder if the fruit will give him greater powers, too."

"Probably. But I don't think he cares about reading minds. Or thinks to do it." She brought some of the powder to her lips. It was bitter, and she resisted the urge to spit it out.

He chuckled. "I should've warned you about the taste. But it will help your neck. Keep down the swelling."

She pushed the rest of the bark away and watched the stream. It burbled over the rocks, clean and clear. At least they would have water, even if they didn't have food. "Maybe the angels will help us."

"The angels concern themselves with God's law, Eve. We've broken it. Inside the Garden we might have been overlooked for a time, but not now. Not when we'll have to kill to eat. They'll come for Adam soon, regardless, and they won't miss us in this wasteland, bumbling about."

"It isn't a wasteland when it has grasses and trees." She picked a leaf from the ground and smoothed it, feeling the black bumps that marred its surface. "I can feel the life humming around us. It's just different." She looked back over her shoulder toward the Garden, looming on the horizon, lush and green, and overflowing with its bounty. "We might pick some fruit from the branches that hang over the walls."

He shook his head. "For tomorrow, maybe. But we can't stay here. We'll need to find shelter, eventually. More than just this tree."

"The sun seems so much brighter here."

"Warmer, too. Almost uncomfortable." He sighed. "This isn't the way I had intended it to be. I thought if we left it would be of our own free will. And with food and nuts and berries to feed us for a few days at least."

"What is that?" She frowned at the sky. Specs of dust seemed to float and hover among the clouds. She climbed to her feet and moved out from under the tree, raising her hand to her face to block some of the sun from her eyes. They were strange motes. Many of them.

Reu came to stand beside her, shading his own eyes and squinting into the distance. "Angels."

As she watched, more and more of the motes appeared, until they made a thick dark cloud. "Are they like birds?"

He offered her his hand, and she took it. In his mind she could see the details which the distance hid from her. Winged men, beautiful and terrible to behold, clothed all in brilliant white. Their wings were all feathered with different colors. Black and brown, gold and silver, red and even blues and greens. But one, with a flaming sword at his waist, had wings as white as his garment, and piercing eyes that saw through her even in memory.

"Michael the Archangel will lead them, with Gabriel and Raphael at his side," Reu murmured. "It will take them time to cross the valley, but they'll be here before nightfall."

§

She had dozed off under the heat of the sun when Reu woke her with a hand on her shoulder.

"They're here," he said.

She blinked and rubbed her eyes as she stood up. That was when she noticed the shade. Like clouds had blocked the sun. A chill run down her spine. There were no clouds. The sky was clear and bright blue. It was the angels. An army so vast, it hid the sun and cast a shadow over the grasslands around them.

Reu took her hand and stepped forward to meet the three who were separate from the mass of winged bodies. They hovered above the earth, their pure white wings making broad strokes through the air without apparent effort.

"Michael. Gabriel. Raphael." Reu nodded to each of them, and Eve thought he only greeted them by name for her benefit.

"We know you, Reu." Michael's gaze slid from him and Eve couldn't look away as he stared into her eyes. Every moment of her life was laid bare before him, sifted through like sand falling between her fingers. Memories were lifted to the top and played within her own mind for both of them to see, and then it stopped as her lips touched the fruit of the tree. The angel's hand hovered over the flaming sword at his belt, and she felt his anger rock through her as though she had been struck. "You have eaten the fruit!"

A cacophony of noise burst forth, like thousands of bells ringing without warning. She covered her ears to try to stop it, crying out and dropping to her knees. Dimly, she felt Reu suffering beside her, even as she thought her ears might burst.

"Silence!" Michael called.

The noise ceased at once, replaced with the soft sound of wings against the air, like the thrum of a heartbeat. She looked up at the angel, his hand still on his sword, ready to draw it forth. The way his eyes gleamed with anticipation sent another chill down her spine, her skin prickling.

"Please," she heard herself say. "Reu only ate of the fruit because of me. To help me."

Michael's lip curled and she knew she had no secrets from him when he looked on her. His grip on the sword relaxed. He dropped to the earth before them and folded his wings to his back. "You are Eve."

She swallowed, unsure of what her identity meant to the angel. "I am. And I ate of the fruit, knowingly. To save the others from Adam."

"God's first son has long flaunted His law. We expected better from His favorite daughter." The angel's eyes narrowed as it studied her, and he reached out, touching her neck with cold fingers. "Adam oppresses God's people with violence." That flash of anticipation rose again, and Eve shivered. "This will not go unpunished."

At these words, the bells sounded again, louder than before. Reu groaned in pain, though this time Eve felt none with the angel's hand still touching her.

"Quiet!" The angel's gaze had shifted to Reu, and Eve saw him mark the black and blue at Reu's side. Michael's hand fell from her and he stepped back, waiting for them to rise to their feet before speaking again. "Your brother has the fruit?"

The sight of Adam, gripping the fruit tightly in his hand rose into her mind. "Yes."

"He has lost the right to live in God's Garden. He will be cast out, just as you have been." The angel raised a hand and two white garments were dropped to him. He tossed the shifts to the grass before them and they lost their brilliance and purity, the white dulling into cream and gray. Michael stared at Reu. "Your sacrifice is noted, but you are still bound by your oath. Adam has twice come too close to his desire. Do not fail her when he is among you once more, for now that they have eaten of the fruit, all will be lost. We will have no other choice but to act, and you will suffer for the results."

"I know my oath."

The angel nodded and spread its wings, rising once more into the air. "Though you have sinned willfully, it was for greater purpose, and this will be forgiven only so that you may serve. God's fire will mark you as the true leaders of your people." He drew the sword of flame, swinging it to the earth like a bolt of lightning, spraying dirt and fire to reveal stone and something else, glinting in the light. "Strike the rocks and metal together over dry grass and branches, and flame will serve you. It is the last protection we will offer."

Reu nodded. "Thank you, Michael, for your mercy."

"The Grace of God is with you both. Protect creation and God's law. Live and serve and give your people peace."

They all rose higher into the sky, moving together so precisely none touched one another, but no sun pierced through their shadow. Eve watched them go, hoping that she would never have cause to meet with them again.

CHAPTER TWENTY-FOUR
343 BC

§

Thor kept a closer watch upon Eve, then, though he had not wished to dwell so deeply on what he could not have. Loki had been as distracted by Hathor and Aphrodite as Thor had hoped, and returned to Asgard, strutting and boasting, which in turn had only driven Sif to greater levels of irritation. Somehow, he had not taken Sif's response to Loki's pleasures into consideration, but watching her snarl and hiss with jealousy made his stomach twist. Surely she could not have loved Loki, of all the gods. Loki, who had teased and taunted her mercilessly in the first years of their marriage, blaming her for Thor's distance.

Or had it been something else, all along? He did not want to credit Loki's accusations regarding Ullr, for he had raised the boy as his own and could not bear the thought that he might have been born of willful betrayal. But he did not know, now, for how long he had been cuckolded. How long had Odin known of it, or suspected, and said nothing? How long had all of Asgard laughed at him while Sif had bedded others behind his back, and he too blind, too in love, to see?

He tried to remember, to think back to those first days when Sif had looked on him with more than friendship. Just after Jarnsaxa had welcomed him to her bed. No one had been pleased with him for consorting with a Jotun, even a Sea Giant, for all Odin had welcomed Aegir into their halls with all his daughters and named him friend and ally. Had it only been jealousy that had motivated Sif, then? But surely he would have seen it, known it in her touch, if she had not truly loved him.

Thor swallowed more mead and brooded, his mood black enough that thunder rumbled overhead. None of the others in Odin's hall dared disturb him, and even when Baldur sat beside him, his brother remained silent, but for his call to one of the Valkyries for a pitcher of mead.

It was Sif who brought it. "Drinking yourself into a stupor again, husband?"

Thor lifted his gaze from the mug in his hands to his wife, and it was as though he saw her, truly, for the first time. Golden hair gleaming, burnished, glowing skin, darkened from so many days spent in the sun, and for all the beauty in her face, the banked fire in her eyes offered no warmth. Sif wore a string skirt, stopping above her knee, and the short tunic left her navel bare. An ivory bangle, carved from boar's tusks, wrapped around her slim wrist.

Thor went still, lightning buzzing in his ears, and the room fading into shades of gray and white, too bright. He caught her arm just above the wrist, the delicate ivory brushing against his finger, smooth as silk. The ivory he had carved with his own hands, filling the grooves of stem and leaf with heated gold and scorching his mortal fingers in the process. His gift to Tora, to Eve, at their wedding feast. The bracelet he had taken from her wrist the night she had died, and kept hidden among his things all these years.

"Do you like it?" Sif asked, her eyes flashing gold. "It was a gift from Loki, after he returned from his exile."

Thor stood so swiftly, the bench beneath him unbalanced. His fingers tightened around Sif's arm, and though he could feel Baldur's hand on his shoulder, he could not hear his brother's words over the thunder of his thoughts.

"And the clothes, too?" he asked her, his voice rough. "Did he choose them for you as well?"

She bared her teeth in what was meant to be a smile. "What's the matter, Thor? Aren't you pleased by the lengths with which I've gone to satisfy you?"

"The bracelet is mine," he growled.

"Is it?" she asked, all innocence. "I wonder what use you could have for such a bracelet, if not to gift it to your wife."

"Take it off." Baldur's grip had turned painful, bruising, but Thor ignored it.

Sif lifted her eyebrows. "What of the clothes? Would you have me remove them as well, strip naked in the middle of Odin's hall?"

"The bracelet, Sif." It was all he could do not to crush the bones in her wrist and tear it from her arm. He wanted to, Odin help him. The clothes were something else. Not Tora's, he was nearly certain, and nothing he had made for her as a symbol of their love. But she wore them now simply to taunt him. And he had no doubt that Loki had been part of it, nor did he care that he had played into their hands, allowing himself to be provoked. The bracelet was all he had of their life together, put behind him in the hopes of reconciling his marriage—a marriage he was beginning to suspect she had never meant to honor.

She sneered, twisting her arm free as if his hold were nothing. "And in return for overlooking this consort of yours, this whore of a goddess you took as your wife, what will you give me?"

"Enough, Sif," Baldur said. "If the bracelet belongs to Thor, it is his right to ask it of you."

Her lip curled, but she slipped it from her wrist, the gold vines within the ivory glinting in the light. Thor did not dare move, watching her fingers. Sif was as much a warrior as the rest of the Aesir, more than capable of snapping bone. Instead, she flung it at his chest so hard it stung him through his tunic. He caught it, but barely, and though he wanted desperately to check it for damage, he did not dare give Sif the satisfaction.

"And where is your justice for me, Baldur?" she asked. "What price ought Thor pay for his disloyalty?"

"Perhaps I paid already," he said, barely stopping from snapping the ivory himself in his anger. That she would stand there before him and speak of disloyalty—"After all, there is Ullr, isn't there?"

She flushed from chest to cheeks. "You dare!"

"It was not I who broke the trust of our marriage. And after what has happened, I dare not take you at your word."

"Thor," Baldur groaned. "Please, you must not—"

"No?" Thor snarled, rounding on him. "How long did you stand by and watch as she betrayed me, brother? How long has Asgard been laughing behind my back, thinking me a fool? No!" Lightning struck the hearth with a sharp crack, scorching the beams and the air around them. Baldur stepped back, and even Sif flinched, her face pale. "I have had enough!"

The lightning came again, then, white and hot with his rage and filling the hall with thunder so loud the stones cracked beneath his feet.

"Thor, please," Baldur said, even his light shadowed in the brightness of the hall. "You will…"

But Thor let the room dissolve, lightning racing through his veins, through his heart, until he stood suspended in its liquid heat, his whole body alive with current.

The last thing he heard before leaving Asgard was the sound of Loki's laughter.

§

"Back so soon?" Athena asked, teasing.

Thor did not so much as turn from the view of the palace stretched below him, all cavalry and soldiers, and the king who demanded more and more again, then turned to his son, snapping orders. The boy raced to obey, glory in his eyes, determination in every line of his body, in spite of its limitations.

"Adam is too hard on his son," Thor said after a moment, determined to keep his other thoughts to himself. Perhaps if he focused on Adam, now Philip the Second of Macedon, he would not be tempted by desire for Eve.

He had not thought overmuch where the lightning should take him, only that he must flee. First, to the House of Lions, who had hardly known him, and then here. As near as he would allow himself to Eve, hidden in Athens as some fool's wife, where she would barely be given the right to see the sun. It infuriated him to think of it.

Athena came to stand beside him, looking out at the palace and the army being drilled. "He plans to conquer the world. Of course he is hard on him. But Alexander is brilliant. Where Philip fails, his son will succeed."

Thor grunted. If Alexander were so brilliant, Athena had no doubt had a hand in it herself, and he dared not argue against such a scheme. Adam pressed into the North and the East already, expanding the influence of Macedon, and as such, Macedon's gods. As if the Olympians did not have enough already, with their fingers in Rome and Etruria thanks to Aeneas, and only limited by Carthage to the south and west, and the Celts and Gauls to the north. Anyone with eyes could see it would be only a matter of time before the Olympian gods reached even to the borders of the North Lands, for Odin's influence expanded further south every year.

Before long, the Olympians would swallow even the House of Lions—unless...

"Would your family object to my presence this night?" Thor asked. "For once, I come only for myself."

"You should know by now you are always welcome at our table, Thor. My father will be pleased to have you as his guest."

"And have I your word you will not abandon me? I fear I will offend Aphrodite unforgivably if I do not have some excuse in your company."

Athena laughed. "Is not Sif enough excuse?"

Thor unclenched his teeth only with an effort, though his jaw was still tight, and he felt the burn of lightning in his eyes at even the mention of her name. She had shamed him so totally in Asgard, and no doubt Loki had completed his humiliation while he spent his days in Aphrodite's bed, spreading word of his blindness to any god who would listen.

He forced himself to breathe, to release the tension knotting his shoulders and turning his hands into fists, and only when he had controlled himself again, did he answer: "Not anymore."

Placed in Olympus, even Baldur's *skáli* would look humble and dull, and Thor's brother was by far the most elegant architect among the Aesir. Thor had seen the city before, but something about the mountain retreat made him strain to see everything again, as if for the first time. Olympus shone more brightly than Asgard ever would, filled with statues of gold and silver, littered with luxury. Huge aqueducts even carried running water through the buildings, and turned immense wheels where the water fell, to power parts of Hephaestus's forges.

Sif would have loved it. He had meant to bring her here, before he had learned of her affair with Loki. He had even spoken with Hephaestus about building her a fine *skáli* in the Olympian style, with hot running water for the bath so that she would no longer have to heat it in cauldrons over the hearth fire while he was away.

"Ah! The Odin-son returns to us!" Zeus slapped him on the back between the shoulder blades so heartily that large and powerful as Thor was, he almost stumbled forward a step. "And what favor do you ask of us this time?"

"I travel for my own pleasure," Thor answered, bracing himself before another of Zeus's gestures knocked him off his feet. "Though, I must admit I do not come without purpose, all the same."

Zeus clapped him again on the back. "You would shock us all the more if you did not! Come, then, and we will speak of it before the wine is poured—Athena, call to your brother, that we might have a proper feast for our guest. You will accept our hospitality, of course, since this business you bring is only your own?"

"If you do not fear my wife's reprisals," he said, following Zeus into a strange garden, fenced with gold and silver. "She will turn her ire to your daughters."

The plants were nothing he had ever seen upon the earth, with leaves of purple and blue, and rainbow fruits. A hissing sound came from beyond his sight, and the smell of wood smoke and heated metal hung thick in the air. A dragon, Thor thought. He had heard of one kept in such a garden as this, guarding the prizes of Hera's collection.

Zeus laughed. "My daughters are well able to protect themselves from jealous wives, and Aphrodite has been quite anxious to see you since she learned of your wife's infidelity. I believe she hopes for an opportunity to assist you in avenging the slight to your honor."

"At the cost of her own husband's?" Thor snorted. "Though I am flattered and honored by Aphrodite's interest, I would not do to

Hephaestus what has been done to me. It would be unkind in the extreme after the welcome he has given me."

"Would you have Athena, then?" Zeus asked slyly. "I am certain you would find her just as willing, virgin though she is. Surely Odin would not refuse you the right to divorce, and Olympus would be happy to gain you as a son-in-law. With one marriage, we could have an entire continent beneath our feet, our families working as one!"

Thor shook his head. He had always known Zeus was ambitious, but he had not ever thought his desires reached so far as that. "I would not do Athena the disservice of a marriage built on less than love."

"No," Zeus said, his eyes narrowing. "I do not suppose you would, after all. My daughter is as ever most discerning. And I suppose she knows what has brought you here, as well?"

"In this, I did not consult with her first," Thor admitted. "And I fear it is a very large favor—more than I have any right to ask."

"Indeed?" The king of Olympus sat down, a vine climbing up and around to offer him a throne. No—not a vine. A tail, mottled brown and green against the earth. And behind Zeus's head, a pair of bright, glowing eyes appeared. The dragon was all but invisible, its hide matching the plants and trees around it to perfection.

Thor was rather relieved when Zeus did not offer him a similar seat, but only leaned back in his strange throne, studying him, and waved a hand indicating he should continue.

"I wish for lands of my own," Thor said, his words even and his voice steady. He did not let himself stare at the dragon, or allow his gaze to return to the beast with any frequency.

Zeus's gray eyes sharpened, and Thor understood for the first time why one of his symbols was the eagle. "Oh?"

"There is a settlement on the far side of the Alps which looks to me, and I have promised them my protection. The lands are not yours yet, but they will be, and I would have your permission to work within them as I see fit, that I might honor my vow."

Zeus tapped his fingers against the dragon's hide. "You are not wrong, Odin-son, it is more than you have any right to ask. And how can you be certain the lands will fall into our hands, and not your father's?"

"If they fall into my father's hands, I will be free to act as I must. I need not apply to him for permission."

"And the Celts?"

Thor smiled. The Olympians were not the only pantheon whose influence reached beyond its borders. "The men on the mainland already turn to Odin. Those who don't will be swallowed by Rome before long. Is that not your intention?"

"Had I spoken to Athena first, she would have warned me not to tempt you," Zeus grumbled. "Now that I have, I can hardly deny our hopes for the continent. But why come to me, and not Ra, who holds our vows?"

"Athena is my friend, and to you and your people, I owe a debt."

Zeus grunted, scratching his jaw. As he shifted, so did the dragon, cat-eyes gleaming pale green. "My daughter was right."

"She is rarely wrong," Thor agreed, "though I do not know to what you might refer."

The dragon's tongue flicked out, tasting the air, and Zeus lifted a hand, causing it to still. "This settlement in the Alps, these people you have promised to protect, it is the House of Lions. Elohim's people. And what would your father say, if he knew you wished to claim them, to nurture them, though they will never give us their worship, the power of their prayers?"

Thor said nothing. He had never told Odin of the vows he had made, knowing his father's opinion of granting favors to those who did not make proper sacrifice. And if Thor had not cared overmuch what became of Eve's family before, after living as her husband, he could hardly turn from them. With that marriage, he had bound himself to them, made them his own kin. Odin could not understand, and Thor could not risk being forbidden to act.

"The lands are yours, if you want them," Zeus said at last. "They are worthless to me. But consider, Thor, that you lend the True God power with every act, and it is only because he yet sleeps that we are suffered here. If their faith spreads and Elohim rises, you will be in no position to keep your vows. We will all be cast out."

Thor bowed, concealing his relief. "I owe you another debt, Thunderer."

"And when you marry my daughter, I will forgive them all." Zeus waved a hand, dismissing him. "Go and feast. Drink until you cannot stand. Dionysus will ensure that none remember whose bed you choose to share."

It was, perhaps, too tempting a thought.

§

Sun woke him the next morning, streaming through the window into his eyes. There was a soft groan beside him. A shapely arm reached for a tassel and then drapes shut out the light. Athena rolled onto her side to look at him, naked but for the sheet that covered her below the waist.

A rising anxiety swept over him as he tried to remember what had happened the previous night, but it was all a blur of wine and laughter.

She laughed and stroked his face. "I'm sorry. I shouldn't laugh at you, but your expression is so comical. Peace, Thor. I brought you here to keep you safe from my sister. We slept, that's all."

The reassurance allowed him to breathe, and he exhaled heavily. "I don't remember much of the night."

"Of course not. One of Dionysus's duties is to keep us from

agonizing over our drunken revelry. Father can't stand when his feasts are ruined by fighting or regret. I assure you, you did nothing more than exchange a few kisses with anyone, and those you did not suffer gladly."

"I thank you, Athena, for not taking advantage."

She lay back, her arms flung over her head as she stared at the drapery above them. "I'm not sure anyone could take advantage of you, Thor, if you did not wish it."

"Aphrodite showed great determination until Ares arrived." He studied her face, wishing that the lines in her brow would smooth. He didn't like the frustration in her eyes.

"My sister is not fool enough to flaunt herself in front of him. Ares would dearly love a contest of might with you, to prove himself the more powerful. And when he lost, he would shame us all by provoking a war, no doubt." She looked at him and smiled, though it didn't reach her eyes. "I think if she had won you, I might have helped him, though I never realized myself so jealous until now."

He propped himself up on an elbow to look at her. "I shall always be flattered by your regard, though I cannot return your feelings."

Her eyes met his and a flush crept up her body from her breasts to her cheeks. "Such pretty words. Odin trained you well not to give offense."

"I do not offer them for my father's sake." He followed the blush to her chest to the edge of the sheet which hid the rest of her body from him. "But I wish I could speak otherwise, Athena. I wish I could offer you something better than this."

She sat up, the sheet falling away, and brought her lips to his. He didn't pull away, nor did he encourage her, and she sighed and turned away. "Perhaps the next time you join us, your heart will not be so unyielding."

"Athena—"

He was stopped by a shake of her head. "You have given me no reason to hope, Thor. I know that. But let me pretend otherwise, just for this moment."

He nodded, though her back was to him, and watched her in silence. He understood now, why she had invited him to her bed. Drunk as he had been, as she had ensured he would be, she had hoped he would turn to her for comfort. But the comfort she offered and desired was pain to him, his heart too sore still from Sif's betrayal, and aching yet, for Eve. It had been, perhaps, an unsubtle test of his resolve, but between her sister Aphrodite, and her brother Dionysus, Athena could be sure that his refusal only came from his heart, and not some twisted sense of honor or allegiance. And she would know it applied to all, not just her, if he denied her sister as well.

It was a relief and a regret that it would come to this, and he hoped in her divine wisdom she would still be able to accept his friendship.

She dressed and when she turned to him again, her expression was pleasant. "Would you like to eat before you leave us?"

"If it would not be an imposition, I could use some food to sop up the last of the wine from my stomach."

"Stay, I'll find you fruit and bread. Perhaps this way my sister will not remember that you slipped away and take offense." She smiled, and then left the room.

Alone, he dressed, wishing that his trouble could be as easily fixed as his hangover.

CHAPTER TWENTY-FIVE
Present

§

"Absolutely not!" Garrit had stopped pacing, and Eve would have been grateful if he weren't glowering instead.

She sighed. Somehow, Garrit's study always made her feel like an erring child, caught pulling hair on the playground. She stood up, hoping it would lessen the feeling if she weren't sitting opposite his desk. She felt as though she was sacrificing Mia for the House of Lions. Or worse, for herself.

"If they're here, we can keep an eye on both of them. I can make sure Mia is safe."

He shook his head. "I don't want him in my home, Abby. Not now, and certainly not more regularly. Mia makes you miserable, and it goes without saying how I feel about Adam. Our entire purpose as a family has been to keep him from you. To protect you from exactly this. You can't expect me to believe that now he knows who he is, he's given it all up and become content to be your brother-in-law."

No, she didn't expect anything of the sort. But she wanted to know if the person she knew Adam could be was still there, hidden somewhere. Paris might have been selfish and arrogant, but he hadn't been a horrible human being. He had only wanted love. She wondered if that was what drove Adam now, too, buried beneath all the hubris. It wasn't something Garrit would understand. She wasn't even sure she did.

"I know what he's capable of doing to her. You want me to just let her run off with him?"

Garrit ran his hand through his hair and took a deep breath, as if gathering his patience. "You said you weren't going to police her. You said you didn't want to mother her. That if this was what she wanted, you had no right to interfere. You said she loves him freely. Or has this changed?"

She knew where he was going, but she could hardly lie. "No, it hasn't changed. He hasn't influenced her."

"Then they leave." His voice was firm. "Mia's made her bed, and you've already made your choice not to meddle."

"But Garrit—"

"*Non*, Abby."

She flinched at his tone, and looked away.

He sighed, framing her face in his hands and kissing her forehead. Eve stepped into his arms, accepting the apology his body offered and hid her face in the curve of his shoulder.

"This family would move mountains for you," he murmured. "We would do anything you asked. Provide for you under any circumstances. But not this, Abby. I won't let him close to you this way."

There was so much of Ryam in him. And Ryam had never been swayed from any course once his mind had been made up. "You won't, or the family won't?"

"It's the same, either way. This is just a new way for him to try to hurt you." He stroked her hair. "Not all mind games are played telepathically. If he had really changed, he wouldn't have forced himself on you this way. You wouldn't have to worry about what he'll do to Mia if you let him leave."

She pulled away and went to the window. The sun was up and the sky was clear for the moment. Juliette and René were out at the stables, and Eve could see them laughing as René gave her a leg up onto one of the mares. He slapped the animal on the rump, and Juliette let the horse have its head, shouting back over her shoulder to René to keep up. There were no dark flecks of odd shaped birds. She'd had the nightmare again last night though, of the sword through her stomach. She couldn't decide which was worse, the nightmares of the mental ward or Michael.

"*Let* him leave." She pressed her palm to the glass and stared into her own eyes. "I'm not letting him do anything."

"Except drive you crazy." His voice was bitter, and she flinched at his casual use of the word.

Crazy. Maybe she was, to think Adam could be something more than this. It had taken much less influence than what Adam was capable of to send her to the mental ward in her last life. "How do you force a man to leave who can make you think you want him to stay as easily as breathing? How are you so sure he'll go at all?"

"Because even a man like me knows when he's been outmatched, sister." She turned at his voice. Adam shut the door behind him and flashed a grin. "I didn't mean to interrupt."

Garrit glared, his jaw tight. "If you hadn't meant to interrupt, you wouldn't have come. At all."

"How can I resist when I'm given such a warm welcome?" Adam smirked.

"You have no business here," Garrit snapped. "Not even as Mia's husband."

Adam's eyes flashed. "You DeLeons are even more arrogant than I gave you credit for. You don't tell the son of God what his business is." His grin was feral, and his gaze slid to her. "But I forgot. You denied God generations ago when you started making alliances with pagans—"

Garrit lurched forward, but Eve caught him by the arm. "Get out of my house and off my land, Adam."

"Stop. Both of you." The room darkened as clouds drifted over the sun, and a chill went down her spine. She put a hand on Garrit's chest and pushed him back a step before he could lunge at Adam's throat. "This is ridiculous."

Adam rolled his eyes. "And I thought Eve was easy to provoke."

"Don't bother stopping to collect your wife on your way out," Garrit sneered.

"That isn't playing fair, *Monsieur* DeLeon. What's mine will come with me. If that means you have to wait another thirty minutes while she packs, that's not my problem. What God has joined, and all that." He glanced at Eve again. "What shall I tell Mia, then? Or would you prefer to explain why you're casting us out yourself?"

Eve kept a hand on Garrit, just in case, though she wanted to slap him herself. *Casting us out.* That he would dare even use the expression after what he'd done—no. She wouldn't let him upset her. Not now.

"You're not doing yourself any favors, Adam. Garrit has been incredibly patient with you, all things considered, and so have I."

He smirked. "I was kind of hoping you'd let him throw a few punches. For Mia's sympathy." Thunder rolled in and he sighed, glancing toward the window. His tone became suddenly reasonable, all insult draining from his voice. "We'll be gone by nightfall, if that's acceptable."

Garrit nodded once and turned away.

She shook her head. Getting to know what made Adam tick wasn't worth this, not now. "I'll go find Mia and explain. In the meantime, please try not to kill one another."

Garrit made a noise that sounded like a strangled laugh. "I can dream."

She raised an eyebrow at Adam. *Touch my husband, and I'll make sure you regret it.*

Adam nodded dismissively, his gaze shifting to the window, and the rain that had begun. *Go to your sister.* Then his lips twitched. *Feel free to upset her.*

She shut her mind to his before he could share anything more than the most general feeling of lust, and left the room before he succeeded in provoking her into an act of violence, too.

§

She found Mia in the entertainment room, watching soap operas on the widescreen television and eating chips.

"Oh, Abby." Mia didn't even look away from the television. "Did you want to watch *Afterlife* with me? What do you do all day when Garrit's working? I thought the reason you couldn't go on a honeymoon was because he had to work?"

"I can't believe you still watch this show." Eve sat down next to her on the sofa. She ignored the rest of the questions. How was she going to explain all of this in a way that didn't sound like a punishment? None of this was Mia's fault, really. She was a victim of circumstance. Eve scrubbed her face. "Mia, you and Ethan need to go."

Mia finally looked at her, startled. "Why?"

"You should go see Mum and Dad. They'll want to meet him." Not that she wanted him anywhere near her parents. But he had given her his word. She had to rely on that now. A little trust, he'd said. And it would certainly make her feel much safer from Michael. She rubbed her stomach again. "And besides, you've got school starting up soon."

"School? As if. I was only doing that so I could get a better job than food service." Mia stared at her, frowning. "This is because you don't like him, Abby. You think I don't notice the way you stiffen when he walks in a room? What is it that bothers you so much about him?"

Eve looked into her sister's eyes and wanted so much to give her an honest answer. It felt cowardly to lie, but she couldn't take the risk. She wouldn't take the risk of going back to an asylum. Not even for her sister. "He rubs me the wrong way, that's all."

Mia's eyes narrowed. "He's your brother-in-law now! Would it kill you to be nice to him? Or are you just mad because I married even better than you did?"

"This isn't a competition, Mia. I don't care how well you married. I'm glad that you think you married so well. You *should* feel that way—" She bit off the rest of her sentence, rocking back against the couch cushions with the realization. Mia should feel that way. How many times had she been married off to men who didn't care at all about her? There had never been a time she didn't know the difference. Never. And she hadn't ever needed telepathy to tell her. Mia would never tolerate a man who wasn't interested in *her*.

"Abby, are you all right? You're white."

She took a steadying breath, then forced herself to smile. "Yes."

Mia wouldn't spend a single day with a man who did not make her the center of his world. She didn't have to trust Adam, but if Adam did love Mia, cared for her—

"But it doesn't change anything," she said firmly. It changed everything. "You have to go. You and Ethan need to start your life together. On your own. Away from us." *Away from me.*

I said feel free to upset her, not manipulate her.

Adam's voice in her head startled her. She hadn't realized he was listening.

"If you don't want us here, just say so. But I don't understand what difference another two people makes, when Garrit's entire family is here."

"If you two go, then they will too, and we'll all have a little bit of peace." *Only you would assume I was trying to manipulate her.*

"Oh." Mia glanced over her shoulder and her eyes lit up. "Ethan, you don't mind terribly if we go visit my parents, do you?"

He was in the doorway, leaning against the frame. *I doubt very much I'll ever have peace, Eve, but that's a nice wish.* He smiled at her sister. "Of course not, Mia. Whatever you like."

Eve shook her head and refused to reply to the thought. The dual conversation was aggravating. "I know they'll be thrilled to meet you."

Mia had always been their favorite. It wouldn't have mattered who she brought home. Tattoos, piercings, bad hair, torn up clothing. He could be a penniless street urchin, and they would hug him and tell him how wonderful he was for Mia.

Jealousy doesn't suit you.

She looked up. Adam studied her, his brow furrowed. Mia was going on about how excited Mama would be to meet him. How thrilled their parents would be that she had found someone so charming and so loving.

"We'd better go pack, then, if you want to leave this evening." Mia took Adam by the hand and pulled him with her back out of the room. "You'll like them so much, Ethan. And then we can go house shopping! But not too close to my parents. Mum will invite herself over if we're not careful."

Eve waited until she couldn't hear Mia anymore before she stood up and turned off the television. Soap operas didn't really hold her attention after millennia of watching it in the flesh. She sighed. Like now. She had the feeling it would be a very long time before any DeLeon was permitted to forget the truth again. The thought didn't give her any comfort.

She returned to Garrit's study. He was still there, sitting behind his desk. But his eyes weren't tracking on his paperwork, and it looked as though he'd been pulling on his hair.

He looked up at her when she walked in, and leaned back. "How did Mia take it?"

"She took it. She's dragged Adam off to pack."

"I'm sorry, Abby. For being so difficult about this."

He pushed his chair back and she sat down in his lap, letting him wrap his arms around her. The rightness of it was a balm. This was where she was meant to be, now. With her family. With her people.

"You're doing what you think is best. Just like Ryam would have. Just like Reu did."

"Infinite patience must be one of your gifts."

"No." She watched the rain against the window. The thunder was distant now. Almost comforting in its rumble. "I can be just as impatient as anyone, given the right motivation."

"You've never been impatient with me. Even when I refuse you."

"You're right to send them away, Garrit." Saying it aloud made it feel even more so. Adam's place was with Mia. Some of the guilt around her heart eased. "They need to get to know each other if they're going to be husband and wife. And Mia will keep him busy."

Garrit smiled. "Then perhaps you'll have your honeymoon after all."

"Somewhere tropical, with lots of sun?" She was surprised how much the idea appealed to her. "All this rain lately has been miserable. I may as well have been living in London."

He laughed, lifting her from his lap and setting her back on her feet. "Give me an hour to make the arrangements, and you can thank me properly. We'll leave first thing in the morning. *Mieux vaut tard que jamais.*"

Yes, much better late than never. She was halfway to the door before it occurred to her to ask, and then she turned. "Just us, Garrit? No security or family or anyone?"

"You have my word, just us." But he was staring out the window and there was an odd determination in his face. She frowned, and when he noticed his face cleared at once. "Go pack, Abby. I'll take care of the rest."

CHAPTER TWENTY-SIX
Creation

§

It took them the rest of the day to learn to strike the stones to spark a fire, though there were plenty of leaves and twigs from the willow tree to act as tinder. Eve shivered from the cold so violently her teeth chattered even after the fire was lit, and Reu pulled her against his body, using the robes for blankets, but it was still a long time before the heat of the fire and Reu's warmth allowed her to stop shaking.

Somehow, the light made the dark around them more intense, blacker and unbearable. She closed her eyes against it, but flames still licked behind her eyelids, and she thought it must be because Reu stared into the fire.

"I thought Adam was exaggerating when he said we would die," she mumbled between shudders in the cold.

Reu sighed and tucked her head beneath his chin. "You can't die from the cold, Eve. Or anything else that might threaten you outside of the Garden. Not before your time."

She clung to his body. "But you can."

"Yes." He stroked her hair. "But I don't think I'll die if the angels intend for us to lead. I don't think they would have said so if they foresaw my death from the cold."

"They're frightening enough to behold without the power of foresight. Even with the fruit, I'm not sure I understand God's intent for them."

He laughed softly. "The angels are not of the world, Eve. But they are concerned with it. Now that God is dead, it will be Michael's responsibility to preserve creation and God's laws on earth. I'm surprised we escaped unscathed by them for our sins. Michael does not usually stop to consider the reasoning behind the acts. Perhaps that changed with God's death as well."

"If God was so powerful, how could He have let Himself die?"

He was quiet for a long moment, and she could follow the ideas in his mind, the possibilities. Perhaps God had not died, truly. Perhaps he had merely dispersed Himself among his creation and his people. Reu rejected the idea almost at once that God had given his power to Eve, to make of her a new Goddess, though he did not doubt there was something more in her than simple humanity. But God did not walk among them anymore, that was certain, and the angels did not behave as he had expected they should.

"I don't know. There is still so much beyond my understanding. I don't think we're meant to understand the mystery of God."

"Do you think Adam knows?"

"It's unlikely. But he often walked with Elohim, and we were not privy to their conversation. Clearly he knew what waited for us outside the safety of the Garden, though he had never been here himself."

She shivered. "I had thought to leave him behind, but it seems he'll follow us here, too."

Reu pressed his lips against her forehead. "Don't worry about that yet. Sleep, for now, Eve. Tomorrow will be difficult enough without borrowing from the future."

§

Sometime in the night, Eve woke to the sound of a great roaring, her heart racing. Reu crouched near the fire, his hand wrapped tightly around a thick brand. He was alert, and his face was grim. The roar was followed by an inhuman scream that made her stop breathing altogether with a gasp, but Reu's calm was infectious. He relaxed at the second noise and came back to her, murmuring reassurance and stroking her hair until she fell to sleep.

§

Eve woke first the next morning, and built the fire back up. It was only after she had tended to it that she saw the carcass on the bank of the stream. A gazelle, its neck bent so far it touched its own back. She knew at once it was dead, and that it had made the scream she had heard in the night. She thought of what Reu had said, about the animals here living off one another, and her stomach cramped with hunger.

A leg had been torn off the animal, and the belly opened. Pieces of entrails littered the mud, along with paw prints larger than her hand. She stared at them, frozen with fear. If the beast which had done this had found them before the deer, would she be staring at Reu's body in pieces now? His stomach devoured, his leg ripped from his body?

She retched in the grass, though there was nothing in her stomach but bitter acid. After rinsing her mouth with water from the stream, Eve forced herself to look back at the carcass again. Whatever creature had done this, it had fed, and perhaps the gazelle would feed them, too. She took one of the stones that Michael had given them, the one with the sharpest edge, and carved pieces of meat from the bones, taking them back to the fire and setting them on the rocks to warm. The meat sizzled on the hot stones, and her mouth watered at the scent.

She cleaned the blood and gore from her hands at the stream, and the rock she had used as a blade. A feeling that she was being watched shivered down her spine, but when she glanced back at Reu, he was still asleep. The feeling intensified, with a great sense of curiosity. Golden eyes blinked at her for just a moment, on the other side of the river, but when she looked again they were gone, and it was only golden grasses waving in the wind.

She went back to the fire and flipped the meat to brown the tops. The sizzling must have woken Reu, because he sat up, blinking for a moment and rubbing his face before coming to sit beside her. His gaze went to the carcass, then back to the meat. He didn't ask what she was preparing, but she felt his understanding.

"Did you sleep well?" he asked.

She squatted near the fire with her arms wrapped around her knees. The morning was still cool, and her skin prickled with small bumps.

"As well as I could." She nodded to the kill. "Whatever did that was very large. It left prints in the mud."

"It sounded like a lion." His expression was grim as he stared into the flames, and she picked the image of the animal from his mind easily. Large and tawny, with claws and teeth she wouldn't want near her skin. "The fire kept it away, but I don't know how long that will save us. We should find shelter. Some caves would be best, with fresh water nearby."

She looked out over the grasses, the same color as the animal's coat, and shivered. "I don't think I want to spend another night in the open, either. Fresh water, or not."

He picked up a piece of the meat, tossing it back and forth in his hands awkwardly. "I never thought to eat the flesh of anything but fruit. Perhaps we should take the fur from the animal before we go. It might help to keep you warm at night."

"Even the beast that killed it didn't leave it naked in death." She pulled her own piece from the fire and nearly dropped it at once, it was so hot.

Reu caught it before it landed in the grass and tossed it back to her. "I think it would be better to use what we can than to leave it to waste away."

"Perhaps." She blew on the meat, repeating his awkward movements until it was cool enough to handle, and then took a tentative bite. It was tough and chewy, but the taste was surprisingly mild, even pleasant.

He took a bite of his own, and she watched his face as he chewed and swallowed. "We'll try to reach the other side of the grassland. There should be caves at the foot of the mountain that we can take shelter in. Perhaps we can forage along the way." But he frowned at the grasses around him. There wasn't much to forage from. "The cave should keep us warmer than we were out in the open."

She shivered again. The feeling of being watched hadn't gone away. But there were too many creatures around them. More animals than she could count, impugning on her consciousness. She shook her head to clear her mind, but it didn't help.

"Are you well, Eve?"

She pressed her hand to her temple. "There's so much here. Whatever power God gave me, it seems to be growing stronger. I can feel so much."

He took her hand and brought it to his face, looking into her eyes. "What do you feel from me?"

Heat flooded her cheeks as a warmth blossomed in her stomach. She pulled her hand away, dropping her eyes to the grass. His want, his love, made her feel lightheaded, and she remembered the images from Adam's mind, of their bodies joined together. "I don't know how to be a wife, Reu."

He ducked his head to look into her eyes again. "I don't know how to be a husband, either. But I'm willing to try. To love you and protect you and bring you joy. If you'll have me."

His eyes were dark, and his love washed over her like a river. And when he touched her, she didn't want to pull away. When he lifted her face and brought his lips to hers, it was nothing like that first kiss from Adam. It was soft and gentle, kind and questioning.

She parted her lips in invitation, and while he kissed her, the rest of the world disappeared. All she felt was his love, his desire, his joy, feeding her own like the leaves fed the flame. And in that moment, she knew who she had been made for, and God's plan for her life. She did not belong to Adam, for from her first moments she had been bound to Reu by his love.

Eve pressed him back into the grass, her senses filled with the warmth of his body, the touch of his skin against hers. She pressed him back and kissed him again as his arms wrapped around her, drawing her in. For the first time, the images of the man and woman, bodies joined, made her shiver with anticipation instead of dread.

Reu stroked her hair, weaving his fingers through it so gently she thought she imagined the touch. She rested her forehead against his, her heart racing in her chest. She could feel his, too, thudding hard beneath her palm.

"Will you show me, Reu?" She asked softly, remembering his words. It seemed so long ago that he had spoken them. "Show me how this is meant to be."

Oh, she cried, mind and body both in exultation. Reu's love washed over her, through her entire being, faster and more powerful than the river current. It was more eloquently spoken than any vow.

My love, his thoughts echoed through hers with his body's release. *My wife.*

CHAPTER TWENTY-SEVEN
218 BC

§

War. The Romans never had their fill of it, and in spite of himself, Thor found himself in sympathy with Adam, an elderly advisor to the Carthaginian general, Hannibal. If it were not for the House of Lions, caught in the middle and ripe for the raiding by both sides, he would have wished them all good fortune and ignored the mess of it. As it was, he had taken the high ground of a mountain, watching the movements of any soldiers who strayed too near. Carthaginians, Romans, even Gauls and Celts, all looking for the path of least resistance across the Alps.

And not for the first time. The entire region had been in turmoil for the last forty years at least, and before it had been Adam urging Carthage to war against Rome, it had been Pyrrhus, attacking from the East. Thor was certain the only reason Pyrrhus of Epirus had done so well in his own battles was because of Eve, born as his daughter Olympias. Athena had taken pity on Thor, in spite of her own wishes, and granted the king her favor, and no matter how heavy the losses, Pyrrhus still rose triumphant in the end, keeping

Olympias from falling into ruin for her father's ambitions. Eve had even ruled for a time, before she had watched both her sons die, then she had seen Deidamia, her granddaughter, made queen, before pretending her own death and retiring west, back to her Lions. Into the heart of more war and far too near to Adam, no matter how aged they both were.

"Have you seen her?" Athena asked. He had noted the owl soaring over the marching columns, but lost track of her in the passing clouds. Of course Athena would be present, just as Tanit was sure to be present among the Carthaginians, being that city's patron goddess, and goddess of war as well.

Thor lifted a shoulder, neither confirmation nor denial, though he would much rather have pretended a lack of understanding. Athena deserved better after everything she had done, and he would not treat her dishonestly. Not that what he had seen of Eve was worth mentioning in much detail. He did not dare show himself, or risk drawing Sif's attention, and to have her so near, on his own lands, and be unable to know her at all….

It was one more reason he hated this war. And he still would not speak to Sif, though he had taken care to spend time with Ullr and Thrud, bringing them both to Egypt, then Olympus. Whatever happened between himself and Sif, he would not have the children they had raised together believe he had turned from them.

"I did not even think of Adam in Carthage when she left us," Athena confessed, coming to stand beside him on the rocky precipice. "I only hoped she would be safe enough with her family."

"So she is," Thor agreed. "You were kind to send me word. There are times I wish the House of Lions was not so near to the North Lands, with the Celts gossiping like Norns between us. Loki seems to hear every rumor of even the slightest events."

"Do they know yet that Zeus granted you these lands?"

Thor shook his head. "The boundary is so ill-defined, they take no notice, assuming it is some patch of Gauls worshipping Woden and Donar."

"And when they learn of it, what then?"

He grunted. If Rome won this war, they would expand, swallowing the Alps and driving the Celts and the Gauls north. When that day came, there would be no hiding his work so far south.

"I will do what I must to protect them, Athena. As I have sworn."

She sighed, her gray eyes softening with something near pity. "And what will you do for yourself, Thor? Even on Olympus, we know the break in your marriage has not healed. Yet you remain Sif's husband, still."

He pressed his lips together. It was not as though he had not considered it. After that night in Olympus, he had returned home, ready to finish it all. But Sif had been prepared, waiting, ready, and when he had found her, she had smiled. A smug and cruel expression that made his blood run cold. Heimdall had appeared a moment later, catching Baldur at the door, and then together they had both turned to look at him, faces grim.

Baldur had shoved through the milling gods and servants to reach him, and Thor ducked his head to listen to the news his brother brought so urgently.

"Famine," Baldur said. "Thorgrim's fishing village starves, and what stores they had for trade were burned to the ground. Heimdall says it was Sif. He said she told the people of the village that they must pray to you if they wished for deliverance."

Thor did not take his gaze from his wife, his vision hazing, but Sif had only smiled wider.

The message had been clear. Leave her, and she would turn all who looked to him, everything he loved and nourished, into dust. This was her warning.

Thor had left the hall without a word. He had not dared to waste a moment in seeing to the village, to Owen's people, his own family. And when he found them, it was worse. She'd sickened them, too. Wasting diseases that lasted months, or even years, all of them miserable with suffering. And Owen's line—every direct descendant of Eve's son was struck down.

If he acted against her, he had no doubt that the next time, she would kill them. And the time after that, when she noticed the House of Lions, it would be the same again. He had no power to protect any people against disease, and there would be no proving Sif had acted so cruelly. Perhaps he had done the House of Lions a disservice, claiming them; were they beholden to Zeus, Sif could not harm them.

"If she loved you once, it does not seem she cares for anything but herself now," Athena said gently, touching his arm. "You deserve better, Thor."

"It is not so simple as what I deserve." A god protected his people, or what good was he? He would not turn on those who looked to him, abandon them for his own gain. "The Covenant will not protect the House of Lions. I am not certain it protects even Eve, herself."

"And if I promised you she would have my protection? That we would not let Sif or Loki harm her? I would even help your House of Lions, if you wished it, to see you made free, and I am certain Bhagavan and Ra would guard Eve as well, if it is needed."

He met her eyes then, and brushed a stray tendril of dark hair from her pale cheek. He could never have asked it of her, and now she offered it so easily, without thought to the pain it might bring her. For his sake.

"You deserve more than what I might give you, Athena."

She smiled sadly, pressing his hand to her cheek, and then turned her face to kiss his palm. "Think on it, Thor. At least promise me that."

He let his hand fall away. "You have my word."

§

Tanit guided Hannibal's army through a pass further north, and Athena forced the Romans back when they strayed too near the House of Lions, but the Celts, allied with Hannibal, felt no such restrictions, and more than once, Thor had been forced to defend the lands he had claimed as his own. Fortunately, the Celts traveled often enough with the Gauls, and once his own people recognized his signs, they urged their companions away, begging forgiveness.

Thor granted it, of course, and when he could, blessed them with clear skies and an easy journey. Obedience should never be left unrewarded, and the work he did turned more hearts to the Aesir. Odin could have no complaints, and Thor was careful to return home each night, even if he did not stay longer than it took to make his presence known.

"Father would see you, Thor," Baldur said, catching him on his way into Odin's hall. "Let Tyr go to guard our people this night."

"Better if it is you," Thor said. He did not dare ignore his father's summons, but nor would he send the Norse god of war so near the House of Lions. Tyr would send the Gauls to sack the rich settlement without a thought. But Baldur he might trust not to abuse an innocent people. His brother would not attack a party that had taken no side. *Athena, I must send a brother in my place.*

Baldur smiled, gripping his shoulder in reassurance. "If that is what you wish, I will see they are treated justly in your absence."

I will meet him, and care for your Lions, she answered. *Do what you must.*

"Athena waits for you at the head of the Roman column," he told his brother. "See that she is treated fairly as well."

Baldur nodded, and with a brief and brilliant flash of silver light, he had gone. Thor took another moment to search the hall, noting Sif with a pitcher of mead laughing among the Einherjar—Odin's warriors, chosen from the slain. It made him ache to see the way she looked on them, the light in her eyes and the seeming joy in her heart as she teased and flirted. She had looked at him that way once, and the more he saw of her now, the more he could not help but think it had all been a lie. A game to her, to see how long he might be fooled. It felt as though he had woken from a dream to fall into a nightmare.

Thor forced himself to turn away, and then he went to find his father.

§

Odin sat alone upon Hlidskjalf, his one eye half-closed, and a raven upon each shoulder, muttering in his ears. Behind the throne, two wolves lounged upon the rushes, ears pricking at Thor's entrance. They were new additions to Odin's menagerie, and from what he had heard in the hall, a gift of the Trickster. At best it made them trouble, and at worst, spies. But Odin was no fool. He would not keep them in his presence if they did not serve his purposes, somehow.

Thor closed the door silently behind him, and waited. From the high seat, a god could see the entire world with a single glance, but only Frigg and Odin themselves were permitted use of the silver throne. A lesser god would go mad seeing everything at once. Some even claimed it was because Frigg had already lost her mind in the seas of fate that Hlidskjalf did not trouble her, but Thor was not inclined to believe his step-mother insane. Inclined to riddles, perhaps, but nothing worse. Certainly she had always shown Thor more understanding and compassion in his youth than he had ever received from his father.

"There is trouble in my house, Thor," Odin said, his gaze still unfocused. Even his voice was distant. "And my son falls prey to the Trickster's wiles."

"Not Baldur, surely."

Odin grunted, brushing the ravens from his shoulders. They squawked, flapping to the rafters and settling there to stare at Thor in accusation. "Sif's foolishness is one thing, but yours, Thor? Did you not learn your lesson from Jarnsaxa, that you credit Loki's lies as truth?"

Thor flushed, his jaw tightening until his teeth ached. "You are wrong, Father, I have learned too well. It seems there are none among the Aesir willing to speak the truth when it comes to my wife."

"And if we had spoken, would you have heard it?" Odin scoffed. "Your loyalty has always left you blinded. To Jarnsaxa, to Sif, to this daughter of Elohim, and before them, to the Trickster, himself. Do you still not understand, Thor? Ymir woke because of you! All the Jotuns you terrorized at the Trickster's behest, calling to their father, drawing him from his slumber. And now you would see us all destroyed a second time, cast out into the void with no people, no world to retreat to!"

"I have done nothing but make peace in this world, at your command." Thunder growled outside, and Thor's hands balled into fists. He had not been the only one terrorizing Frost Giants in those days, and until Thor had involved himself with Jarnsaxa, Odin had been all too happy to overlook his excursions with Loki. Indeed, Odin had overlooked him altogether. "What happened with Ymir was Loki's doing, and if in my fool youth, I served as his tool, where was my father to stop him? To stop me? Or is that what you did—is that what Sif was?"

"Jarnsaxa was beneath you!" Odin rose from his high seat, and the wolves rose with him, heads low and hackles rising, responding to his father's fury. "Sif saw the truth, even if you could not. She knew her duty. But you, you are your mother's son, more interested in what lies beyond the next mountain than in your family, loyal to everything but me!"

"All the wisdom in the universe, and this is what you believe." Thor curled his lip and lightning flashed outside, leeching the color from the room. But even after it had faded, Thor saw only blacks and grays and whites.

His whole life, orchestrated by his father, manipulated by Sif to bind him to Asgard, to the Aesir. He could never have believed it, no matter what the Trickster said, but to hear it from Odin's lips— his body buzzed and crackled with lightning, fire licking at his veins, but his head was clear. For the first time in eons. Odin's wolves slunk back into their corners, tails between their legs.

"How many Jotuns did you betray," Thor asked quietly, his voice utterly calm, "then call upon me to defend Asgard when they dared object? And every time, I did as you asked, without question, without a moment's doubt. Every time I slaughtered them, to prove myself, to make you proud."

"Until Jarnsaxa bewitched you," Odin said, throwing it all away with a flick of his fingers, and the bite of bitterness in his words. "Until she gave you two bastard sons and whispered peace in your ear. Well, I have given you peace, Thor. I have given you this world, where you need not war, and still you betray me! Still you turn from us! For what? What is it this earth goddess promises that I have not already given?"

"The only thing I ever wanted of you, Father," Thor sneered. "The only thing I ever asked of my wife. Though fool that I am, I did not know the lie until I experienced the truth. Love is what she promised me, and unlike you and Sif, it was no hollow thing." His skin burned white hot, static skating over his body, tickling his palms, but he would not accept its pull. Today, he would not storm away from Asgard, would not flee his father with the expedience of lightning. Today, he would stand firm. "And as long as she lives, as long as she thinks of me with fondness and the memory of our life together brings her comfort, I will honor her for it. I will love her above all else in this world and the next. And there is nothing you can do to stop it."

Thor turned his back on his father, on his king, with deliberate insult, and left the hall.

CHAPTER TWENTY-EIGHT
Present

Eve was unpacking her things when she realized it was missing. In spite of weight restrictions, she had brought several books along with her on their honeymoon, to read on the beaches of Mau Piti. Garrit had teased her, but when she had lain out in the sun, she noticed he brought a few of his own, too. Pleasure reading. And neither one of them would have brought anything so delicate as the journal.

"Garrit?" she called back into the hall.

He laughed when he found her in the library. "Checking to be certain everything is still in its place?"

She smiled, but she didn't mean it, distracted by the absence within the glass case.

The humor in his expression faded almost immediately. "What's wrong?"

"I can't find the journal." She pulled books from the cabinet, careful of the more fragile items. Old leather fragmented and flaked in her hands. Garrit had mentioned sending several for restoration and recopying, but surely he wouldn't send the journal without telling her. She put the books back gently. "Did you do something with it?"

"No." He checked the cabinet again, and the end table near her favorite chair. "Did you leave it in the bedroom?"

She frowned. "I don't remember taking it out of the library. I left it right here." She touched the spot beneath the bronze lamp. A scrap of paper poked out from beneath the base, tucked there as if to keep it from being lost. She pulled it out and unfolded it.

You'll get it back.

She stared at the script until Garrit took the paper from her. A muscle along his jaw twitched, and he murmured something in French she didn't catch. A curse, she thought, flinching from his anger, poorly banked. "Adam."

"He said he wanted to read it while he was here. I wouldn't let him." She should have known it would only encourage him when she refused to allow it.

He crumpled the note in his fist, his eyes dark. "Predictable of him, really. The man believes he is above any decency of manner. I begin to think he does not understand the word no."

"You don't know him." She took the paper back, opening it up. In all these years, she'd never seen his handwriting. During her life as Helen, no one but scribes and record keepers wrote anything, though she had made it her business to learn what she could.

Garrit tilted her head back up with a finger beneath her chin. His lips were pressed into a thin line as he searched her eyes. "Neither do you, Abby."

She pulled away from his hand and looked back at the note. The whole situation made her resentful. Of Adam. Of Garrit, for being right. "So what do we do?"

"Call Mia and ask her to return it. I doubt she'll believe he stole it, but we could say it was mistakenly packed with their things." He shrugged. "If I have to, I'll go retrieve it personally."

"You don't think he'll give it back willingly? He hasn't yet broken his word, has he?"

He turned away, running his hand through his hair. "He hasn't had a choice, Abby. Crossing into our lands is one thing, thieving a family heirloom is something else entirely."

"Garrit, that doesn't make any sense."

He sighed. "No, I suppose it doesn't."

She studied the way his shoulders tensed while he talked. The uneasy way he looked toward the window. The way everyone had been jumping at the thunderstorms. Even Ryam. And Adam, keeping his own secrets. Or maybe they were the same secrets. All of it.

"What exactly is going on?"

He looked back at her then, his lips pressed thin. There were too many lines in his face, for a man who wasn't even thirty. "There are things at work here that are so far beyond me I wouldn't be able to explain even if I wanted to. Even if I was permitted."

"Permitted?" She took his hand and pulled him around to face her. "I could lift it right from your mind, Garrit."

"But you won't." It was said so quietly, his gaze holding hers. "Will you?"

She dropped his hand as though he'd burned her. She wanted more than anything to think there was something more about her family, something she didn't understand, something that would keep them safe. God's protection, perhaps, lingering somehow through Reu's children. But stealing the knowledge from Garrit's mind was a step closer to Adam. And the idea of doing that to her own husband made her sick.

Garrit nodded, some of the lines around his mouth easing. "There's another copy of the journal in the vault. The original. I cannot promise it's legible anymore, but we might restore it if the other is lost."

She looked at the door, unable to meet his eyes. She'd been tempted, so tempted to simply take the answers she sought, and Garrit stood there, more relaxed with every word, trusting her in spite of it. "I've been meaning to go down there anyway. It's been nearly five hundred years since I looked at any of it."

"It would take you months to sort through it all." He caught her hand as she stepped back and pulled her into his arms. "Abby, I love you. If I could tell you everything, I would."

"But you can't."

"I'm sorry." He rested his forehead against hers, his hands framing her face.

She closed her eyes and wished that Adam had never come into her life again. That things could go back to the way they were, without any secrets.

She touched his face. Ran her fingers through his hair. And then she kissed him. Her husband. Her family. Her love.

Having just arrived home from their honeymoon, a kiss was the only encouragement he needed, and for a time, it was enough to make them both forget what they were fighting about.

§

Eve lay awake in bed for a long time afterwards, wondering if she carried a child. Motherhood had never frightened her after the first time. She had always known it was part of her purpose, part of what made her unique. Her children, with rare exception, were always born strong and healthy. And those exceptions had been miscarriages, early in the pregnancy, and only in situations where she hadn't cared for her body as well as she could have. God had made her strong, but the babies in her womb were only human. Mortal and weak, as Adam would have said.

She had known her fair share of poor households, and lives of poverty. She had been a pauper more times than she could count. In those lives, she had been careful of pregnancy, seeking to avoid bringing a child into the world until she knew she could care for it properly. Simple things that ordinarily she wouldn't worry about for herself. Food, water, shelter, clothing. But as a woman of means, in the DeLeon household where any child would be celebrated and cared for, there was no reason to worry. No reason to wait. Garrit would make a fine father, as Ryam had. It was only Adam that worried her. So close now, no matter how far away he was, as the husband of her sister. It wouldn't be the first time he had threatened a child of her body. Or the first time his presence had been a threat to her and her family.

She pressed her hand to her belly, below her navel. Would whatever protected her here on the estate also protect her child from his threat? Did she dare trust that Adam would keep his word, and do no harm to her family now that he was married to Mia?

"Abby." Garrit's hand covered hers on her stomach, and he kissed her cheek as he pulled her against his body. "You're worrying again."

She turned her head to look at him and smiled to see him studying her. He must have been watching her for some time. "How can you tell?"

He raised his hand to her face, smoothing the hair away from her forehead. "You scowl." He touched his fingertip to the spot between her eyebrows. "And your brow wrinkles right here."

"You imagine it, I think." She kissed his temple and nestled against him.

He tucked her head beneath his chin and she felt him sigh. A contentedness leached from his body into hers without conscious effort and eased her mind into a pleasant lassitude. "*Ma jolie femme.* Always with the weight of the world on your shoulders. I never imagined I would be here, in the heart of this madness, but I would not trade you for anything in the world."

"Even when I frustrate you to the point of shouting?"

He chuckled. "Even then. Those same things that frustrate me, I love." But she caught the shift in his mood as the silence stretched between them. "I could wish your damned brother hadn't stolen that book."

"He'll return it." She wasn't sure what made her so certain, but she was sure. "I think he just wanted to understand."

He shifted slightly, his body stiffening beside hers. "You forgive him too easily."

"It was a long time ago, Garrit. It's only right to allow that people change, and most do so within decades, never mind the generations he's spent suffering for his sins." She propped herself up on an elbow to see his face. He was scowling at the ceiling and she smoothed the lines away. "But this isn't about forgiveness. The weight of all those years of war and pain, being unable to learn from the mistakes of each previous life, but forced to look back on them all at once from this lifetime. I pity him for it, more than anything."

He raised his hand to her face again, caressing her cheek. "I fear I was not raised to sympathize with his plight."

"Maybe it's for the best that you don't." She contemplated her stomach again. "I sometimes forget there are other things worth fearing in this world beyond my brother's arrogance."

His hand covered hers again and he studied her. "What is it that's worrying you?"

She sighed and lay back on the bed, covering her eyes with her arm and trying not to let her memories crowd out her present. She couldn't repress them all, but she was married now. She did not need to fear Michael as a married woman and she would not terrorize Garrit with her nightmares.

"The last time Adam knew himself and knew me, he wasn't

above threatening my children."

"Ahh." His touch became almost reverent, even as his mood blackened and his voice dropped to something rougher than whisper. "I am certain this will not be the last time I say it, and I wish I could offer you some kind of proof. But you have no reason to fear for our children."

She pulled her arm away to meet his eyes. "How can you be sure?"

He shook his head. "Because he wants you, Abby. Even if he could harm them, if he's half as smart as you are, he must realize harming the people you love will only drive you further away."

"Marriage isn't in any way the commitment it used to be. He could just as easily leave Mia as stay with her." She frowned at her own words. And Garrit's explanation troubled her deeply. He was right. None of this would end in this life. Married or not, as long as they both lived, as long as Adam remembered, Michael would be watching. And if somehow, she forgave him, learned to treat him as a brother in truth as well as word, let her guard down for even a moment….

"It wouldn't serve his purposes to do so, and if he did we'd all be better for it. Though, he seems to me too traditional for divorce." His scowl deepened. "Not unlike you, much as I prefer not to consider the things you have in common."

She shivered, more from her own thoughts than his words. "I don't like to think about it either."

"Then do not think at all, *mon amour*." His fingers twined through hers and he brought her hand to his lips, kissing her palm. "Not of him."

And then he distracted her the way only a French man could, utterly and completely.

CHAPTER TWENTY-NINE
Creation

§

They set out under the glare of the sun, the warm roughness of Reu's hand in hers Eve's only comfort. The robes protected much of their bodies from the light, which turned their exposed skin pink and then red, but it did nothing to save them from the heat. Reu draped the scraped hide fur-side down over their heads as they walked, shading their faces from the sun, and it eased some of the discomfort for a time. But even that wasn't enough, and Eve nearly cried with relief when they stumbled across another stream in the grasses.

She dropped to her knees in the mud and cupped the water in her hands to drink, cool and clean. The wetness of the mud soothed her skin where it had burned and she rubbed it on her arms until Reu saw what she was doing and stopped her, washing the dirt from her body and suggesting she lay in the water instead.

He sat on the bank, the skin draped for shelter, and watched as she immersed herself, not even stopping to remove her robe first, though she did not feel as self-conscious about her nakedness now that her body had been joined to his. She closed her eyes and let the water flow over her reddened skin, keeping only her face free of the stream so she could breathe.

Distracted until that moment by her discomfort, she felt again as though she were being watched, studied with intense curiosity. It had begun to take a greater shape now, though there were no words. A sense of otherness, strangeness. She opened her eyes, looking to the banks around them, but there was nothing in the grass she could see.

Eve pushed it from her mind, and made no mention of it to Reu, as he seemed troubled enough by the search for shelter and the need for food. They had made another meal from the carcass before they had left it, but they would both be hungry again before night fell, and the idea of hunting and killing another animal themselves made her uneasy.

"We should make it to the other side before the sun sets, I think," he said.

She left the water reluctantly, and moved to sit beside him. The wetness of her garment was comfortable, though the sun leeched the moisture from it almost at once. What they might have seen of the Garden was obscured by the masses of angels that had flocked to it, waiting just outside its walls. She didn't know what made them wait, or when they would act. Perhaps Adam had not eaten of the fruit, and they would not cast him out after all. Or maybe they were waiting for him to eat of it. Either way, she and Reu would have that much more time together before he arrived.

"Do you think there will be fruit trees?" It was a hopeless question. Nothing here was what they wished it would be.

Reu spread the skin over her when she was settled beside him. "I can't imagine that God would make this world devoid of fruit trees, save for the Garden. But I would be happy for bushes of berries."

"Or trees with nuts," she agreed.

He laughed. "We could live very well off acorns and almonds." He sighed and rose, offering her his hand and pulling her to her feet beside him. "We should keep going. I'd like to find shelter before the others are cast from the Garden. It will go easier for them, if we are not all wandering endlessly."

She let him lead her on, keeping her hand in his. These golden grasses scratched her skin, and her feet were sore. "Will they come to us? When they have Adam?"

"I hope they will. That they'll see Adam has led them falsely."

"We're only two, Reu. Even with the help of fire, if they follow Adam still, and he wants to harm us, I'm not sure what will happen."

His hand tightened around hers. "We'll find a way. The greatest threat has passed, now. As my wife, he cannot touch you. If you had not wanted me, I would have suggested you take Lamech as your husband when they joined us. He would have been willing."

She considered his words, and the words of the angels the previous day, as they walked on in silence for a time. Something had bothered her about what they had said, and the serpent before them. "What was the greatest threat, Reu? That you are oath sworn to protect me from?"

He was silent for such a long time she wondered if he had heard, but in his mind, it was clear the question troubled him as much as the answer. She waited for him to find the words, or the strength to speak them.

"The angels fear that if you join with Adam, you will create a Godchild. Lucifer told me something similar, though I wasn't sure I believed him. That's all I can tell you. They didn't explain themselves further."

She frowned, picking her way through the grass as carefully as she could to avoid further discomfort to her feet. "Having a husband will stop him?"

"God's law stops him. He cannot take a woman who has chosen another. It is forbidden."

"What will stop him without God?" She knew too well the ease with which Adam had thrown away the limitations of God's laws. He had no respect for any law but his own.

"We will." There was a new determination in his voice. "We have already, with our marriage. As long as we love one another, that binding protects us both even from his power. And the others will help us. I will not let him force you to live in fear. I know the law, and if he will not abide by it, he will not be welcome among us."

She saw the tension in his jaw, the way his eyes darkened with anger and resolve. It was easy to believe when there was no room in his mind for failure. Before, Reu's protection of her had been yielding. He had hesitated to act until she had known her own mind. Now that she had chosen, there was no uncertainty, nothing to give him pause. He would find a way to protect her, whatever that meant.

They found caves at the base of the mountain, but it was well after dark, and they were stumbling by the light of a torch and the crescent moon. The shelter was shallow, and they did not see water nearby, but they were both too tired and too cold to continue looking.

They used the torch to light a fire near the mouth and Reu curled his body around hers, under the fur from the gazelle, and not even the cold kept her from falling asleep.

§

Eve woke to soft footsteps on stone and a softer whuffling. Hot air blew against her face and she stared into gold eyes and ivory teeth the length of her smallest finger. The animal's curiosity overwhelmed her, and she scrambled back from its reach.

The lion snarled at the sudden movement, its eyes becoming slits, and one massive paw, claws unsheathed, grasped the edge of her robe, stopping her. She tried to tug it free, but the lion snarled again. She froze. Its nose and whiskers twitched delicately as it sniffed the air around her, tickling her skin.

She glanced to where Reu still lay under the fur blanket. His eyes were open, his face tense, his hands in fists. She felt his caution and fear, warring with the desire to act. She swallowed against the tightness in her throat and held still.

The lion released her robe, though its nose didn't stop twitching. It sat back on its hindquarters and began to lick a paw without taking its eyes from her. This was the curiosity she had felt yesterday, the interest in her otherness. The lion had followed them across the grassland, staying out of sight, waiting for an opportunity to inspect them. Now that it had backed away from her, she could see blood on its muzzle, which it began almost at once to wash away.

Reu shifted, and the lion turned its head, ears perking and narrow eyes focusing on him. It growled and stalked forward, stopping to smell the fur. Eve could sense its confusion. A roar from outside the cave caught its attention, and the lion turned abruptly away, padding back out. Eve exhaled, relief flooding through her, but the lion did not even go a stone's throw from the mouth of the cave before it gave a roar of its own and lay in the dirt and grass.

She was shaking, trembling, her heart pounding in her chest. Reu crept to her then, and pulled her with him to the back of the cave, wrapping her in his arms and holding her against him.

"Shh," he said, when she started to weep, gulping back sobs. His eyes were on the lion, which rose to its feet at the approach of another of the tawny beasts. She watched it through his eyes, her face hidden against his neck. The lions greeted one another, rubbing their heads against each other's bodies and making rumbling noises.

He stroked her hair, trying to calm her, though she could feel his own worry. Her heartbeat slowed and her breathing became more regular again. The two lions threw themselves back to the ground and yawned.

"They hunt at night," Reu was saying, his voice just a breath against her ear. "They should sleep soon, and perhaps we can get around and away without waking them."

"What do they want?"

He held her closer and she felt him shake his head. "You would know better than I would. A full belly, and a place to sleep out of the sun, maybe. And we're lucky their stomachs were already full, or I might have been their next meal." Then he hushed her and stroked her hair again, because she began to tremble. "You're safe, Eve. A lion can't kill you. Nothing in this world but Michael's sword will kill you or Adam before your time. Elohim has made it so. You're safe."

But it wasn't her life that she feared for. It was the image in her mind of the carcass on the bank of the first, wide stream, and what those teeth and claws could do to Reu's warm skin. Reu, her husband and protector. Reu, who she loved, who she knew she was meant for, whose children she was meant to bear.

She had to keep him safe.

CHAPTER THIRTY
180 BC

Odin refused him the right to a divorce, of course. And refused, too, to forbid Sif from Thorgrim's village on the coast. Between Sif's threats and his father's determination, Thor was tied more closely to Asgard than he had ever been. During the days, he might go out, traveling by lightning to any lands he knew, but he could not risk an absence of more than a night, for fear of what Sif might do. Nor did he dare to frequent the House of Lions and the lands Zeus had ceded him. Ra took pity upon him, and Athena, too, watching over them, even reminding them of their history when they lost their way.

But with Thor's declaration of loyalty to Eve, Sif and Loki gave up all pretense of disinterest, flaunting themselves before him at every opportunity. It wore at his patience and his pride, leaving his temper badly frayed, and the thunder of his anger lurked much too near. So Thor walked the Earth, and when he returned to Asgard, he drank to drown the fire in his blood, but his mind wandered, reaching toward Eve, and what he could not have. So he drank more, to keep himself from thinking and let the Valkyries flirt and tease him to distraction.

Perhaps he drank too much.

"Thor."

He lifted his head from the table and tried to focus his eyes on the person before him. Too much mead. The voice was odd, though without seeing who spoke, he couldn't put his finger on why.

There was a sigh, and then he was slapped across the face. Hard.

Anger and lightning burned away the blur in his eyes, and when Athena raised her hand to slap him again, he caught it by the wrist, rising to his feet with a growl. "You have no business here, Greek."

"Because you're so obviously drunk, I'll forgive the intended slur." She pulled her arm free from his grasp and her eyes flashed as she glared up at him. "I came at your brother's invitation, though I cannot say Odin is entirely pleased."

Thor grunted and dropped back to the bench, rubbing his face and trying to calm himself. Athena was his ally. Eve's protector. Tora. His Eve. His lovely, brave Eve. "She is well? Sif and Loki—?"

Athena's gray eyes narrowed. "This is neither the time nor the place for that discussion, Thor. How could you allow yourself to become this—what could you possibly be hoping to accomplish by drooling on the table?"

"Peace," he grumbled, but he let the lightning consume the alcohol in his blood and tried to clear his mind. Using his power this way always left him with a ferocious headache, and he did not love Athena overmuch for giving him need to abandon his stupor. "As long as I remain here, drooling, as you put it, Tora's village is left alone, and so are the others. But I can hardly tolerate that—" he jerked his chin up, indicating Sif, where she sat upon the Trickster's lap, "without help."

Her voice softened, and she touched his arm. "This is not peace. This is poison and pain. Your brother says you spend your days drinking until you black out, and he carries you to your bed. If she is holding your people hostage—"

"What?" he demanded, unable to hide his bitterness. "I should appeal to my father?" He barked a laugh, but didn't look at her. Didn't want to see the judgment in her eyes or the pity in her face. Easier to watch Sif, feeding Loki bits of fruit and cheese, tracing her fingertip over the curve of his ear. "It is no business of yours what goes on in these lands."

"It is not the lands I care about, nor even the people. We have need of you. Sif and Loki have not been idle while you were leashed to Asgard."

He watched Sif rise, casting him a sly smile as she took the Trickster with her from the hall. It seemed she did not even care enough to be jealous of Athena, now that she had Loki to satisfy her. "No, I do not suppose they have."

"Thor." Athena's hand tightened on his arm, her fingers digging into the muscle and drawing his attention. He glowered at her, but her expression stopped him. She looked gray with stress and worry, lines fanning out from around her eyes that had not been there before. "They are calling for Eve's death."

Thunder cracked so loud overhead the rafters shook, a rain of dust falling from the ceiling. "The Covenant—"

"Makes room for sanctions against another god or goddess, if it is agreed to in Council. But Adam and Eve are not part of the Council, and the angels refused to take part in the agreement when it was made. She has no defense."

His eyes burned, and the headache he had thought ferocious before became blinding. Or perhaps that was the lightning, hazing his vision. "She has done nothing wrong, made no threat to any of us. She does not even know we live! What reason could they possibly give for this?"

"Loki argues her very presence is a threat. And if she does learn of us, she might choose to give herself to Adam. The two of them together, and the godchild they might create will unmake the world, destroying every living thing upon it, and with a god of that power laying claim, we will be fortunate to escape with our lives. He says it is the only way to protect our people."

Thor sneered, rising to his feet. "Loki argues, does he? And his silver tongue serves him well, I am sure, no matter how offensive the lie."

"Thor," Athena's tone held caution, her nails biting into his skin. "If you lose your temper now, lash out blindly—"

"Not blindly," he said. "No, I would not miss the sight of it for anything after all I've suffered. Have you any idea how long I've wondered why Odin tolerated that filthy cur? But I see, now. I see exactly what purposes he serves, and I have had enough. The Covenant that binds us will be honored in letter as well as spirit, whether that is my father's will or not!"

He shook off Athena's hand, and ignored her call for him to calm, to see reason. He'd had enough of reason, enough of wisdom, for it had only brought him to this place, leashed like a dog to his father's throne. If Odin wished him to remain in Asgard, so be it. But Thor would not stand by and let them strip him of his honor, too. He would not let Loki, Sif, or Odin use the relationships he had built for the Aesir for ill-purpose. He had a right to extract payment for the insult and dishonor, and he would do so now.

Thor shouldered his way past his brothers, past his sons, snarling at their questions and concerns. Of course it did not stop Baldur from following, or Athena, her pale face even whiter still, but he did not care. It was better to have witnesses, besides. Baldur would defend his right to justice, and what Baldur judged fair, no Aesir would argue. Not even Odin, though he might still punish Thor for disobedience of some kind.

As long as he silenced the Trickster before he spread more lies about Eve, it would be worth it.

"Loki!" he bellowed, thunder rumbling beneath the word. He knew where they would be. No god could have failed to notice after all these years. And even Sif was not foolish enough to bring the Trickster back to the cottage, now that Thor spent his nights at home.

The god was lounging in the courtyard of his hall with a group of women, Sif and Sigyn among them. Servants darted in and out from the kitchens bringing food and drink to Loki's guests. Unlike the Aesir, Loki did not care for the cold, and had built an external hearth in his garden. A fire burned low, now, for the sun was still warm. Until Thor covered it with storm clouds.

Loki did not rise, but smirked and raised his mug. "Thor, what a surprise. Sigyn, my love, find some mead for the Odin-son. As much as he can drink!"

Sigyn rose lazily from her position, draped against his chest. "Of course, husband."

Thor did not watch her go. That any goddess had found the Trickster worth marrying, and could suffer his infidelities thereafter, was beyond his capacity for understanding. As it was, Sigyn seemed to do little else beside wait on her husband.

Sif smiled at him, her fingers playing in Loki's hair. "Husband, how kind of you to join us."

"Kindness has little to do with you, I promise."

"Pay him no mind, Sif. Thor is blustering because we found his mistress at last. His honor demands he make threats until I am cowed." Loki smirked, but still did not move to dislodge Sif, and nor did she stir, though her skirts were in clear disarray, the Trickster's hand on the bare skin of her thigh.

Lightning crackled behind his eyes, but he banked his fury, letting his anger cool into the calm of anticipation. Loki would pay for his insults today, and the knowledge settled his temper nicely.

"You will stop spreading your lies by treading on my honor, Loki."

"All in good fun, Thor. You can hardly deny me this smallest of entertainments, when you run about the world fathering children and taking lovers as you please. Though I should have thought you had better taste, Athena. Or is Thor the sexless wonder you've been waiting for?"

Baldur shifted uneasily, behind him. "It is unwise to say such things, Loki, of any god."

"No, brother, let him go on. Let him continue to perjure himself, so there can be no doubt by any who witness that my response is justified." Thor hefted a hammer that had been left beside the fire. No doubt Loki had been attempting to smelt and forge, tired of having to trade with the other pantheons for metal arms, now that there were no dwarves to work for them.

"Perjure myself? Do you deny you took a wife during the exile we shared on earth?" Loki grinned. "I suppose I couldn't blame you if you were only practicing your arts, knowing that when you returned to Sif's bed you would have to live up to my skill."

Thor was surprised by the weight of the hammer, the power. Sparks of lightning wrapped around the shaft, and lit the heart of its head, the weapon magnifying his own strength. This was a hammer brought from the old worlds, then. Stolen from the dwarves themselves. He should not have been surprised to find it near Loki, he supposed, for that one had always taken what he wanted for himself with no regard for the person who possessed it.

"Are you sure you want to keep insulting me, Loki?"

"No insult, Thor, merely fact. Is it not true, Sif? He's so intimidated by you he cannot even perform his husbandly duty, though I would venture he might not be so unmanned if you took the guise of his mortal wife."

Sif glanced over him lazily, her eyes glowing golden. "Shall we test your theory?"

Perhaps he had been mistaken, and this hammer was not for the forge, but forged itself. The Dwarven war-hammer? *Mjölnir*? And Loki and Sif provoking him while he held it. Unwise indeed.

Loki's grin twisted with malice, and Sif rose, her body shifting in the same motion. Golden hair darkened, turning to a rich, chestnut brown, and the lean, hard muscle of her body slimmed and softened, even the glow of her eyes faded into the startling green of Eve's.

Thor stiffened, his grip on *Mjölnir* tightening. She might look like Tora, but her expression lacked Eve's warmth, her love. He growled.

"Change back."

Sif smiled with Eve's face and stretched Eve's arms above her head, like a drowsy leopard, toying with its prey. "What is it about this form, Thor, that drives you so mad?" Her gaze shifted briefly over his shoulder. "I suppose you always favored fey-colored creatures. Is that why you prefer Athena to Aphrodite, too? For her dull, dark hair?"

"Sif," Baldur warned. "You may not insult a guest of Asgard in my presence."

"I do not take offense," Athena said, her voice cool. "We in Olympus have known for some time the worth of Sif's words."

Sif's lip curled, and Thor freed himself from her spell, shaking his head to clear it. Eve would never look on anyone with such open loathing and hostility. Sif brushed by him, and so help him, but even her scent was Tora's. Sunshine and spring rains. But she was not Eve. And if she had her way, if he did not silence Loki, Eve would not live long enough to know him again.

Thor caught Sif by the arm and threw her back to the Trickster.

"An unconvincing display," he growled. "Your game is played and lost. Change back, and do not test me further, Sif, I warn you."

She laughed, falling gracefully to the couch beside Loki, who had not bothered to so much as stretch out an arm to steady her. "You warn me? And what will you do if I disobey? Your precious honor will keep you from striking me, doubly so while I keep this form. And Odin has granted me his protection, besides. I am free to do as I will."

He bared his teeth. "If you wish to test that theory as well, then stay where you are and we will see which of us is more determined. Because I assure you, wife, the bars of my cage are broken."

Maybe it was because the sky had gone black above them, or perhaps because of the calm in his voice, for he had firm control of his temper as he lifted the hammer, but Sif rose, stumbling back, as he advanced. She had too much pride to run, and too much sense to stand between him and the Trickster. He was not certain he was glad of it.

Loki did not so much as sit up when Thor's shadow reached him, his silhouette stretching toward Sif where she had pressed herself to the wall.

"You know what I love most about you, Thor?" he drawled, examining his fingernails.

"I'm sure you have every intention of telling me." *Mjölnir's* handle was shorter than he might have liked, but he'd make do. He tested his grip, but the hammer fit perfectly to his hand, its thirst burning the back of his throat.

Loki lifted his gaze, a terrible grin splitting his face. "You are so easy to drive into a rage. So predictable. And yet, still, you surprised me. I should have known from the beginning it was Elohim's daughter, but you had us all so convinced of your loyalty to Sif. I cannot wait to go to her, dressed in your skin. How startling it will be, when the man she loved appears before her eyes. I think I shall kiss her first, to see how sweet she is, before I beat her bloody and—"

Thor brought the hammer down on his face.

A gasp sounded behind him, and he glanced over his shoulder. Sigyn stood by the kitchen entrance, a mug clutched too tightly in her hands.

"Have no fear, Sigyn. He won't be killed." Even as he said it, Loki was scrambling back, barely stunned by the blow.

"What do you think you're doing, you oaf?" Loki demanded.

"You seem only to understand one language, Trickster."

Thor swung the hammer up with both hands, catching Loki by the chin and throwing him back against the hall. He was sure he heard the crack of his jaw that time, and Loki screamed. The first strike had merely been a warning, without any of his strength behind it. This one was something else entirely, and *Mjölnir* hummed in his hands.

"Thankfully, it is one I speak."

Sigyn began to weep, but Thor ignored her and dragged Loki to his feet by his tunic. Blood poured from his nose and mouth, and Thor guessed he had bitten his tongue. Good.

"If you so much as think of touching her, Loki, or dare whisper another word against her life, no power on this earth or any other will stay my hand. The lesson will last much longer, and damage done to more than just your mouth."

Loki jerked himself free, and spit blood in Thor's face, though his expression did not hide the pain it caused him to do so.

Thor wiped the blood away with the back of his hand, and lightning crackled overhead, though his voice remained eerily calm. "Do you understand me?"

Sigyn pushed past Thor where he stood, still holding the hammer. Loki could not speak around his tongue, and spit again, glaring sidelong as he turned away to the comfort of his wife. It had always galled Loki that he couldn't read minds as Thor did, though he used what strength he had to plant suggestion, and those were powerful enough. His contempt and fury was obvious in the single thought he shared.

As you say, Odin-son.

Thor left his wife behind, but the hammer—the hammer he took with him.

CHAPTER THIRTY-ONE
Present

§

"Oh, Abby! Look at you! Big as a house!" Her mother hugged her while Garrit welcomed her father. "Has Mia arrived yet? Garrit is so kind to invite us all here for the holidays."

"Yes, he's very thoughtful." She stepped back to let her parents into the house.

Not that Garrit was at all thrilled with the idea of inviting Adam back into his home. They had discussed it for weeks and ultimately, there had been no other choice. Eve was safest in France, and the less travel at this point in her pregnancy the better. Since Garrit couldn't invite her parents without Mia, and he couldn't invite Mia without Adam, he would suffer her brother's presence once more. And Eve would reassure herself that her sister still wasn't being manipulated while she tried not to have nightmares of Michael.

"Maybe we'll get lucky and Adam will return what he stole from you without further threat," Garrit had muttered the morning her family was supposed to arrive.

"Garrit. Try to be civil."

"Have you ever known me to be anything otherwise?" She raised an eyebrow at him, but he only kissed her cheek. "I'll be civil. Unless I'm provoked."

"The trick is to be civil even after you're provoked."

He laughed. "Yes, and you do that so well when it comes to Mia. I can only imagine how long that civility will last faced with your parents, your sister, and your brother-in-law."

In spite of the challenges, and Garrit's doubts, Eve was pleased she wouldn't have to travel. Even climbing the stairs took more energy than she had lately. Just standing in the foyer with her parents was making her feet swell.

"Come in, please. Make yourselves at home." Garrit had waved to one of the staff to collect their luggage from the car. That was another argument she had lost as her stomach had swelled with his son. Staff to cook and clean and do all the things she normally would. "Abby, I am certain your parents cannot expect you to wait on them in your state."

"Oh, dear, no!" Her mother immediately ushered her to one of the sitting rooms. "You shouldn't be on your feet. You look as though you're going to give birth any moment. Really, Abby. There's no need for ceremony."

"Yes, Mum." She sighed and let herself be persuaded into a seat on the couch. Of course if she hadn't been at the door, her mother would have insisted she not laze about. It was only Garrit's obvious desire that she rest which saved her from her mother's censure. She stroked her stomach.

Not much longer now. Less than a month. But Garrit really didn't need to fuss. She had explained to him repeatedly that she was made for this. As long as she ate properly and slept enough, the baby would be just fine, and she would too. Hadn't she borne Ryam six children, all healthy, without a single stillborn baby? That two had died of illness before their fifth birthday had been due to circumstances beyond her control. That she had only lost two had been a miracle in itself in those days, though it paled in comparison to six healthy and easy births. But it was a husband's prerogative to fuss over his wife, she supposed. Ryam had done the same.

"Now, when are you expecting your sister?" her mother pressed.

Garrit poured her mother a glass of wine, and her father a tumbler of port before sitting down beside Eve. "Before dinner, I'm sure," he answered for her. "I was surprised you didn't all choose to travel together."

Her father sat down with his port and an appreciative sigh. "Oh, well. That Ethan has his own way of going about things. Wouldn't hear of taking the train. Of course, your mother and I can't stand to fly. Will your parents be joining you for the holidays as well, Garrit?"

"*Oui*. They'll be here after dinner, with Aunt Brienne and her family."

Eve tried not to grimace. Garrit wouldn't let Adam into the house without at least his father for help if needed. And Brienne, as matriarch, had been impossible to dissuade. She wouldn't be surprised if Jean arrived at the last minute, too, just to reassure himself Mia wasn't being mistreated.

"A full house, then. Won't that be merry!" Her father raised his glass, using the excuse to drink a good portion of the port.

Garrit smiled politely. "I expect you'll hardly know they're here. It takes quite a number of us before anyone gets crowded."

Eve squeezed his hand. He raised hers to his lips, brushing a kiss across her knuckles. A tendril of jealousy slipped into her mind, followed by a presence she recognized immediately as Adam. She shivered and hoped Garrit would think it only a response to his caress. But something must have shown on her face, because he frowned and stood, excusing himself from the room.

"What was that about, Abby?" her mother asked.

"Ah." She blinked, trying to ignore Adam's soft chuckle in the back of her mind. "I think he heard a car. Mia and Ethan."

"Oh, how wonderful!" Her mother rose and left as well. No doubt on her way to the front door.

Eve sighed and glanced at her father, who didn't seem to be interested in moving further than the table with the rest of the port. He was refilling his glass. "I thought Mia and Ethan were close by?"

"Oh, they are." Her father agreed, swirling the contents of his glass. He sniffed at it, his eyes half closed in pleasure. "But you know your mother. She and Mia have always been thick as thieves. And Ethan keeps your sister busy. He's making her finish her degree at University. Mia wasn't happy about that at all. As quickly as they got married, I wonder if the poor man just didn't want an excuse for a bit of peace and quiet."

She tried not to smile at the idea that Adam had bitten off more than he could chew with her boisterous sister, but it was difficult not to. "Mia can certainly be a challenge."

Hardly, he said in her head.

It's rude to eavesdrop. She cleared her throat, watching the car pull up through the window. "Do you like Ethan?"

Her father smiled, sitting back down on the couch. "What's not to like about him? I never expected Mia would have the sense to marry someone with that kind of stability, but he seems to take good care of her. I think marriage was an adjustment for her."

"No doubt." She tried not to think of the number of ways Adam could be abusing Mia. He had given her his word, and she'd know soon enough anyway. Certainly there was no cloud of influence in her father's mind, and what he described seemed bizarrely normal. "As long as she's happy, I suppose that's all that matters."

"You'll see for yourself, Abby. He's a good influence on her." Then her father grimaced, as the noise of the two women reached them. It sounded remarkably like the squealing of girls on the playground. "Your mother on the other hand..."

Eve didn't need him to finish. Her mother had always fed Mia's histrionics. She could hear them in the hall now, and she pushed herself to her feet with an effort. But it was only Mia and her mother who walked into the room. Eve frowned. That couldn't be a good sign.

"Oh, Abby! Look at you!" Mia laughed and hugged her. "I don't think you'd even fit on a plane. No wonder Garrit invited us all here."

"Did you have a comfortable trip?" She was faintly concerned that Adam was alone somewhere with Garrit. "Where's your husband?"

Mia had already taken a seat next to their mother after a perfunctory greeting to their father. "Garrit whisked him off somewhere." She waved a hand dismissively. "I'm sure they'll be along shortly."

Eve was torn between the need to play host to her family, and the desire to go find them before someone started throwing punches.

Please, Eve. A little bit of a faith, if you don't mind. Then she heard him sigh in irritation. *Your husband asks me to tell you to stay with your parents. Why didn't you ever tell him we could talk this way? He doesn't seem very happy about learning it from me.* He chuckled. *If I had known you were keeping secrets...*

You would've told him anyway. But she did sit down again. Thankfully with Mia's arrival the burden of carrying a conversation with her mother was lifted. She wished she could go take a nap. When Garrit came back, perhaps she could close her eyes for few minutes.

You're exhausted. There was a hint of alarm to his tone. *I didn't realize—Mia never told me that you were pregnant.*

Of course not. It probably hadn't occurred to her to mention the reason they were celebrating the holidays in France. *I'm fine. What are you two doing?*

Oh, the usual. I'm signing away my soul in exchange for permission to cross into DeLeon lands. Promising I'll be on my best behavior. Though, it makes more sense now I know you're pregnant. I thought they were just being more difficult than usual to irritate me.

Signing away your soul is normal?

Her question was met with silence, and the abrupt disappearance of Adam's mind from her senses. She rubbed at her forehead. At least she was already sitting down. If Garrit had just knocked him unconscious, she wouldn't have to worry about falling when she went with him. Garrit wouldn't risk it unless Adam had done something extreme. Not that extreme behavior wasn't beyond him.

She turned her attention back to Mia and her mother, but she had no idea what they were talking about anymore. Her father was already on his third glass of port. She tried not to fidget while she waited. What was taking them so long?

"Ethan promised me a new car if I finished in the top of my classes," Mia said.

"How exciting, Mia!" Her mother fluttered. "When will you get your grades?"

"At the end of the week. But I'm sure I did well. He was impossible about it. Always nagging at me about my class work. And studying. I'm sure he'll be an absolute prat again when the next semester starts."

"How do you put up with that, Mia?" Eve regretted saying anything the minute her mother looked up at her, her lips pursed.

"I imagine she puts up with it the same way you put up with your in-laws always inviting themselves over."

"They don't invite themselves over. This is their home. Mother, really. I don't see why you're so upset about it. I knew what I was getting into when I married Garrit."

"And your sister didn't?"

She opened her mouth, then shut it at once. There was no possible way she was going to win this argument. And she wasn't even sure why she was having it to begin with. "I was talking to Mia, Mum."

"Ethan isn't any more difficult than Garrit is, I'm sure. Besides, he always gives me plenty of incentive." Mia smirked in a very satisfied manner, and Eve flinched at the lust of her sister's thoughts, taken aback by the strength of them. "Anyway, it doesn't matter. I only have a year and a half left. It seemed silly not to finish."

Eve didn't waste her breath pointing out that Mia had been dead set against finishing her degree not eight months earlier. Regardless of how or why Adam had convinced her to do it, she was glad. It would be easier on her sister to have a degree if Adam abandoned her, or she decided she wanted nothing more to do with him.

She still wasn't sure Adam wouldn't divorce Mia when he had accomplished whatever it was he was trying to do. And he had to be trying to do something. If it was to learn about her, her sister was hardly the most effective tool for that particular endeavor. Mia was much more interested in herself than anyone else. The only thing that made sense made less sense than anything else, and Garrit would never believe Adam was actually in love.

Mia stood up suddenly, smiling and holding her arms out to Adam. He had the nerve to wink at Eve before he took Mia's hands and kissed his wife's forehead.

"Sorry, darling. I didn't mean to keep you waiting." He turned to her mother and bowed over her hand. "Always lovely to see you, Anne. How was the train? Were the seats to your liking?"

"It was wonderful, Ethan. Thank you. Very kind of you." Her mother was smiling at her son-in-law with an expression of absolute adoration.

Eve frowned.

Garrit sank to the couch beside her. "I didn't mean to worry you."

"What took you so long?"

He shrugged, but his eyes were creased with stress. "*Rien de particulier.*"

Nothing in particular, indeed. It had sounded completely particular and incredibly specific from what Adam had said. But her brother turned back to them before she had a chance to voice her disbelief.

"You look radiant, Abby."

Garrit stiffened next to her, his eyes narrowing. Eve searched Adam's face for some kind of barb, any hint that he was mocking her. But there was nothing. His expression was warm, and his smile wasn't even all that charming. Just a smile. Almost brotherly. "Thank you."

He nodded, his eyes flicking to Garrit beside her so quickly she thought she might have imagined it. And then Adam turned to her father, and offered to refill his glass while he was getting his own drink.

Garrit put his arm around her. She rested her head against his shoulder, trying to soothe the worst of his tension away. At this rate, sitting down to dinner would be a relief. She did hope René would be reasonable when he arrived. She wasn't sure if she could take two DeLeon men waiting for an excuse to leap at her brother's throat.

CHAPTER THIRTY-TWO
Creation

❧

As the sun rose, the lions drowsed, and Eve flicked a pebble into the grass near them. Barely an ear twitched in response. Perhaps it would be safe for them to leave the cave. She was starving with hunger, and she knew Reu suffered even more than she did. For her, it was only a mild discomfort, but for him it meant exhaustion and weakness as the days wore on. Adam had been right about that much; God had made her differently than the others.

"We can't stay here," she whispered, though she knew he thought it too. "You need food and water. With the lions asleep, it's the safest opportunity for you to go." She reached for the hide, watching to be sure the noise and movement didn't startle the animals outside. They didn't move.

He grabbed her by the arm, keeping her from rising. "I'm supposed to be protecting you, Eve."

She shook her head. "You said the lions can't hurt me. If they can't hurt me, you don't have to protect me. I have to protect you."

He sighed. "It isn't right for me to leave you."

"Either I'm safe or I'm not, Reu."

"I said they can't kill you. You can be hurt like anyone else, even if you heal without difficulty." He ran his fingers through his hair, staring out at the lions. "Either way, I don't want to risk you. You'll be trapped here if I disturb them."

"And if you don't go first, and the lions wake, there isn't anyone left to protect me when Adam arrives."

He set his jaw, and agreed with a stiff nod. She squeezed his hand and then wrapped the stones Michael had given them inside the fur, pressing it into his hands. "Take this. I'll follow when it's safe."

He crept to the mouth of the cave and waited to see if the lions would notice. When they didn't even flick their tails, he stepped out into the sun and moved cautiously from the cave, giving the animals as much room as possible.

The rocks shifted in the fur, clacking together, and one of the lions lifted its head, looking directly at Reu. He froze, and Eve held her breath, praying for the lion to close its eyes again and go back to its nap.

The cat looked away. Reu crept forward again, moving around a boulder with a final glance over his shoulder. One of the lions rose to its feet and Eve could feel its interest in Reu.

She stepped out of the cave where it could see her, and the lion flicked an ear, its nose twitching and golden eyes slitted. It started rumbling as it had earlier, and then it turned away and padded silently off into the grasses.

The second lion watched her, too, ears following her movement. Eve strained to glimpse where the first lion had gone. It might yet circle back to Reu, where she couldn't see. She turned her back on the second lion, relying on that curious other sense which allowed her to feel it, and followed after Reu. The second lion lost interest, too lazy in the heat of the day to bother.

There was a steep path of loose rock and dirt on the other side of the boulder, and she could see where Reu had slid down the hill side. A curse rose from the stone outcropping below and she slipped down, her feet protesting every bite of the rough stone, her palms and knees scraped raw by the time she reached the bottom. She picked herself up and followed the sound around a pile of rock.

Reu was cornered by the other lion, stretched out in the grass. The cat stared at him, something she couldn't make out struggling in its paws. The lion lowered its head, trapping the wriggling mass, and bit. The crunch and snap of the bone sent a shiver down her spine.

The lion rose, dropping the rabbit, now dead and limp, at Reu's feet. It rumbled and then turned away, walking toward her. She didn't move, not sure what to expect. But the lion only rubbed its head against her hip as it passed her, the rest of its body following with such force that she stumbled sideways.

It disappeared into the grass again and she looked back at Reu. His face was white with shock, and it was several heartbeats before he lifted his gaze from the rabbit and met her eyes. Then he was moving, and his arms were around her, hugging her tightly. She wasn't sure if the tears that came to her eyes were from fear or joy, but she cried, and he held her until she stopped and then wiped away the moisture from her cheeks.

"We should find shelter. And water." He let go of her only to pick up the rabbit from the ground. "And we'll build a fire and eat."

She shook her head. "I don't understand what happened."

He stared at the rabbit in his hand. "I thought when that lion found me again it was over, but it just laid down with the rabbit and stared at me until you came around the rocks. It was as if it was waiting for you."

She frowned, looking after the lion. "Do you think it left the gazelle for us by the river yesterday on purpose?"

"God wouldn't have sent them from the Garden if they couldn't harm us. You saw how easily it killed the rabbit. One bite to the back of its neck." His fingers moved over the body of the animal, feeling the bones where they had been snapped.

She had never seen anything killed before, and it wasn't something she could have imagined doing herself. "Would you have known what to do with it if the lion hadn't killed it for us?"

He grimaced and said nothing, moving from gap to gap between the rocks, looking for a suitable cave, but she felt his discomfort. The idea of taking a life was upsetting to her, too. But not as upsetting as the idea of losing Reu, watching him die like Adam had said she would.

Adam said the world had been made for him. For the two of them. All creation, all the animals and plants, made to serve him and give him pleasure. Made to serve them both? If Adam could impose his will on Lilith, a woman, what could he do to animals? To a lion? If he wanted something badly enough, would they obey, even without his conscious command?

What about what she wanted?

"Here, Eve," he called. She followed his voice and found him on a rise, standing in the mouth of a cave. He smiled and took her hand. "There's water in the back, and several more chambers on either side. Large enough for the others, if they want to join us."

The others. Adam. Adam with an entire pride of lions at his back, obeying his every thought. Her stomach knotted as she walked through the cave. There was a crevasse in the ceiling of the largest chamber that allowed more light than just what the mouth could provide.

Fire wasn't going to be enough. Not to save them from Adam if he could command armies of beasts. She had to know what she was capable of, what Adam was capable of.

"Eve?"

"I'll bring back kindling." She left the cave before he could respond.

§

The lions were still sleeping in the sun. But there were more of them now, including one that was much larger, with a heavy mane around its neck and head. It yawned, showing teeth that made her heart race. She wondered if they could feel her fear the way she could feel their indolence.

She pushed away the worry and focused her mind on what she wished to accomplish, though she had no clear idea of how to go about it. Adam had used touch when he had attempted to manipulate her, but that was before they had eaten of the fruit, and clearly she had not needed to touch these lions to compel them to hunt for her.

It didn't help that she questioned the rightness of her desire. If she forced these lions to obey her, was she any better than Adam? Should not the animals have wills of their own as well? She thought about going back to speak with Reu, but she didn't want to admit she might have forced the lions to act on her behalf. She didn't want to admit she might share that ability with Adam—not just to read minds, but to control them.

None of this would stop Adam from acting, if he thought he could regain control. She was sure of it. But she did not want to control the others or these beasts. Nor did she want to lead, though that seemed to be what she had been made to do. Why had God not given her the desire for it, if it was his intention? Why did Adam seek control and power so fiercely, while she, who seemed meant to lead these people, wanted little to do with any of it?

She sat down in the grass with a clear view of the lions as they lounged in the sun. It was not a blistering heat, yet, but Eve imagined she would be grateful for the shelter and shade of the caves before long. She wondered if the lions, too, would seek some kind of shelter. She plucked at a piece of the tall grass, ripping it into pieces with her fingers. Maybe that would be a good way to test things. They certainly didn't seem to want to do much in the heat. She focused on the largest lion, the one with the big mane of darker fur, and pictured it standing up and walking to the shelter of the shallow cave where she and Reu had spent the night.

The lion sat up, looking back over its shoulder at the cave. She felt it consider the idea. Although, consider might have been too human a word. She pictured the lion moving again, imagined the coolness of the cave, out of the sun. She remembered how good the stone had felt against her skin in those first days. How much more comfortable it would be than sitting in the sun.

One of the other lions rose to its feet, padding the short distance to the cave and throwing itself back down on its side. It rumbled with what seemed like pleasure. The largest lion followed, sniffing around the cave and what was left of their fire before lying against the stone in the shade.

There were two more females. Eve repeated the same images. Moving into the cave. The coolness of the stone. The relief from the sun. Their tails switched and their ears flicked before each, in turn, rose and moved into the shade of the cave.

The sun beat down on her, and she gathered some of the dryer grasses for kindling. Maybe they could make the fire outside, to keep it from heating up the cave. But it was cooler on the edge of the mountains than it had been in the valley, and there were more trees and bushes, though none seemed to bear any fruit. She decided to take her own advice and find shelter from the sun and heat. This first attempt had been successful, and she didn't think the lions were hurt by it, perhaps they had even been helped. Maybe all she had to do was provide suggestion and encouragement. Maybe these animals would learn to trust her, and from that trust they could work together, and bond not just with her, but with Reu too.

She went back to the new cave. Reu was sitting just inside, working the sharp edge of the stone against the fur from the rabbit to scrape the flesh from the skin. The rest of the carcass was tied around a thick branch, suspended between two larger stones.

He looked up when he heard her and nodded to the kindling. "I was beginning to worry you'd been caught by something."

She sat down next to the carcass and laid the grasses in the middle of the stone circle, picking up the angel's stones to strike sparks. "I don't think they'll hurt me."

The grass caught and flared. She felt his eyes on her, but she kept her focus on the flame, feeding more grass, and then smaller sticks.

He came to sit beside her, turning the meat of the rabbit so it was closer to the fire. "I hope you're right, Eve. That they will be our friends and not our enemies. But I don't think they were made to be."

"I think I can find a way."

She felt him watching her again. "You feel them, don't you?"

She nodded, and looked up at him. "I don't want to force them to do anything. But maybe I can find a way to ask them?"

"Promise me you'll be careful." His expression was serious.

"I'll be careful," she agreed.

He sighed and looked away, out at the grass and the bushes. She felt the conflict in his thoughts, between asking her not to, and encouraging her to do more. He looked back at her face, and his eyes searched hers.

"If I can do it, Reu, there's no reason Adam can't."

His eyes darkened and his mind cleared. He nodded. "Tell me how to help."

CHAPTER THIRTY-THREE
172 BC

Thor bowed respectfully to the immense statue of a seated god, hewn from the rock. The stone scraped as the massive head inclined.

The god was everywhere in his lands as Brahman, taking many forms, but it was only respectful to address him in a manner which allowed response. Bhagavan had been the first to join Ra in the world, and between them, they had created the Covenant, by which every god was now bound. Every god but Elohim's twins, Adam and Eve.

"Bhagavan-Shiva," Thor said, "I beg your forgiveness and your indulgence for my intrusion, and thank you for allowing my passage."

One massive arm stretched out, grinding rock against rock, acknowledgment and invitation both. Thor bowed again, and entered the temple.

The dampness of the jungle around them brought sweat to his brow, but the temple was cooler, if not dryer. Thor followed the path of recently trampled vines, and unlike his last visit, it led him upwards. Crumbling staircases seemed held together by vegetation, and Thor had no choice but to trust that Bhagavan would not let him fall.

He had visited the god before, of course, while journeying for Odin, and found Bhagavan to be a most understanding and excellent host. But this trip was different, made for Eve's sake, and he hoped, without the knowledge of his father. This far east, and shrouded in the veil of the jungle, itself a part of Bhagavan's power so near to the temple, Odin would have difficulty seeing them, even from Hlidskjalf.

At last the corridor led into a large room, with wide, open windows, and Thor bowed again to the gods already present. Ra and Athena, of course, but also a second statue, this one of blue-skinned and four-armed Vishnu, the most omniscient of Bhagavan's aspects, and beside the stone figure stood elephant-headed Ganesha, the most wise, in the flesh.

"Thor of the North," Buddha greeted him, returning his bow. "It is a great honor to meet you at last."

"The honor is mine, Siddhartha." None of the western gods were certain where Buddha had come from. Some called him an Avatar of Vishnu, merely another aspect of Bhagavan himself, but Thor was not so certain. He did not have the same flavor within his aura as Ganesha and the others Thor had met. "Rarely have I heard of a god spoken of so highly by so many."

"Then you have not heard how the others in this world speak of you, Odin-son," Buddha replied with a serene smile. "Bhagavan-Shiva begs your forgiveness for not meeting you as well, but I am certain you will be satisfied by Ganesha's counsel. His decision will be binding for all of the Brahman."

Thor nodded to the Elephant-headed god. Ganesha's supple trunk curled, his ears flapping idly in something like a smile, judging by the god's eyes.

"If it would not be too much trouble," Thor said, avoiding Athena's eyes, "might I see her?"

"Ra suggested you might wish it." Ganesha's ears flapped again, and he gestured toward the windows. His voice was deep and brassy yet, oddly distant. "I have, ah, removed the obstacles between you, in a sense. The windows look out upon the village, rather than the temple grounds. You must forgive me for not offering more, but it is safer for everyone this way."

Thor crossed the room, finding a lush river where the courtyard should have stood, and a village set back upon its bank. The scaled back of a crocodile surfaced in the water, green-gold eyes slitted as it searched for prey. The children played far enough back to be safe, dogs chasing them with wagging tails. A girl's voice rose in a curse as a monkey darted off into the trees, some prize caught to its breast. Thor smiled. It seemed a peaceful place, thieving monkeys or not.

"We have your vow, then," Ra said, behind him. They had not the time to wait for him to look his fill. A gathering of gods such as theirs would not go unnoticed if they lingered, if not by Odin, then another, and few gods were known for their ability to keep a secret. "As long as she remains within your lands, you will keep her from harm?"

"We have no reason to do her harm, and every reason to wish her peace," Buddha said. "She is safe here."

"And among the Brahman as well," Ganesha agreed. "But if the Council moves for her death, even Bhagavan cannot protect her for long."

A woman knelt by the water, skin like cinnamon and hair like ink. She bent to draw water, dipping a large earthen jug into the river. The crocodile's tail twitched and it submerged, invisible while it hunted. Just as Odin had shielded his own motives, holding Thor out as proof of his good will and claiming the Trickster acted alone. Had he always? Thor could not be certain, looking back, but he knew what Odin wanted, now. His father would call for Eve's death.

"Then we must stall the Council," Athena said. "Even under the best of circumstances, it might take a century, but the longer it waits, the less urgency they will muster. By the time all the gods have been gathered, Loki's work could be undone. And there is still the question of their godhead to be decided before any judgment is passed."

From the vantage of the window, Thor could see the barest ripple of the water where the crocodile lurked. The woman only hummed to herself, seeming unconcerned, even careless. He gripped the windowsill, stone crumbling beneath his fingers.

"Better for Loki and Sif if she were not recognized, but calling the Council at all works against their cause." Ganesha said. "They might have acted first, claiming ignorance, and begged forgiveness later. Now they will be bound by the outcome, and with the Trickster's silver tongue silenced, we might work our own wiles."

The beast sped forward, intent now on its prey. A hoarse call of warning broke from Thor's throat, and her head turned, away from the river. A soft line formed between her eyebrows as she searched the trees with emerald eyes, her body still bent over the water, in easy reach. Too close.

The crocodile lunged, maw gaping, and she sat back, the jug of water slowing her response. Its jaws snapped shut with a crack, and then…

"Aphrodite might help, even if Hermes sides with Loki," Athena said, coming to stand beside him. She snorted at what she saw and turned away, back to the others. "Together, we will speak to Zeus."

Laughter floated on the wind, clear and sweet and joyful. Eve stroked the crocodile's nose, leaned down and kissed its leathery snout.

Thor forced himself to relax, and let go of the static that filled the air around him. Of course she was fine. No living thing of this earth would do her harm. Not truly. And even if it had wounded her by some strange chance, she would have healed quickly. She always healed quickly. He should have known better than to worry. Even in the most deadly of circumstances, Eve survived. Unfortunately, the same could also be said for Adam.

"But what will they say?" Buddha asked. "Speaking against her death is not enough; we must argue for her life, some purpose she fulfills in the world—she must serve it somehow."

The other gods fell silent, and Thor became aware of their scrutiny, the weight of their gazes upon his back. He shook his head and did not take his eyes from Eve.

"Eve could not tell me her purpose," he admitted. The crocodile had sunk back beneath the water and slithered away. Eve had turned again, staring into the trees, into his own eyes, though he knew she could not see him. "Adam hid it from her, and Elohim fell into his slumber before she might ask."

But there was a pattern, he knew, which spoke of something more than bloodline and chance. Elohim would not have risked the godchild for nothing, and even if Thor knew little else, he knew what she had given him, and seen that gift spread, rippling out and flowing over an entire village, bringing them peace and joy and happiness. Looking into her eyes, he longed for that peace again, ached to hold her in his arms.

He had nothing left in Asgard, but he was still tied to the North. If he appeared to her now, offered her his love and a home, what would she think? He was not certain she thought of him at all, anymore, but for when he used those memories to soothe her. And she could never be happy in Asgard, torn from the earth, from her people and her family, from whatever purpose she was meant to fulfill, besides love. Even if he were wrong about her happiness, Sif would never give her peace.

What is it? Athena asked, touching his hand. *What do you not say?*

He forced himself to turn, tearing his gaze from Eve, though it had been near a thousand years since he had met her eyes. Now was not the time to reveal himself, with Loki and Sif spreading lies about how Eve might respond.

"She is Elohim's love," he said, glancing briefly at Ra. Thor thought for a moment he saw the old god's lips twitch, a smile quickly repressed, but he could not understand why. "I am not certain the argument will give much peace to those afraid of being cast out into the void, but I know she brings love to every land where she is born. It is very much like Divine Grace. A blessing to renew her people."

Buddha smiled, even as Athena's hand fell away. Thor watched her, guilt and grief squeezing his heart. *Forgive me, Athena.*

She shook her head. *Only tell me it was not just for the nimbus of her grace and love that you came to Olympus so frequently while she lived among us.*

He straightened, catching her by the arm. That she might think it—but he could not blame her for fearing he had used her, knowing her family. Aphrodite and Ares would think nothing of cultivating another god simply to have their way.

"We are friends, Athena." He kept his voice low, but firm. Ganesha and Buddha did not speak, but it was clear they communed, their faces turned to Vishnu's stone form. "Even for Eve I would not suffer through so many feasts upon Olympus. I came for the pleasure of your company, and you need never doubt it."

She smiled sadly. "I am ashamed for thinking otherwise, even for a moment." *Seeing the way you look on her… I thought for many years I was above my sisters, my queen, that I had escaped the pettiness of their temperaments, but when it comes to you, I am as jealous as Hera.*

But unlike Hera, you do not let your jealousy rule you. He squeezed her hand and let her go. *It is a very great difference, Athena, and one which sets you very much apart.*

"We have decided," Ganesha announced, his long trunk curling up to his broad forehead. "The Brahman will assist as we may and Bhagavan himself will delay this assembly. If Eve is indeed Elohim's Grace, we dare not risk her loss. Without Grace, the world will wither, and its people will fail, just as surely as if the godchild unmade it."

Ra bowed, relief more than evident in his features. "Then we must leave you. I fear we have already lingered too long."

Thor hesitated, casting one last look out the window. Eve balanced the water jug upon her head as if she had done so a hundred thousand times before, and made her way back to the village.

"Come, Thor," Athena said gently. "You will see her again. And if we succeed, perhaps one day she will even know you, again, too."

He let her draw him away and bowed farewell to Vishnu's form, thanking Buddha and Ganesha for their time, for Eve's protection. They left the temple together, Athena's hand firm upon his arm. As if she knew how much he wished to turn back, to take himself to Eve.

"Spend this night in Olympus," she said when they stood again beneath Shiva's stone gaze. "Let us offer you at least that small comfort."

"Better if my father sees me hollow-eyed and heartsick." He covered her hand with his, then brought it to his lips. "Perhaps he will choose to see it as remorse. And I must try to reason with him, Athena. The Aesir have too much influence to do otherwise."

She shook her head, catching his hand in both of hers and pressing it tightly between them. "It is not the Aesir who have influence, Thor. No matter what your father decides, no matter what he says in the Council meeting, it will be your words that hold sway. You are the god they know, the god they trust. Not Odin."

"If I speak against him so openly, there will be no healing the breach."

Athena let him go and stepped back. "I cannot help you decide how far you are willing to go to protect her, Thor. I can only say that if Odin has lost your loyalty, the fault is most assuredly his own. And if he acts unwisely now, unreasonably, he does not deserve your support."

He watched her open her arms, thick with feathers, and shake them into wings. With another breath, she was all owl, and lifted herself up into the trees, and then the sky, leaving him behind.

"She would make you a very fine wife, Thor," Ra said at his shoulder. "If I were free to choose…" The Egyptian god sighed the rest away and smiled dryly. "I fear I am too old to give her what she deserves, now, but she would make a better match for you than Eve, if you could turn your heart."

"My father is not wrong about me, Ra. Once my heart is set, it does not change so easily."

But for a moment, that moment, he almost wished it could.

CHAPTER THIRTY-FOUR
Present

Eve slipped away to the library, hoping she might escape both the DeLeons and the Watsons for a time. It was a struggle to find a comfortable position anymore, but she leaned back in an armchair with her feet up, hands resting on her stomach, and felt some of the knots in her back unkink. When she concentrated, she could feel the baby inside her, contented and calm. The unique mind and presence within her own body had always fascinated her, utterly trusting, so totally innocent, untouched by the world but still part of it.

"Am I intruding?" Adam asked.

She looked up, surprised to find him in the doorway. He had seemed to be avoiding her since his arrival, though she wasn't sure if that had been his own idea, or Garrit's. "Only if you're intending to fuss over me. I've had quite enough of that for one day."

"No." His lips curved, then thinned in what she thought might have been a repressed smile. "I wouldn't dream of insulting you that way."

"It isn't an insult."

"Isn't it?" He came into the room, perching on the edge of the ottoman beside her feet.

"I appreciate their concern," she answered, trying to keep the note of challenge from her voice. She didn't have the energy to fight with him, and she was just uncomfortable enough that she wasn't interested in defending her family, either. "But Garrit fusses over me enough without his parents and his aunt doing it too."

He tore his gaze from her stomach to stare at the book in his hands. Ryam's journal, by the dates on the spine. "They've made an art of hating me, haven't they?"

"You shouldn't have taken it."

"I thought it might answer some of my questions." He met her eyes and smiled, offering it to her. "He loved you a great deal to go to all this trouble. To set his family the task of caring for you in perpetuity."

She frowned slightly as she took the book, following his thoughts. He was thinking about what Juliette had told him. The things he had forced her to tell. "You don't know who they are, do you?"

He raised an eyebrow. "I'm not sure I understand your question."

"This is Reu's family, Adam. My House of Lions."

The warmth drained from his face almost at once, and he stood up, turning away to the window. *No wonder they hate me so much.*

"They don't hate you."

He laughed, but it was an awful sound. Bitter and angry. "Even you hate me."

She sighed, watching him lean against the frame of the window, his head bent. The last few days had been easy. He had behaved himself perfectly. Garrit hadn't even had cause to gripe. Not that it meant he relaxed at all. But she felt at least they had come to some kind of truce. René had been as reasonable as she had hoped, and Juliette as calming. The change in Adam had been fundamental, though she couldn't quite identify it. He had been no more and no less than kind. His arrogance and the hurtful sarcasm of his last visit all but gone. If she was honest with herself, she found it more disconcerting when he was nice, and she saw glimpses of Paris.

"I don't hate you, Adam." She wouldn't lie to him. It was fear, more than anything. Anxiety for what his presence could result in. Maybe she shouldn't worry. Maybe she didn't have to. Maybe she was safe. But that was no reason to tempt fate.

He turned to look at her. "But you don't trust me."

"No." She hadn't trusted Paris, either, and that Adam hadn't threatened her at all. But she wanted to trust him now. That was the most frightening part.

He smirked. "I'm not sure I would trust me either. Though I think your husband distrusts me enough for both of you."

"They have a long memory, this family—Oof." The baby kicked and she stroked her stomach, trying to soothe it.

He sat down again on the ottoman, reaching for her, and then stopped suddenly, his hand suspended over her stomach.

"May I?"

She raised an eyebrow at his tone, so strangely reverent. "If you like."

He pressed his hand to her stomach and she tried to ignore the heat of his touch, the way it seeped into her body. The baby kicked again, and his eyes lit. He smiled, and it was the most artless expression she had seen on his face since he had arrived before her wedding. Full of an innocent joy. Like the day in the Garden when he had offered her strawberries for the first time. Her heart started to race and she scowled. The baby, feeling her stress, began moving more forcefully and she winced.

He pulled his hand back at once, almost guiltily. "I'm sorry."

She shook her head. "No, it's fine. It isn't you." She closed her eyes to soothe the mind within her. So undefined but so sensitive. The baby calmed and she looked up at Adam. "See? All better."

He smiled, but it was forced, as though he were distracted.

Adam?

He shook his head and stood up, walking to the door. He stopped before he opened it, but he didn't look at her. *They're right to mistrust me.* There was an anguish in him she hadn't noticed before, an ache that ran deep and made her own heart hurt. "I'm sorry for disturbing you. I just wanted to return your book."

And then he left, the door swinging shut behind him.

She stared after him for a long moment, at the place where he had been, puzzling over the exchange. If they were twins, shouldn't she have some idea of his thought process? If they were so similar, how were they so different? Adam was the most confounding man she had ever known.

She picked up the journal and let it fall open in her hands. The sketch of Adam in its plastic sleeve stared back at her.

Maybe she was being unfair. It seemed more and more lately that the title of most confounding really belonged to Ryam. At least Adam she could question. Ryam was still baffling her centuries after the fact.

She wasn't sure what was worse: not knowing the answers, or knowing Garrit seemed to have them but was forbidden to tell her.

§

They served lamb for dinner, and Eve did her best to ignore the associations. Juliette must have made the menu, she thought, and Garrit must have decided she didn't need to be bothered by it. As if choosing a main course was going to send her into early labor.

She hadn't eaten lamb since Troy. Eve stared at her plate and pressed the memories back into the darkness where she had kept them locked away. Before she had married Menelaus, when she had still believed she might escape her fate and the horrors of war with Troy which would follow, she had fled to Athens, throwing herself upon the mercy of Theseus, its king. She hadn't thought, even for a moment, that she would fall in love—but Theseus! Her throat closed, tears pressing behind her eyes. Theseus had sacrificed a lamb to the gods every day for the two years of their marriage, until her brothers had come and stolen her back to Sparta. For lives afterwards, she hadn't been able to even smell lamb stew without her stomach turning into knots. If it hadn't been for Theseus...

She rubbed her chest, over her heart, trying to dispel the ache of his loss. Another husband who had loved her more than she deserved. Thinking of Paris was preferable, but with Adam sitting across the table, she didn't dare.

You're not eating.

She nearly bit her tongue in surprise, but she brought a piece of the lamb to her mouth and swallowed before she could taste it. *You were saying?*

Adam's eyes narrowed, but the stone in them had softened to storm clouds, and she could feel his concern. *You can't afford not to eat with a baby in your womb, Eve. Is there something wrong with the lamb? I didn't think you could suffer from cravings or morning sickness.*

It doesn't have anything to do with the baby. Except it had, once. A baby she had born for Theseus, and lost. How many hours had she spent on her knees, praying to Michael to let her keep her child? She'd even made offerings to Poseidon and Aphrodite, Hera and Zeus, desperate enough to beg even for their intercession. For nothing. False gods, and worthless angels. How did anyone ever convince themselves of faith?

"Are you all right, Abby?" Garrit asked, frowning. "You look a bit gray."

She forced a smile. "Just fine, Garrit. I bit my tongue, that's all."

You're lying.

Eve didn't look at Adam, but kept the smile on her face until Garrit went back to listening to her mother. Something about how she wished they would purchase a summer home in England, so she would be able to see her grandson when he was born.

Eve?

The way he said her name brought Paris to her mind, and she latched onto the memory to chase away the sorrow. Paris, at least, had never fed her lamb. Not that he hadn't sacrificed enough of them to Aphrodite.

Adam was smiling at Mia as he poured her another glass of wine. He'd done the same for her, once, at a banquet in Sparta. She could still see the lines of Paris in his face. The curve of his ears, the straightness of his nose, the strength of his jaw. He had changed, of course, skin color, face shape, the rise of his cheekbones and the color of his hair, but the essentials stayed the same.

He turned to look at her, his forehead furrowing in the same place hers did. A wrinkle between the eyebrows that could have been her own. She realized she was staring and looked away, focusing on the napkin in her lap, but he was already in her head. Gentle, but present, like a lazy day in a hammock with an insect buzzing in your ear.

Paris? He asked. *What about Paris?*

It had been sloppy to let her mind wander, but it had been that or cry with old grief, and at least the scene these memories could make would go unnoticed.

Nothing, she said, even though he wouldn't believe her.

There was a long silence, while he listened and she tried not to think about it. It didn't work. It never did. Not thinking of something inevitably brought it to mind, even if all that came was the thread of reminder. *Not Paris. Not Troy. Not Helen. Not Theseus.*

Oh God, please, not Theseus. Not Helen. Not Troy. Not Paris.
You knew me?

Mia was talking about the car she was going to buy, asking her father what he thought. She turned to Adam, asking him if he agreed. Somehow he managed to have the right answer, though Eve could feel his mind churning with the memories slipping through the cracks of her consciousness. Paris, holding her in a dark room. The whites of his eyes had been the only thing she could see, but she would have known his touch anywhere. The warmth of his hands against her skin, one palm pressed against her cheek, turning her face to his.

Helen, he said.

The wineglass in Adam's hand slipped and spilled, the red liquid crawling across the table to her plate, staining the linens the way blood had once stained the fields of Troy. She stared at it, to keep from meeting his eyes. Watching it draw closer and closer. She couldn't bring herself to stop it.

"*Merde!*" Garrit blotted it with his napkin, and shot Adam a dark look.

"Forgive me," Adam said, mopping up the spill on his half of the table. He cleared his throat, and did not so much as glance in her direction. "A shame to have wasted a cup of such a good vintage, too. The wine your family makes is exceptional, Garrit. Is there any way I might buy a case?"

"Oh! Yes!" Mia said. "That would be perfect! It isn't as though Abby can drink wine now, anyway."

Eve closed her eyes and took several deep breaths, emptying her mind as she exhaled. She could feel the baby, and let its consciousness fill her thoughts, crowding everything else out.

"Of course," Garrit answered through his teeth. "I'll see what we have in the cellar after dinner."

"I think I need to go lay down," Eve mumbled.

And then she fled.

CHAPTER THIRTY-FIVE
Creation

৯

A short and easy climb brought Eve to the vantage point with a view of the entire valley, the Garden at its far edge. The stone precipice sheltered them from the heat of the sun during the day, as well as the rain.

The largest of the lions, the male with the dark shaggy mane, followed her with one long leap. She leaned against his tawny body, sitting cross-legged on the sun-warmed stone and frowned at the Garden.

"Why haven't they acted yet?"

The lion chuffed beside her, but she knew it didn't understand more than her frustration. She scratched behind its ear until it purred. Reu had been growing more anxious about leaving her alone with each passing day, but the angels still flocked around the Garden without entering it, and so he had taken the other lions of the pride with him to hunt. Eri, the male, never left her side, and Tzofi, the female who had given them the rabbit that first day, followed Reu wherever he went.

It had been nearly seven days since they had met the lions and she had resolved to find a way to train them. Seven days spent learning to master fire and beast. That it had only taken a week to convince the lions they were best served as their friends made her uneasy. Maybe because it added truth to some of what Adam had told her about how they were meant to rule.

She sighed. Eri painted her arm with his rough tongue, and purred loudly. That was always his answer to her apprehension. Grooming reinforced the bonds of the pride. It was affection and promise and companionship. She threaded her fingers into his mane and let the lion's confidence leach into her mind. If she was meant to lead, she would do so, but it would not be the way Adam had shown her.

Of course, none of it mattered until the others found them. And none would until the angels drove them from the Garden into the wild. Reu had already begun to anticipate the arrival of the others. They collected wood and roots for burning, as well as the dung of the animals. The dung of the elephant worked especially well for their fires. He patiently skinned every kill and scraped the hide clean before stretching it to dry and cure. Eve had shaped several bone needles for stitching the hides together to make clothing and blankets using the gut. They dried meat as well, so there would be enough food for everyone until the others learned to hunt.

She grimaced. If it hadn't been for the lions, Reu might very well have starved by now, leaving her no choice but to watch. She still wasn't sure if it was a blessing or a curse that she was assured of her own survival. Neither one of them liked having to kill to eat, but they were a long way from the nut-bearing trees of the Garden, and the closest thing to fruit trees they had found were berry bushes. She had made salads from greens and other grasses, but they were bitter and tough.

Movement caught her eye, and she looked back to the Garden. A rainbow of angels had risen into the sky and from this distance she thought she could make out the stark bright white of Michael's wings as they flared, and then disappeared in the greenery.

It was time, then.

She climbed to her feet, Eri rising beside her, and searched the valley for Reu and the other lions. It would take the others at least a day to cross the grassland to where she and Reu had made their settlement. Still. It was good she had seen this.

She placed her hand on Eri's head and looked down into his golden eyes. "Can you call to the others?"

His fur shivered under her touch and he looked into the distance, his nose twitching as he drank in the scent of the wind. Then he turned unerringly, his tail flicking against her leg, and roared.

Even expecting it, the sound still made her tremble, and she was glad Eri and his pride guarded them, for she would not have been easy knowing the cats hunted for their flesh. She slapped the lion on the flank and turned her attention back to the Garden.

There were fewer angels outside, now. She wondered if Michael had sent them off, or if the Garden had swallowed them. She wished she could see or hear what was happening. Maybe if she closed her eyes and focused…

Reu and the lions were the first thing she felt, familiar presences, clear and crisp. Reu had already been on his way back, and now moved more quickly at the sound of Eri's roar. The females did not hurry, unconcerned by Reu's human anxiety, but Tzofi kept pace with him. Eve probably could have called Reu herself, but she found the idea was distasteful to her, too similar to Adam's methods of control.

She pushed beyond them, opening her mind to the rest of the valley slowly. Birds hunting and soaring high above them, and more on the ground with the rodent-kind, looking for bugs and seeds and flowers to eat. Then the larger beasts, prey animals, skittish and wary, ready to flee at the slightest noise or movement.

She pressed further, visualizing the Garden in her mind, the path through the trees from the gate to the caves Adam had made their shelter, until she felt the others there. Hannah's quiet calm, even as the angels surrounded them, their faces hard as stone. Lilith's terror, colored by Adam's fury, as she cowered before the sword of fire. And Adam himself, arrogant and unmoved by the demands and the threat in Michael's eyes.

She wondered at his conceit. It had not taken more than the sight of the angels massed above to inspire fear of God's Law in her heart. Yet, she felt Adam's dismissal of these beings, powerful in their own right, and their judgment of him.

The impressions were more confusing than enlightening. A blend of perspectives growing more entwined the more she tried to see, colored heavily by fear and trepidation. She could not hear the words spoken by the angels, though she could clearly see their lips moving, nor could she hear Adam's verbal response. But his anger was like a beacon to her, burning bright in her mind. A flash of surprise was her only warning before the focus of his mind narrowed and she cried out in pain, her eyes opening as she lost what connection she had managed to create.

Eri rumbled under her hand, more a vibration than sound. She dropped to her knees and pressed her face into the fur of his neck. She felt drained. It was more than she had done with her power since the lions had been tamed. Too much to have attempted all at once.

"Eve?"

She leaned over the ledge. Reu stood below it, a small gazelle across his shoulders. He frowned when he saw her face and dropped the kill to the grass. She let herself fall from the edge of the precipice and he caught her around the waist to set her lightly on the ground.

He searched her eyes. "Are you well?"

She nodded, rubbing the back of her neck. "The angels have entered the Garden. Michael is speaking with Adam right now."

"How do you know?"

"I saw them, and then I felt it. They're all afraid. Except for Adam. How can he face them without fear?"

"Adam spent time with the angels before God's death. Before the rest of us were made." Reu frowned slightly and picked up the gazelle again, carrying it to the area where he dressed the kills.

The lions were already there, waiting with gleaming eyes for the offal he always shared with them while he worked. Tzofi was washing blood from her whiskers, and she greeted Eri with a chuff and a purr. Eri rubbed his head against hers and lay down in the grass, rolling onto his side with lazy grace.

"I'm not sure I can lead, Reu. I've only just learned to live."

He smiled at her as he set down the carcass and squatted in the grass with his flint knife. "In all Adam's days in the Garden, he did not do what you've accomplished in just seven. You've done more than just learn to live, Eve."

She sat down beside Eri across from Reu, wrapping her arms around her knees and watching him as he began his work, carefully peeling the skin from the flesh and throwing bits to the lions as he went. "Instead, he cowed our people into submission. I think his accomplishment is still the greater."

"Have faith, love."

"If God is dead, Reu, what is there left to believe in?"

He stopped and looked up at her. She could feel his thoughts as they swirled around her question, and she knew his answer before he spoke. "I believe in you, Eve. God's Grace is in you."

She shivered and wished once again she had known God. To know his plan for her firsthand. To know what it all meant. But Reu didn't have those answers either. "They could be here as soon as tomorrow."

"And we'll be waiting," he said, confident. His thoughts were so calm. Things would be as they were meant to be. The angels had said they were meant to lead, and so they would.

She sighed and stroked Eri's head while he purred beside her. Watching Reu work the skin from the animal could be mesmerizing, especially combined with the attention of the lions. It tugged at her so strongly she even felt their hunger for the meat. She shook her head to clear it and stood up. "I'll start a fire."

Reu nodded. "I won't be much longer."

After they ate and arranged the rest of the meat to dry, they climbed the rocks to the overlook. It was her favorite part of the day with Reu, when they took this moment just to be together, putting the day and all its work behind them. It had become their ritual to watch the sun set behind the mountains each night, painting the sky with the reds and oranges of flame. The stone held the heat from the sun for hours after, keeping them warm enough from the night chill. When it was clear they slept there, under the open sky, and Reu would tell her the stories of the stars as they came out, one by one.

She rubbed the back of her neck. Her skull still ached from her earlier effort to discover what was happening in the Garden with the others. Reu noticed and brushed her hand away, taking over with his strong fingers and working the knots from her neck that she hadn't known were there.

He chuckled softly at the noises she made, and kissed her shoulder. Eve curled up against his body, her cheek against his bare chest, and listened to his heartbeat in the fading light. Tonight might be the last night they had alone together, without fear, without worrying about Adam.

"Sometimes I wish we could stay this way forever. Just us. Without any of the others."

Reu kissed the top of her head. His hand slid from her neck to her arm and then the curve of her waist. "As long as we're together, as long as I can hold you in my arms at night, it doesn't matter how many others are with us."

She smiled and tilted her head to look up at him. "Not just hold me, I hope?"

He laughed and brushed her hair from her face. "Hold you and love you and protect you and treasure you always, Eve."

His kiss distracted her from the realization, sudden, sad and complete, that his always would never be hers.

CHAPTER THIRTY-SIX
15 AD

Thor spent as little time in Asgard as he could, frequenting Thorgrim's village to ensure their safety, and sleeping under the stars, wandering from place to place. He didn't stay in the North, either. The feeling of Sif watching him, breathing in his ear, made his shoulder blades itch.

At first, he had ignored the star when it had glowed bright and high in the sky, though he had heard the prophecy whispered in Egypt and Rome, even Greece. The House of Lions had asked him about the king of kings, but he hadn't had any answers for them. It was unlikely the baby was anything more than just a child, but with Eve in that part of the world, he felt it the better part of wisdom to investigate.

He had barely passed into Syria when he met a man on the road, hungry and dirty. As this land, strictly speaking, was controlled and governed by the Olympians, he didn't think much of it when the man appeared to have an immortal aura, but offered him some of the water he carried to drink.

The man studied him with piercing eyes as he drank from the bladder, and Thor found himself thinking of Eve, as he waited. It would be faster to teleport the rest of the way, but he wanted to learn more about this prophet, and gathering information from strangers was easier to do when one was covered in the dust of the road, disguised as a traveler.

It would be good to see Eve again. He sighed and dwelled in the memory of her kiss, the softness of her body in his arms. He shook his head and jerked himself free of the reverie.

The man was still watching him and his eyes had hardened. "You interfere with God's daughter."

Thor frowned, taking the bladder of water back and giving this traveler a second look. His sandals were beaten and abused, his skin coated in dust. "Athena? I would hardly call a friendship interference."

The man's face twisted into a sneer. "Pretenders and thieves. I do not speak of Zeus, or his family." Wings of brilliant white flared out from his back, and Thor took a step back, not quite sure whether he should be calling *Mjölnir*, or offering some kind of homage. "The True God gathers power even now. It will not be long before your time is at an end, Thunderer."

"I mean no disrespect to your creator, Archangel. Nor to you."

"And yet you take advantage of His lands, His people. You have the nerve to think you are deserving of His daughter! I warn you, interference now will not be tolerated. Gabriel has his role to play, and it is my duty to see it is done."

"His daughter?" He wasn't sure what to make of it. Any of it. All this time he'd spent wandering the earth and he'd never come in contact with an angel before, though he had looked. "You mean Eve?"

"Mother of men. Savior of her people. She plays that role again now, so the scriptures can be made true, and God's people returned to Him. Returned and made to turn away from the likes of you."

He shook his head. There was so much hostility from this man, this angel, and Thor had no interest in a fight. "I was merely seeking information about the prophet. I would not involve myself in Elohim's business, and these are not my lands, besides."

The angel sniffed and raised his chin. "A long time have We watched you, Thor Odin-son. And never have you allowed the boundaries arbitrarily drawn to stop you from accomplishing your goals. All due respect is paid, yet somehow you always get your way in this world. Have you never wondered why?"

"I imagine it has something to do with my diplomacy." But his temper was wearing thin, and he could not afford to summon lightning in Olympian lands. Zeus was not so understanding that he would overlook it. "What's your name, Archangel? That I may know to avoid you in the future, if this is how you would treat your allies."

"You and all your brethren are invaders and intruders, seeking to take advantage of God's weakness. If you were other, I would treat you with greater respect."

"You fail to see the difference between myself and my brothers, Angel. Even if I am not deserving, I still desire to see Eve live. And that is more than can be said for many."

The angel sneered again. "Nothing of this world can harm her."

Thor acknowledged that truth with a slight nod. "Then I suppose the only threats to her are those of us who merely live in it." He turned then, and continued on along the road. He had no interest in fighting with this angel any longer, especially when the creature would not even give him his name.

He had his suspicions, of course. There were said to only be three Archangels, with wings that white. Eve herself had told him as much. And since the angel had spoken of Gabriel, he assumed this must be either Michael, or Raphael. But Raphael had not been seen since the dawn of time, and Ra had spoken often enough of Michael's twisted arrogance that Thor felt certain enough of his identity.

Not that he had expected to stumble across a scheme of the True God's angels in the midst of this prophet nonsense. Less nonsense, he supposed, if it was Gabriel disguised as a man. It was Eve's role he didn't understand. Savior, the angel had called her. But how? Not only by sharing Elohim's Grace, surely.

"If you allow her to be destroyed, you destroy all hope for the world, Aesir," the angel called after him.

He glanced over his shoulder. The wings were gone again. Hidden somehow, but the angel stared at him fiercely, and Thor thought he saw an edge of flame around him. Just for a moment, and then it was gone. And when he blinked, the angel was gone too.

He shook his head again and continued on, wondering how the threat of the godchild and the unmaking of the world could somehow be perceived as hope.

§

Eve was weaving by the window. How many looms had she had in her existence? How many reams and reams of fabric had she woven? Her fingers deft and quick, she hummed softly to herself as she worked, and Thor watched just out of sight.

Her husband was in his workshop, teaching their oldest son how to join wood most effectively. If he hadn't witnessed her sons before, known she never passed on her immortality, he would not have recognized the young man for what he was. Not a man at all, but something else. Something more. Gabriel, if Michael was to be believed.

Eve stood, and he noticed the rounding of her belly. Pregnant again. He had seen her give birth well into her fifth decade before, though she could not be much older than thirty now, and her husband seemed to take good care of her. Provided well for her.

A little girl ran into the room shouting for her attention, and Eve laughed and swept her into her arms, lifting her up and kissing her cheek. The little girl could only be Eve's daughter, and she reached for the loom. Eve sat down with the child in her lap and guided her fingers, showing her how to weave the threads, patiently.

The sound of male voices carried into the room, interrupting them, and Eve set her daughter back on her feet, sending her running back out of the room to greet her father and brother. From where he was standing, Thor could see the angel-man kneel and catch her, tossing the little girl into the air. Eve followed more sedately, and her husband, Joseph, looked on her with love. His hand touching her stomach briefly, reverently.

Gabriel, or Jesus, as Eve called him now, kissed his mother's cheek, still holding his little sister in his arms.

The contrast between this young man, and the one Thor had met on the road was astounding. Gabriel's eyes were kind and patient. How much of that disposition was due to Eve's mothering, even for so short a time? Certainly she seemed to have a loving household. A joyful household. If Michael had been chosen as the prophet to be born, would he have benefitted in the same way?

Thor crept around the house to the next window, following Eve as she moved and staying in the shadows where he could. She went to the hearth, uncovering loaves of bread to bring to the table. There was another girl, there, stirring a pot. Another daughter? And another boy came running in from the workshop.

It seemed to be some kind of occasion, and Thor barely had time to slip out of sight as a young man not much older than Jesus arrived at the house. He did not have the look of either Eve, or Joseph, and Thor didn't think he was another child, but Joseph clasped hands with him, and welcomed him to the table. Jesus broke the bread, sharing it with his siblings and their guest, while his sister served bowls of some kind of stew and Eve poured wine cut with water for everyone.

After they were served, and before anyone ate, Eve took the hands of those on either side of her, and the family bowed their heads while Joseph said a prayer of thanks, offered to the True God. Eve's God.

Gabriel alone did not close his eyes, and it was in that moment he looked up directly at Thor. He barely nodded, smiling reassurance, his expression knowing and understanding.

Your time comes, Odin-son.

Thor stared, feeling almost as if he couldn't bring himself to move. *My time for what?*

She'll know you, Thor. You'll have her love again. Go on as you've begun.

He shook his head. *I don't understand.*

The angel, the man, the prophet, smiled again. *God doesn't forget what he owes you, Son of the Earth. Son of Jörd. Did you never wonder what drew you here?*

More riddles. Do angels never speak plainly?

Gabriel twitched one shoulder. Not enough to draw the attention of any of the others. *Some secrets are meant to be kept. We offer you enough to cause you to wonder. To cause you to ask the questions you are meant to ask. It is God's greatest gift to his children, curiosity and even doubt. Free will to choose your fate, to choose your path. Free will to choose love.*

And then the prayer was ended. Gabriel turned to smile on his mother, and though Thor waited, he offered him no further explanation.

He did not linger for many more days, for fear of drawing Sif's attention, but the life Eve seemed to be living brought him peace, and he thought perhaps with the angel at her side as her son, she would be safe. For a time, at least.

He left Syria for the House of Lions, to give them the truth of what he had learned. Jesus was not a true prophet, in the way they believed, but he still spoke with the True God's voice as his angel, and as Eve's son. Humanity could do much worse than to listen.

CHAPTER THIRTY-SEVEN
Present

It was getting close, Eve decided, as she tried to ignore the twinge of what seemed like false labor. She closed her eyes and swallowed against the discomfort. If she could just get through tonight and tomorrow, she could have her baby in peace without Adam or Mia or her parents. The front sitting room was her latest retreat, and fewer people thought to look for her there when she had established herself so firmly in the library. But that afternoon, her father had joined her with his drinks and his bluster and his rattling snores, and she couldn't find a comfortable position in her seat, to save her life.

Not that there was much pain, yet. And the spasm in her back, combined with the ever so slight ripple of contraction across her stomach didn't feel like the real thing. But it had been a long time since her last child, and she didn't like the waiting. With everything else, it just seemed like an extra set of anxieties she didn't need.

She would be happy when the baby finally came and she could be comfortable again, even if it meant sleepless nights. Though she did have the advantage there. She would always know what the baby needed when it cried. It amazed her how other women managed to raise their children without the advantage of telepathy. Every time she became a mother, she was reminded of how precious and powerful that gift was. But even with it, she was still so baffled by the choices people made, the things that people did; how much more difficult was it for everyone else, who didn't have her advantage?

A car door slammed outside and Eve frowned. As far as she knew, they weren't expecting anyone, coming or going. She ignored another twinge and moved to the window, looking out at the drive. Adam was loading a suitcase into the trunk while Mia watched, pouting.

Eve frowned. *Leaving?*

Adam stiffened, but didn't look back. *A happy surprise, I'm sure, for your DeLeon family.*

I don't understand. She could see him speaking to Mia, but couldn't hear the words. Mia's forehead furrowed, her expression crumpling.

I thought you would be relieved. He slammed the trunk of the car and crossed to Mia, placing his hands on her shoulders and kissing her forehead. Mia seemed to relax, though she was still scowling. He touched her cheek and brushed her hair back behind her ear. Eve pressed her lips together into a thin line as she caught the conversation from his mind.

"I'm sorry, Mia. I don't mean to ruin your holiday. Stay. Enjoy the time with your sister."

"I hate that you're leaving me. You've never had to cut anything short because of work before. Why now? Tomorrow is Christmas! Just stay one more day, then you can go and I won't even argue."

He laughed and pulled her into a hug. Eve even felt his affection for her and the way Mia softened in his arms. He spoke into her hair. "If I could stay, I would. When you get home, we'll have another holiday of our own. We'll go pick out your car, if you like."

"Promise?"

"Yes. Of course." He let go of her then, tilting her face up to his and kissing her. "Give your family my regrets, would you?"

Mia pouted again. "Are you sure you can't stay? Just one more day?"

You don't actually have to work, do you? Eve asked.

It's better if I go. He held Mia again, hiding his face in her hair.

Eve shook her head. *She's your wife, Adam. And it's your first Christmas. You should be together. It isn't right for you to go—*

Enough, Eve. The sharpness of his reply surprised her, and she was sure he felt it because when he continued his tone had softened. *Please. Just let me go. I'll make it up to her.*

The anguish in his thoughts made her flinch, and she withdrew from his mind. She didn't hear what Mia said after that, or what he said in reply. But she saw him set her away and walk to the car.

He looked at Eve, their eyes meeting through the glass. His expression was unreadable. She winced at another pang in her stomach. He got in the car, waving to Mia, and then pulled away.

Poor Mia. She looked as though she was going to cry, watching the car disappear. Maybe it wouldn't be so wrong, just this once…

She found her mother's thoughts in the bedroom, suggesting gently that she should look for her daughter. It was only a few moments until Anne Watson came out of the manor and Mia all but tripped into her arms.

Eve turned away from the window, and sat back down with her book. Her father still snored in the armchair in the corner, oblivious to everything that had happened. Oblivious to his daughter crying outside in his wife's arms. Eve envied him. She sighed and reached for her brother. If he was leaving Mia this way, really leaving her, she would never forgive him. He had promised he wouldn't hurt her. He had married her. That wasn't something he could turn his back on. Mia loved him.

His mind was a maelstrom of regret and sorrow. And something else. Something which distressed him more than anything else. She felt him bury it beneath all the other emotions. Walling it with anger and pain.

Adam?

His mind stilled, abruptly blank. *Give my regards to your husband.*

Adam, I don't understand.

I had to leave. It's for the best.

The day before Christmas? With some specious excuse about work?

Kinder than the truth, in this instance. Don't worry, Eve. Your sister is resilient. She'll forgive me.

Why?

Why didn't you tell Garrit you could reach me this way? Why didn't you tell him you spoke to me directly about that journal, to remind me to return it?

She tried not to let her frustration show, but he chuckled in the back of her mind all the same.

It didn't seem important. He knows I can feel you. Sense you.

You didn't tell him because you knew he'd resent it.

What does that have to do with Mia?

It's none of your business, Eve.

She's my sister! You gave me your word you wouldn't hurt her.

And I haven't.

She's crying in my mother's arms!

Adam sighed, losing some of his control. And suddenly she felt what he had been trying to hide, heat and sorrow filled her body. So strong it overwhelmed her. *I didn't know. I didn't know she was your sister when I met her.*

She tried to withdraw, to filter it out, but his mind held hers fast, and he wouldn't let her go. So much heartbreak, like an ache in her soul, a knife cutting through her heart. And then the pain dropped, shifting lower.

My Eve, he said, *my love.*

She must've cried out because Garrit came into the room. He was never far from her these days. "Abby?"

"No!" The baby kicked and then moved, and she felt the wetness of her water breaking. A true contraction made her double over in pain.

Adam released her immediately, and Garrit's arms wrapped around her as she gasped from the shock. "Abby, what's happened? What is it?"

Call the doctor, you fool. She's having your son! Garrit spun to grab the phone, but he didn't seem to notice that Adam's voice had come from inside his own mind.

Thunder rolled in time with her next contraction, though the sky was blue, and Adam's presence disappeared completely from her thoughts. She could have sworn she felt something else, hard and sharp and burning fire, but then that was gone too.

§

It was an easy birth, as Eve had assured him it would be. Garrit sat on the edge of the hospital bed as she cradled the baby against her chest, dry and fed and sleeping.

"He's beautiful."

She smiled. "He looks like a DeLeon. I expect he'll even have your eyes when he's grown."

Garrit stroked her hair back from her face and stared down at the sleeping baby. "Hopefully he'll have his mother's grace."

"Who needs grace when they have DeLeon charm and good looks?"

He chuckled and leaned down to kiss her forehead.

The door opened and Mia peeked in, her face flushed with excitement. "Can we see, yet? Please, Abby!"

She smiled. "Quietly, please, Mia. He's sleeping."

Her sister closed the door as softly as possible and tiptoed across the room to peer down at the baby. "I can't believe I'm an aunt!" She sighed. "I wish Ethan hadn't missed this."

Eve's smile faded. Mia didn't seem to notice, but Garrit did. He squeezed her hand, and she felt his reassurance. "You'll just have to tell him about it," she managed to say. "I'm sure he wouldn't have gone if it weren't important."

Mia waved a hand dismissively. "Oh, I'll live. It just means I get one more year of ripping open my presents like a little girl before I have to pretend to be dignified about it."

"Ethan's too, if you like," Garrit said.

Eve frowned at him, but Mia laughed. "Serves him right for missing Christmas. Maybe I will. You're so lucky, Abby. I bet Garrit won't let those stuffed shirts he works for drag him away from you now."

"Not for anything." He smiled. "It's my son's first Christmas."

"Oh!" Mia clapped her hand over her mouth when the exclamation came out louder than anything else in the room. "Oh no! We haven't gotten him any presents!"

"I don't think he'll notice," she laughed. "He barely even registers that anything exists beyond his own nose."

"What are you going to name him, Abby?"

She looked at Garrit. His brow creased as he studied the baby thoughtfully.

"We hadn't decided yet. I thought we'd have another week or two. A family name, I think. If Garrit will choose one."

"Alexandre," he said softly, and then he smiled at her. "Let's call him Alexandre Ryam."

She felt tears prick her eyes. Alexandre had been one of Adam's names, when she lived as Helen. The name he had earned for his bravery, for a selfless act. Garrit couldn't have known what he suggested, not really, but it seemed fitting, somehow, after Adam's departure. "That sounds perfect."

Mia touched the baby's hand with a finger. Alexandre wrapped his little fist around it, even as he slept. "I'm going to be your most favorite aunt, Alex. You can come visit me whenever you want, and I promise I won't make you do anything except play. And when you have brothers and sisters, I won't make you share any of your toys with them. I'm going to spoil you rotten."

"Why don't you go get Mum and Dad, Mia?"

She sighed. "Do I have to?"

"Please?"

Mia left, and Garrit tore his gaze from the baby to look at Eve. "What happened to Ethan? In all the commotion I honestly didn't think of him."

"He left just before." She fussed with the baby's blanket as an excuse not to meet Garrit's eyes.

The memory of what Adam had revealed to her was still raw. The way he had held her to his will in that moment, showing her the love which had overtaken him, though he knew she couldn't return it. And even if she hadn't been married, his awareness that she would have refused him, had no choice but to refuse him. It was a love laced with agony, and her heart broke for him.

"I would have sworn he was with us when I called the doctor, and we raced you to the hospital."

She shook her head, looking up at him, her lips pressed into a thin line. He studied her expression for a moment, and she waited for him to understand.

When it came, he turned his face away, and the muscles along his jaw revealed the clenching of his teeth. "He knew you were going into labor because he was in your head. He was in my head."

"I saw him drive off, and Mia was so upset."

He was still stiff, and his eyes were dark with a mix of emotions. "Why did he leave?"

It wasn't a question she wanted to answer honestly. "He said to give you his regards. That it was for the best that he go." That he loved me. That he was leaving for me. For Mia, too, so he wouldn't betray his love to her. To be faithful to both of us, she realized.

Garrit nodded. "If you speak with him again," the words came out resentfully, "give him my gratitude."

She dropped her gaze back to the baby, then her parents came into the room with Mia, and René and Juliette, and she was spared the problem of answering him.

§

Eve woke in the dark, gasping. The dream had not been this vivid since she had lived as Helen, and she pressed her hand against her womb, the phantom sword a fire in her belly. She reached to touch Alex, sleeping peacefully in his bassinet, to reassure herself he was still breathing and warm and safe. The doctors had insisted on keeping them overnight, to give her body time to rest, though how much of it was Garrit's worry and how much a medical necessity she didn't know. But Alex was well, his mind the pleasant susurrus of infant dreams, swirls of colors and impressions. Undisturbed.

"For the moment."

The voice froze her, cold and hard, and the burn in her womb throbbed painfully. Michael stepped forward from the shadow, white wings folded neatly to his back, gleaming so brightly she wondered how she had not seen him until now. The Archangel laid a pale hand over Alex's fluttering heart.

"But that can change swiftly, Eve. And I would not even need the sword to steal the breath from your son's body." The hand rose higher, hovering over Alex's mouth and nose, but not quite touching. "Should I kill him for this treachery, to remind you of the risks you take? Evidently dreaming of the death that will come no longer suffices."

"No," she whispered, lurching forward and knocking the cradle away. "I haven't forgotten! I need no reminder!"

"But you soften toward your brother." Michael's eyes met hers, glowing with blue fire.

"No!" She stepped between Alex and the angel, hiding the baby behind her. As if that would stop Michael. As if he could not force her to do anything he wished. Her gaze fell to the sword at his hip. "I am in love with my husband. Adam has no power here. No power over me!"

Lightning flashed outside, thunder crackling like fireworks. Michael's eyes narrowed, his head turning to the window. Rain pelted against the glass, turning to hail in the space of a heartbeat. The angel's nostril's flared, and Eve felt his fury wash over her, blistering her thoughts. Her hands went to her temples and she fell to her knees with a strangled cry, gripping her skull.

He glanced back at her again, his lip curling. "If you let him touch you, there will be no power on earth that will stop me from delivering your punishment." He bent down, bringing his face to hers, so near she could smell the brimstone of his skin. "You and all your people will die."

Before she could respond, Michael was gone. The sound of the rain against the window seemed to quench the fire in her soul, though she did not have the strength to rise. Her whole body trembled, and she dropped her face to the tile floor, her eyes flooding with tears.

Never, she promised herself, shaking with silent sobs. *Never.*

§

Eve had no memory of returning to the bed, spent from weeping, but somehow she woke up there, snug and warm beneath the blankets with Alex's bassinet within reach. When Garrit came to take her home, a fine mist still hung over the earth and for a moment she could have sworn she glimpsed a man standing out by the tree, so often struck. But he had no wings, and somehow, with the dampness against her face and the roll of thunder in the sky as she ducked into the house holding Alex in her arms, she had never felt safer.

CHAPTER THIRTY-EIGHT
Creation

§

Eve watched the others cross the grassland from the precipice. Eri rumbled against her side, his skin shivering beneath her hand. It was Hannah, she thought, by the golden hair, and Lamech with her. He was tall and brown and when he looked at Hannah, she could see the love in his face. Reu would be pleased if Hannah and Lamech had married. They had been his closest friends while living in the Garden. Before Eve had been made and God had died.

Eri sniffed delicately at the wind, and dropped to the stone, watching the movement in the valley through narrow eyes. Eve sat beside the lion, her legs hanging over the ledge. Reu stood beneath them with Tzofi, but Eve had sent the other two lions ahead into the grasses to keep the hyenas away. An early hunt had resulted in a good sized antelope roasting over the fire, ready to feed the others when they arrived.

Reu tickled the bottom of her feet and Eve laughed, pulling them back up. He smiled. "You're almost as brown as Lamech, now. They'll hardly recognize you."

She could see others behind the pair, but they weren't close enough to tell apart from one another, and the bird she had used to identify Hannah had found other interests.

"Perhaps that's just as well. Should I take a new name? Maybe Adam won't know me." She could already feel the touch of Adam's mind against hers, searching, and knew the idea was worthless.

"You'll be safe, Eve. Hannah and Lamech will help you, too."

She scratched Eri behind the ears. "Adam's angry."

"I would expect nothing less."

"I don't see the angels anymore." She frowned at the sky and dropped to the ground beside Reu. "They must have left in the night. Where do they go?"

He shook his head, putting his arm around her shoulders. "I don't know. Adam might."

She sighed. "There are so many things he keeps from us. So many things we'll never know because of him."

He kissed her forehead. "So many things we'll learn on our own without his help. We have God's law, we know right from wrong; nothing else matters anymore."

She let herself be reassured, but the problem had nagged at the back of her mind since they'd left the Garden. Adam knew so much about God. Maybe he could be convinced to tell them. Or at least to tell her. She wanted to know where she came from. She wanted to know God, her creator, her father.

They sat together in the shade of the stone as the sun rose higher, hoping the trail they had broken through the grasses and worn into the dirt would be enough to lead Hannah and Lamech to them. The shadows shortened and then stretched, and when Reu's two friends arrived, exhausted and parched, Reu fed them and Eve brought them water. The lions watched the new-comers closely and Eve twice hushed Eri's snarls. If they were fortunate, Adam would be as frightened by Eri as Hannah and Lamech were.

"The angels told us to find you," Hannah said after they had eaten. "They said you could teach us to live outside the Garden. Adam was furious. He tried to order them to kill you both. He shouted at Michael until the Chorus brought him to his knees, and we all wept from the pain."

Eve sat against Eri's flank, and Reu crouched beside her, carving the remaining meat into manageable pieces. "The others?" he asked.

Lamech shrugged, wary eyes on the lion at her side. "Lilith will follow Adam. Sarah means to come here. Those who were afraid of Adam were even more afraid of the angels. They'll come to you and Eve."

"And Adam?" Eve asked.

Hannah met her gaze, her expression filled with sympathy. "Lamech thinks his pride will prevent him from joining us, but I think he'll come, if only for you. It does not sit well with him that you chose Reu."

Eve nodded, pulling her knees to her chest. If she cleared her mind, she could feel him even now. Circling. Waiting. Watching. How much could he feel of her? Did he know she was afraid? Did he know she was curious? Lately she had begun to wonder if her curiosity was his or her own. She wasn't sure if she could tell the difference anymore.

Reu touched her cheek, and she tore her gaze from the fire to look at him, unable to avoid seeing the concern in his face. Feeling the worry as his fingers twined into her hair. "With Lamech and the lions there is little he can do. If he comes, he will follow our rule, or he will be made to leave."

"If he ate of the fruit, it isn't that simple. What he's done to Lilith could be done to another." Eve shivered in memory. The taint of Lilith's mind, the way he had choked it, still made her feel twisted and sick. "What I've accomplished with the lions will be nothing compared to what he will do to you."

Hannah frowned. "Surely the angels would not have sent Adam to you, sent all of us into your care, only to deliver us further into his power? They said he's lost the right to rule. We're to follow only you and he's forbidden to threaten us."

"I don't know, Hannah." Eve looked back at the fire. "I don't know what to think of them or what they'll do. They said they wouldn't help us any further."

One of the lions roared outside the cave, and Eri rose to his feet, padding to the entrance, tail switching and nose twitching. Eve closed her eyes, letting herself see through the lion's eyes, smell with its senses. It was getting easier to do, and not just with the lions. Birds were the easiest, and the most helpful. She could see the entirety of the valley if the right bird soared overhead.

Eri made a rattling noise that wasn't quite a growl, and she saw the movement in the dark. More people. Terrified and stumbling.

"It isn't Adam," she told Reu. "Not yet."

She heard him stand and leave the cave, stopping by the fire to choose a good-sized brand as a torch. She could hear the lick of the flames and the shift of the wood with Eri's ears.

She cleared her head with a little shake and smiled at Hannah and Lamech. "If you feel up to it, I think it would reassure them if they saw you with Reu, alive and well."

Lamech made to rise, but Hannah put a hand on his shoulder, pressing him back to the cave floor. "I'll go. Stay with Eve."

She followed Reu's steps, giving Eri as wide a berth as possible. Eve called Eri back to her softly. His tail flicked again and he rumbled so low she felt it in her bones, but he came and sat beside her.

Lamech shook his head. "I never thought I'd see a lion tamed to obey like a dog."

She smiled and stroked Eri's mane. "Not quite like a dog, from what little I saw. The dog wants to please its master. Lives for praise.

Eri only does so to serve his own interests. The pride eats better with Reu's help hunting, and fire keeps the hyenas and vultures from their kills."

"Only Elohim could tame the wild beasts, Eve. Until you."

She looked away from his face. The earnestness. The belief in his eyes and the faith in his heart. He was so much like Reu. "If I can do this, Adam can too."

Lamech made a noise in his throat and she could feel his disgust. "Can, perhaps, but would never lower himself to bother with lesser beasts. And he would not think to help them in exchange."

Reu and Hannah returned with the others before she could answer. There were many this time, and Eve recognized Seth and Sarah and Enoch among them. She rose to welcome them, offering food and water, and the softer furs she'd been able to sew together into blankets. Eri slunk away from so many strangers, his teeth bared, but Eve calmed him and sent him outside.

In the end, she and Reu slipped from the cave to sleep on the stone above with the lions for warmth and the stars for privacy. She wondered how long it would be before she was used to all their thoughts and emotions washing over her like water in the stream. There were so many dreams, and even prayers floating through her mind. But then Reu kissed her and all of it dropped away.

§

Eve woke before the sun came up and it took her a long moment to understand what had pulled her from her dreams. Then she heard Eri's angry snarl and Tzofi's answer from below. She sat up, careful not to wake Reu, and crept to the edge of the overhang where Eri stood, head low, body crouched.

It was barely more than a whisper on the wind, but she knew the voice and she shivered. Eri snarled again, ready to leap, but she put a hand on his shoulder and climbed quietly down to the earth.

Tzofi had him cornered against the rocks. His fingers closed around a stone that looked deadly sharp in the pre-dawn light, and his face was a mask of arrogance and anger. He stepped forward when he saw her, and Tzofi growled. She did not call the lion to task, but stared at him, covered in dust and dirt.

Adam had come.

"What do you want?" she asked.

He straightened, confident still, even with the lion ready to leap at his throat. But then she remembered he couldn't be killed either, and her stomach wrenched. Perhaps she should have woken Reu.

"Food, shelter. The same as these others you've welcomed." *Weak fools, pathetic, really.*

"You need neither," she said, wondering if he realized she had heard him. Better if he didn't.

"You would let Lilith starve to spite me?"

She looked back at Eri on the precipice. His silhouette golden with the first of the sun. "Maybe letting her die would be a kindness, instead of living under your control. And how do I know you won't do the same to the others too, if I give you what you ask for? If I let you live among us?"

"Is it your choice to make? To condemn her to death? You rejected me and the power I offered you. You chose not to be a goddess when I would have given you the world. Who are you to decide if her life is worth living or not?"

"You are a threat to all of them, Adam." His face was smooth, anger no longer hardening his eyes. But she could taste the bitterness of his emotions, still, on the back of her tongue, and the black fury, so well hidden from his expression, lashed against her mind like a pacing lion, snarling and snapping its tail. The others would not have her advantage, they would not realize he only waited for his moment to strike. "To all of us."

"Not you." He flicked his fingers to indicate the lions. "And you seem to have found a way to protect the others. But I could have done them harm already and I didn't. It isn't them you fear for, is it Eve? Did you give yourself to that dog?" His eyes raked over her body, his gaze burning. "Did you let him plant a child inside your womb?"

She wrapped her arms around her body, hating the way he looked at her. "Reu is my husband and he leads at my side, here."

He laughed, harsh and low. "You would have done better to stay with me."

"Lilith can come to us. I will not refuse her," she said, speaking over him. "But you'll have to ask Reu if he'll have you."

He grinned and stepped forward, only to be stopped once again by Tzofi, her tail switching wildly and teeth bared. "I can answer all your questions, Eve. I can help you here. Reu will know that. That's why you want me to go to him. You want me here."

She shook her head and turned away. "You can speak to him when he wakes. In the meantime, Tzofi will guard you to be sure you harm no one. Perhaps she cannot kill you, but she can hurt you, Adam. And she will, if you do anything to us."

"And Lilith?"

The sun streamed over the stone, warming her face and arms. She hadn't realized how cold she was, standing there, until the sun touched her again. "The lions will not harm her. She'll be fed and sheltered. But if you hurt her again, I'll have the same taken out of your hide by Eri."

"I'm at your mercy, Eve." But she didn't like the way he smiled, or the flash of triumph in his eyes. She didn't like the feeling that somehow she had done exactly what he had hoped she would.

She stroked Tzofi between the shoulder blades, encouraging her to watch Adam, to keep him from the others, to protect Reu most of all. And then she walked away, back to her bed on the precipice.

Back to Reu's side.

But her peace was shattered, and as long as Adam was near, she wasn't sure she would ever get it back.

CHAPTER THIRTY-NINE
154 AD

§

"Father, you cannot honestly be considering this!"

"Elohim's daughter is a threat to all the gods, a threat to the very world we live in. The way these Christians are growing, we need every advantage we can gain. And was not the movement begun by her son? Only a fool would not consider it." Odin sat back on his throne, a raven on his shoulder and the other high in the rafters.

Thor inhaled deeply through his nose and began to count, trying to keep his temper under control and the thunder from the sky. The Council was tomorrow. Losing his temper now would destroy any chance he had of convincing Odin he could not sentence Eve to death. "This can't just be about us, Father, about our people. This has to be about the world. You say she is a threat to it, but I tell you she is its nurturer! The angels told me—"

"Of course the angels told you she was necessary. If she is the True God's tool, his means of working within this world, then they would spare no lie, no deceit to keep her. They play on your emotions, Thor. You're being turned against us, against your family, your people, your fellow gods. For what? Love of a woman you can never have? She would turn us all out into the void the moment you revealed yourself!"

"You know *nothing* of her, and worse, you have shut your mind to all reason." He felt his eyes burn, and tried to calm himself again. The sky had begun to darken, but no thunder broke. He took another breath, and struggled to keep his tone even. "It only makes sense that she is here for a purpose. That she is made to protect humanity. To save it. We should not interfere in things we do not understand, Father. Surely you, in your wisdom, recognize this truth?"

"In my wisdom, I recognize that you have been subverted. I cannot be certain of your loyalty to me or mine, nor can I trust your judgment when it comes to the woman you call Eve. I have made up my mind." Odin stood then, and glowered. "You will obey the Council's decision, Thor, no matter what it is, and you will obey me."

"I will speak my mind, Odin. And I will fight for her right to live tomorrow. If that means disobedience, so be it." He turned and left the chamber, slamming the door on his way out. He heard the startled squawk of Odin's ravens and found at least some satisfaction in disturbing something, even if he had not changed Odin's mind.

Odin sides with Sif. He sent the thought to Athena, and in his anger, thunder cracked, lightning flashing overhead. It began to rain, but he found the water beating onto his shoulders and head to be more comforting than anything else. He belonged to the rain, to the storm, to the sky. And it belonged to him. An outward expression of his feelings, of his person.

It won't matter, Thor. It won't be enough, she replied. *Calm yourself. The threat of the Christians works in our favor, now.*

Not with Odin. He blames Eve. It disgusted him. Odin had always prided himself on his wisdom, on his justice. It was not wrong to protect the defenseless, and it would cost the Aesir nothing to stand for Eve. It was not as though she joined in preaching the Christian doctrine! The sect could be crushed without killing her, but Odin looked at her, and saw only the author of his troubles. He blamed her even for the break in Thor's marriage, though Sif had carried on her affair with Loki long before Thor had ever thought of loving Eve.

Athena sighed. *We are all selfish, concerned only with ourselves, or preserving our power, our domination, our people. It is rare we look outside our small areas of influence and care for the larger world. The Covenant does not really allow for it.*

Do you believe Michael spoke the truth? Her death will undo the world?

Bhagavan believes it, and I have never known the angels to lie, but that does not mean they will not do what they must to preserve the True God's creation. If nothing else, you are right that we should not interfere in what we cannot fully understand.

He grunted and sat down on a stone bench, letting the rain soak through his clothes to his skin. He closed his eyes and turned his face to the sky. *I have lost my father's trust, the trust of the Aesir, for Eve.*

You've acted only as your conscience dictated. There is no shame in this. Those of us outside Asgard still trust in you, perhaps all the more so because of it. Have peace, Thor, it will be over soon.

Her mind faded from his, and he was alone with his thoughts again.

The rain had softened to a sprinkle, and he rubbed the water from his face, opening his eyes to stare at the world tree. World to world, place to place, always offering its golden fruit. His mother's tree, but Thor had no memories of her.

Odd that Gabriel had mentioned her. How could the angel have known his parentage at all? Known his mother's name was Jörd? It had been another plane, another world, another time. Before this world and its angels had even been created.

He had been puzzling over Gabriel's words for more than a century now, and come no closer to their meaning. What could the True God owe him? What had he done to deserve any gift from Him, any attention? It couldn't be his love for Eve that Michael found so distasteful. So simple a thing, not worth any reward. It wasn't as if it had been done purposefully. Indeed, for the last thousand years it had felt as though he carried his love as a curse.

But Gabriel had said he would have her love again. That she would know him, someday. And it had filled him with a hope he hadn't felt since before he had watched her die as Tora. One more reason to preserve her. One more reason to save her. If she was meant to know him, to love him again, he couldn't let her be sentenced to death by the Council. She had been his wife, and he had been her husband. He could not sit by and watch her be consigned to death any more than he could do nothing if it was Baldur's life in question. And no matter what Odin said, he would do the same now for any of the Aesir as he did for Eve. Argue for their lives just as fiercely. Even Sif, for all her cruelty, he would defend.

Odin would disown him completely after the Council meeting tomorrow. Thor would have no home, no family, no place. Magni and Modi, Ullr and Thrud would be forbidden from speaking with him. Thor would be exiled, left to care for the people who looked to him alone. He snorted. There were worse things than to walk the earth.

The earth. Isn't that what Gabriel had said? Son of the earth?

He shook his head. Perhaps when this was over, he could consult Athena on that issue. Perhaps she would be able to make more sense of it than he had. But the Council meeting must come first. He must focus his thoughts on that. On Eve's defense.

That someday she might know him, and his love for her, again.

༄

At Ra's suggestion, the Council meeting was held in Egypt. No one could argue he was not fair or just, or that he would not listen to reason. His opinions were well respected among the gods, as he was the oldest of this plane but for the Hindu Lord, Bhagavan. But because Bhagavan had taken the form of Shiva, the gods could not count on him to mediate without prejudice or preference. Shiva favored destruction and chaos. That much had been Ra's idea, but Thor still remembered Bhagavan's booming laughter at the suggestion.

"Ah, Thor. Good. Your timing is perfect." Ra did not even turn away from the window, but he flicked his fingers in the direction of a table when the lightning of Thor's journey had faded. Ra's personal chambers were, as ever, well supplied with refreshment. "Help yourself to the wine. Athena said to give you her regrets. She is still arguing with her father, and does not dare to leave his side before the Council meets, for fear he'll change his mind."

Thor grimaced, but poured himself a taste of the fine red wine, cutting it with water to quench his thirst. "I was given to understand that Zeus would not be a problem."

"He wasn't. He won't be. Athena has him well in hand with Aphrodite's assistance. As long as she does not leave him open to the suggestions of Ares and Hermes. Loki found great allies in those two." Ra finally turned away from the window and studied him. "She told me about Odin."

He drank down the wine in two gulps and poured another glass. "I once thought myself to be my father's favorite son. Nothing I did could displease him, once I had grown into my power. Now he seeks the death of the woman I love. How else does he expect this to go between us? Does he think I'll roll over and beg his forgiveness if he succeeds?"

Ra's face was lined, his eyes full of sympathy. "Odin wants what is best for his people, Thor. To the exclusion of all else. You know this. He wants what he believes is best for you. To free you from the enchantment he imagines has been placed on your heart. So yes, I think he does believe that with her destruction, you will turn back to him, your eyes suddenly opened."

"Eve does not have that kind of power. I have told him so, repeatedly."

"What power she does and does not have, I cannot say. But *I* do not believe you are controlled by her influence." Ra sighed and sat in his throne. "You are prepared? You know what you are to say?"

Thor nodded, sipping the wine though he would have preferred to drink it by the mug to settle his nerves. He dared not lose his wits before this meeting by too much drink. "Backwards and forwards."

"Let the others have their say. Let them shout for her death, and make their own suggestions. Speak for her only after they've aired their grievances. I suspect it will go quickly."

"This meeting should not be about Eve, Ra. The true threat to them, to all of us, is the Christians."

Ra smiled. It was thin and humorless. "Yes, Michael and Gabriel outdid themselves. It will be fascinating to see what develops." Then he waved a hand in dismissal. "Go on ahead. The longer you dally here the more likely someone will suspect where you have gone. Have faith, Thor. A body this large is always better at inaction than anything else. Democracy does not favor bold acts." He shook his head. "It is a wonder the Greeks ever accomplished anything."

Thor finished his wine, bowed, and left for the temple where the meeting would be held. He took up a seat in the shadows and waited.

"All who have joined together within this temple have accepted the Covenant," Ra began, formally calling them to order. It did not take long for the room to quiet.

"And it shall not be broken," Thor replied with the assembled.

"We gather today to discuss what action must be taken to preserve ourselves and our people from the threat of Adam and Eve," Ra said.

"Let us just kill them and be done with it," Loki called from among a group of lesser gods. Celts mostly, Thor thought, and Lugh among them, leaning back into the lap of a goddess. Thor narrowed his eyes. Hermes sat with them as well, declaring his allegiance, but Ra and Athena had expected as much from the patron god of thieves.

Zeus stood, robed in gray, and waited for Ra to allow him to speak. The king of the Olympians stared Loki down with an expression like a thundercloud. "And when Elohim stirs in anger, and his angels come to smite us for our sins, what then, Trickster? Eve is harmless enough on her own, unwilling to hurt so much as a mouse if it can be avoided, and Adam is without his memory. The only threat he poses is as a warmonger among men."

Zeus retook his seat, and Ra nodded to Buddha, who did not stand, but floated upwards from his cushion while maintaining the lotus. "As a warmonger he has already served as a great threat to all our people. I do not advocate the destruction of either of them, but perhaps there is some way we might limit his influence."

Clever of him, Thor thought, to redirect their concerns to Adam alone, after what Zeus had said. And of course Adam's violence would distress him. Thor glanced at Sif, seated by his father. She leaned over, whispering something in the Allfather's ear, but he could not tell from her expression if she had expected the shift.

Odin stood, his fur lined cloak made him look even larger than Zeus, and Thor did not fail to notice his father displayed his missing eye. A gaping black hole, made even more horrendous by the scar that ran over the socket. If Odin sought to impress this assembly with his sacrifice and strength, he had begun well. No one who met his single eye, or stared into the empty socket would forget Odin was a god both of wisdom and war, and had earned the honors with blood.

The Lord of Asgard barely waited for Ra to acknowledge him, his disgust clear on his face. "Just a moment ago, Zeus warned that interference will earn the wrath of Elohim, and now you speak of meddling with Elohim's son? The True God may as well be dead, for all it matters. The angels are no threat to us, provided we stand together, but the Christians, born from Eve's own womb, already swarm like flies. You say she is harmless, but she threatens the very heart of our power with her new faith. Kill her and the Christians will die with her. Kill her, and Elohim's power will wane, leaving us this world uncontested!"

Thor rose out of the darkness, catching Ra's eye. "I disagree."

He paused and felt all eyes turn to him. Even from across the room, he could feel the lash of Odin's anger, but he avoided his father's gaze. None of what he was about to say was a surprise to any of the Aesir.

"The woman who has been called Eve is essential to the wellness of humanity. Without the renewal of the race through her children, they will rot. I have watched her for many generations, as she moves from people to people, and she is always born into the community most in need, where love and compassion have been trampled, and healing must take place. Her purpose is larger than we have understood it to be. After all, what good is this world if there are no people to offer sacrifice and prayer? We may as well wander the void, or return to the dead worlds we left."

"What do you propose?" Ra asked.

"If Adam's warmongering is the problem, restore his memory. Make of him an ally instead of an enemy!" Thor measured the responses of the others as he spoke. Athena's expression was carefully neutral beside Zeus, but she leaned over to murmur in his ear. Bhagavan-Shiva, across the room, was grinning at the potential for chaos. "He is less scrupulous than his sister and may be persuaded through riches and power to do as we ask."

"And if he does not?"

Thor shrugged. "If you destroy Adam, you destroy Eve. If you destroy Eve, you destroy humanity. If humanity is destroyed, this plane of existence is worth nothing to us, just as surely as if the godchild to come had cast us out and remade it all."

There was an uproar of angry objections. Ra waited until it had become a mumble before he raised a hand to gesture for quiet. He had to stare down many into silence before he nodded to Isis and the goddess could be heard.

"Perhaps it would be best to leave well enough alone. We must first face the Christian movement, as Odin has said. If Adam and Eve have not found each other by now, surely they will not in the near future. If Eve is as Thor and others have described her, she will instinctively avoid Adam and his destructive ways. She has her memory. She knows the danger he is to all. I cannot imagine she would willingly give him a child of her womb."

Hera stood, the gold cuffs on her wrists catching the light. "Isis is correct. Eve is a discerning woman." She smirked slightly. "Even Zeus failed to bed her."

Again, Ra had to wait for the temple to quiet, although this time it was laughter that drowned everything else out. Thor hid his own amusement. Zeus waved a hand in dismissal of the insult, a tolerant smile curving his lips, but there was a spark in his eyes when he looked at his wife that suggested Hera would pay for the remark later. Not that it would be the first time they disagreed. Zeus had a habit of ignoring his wife's needs in favor of his own, and Hera took great delight in punishing him for the results.

Bhagavan-Shiva stood, when all had quieted, a garland of skulls rattling as he did so. "In the void, there is no chaos, no order, no sustenance. I would not hasten our return to it by foolish action when we might yet enjoy many more centuries of prosperity and madness. And I find it strange, also, that these two lesser gods have inspired such fear in even the most powerful among us. Elohim's children are but two, and we are many. Even this godchild will be mewling and weak upon its birth, leaving time enough for action, should that day come. But for myself, and for the Brahman, I will add this: to destroy another god or goddess without warning will be seen as a breach of the Covenant to our people. And if we are so threatened, we will not hesitate to go to war."

Thor was not the only god who drew a startled breath at the words. Shiva smiled with all three of his eyes, and reseated himself in the silence that followed. His third eye swept the room before his gaze settled upon Thor, blinking once. The wink did not comfort him at all. To promise war—it was nothing they had agreed upon. If the Covenant broke, with so many disparate pantheons already present, the world would not survive it.

"Will one of this body appoint himself to watch the twins to ensure their separation while the rest of us concern ourselves with our flocks?" Ra asked, at last, when no one else rose to speak.

Murmuring spread throughout the chamber, but none objected after Bhagavan's threat. Thor hesitated to volunteer himself, though having an excuse to follow Eve for generations made his heart soar. Sif would not like it, Odin even less, but across the room, Loki had a very thoughtful expression on his face. Thor dared not allow the Trickster to interfere in their lives, or in any way guide the fate of humanity. He could not trust that Loki would not act as Odin's hand, and Odin had made his feelings clear—he wanted Eve dead and gone, and Thor returned to the wife he had chosen for his son. Not that Sif would have him, or he her. Not that it would bring Thor back to heel. He would never be his father's dog again.

Thor stood, and once more, all eyes turned to him.

"I will do so." He kept his gaze on Ra, though Sif's gaze burned through his heart with bitter fury. "I have already been observing them. If anything out of the ordinary occurs, I will be able to notify the Council."

"So it shall be," Ra said quickly, before an argument offered itself. "You are bound by the Covenant, Thor of the North. Until some course drives them together, united against us, no action will be taken by this body." And now he looked hardest at the gods whose specialties were trouble and trickery: Lugh, Puck, and Loki; Hermes and Eris; Set, Anansi and Legba; Coyote, Raven, and Crow; Kaulu and Olifat; and of course Hanuman. It was only natural that they had found seats all together, though others still were sprinkled among their respective pantheons.

"Are we in agreement?" Ra asked.

"The Covenant has been made," they all replied, though some voices and faces were clearly disappointed.

"And it shall not be broken," Ra finished. "Very well. This session is concluded."

Thor seated himself and watched as gods began to file out of the temple in groups of two or three, trying to sense those who had been disappointed by the outcome of this meeting. He did not miss Loki's sneering scowl, or the look the Trickster exchanged with Sif. When all had gone, Thor stood, staring at the empty chamber.

He knew he should return home to Asgard while he was still permitted within its walls, but he couldn't bring himself to go without checking on Eve first.

After all, this time it was his duty.

CHAPTER FORTY
Creation

§

Hannah and Sarah had brought seeds with them from the Garden, and planting them was their first concern. They found a place near the stream with good earth and marked it with stones. The presence of the lions had driven the smaller animals away, so they didn't need to worry about rabbits or rodents nibbling the stalks as they grew. Someday they would have fruit and nuts to supplement the meat Reu was teaching the other men to provide.

Most of the women settled into their new land easily, finding a routine for themselves and work to keep them busy. As the weeks passed, it was not just the seeds that sprouted and grew, but Tova's stomach as well, becoming heavy and awkward. No one quite knew what to do to help her. Reu had mentioned watching a dog give birth once, but could offer little more than his witness that it had been messy and difficult for mother and child. Worse, Reu was certain the baby belonged to Adam, not Tova's husband Enoch. One of several, it seemed, but Adam showed no interest in any of the women.

"I don't understand," she told Reu one night. Several moons had come and gone since the others had arrived. "Why is he still here? He does as he's asked, keeps the terms you set without complaint. It's not right, Reu. It isn't like him to remain so subdued."

Lilith had married Adam and lived with him outside the shelter of the caves. When Eve realized she was sleeping in the cold, she had given her the fur from an antelope to warm herself, but Lilith had sneered at her and the gift, even as her waist thickened. Adam kept his word, and no new bruises appeared on Lilith's body, but there was little Eve could do to help her, and she did not trust Adam, even so.

Reu shook his head and settled her more comfortably against his body under the fur they kept as a blanket. "Maybe he's changed. Maybe being thrown from the Garden taught him humility."

"I wish I could believe that."

"This has been difficult for everyone, Eve. Losing the abundance of the Garden, hunting to feed ourselves. I would be more surprised if he moved through this life unchanged and untouched." His hands were warm and rough, calloused now from the work he did with them.

She drew his hand across her waist and pressed herself as close to him as possible.

He chuckled softly in her ear and then stopped, his hand passing across her stomach and abdomen again more firmly, searching. "Have I given you a child, Eve?"

"I have begun to wonder, too." She twisted in his arms to look at him in the darkness, reminded suddenly of the first time they had spoken, when all she could see of him was shadow in the cave. "But I'm not sure I know how to be a mother, Reu."

He kissed her, stroking her hair and face. "Nor I a father. But there will be other children before ours to learn from, and God made us for this more than anything. You mother us already, caring for Tova when she sickens in the morning and making sure we are all fed and clothed."

"You give me more honor than I deserve, husband."

"I give you the honors you have earned, wife." He pressed his forehead to hers, and his voice became rough. "Keep Eri close."

"Always," she agreed, though the reminder made her frown. Eri protected her from Adam, first and foremost.

He sighed and held her close. "I love you more knowing you have my child within you. I cannot let any harm come to you now."

"I'm safe, Reu. Here with you, I always feel safe."

"It will be many months before the baby comes," he said softly.

"Hannah says Tova's child will come any day now. We stay by her side, waiting for signs. I think it will be reassuring to all of us to be able to witness our own futures, but I know she's frightened."

"Keep some of the willow bark at hand. If there's pain, it should help." He stared at the stone above them, his eyes unfocused. "I wonder if Adam knows anything of this."

The idea he might had occurred to her, but she had not wanted to ask. "Perhaps."

"I'll speak with him during our hunt tomorrow." He sounded determined. Eve silently wished him luck, though it was unlikely he would meet with much success. He yawned, and she felt his exhaustion creeping over her.

"Sleep, love," she said, curling up against his body. "Sleep well."

§

It was late the next day when Tova went into labor. Her cries echoed so loudly, Eve worried it would bring the hunters running in concern. Eve did her best to soothe her with soft words and cool water, but each time Tova's body rocked with labor, her screams ripped through them all. Then the baby's head appeared between her legs and Hannah was able to draw out its little body as Tova pushed and wept. It was a little boy, wet with blood. He cried almost as loudly as his mother, and Eve smiled.

"He's strong like you, Tova. And beautiful. What will you name him?"

She looked startled at the idea, searching Eve's face. "But he is yours, Eve. Won't you name the children, as Adam named us?"

Eve shook her head, sitting back on her heels. It had never occurred to her the women might expect such a thing. "He is of your body, Tova, and it is your right to name him. I would not take that away from you. We live by Adam's rules no longer."

Tova looked back at the baby, her brow furrowed. "But what is a good name?"

"Any name you desire." Eve stroked her hair back from her face and sighed. They had been living under her leadership for so many moons, and they still did not understand their own freedom.

The baby continued to cry, long and loud, and Eri joined them, his ears flattened against his skull, sniffing at the baby and its mother. There was a roar from outside, and Tzofi appeared with Reu not far behind. The lioness went to the baby and began licking the blood and fluids from his body, purring loudly. Eve watched carefully to be sure the baby would be safe, but there was nothing to alarm her in Tzofi's mind.

Tova laughed when Tzofi's rough tongue lapped over her arm, and Reu called both lions away, kneeling where Tzofi had stood.

"The first son," he said, glancing from the baby to Eve, his eyes full of affection.

"Maybe I should call him Kefir." Tova smiled. "Since the lions like him so much, and he roars like one. My little lion."

"It is a good name," Eve agreed, returning her smile. "Perhaps he will grow to be as strong and as skilled a hunter."

Reu laughed. "If only it were so easy. That we could name

ourselves lions, and become them." He stood then. "I must return to my work. May God's spirit bless you, Tova, and your son."

Eve stayed with Tova until the baby fed and her exhaustion overcame her joy. Tova passed the baby to her, and Eve cradled him carefully to her chest. He slept too, like his mother, no doubt worn out from all his crying. Reu had carved steps in the rock to their overlook, and she took the baby with her to look over the valley. Eri followed at her heels.

It was a shame this boy would never know where he had come from. Would never know the bounty and splendor of the Garden, or the journey from it. She prayed he would never have cause to meet with the angels. He was a child born of the mountain and the grasses and the earth. Adam's child, if Reu's thoughts were true.

"You look out at the Garden as though you loved it," a voice said behind her.

She did not have to turn to know who spoke. "Would you like to see your son, Brother?"

Adam came to stand beside her, ignoring the baby in her arms, and the warning snarl from Eri. "Do you miss it, then? What you chose to leave so quickly?"

"You exiled me, Adam. I did not choose to leave." She frowned at him. "If not to see your baby, why do you come to me?"

He stared into her eyes for a long moment, silent, before looking out at the land. "I will have it back, Eve. Come with me. The angels can't deny us. It is our right, our home, and I *will* have it back."

"You're mad." She held the babe more tightly and stepped nearer to Eri. "Michael guards the Garden himself. At night, his sword of flames is a beacon. He'll never let you pass."

"I am the son of God, as you are His daughter!" His eyes flashed, his lip curled with disgust. "I will not live like this in the scrub, when I should live as a god in the bounty of the Garden!"

She shook her head. She had only known Michael for the briefest of moments, but it had been enough to know he was her superior in all ways. More powerful than she could dream. "And what of Lilith, who carries your child even now? Will you abandon them?"

"She is nothing." He looked back out at the Garden, his eyes sliding over Kefir in her arms. "The only child I want is of your womb, Eve. I will not waste my time on any others."

His callousness astounded her. After all this time, when he had worked side by side with the others. Hunted with the other men, shared meals with the women. Still, they were nothing to him. People he would leave to die without concern. All he wanted was his power. The Garden. Herself as his wife.

"Try, Adam," she said softly. "Try to take it back, and I hope you succeed. Perhaps then we will be free of you forever."

She left him there, sneering at her refusal, and went to find Enoch to show him the baby who would be his son.

§

Smoke woke her, thick in the air. It had been a clear night, and Kefir's wails had driven most of them out of the cave to find a more peaceful sleep elsewhere. The sun had come up, but the light was choked by the dark clouds of ash. She stood to see where it came from. No fire of theirs could have created so much smoke.

That was when she saw it, and she heard herself wail as loudly as the baby.

The Garden burned.

It was Adam's work. Adam's anger. Adam's spite.

"Eve?" Reu called, then coughed. "Eve? What's wrong?"

She couldn't tear her eyes away. Most of it was char and black ash now, but flames still licked at trees further out. How bare it looked inside the great golden gates with no fruit trees bursting against the walls, reaching with lush, leafy fingers to the world beyond.

"Wake the others, Reu. Tell Hannah and Lamech to dig up the plants that have sprouted and pack them with dirt in those baskets she's woven. I don't want to leave them behind now that they're all we have left."

If she squinted, she thought she could see him, standing there with a brand in his hand, waving it over his head. She lifted her gaze, searching the sky. A falcon soared, just near enough, perhaps, if she could only catch hold—

And then she saw Adam clearly from high above, the wind whipping at her face as her mind soared with the bird. The falcon circled lower with her encouragement. Closer still, and she could hear him too, screaming his anger.

"I will turn it all to ash, every tree, every bush, every meadow. I will set the world aflame until there is nothing left but Eve, broken to my will at last, and once I have her power, her child, I'll see you burn, too!"

The angels wept for the destruction he had caused. Tears of blood and gold falling to the earth. But not even their power could save the Garden now. Adam had turned it all to ruin and wasteland.

Dimly she knew Reu stood beside her, coughing, horrified, and as if from a great distance, she heard him shouting. Following her instructions. But her attention was on Michael. The angel dropped lightly to the earth at Adam's back and raised his burning sword. Lightning flew out, dancing over Adam's body and bringing him to his knees with a cry. He fell face down into the ash, all that was left of what had once been fertile and green.

Michael's beautiful and terrible face distorted with pleasure, and he kicked Adam so hard Eve felt her own ribs ache. The angel grabbed him by his hair, jerking Adam's limp body up until his feet dangled.

"You think because Elohim is gone, you are the only one with the freedom to act?" He sneered. "In His absence, the world is mine to guard, mine to keep, and God's son or not, you will suffer for your sins." He dropped Adam, then, boneless to the ground.

Raphael stepped forward, his face impassive, and knelt beside Adam, checking his ribs. "Would you finish what he has begun? For the world, he must live."

Michael's face twisted in disgust. Hate. Lust. "Then let the knowledge he coveted burn with the rest. Even if he must live, he need not remember."

She saw the same look in Michael's eyes that had been in Adam's when he had spoken of the fruit, of the power of God, and she knew a fear that caused her stomach to twist. Michael had more power than Adam ever would, and there was nothing to stop him from using it.

Tears burned her own eyes, washing down her face. The falcon flew on, and Eve blinked free of its sight. What was left of the Garden was distant once more.

Eve turned away. There would be time enough for grief once her people were safe. But it wasn't only Adam she feared anymore.

Better if they never saw Michael again.

EPILOGUE
The Redwood Hall

An old man stared into the living flames of the redwood hearth. The roots of the great tree formed a chair beneath him, cradling his ancient body and rocking it gently. The leaves rustled, whispering their news, and he lifted his gaze from the fire.

"Thank you," he said softly.

The leaves rustled again in answer, then stilled as the angel stepped forward into the red-gold light. Michael's white wings flared, then settled to his back, his face unreadable in the shadow.

"You called to me."

"I did." The old man studied the angel, his fingers drumming on the rooted arm of his rocking chair. "And as my servant you must obey."

The angel's jaw tightened, but he dropped to one knee in the carpet of leaves, bowing his head. "Command me, my Lord."

"Your sword, Archangel."

Michael lifted his head, his eyes narrow and hard. He gripped the hilt of the weapon on his hip, knuckles white. "What?"

The old man held out his hand, his expression as still as the leaves above. "The sword."

Silence pressed down around them, so heavy and thick even the fire did not dare flicker or pop.

Metal scraped on metal at last, cutting through the quiet, and Michael rose, offering the sword hilt first. The old man held it, laying it across his lap. His fingers followed the edges of the blade.

"So finely wrought." He sighed. The blade, sharp as it was, did not draw his blood. "As it must be, to slice souls free of hearts without damage, and teach death to an immortal." The old man looked up, his face lined with eternity. "Do you think in all this time, I have not heard my daughter's cries? You have left her to suffer needlessly, allowed her to be tortured by false gods, and now you threaten her child. How many would you slaughter to eliminate her blood from the earth and take what is mine?"

"As many as I must to keep it whole, to prevent her rebirth if she threatens the world. As you have demanded of me."

The old man leaned back in his chair, still holding the sword. "That time is done, Michael. My son has learned his lesson, and my daughter knows her duty. Eve will teach Adam all that is required, now. You have paralyzed her with fear for long enough. She will be free in her next life to do as she must."

"You risk everything!" Michael's hands were fists at his sides, his words spit from between clenched teeth. "Do we mean so little to you, that you would allow us to be destroyed?"

"Have you no faith in your Creator, Archangel?"

Michael's wings flared again, his gaze locked on the sword in the old man's hands.

"You ask me to leave my creation in your hands, but to keep it you would destroy my greatest achievements. The world will not survive without my daughter, Michael, and I dare not leave her life in your power any longer. The sword will remain with me, and when the child is born, you and your brother will bring the babe here. This is my command."

"The other gods will never allow it."

"Won't they?" The old man smiled, ancient eyes twinkling. "When my first born has returned to me, at last, to guide them?"

Michael hissed and turned away, one stroke of his broad wings lifting him into the air. "So be it."

The old man nodded and closed his eyes, his fingers still tracing the lines of the sword. So well made. He had not the strength for it now. He would never have the strength for such a making again. But all was not lost. Not as long as Eve lived and loved. Not as long as Adam loved her. He sighed.

Today, he had earned his rest.

Coming Soon:

The next installment in the Fate of the Gods Trilogy:

A FATE FORGOTTEN

Fate of the Gods Trilogy: Book Two

Amalia Dillin

ABOUT THE AUTHOR

Amalia Dillin began as a Biology major at the University of North Dakota before taking Latin and falling in love with old heroes and older gods. After that, she couldn't stop writing about them, with the occasional break for more contemporary subjects. She lives in upstate New York with her husband, and dreams of the day when she will own goats—to pull her chariot through the sky, of course.

Find her online at AmaliaDillin.com,
or follow her on Twitter @AmaliaTd.

ALSO AVAILABLE FROM WORLD WEAVER PRESS

Shards of History
a novel by
Rebecca Roland

"Five out of Five stars! One of the most beautifully written novels I have ever read. Suspenseful, entrapping, and simply…well, **let's just say that *Shards of History* reminds us of why we love books in the first place.**" —Good Choice Reading

Like all Taakwa, Malia fears the fierce winged creatures known as Jeguduns who live in the cliffs surrounding her valley. When the river dries up and Malia is forced to scavenge farther from the village than normal, she discovers a Jegudun, injured and in need of help.

Malia's existence—her status as clan mother in training, her marriage, her very life in the village—is threatened by her choice to befriend the Jegudun. But she's the only Taakwa who knows the truth: that the threat to her people is much bigger and much more malicious than the Jeguduns who've lived alongside them for decades. Lurking on the edge of the valley is an Outsider army seeking to plunder and destroy the Taakwa , and it's only a matter of time before the Outsiders find a way through the magic that protects the valley—a magic that can only be created by Taakwa and Jeguduns working together.

Turn the page to read an excerpt!

"Fast-paced, high-stakes drama in a fresh fantasy world. Rebecca Roland is a newcomer to watch!"
—James Maxey, author of *Greatshadow: The Dragon Apocalypse.*

Excerpt from
SHARDS OF HISTORY

Soon Malia neared the spot where the Jegudun had fallen from the sky. She slowed, scanning the area for any signs of it. Wind rustled aspen leaves, the only sound other than her soft footfalls. The lack of animal sounds raised the hairs along the base of her neck.

Something rustled in the tree above her. Malia's hand flew to her dagger as she crouched and looked up. A squirrel chattered at her, then bound along the tree limb. Malia pressed a hand to her chest and took a deep breath. Her heart raced as if she'd just run uphill. Then she grinned and shook her head at her reaction, glad nobody had been around to see her jump at a squirrel.

A few steps later, the aspen opened to a meadow about twenty paces across. The grass grew as high as Malia's waist in some spots. Yellow cinquefoil bloomed along the perimeter. The wind died, and everything went still.

To Malia's left lay the Jegudun, a small, human-like figure with wings. Standing, it would probably be no taller than a five year old child.

The creature's face reminded Malia of a wolf. Sharp teeth lined an elongated snout covered with down, and a short beard clung to its chin. Its eyes, set forward in its face, were closed, and its tufted ears, although pointed, seemed relaxed.

Feathers on one side of an outstretched wing melded from light gray to dark gray on the other side of the wing. Blood covered its right shoulder.

Feathers gave way to down on its face and barreled chest, but that was the only thing soft about the Jegudun. It had squat, heavily muscled legs, and arms separate from its wings. An outstretched, human-like hand ended in curved, sharp claws that could easily tear flesh.

The tension in Malia's muscles eased as she realized the Jegudun was dead. She imagined those men at the cliffs, facing a horde of these creatures, and shook her head. She didn't think she could stand up to one living Jegudun, much less a bunch of them.

Malia swallowed the knot in her throat and inched forward. She reached a trembling hand towards the wing. The feathers were soft and smooth beneath her fingers. Emboldened, she ran her hand along the forward edge of its wing, moving to its bloody shoulder. Hard muscle lay beneath the down.

The Jegudun's other arm whipped around to grab her leg. Claws dug into her flesh. The creature yanked, toppling her onto her back. Malia hit the ground hard. She kicked her leg, trying to pull free, but the Jegudun's grip was a vise.

It sat up, snarling, showing two rows of sharp teeth. Malia cried out and fumbled for her dagger, but it was pinned between her hip and the ground. The Jegudun pulled her towards it, her skin scraping against the ground. She imagined the creature's teeth clamping on her leg and tearing out flesh, or burying its snout into her soft belly until it reached her intestines. *I won't die this way.*

**Available now in ebook,
and in paperback May 21, 2013!**

ALSO FROM WORLD WEAVER PRESS

*White as snow, stained with blood,
her talons black as ebony…*

Opal
a novella by
Kristina Wojtaszek

The daughter of an owl, forced into human shape…

"A fairy tale within a fairy tale within a fairy tale—the narratives fit together like interlocking pieces of a puzzle, beautifully told."
—Zachary Petit, Editor *Writer's Digest*

In this retwisting of the classic Snow White tale, the daughter of an owl is forced into human shape by a wizard who's come to guide her from her wintry tundra home down to the colorful world of men and Fae, and the father she's never known. She struggles with her human shape and grieves for her dead mother—a mother whose past she must unravel if men and Fae are to live peacefully together.

"Twists and turns and surprises that kept me up well into the night. Fantasy and fairy tale lovers will eat this up and be left wanting more!"
—Kate Wolford, Editor, *Enchanted Conversation:
A Fairy Tale Magazine*

Available in ebook and paperback!

Who knew one gaudy Velvet Elvis could lead to such a heap of haunted trouble?

The Haunted Housewives of Allister, Alabama
a novel by
Susan Abel Sullivan

"Funniest novel I've read since *Hitchhiker's Guide to the Galaxy*."
—NewMyths.com

When Cleo Tidwell said, "I do," for the third time, she had no idea her marriage vows would be tested by a tacky piece of art. But Cleo's not the kind of woman to let a velvet-offense-against-good-taste just hang—oh no, she's on a mission to oust the King. Trouble is, Elvis won't leave the building. And he's attractin' all manner of kooks, fanatics, and lookie loos to Cleo's doorstep, including the entire congregation of the Church of the Blue Suede Shoes.

Everyone wants a piece of the painting, but Cleo's starting to suspect that whatever's haunting the Velvet Elvis wants a piece of her husband. Why else would her hubby trade in his car for a '56 pink Caddy, moonlight as an Elvis impersonator, and develop a sudden hankering for fried peanut butter and banana sandwiches? Certainly it can't be anything as simple as a mid-life crisis, because Cleo is *not* getting divorced *again*—her mother would never let her hear the end of it.

Cleo's life is all shook up by crazies with death threats, psychic warnings "from beyond," kidnapping attempts, invitations to join the Blue Shoe Loonies, and even murder! Cleo Tidwell is in a fight for her life, her marriage, and the perseverance of good taste everywhere.

Available in ebook and paperback!

Beyond the Glass Slipper
Ten Neglected Fairy Tales to Fall in Love With
Introduction and Annotations by
Kate Wolford

Some fairy tales everyone knows—these aren't those tales. These are tales of kings who get deposed and pigs who get married. These are ten tales, much neglected. Editor of *Enchanted Conversation: A Fairy Tale Magazine*, Kate Wolford, introduces and annotates each tale in a manner that won't leave novices of fairy tale studies lost in the woods to grandmother's house, yet with a depth of research and a delight in posing intriguing puzzles that will cause folklorists and savvy readers will find this collection a delicious new delicacy.

Beyond the Glass Slipper is about more than just reading fairy tales—it's about connecting to them. It's about thinking of the fairy tale as a precursor to *Saturday Night Live* as much as it is to any princess-movie franchise: the tales within these pages abound with outrageous spectacle and absurdist vignettes, ripe with humor that pokes fun at ourselves and our society.

Never stuffy or pedantic, Kate Wolford proves she's the college professor you always wish you had: smart, nurturing, and plugged into pop culture. Wolford invites us into a discussion of how these tales fit into our modern cinematic lives and connect the larger body of fairy tales, then asks—no, *insists*—that we create our own theories and connections. A thinking man's first step into an ocean of little known folklore.

Available April 16, 2013, in ebook and paperback!

ALSO FROM WORLD WEAVER PRESS

Wolves and Witches
A Fairy Tale Collection
Amanda C. Davis and Megan Engelhardt

Cursed: Wickedly Fun Stories
A Collection
Susan Abel Sullivan

Specter Spectacular: 13 Ghostly Tales
Anthology
Edited by Eileen Wiedbrauk

Coming soon!

A Fate Forgotten
Fate of the Gods Trilogy: Book Two
Amalia Dillin

The King of Ash and Bone, and other stories
A Collection
Rebecca Roland

World Weaver Press
*Publishing fantasy, paranormal, and science fiction
that engages the mind and ensnares the story-loving soul.*

Made in the USA
Lexington, KY
04 May 2013